THE
ARMS MAKER
OF BERLIN

THE
ARMS MAKER
OF BERLIN

DAN FESPERMAN

ALFRED A. KNOPF · NEW YORK 2009

THIS IS A BORZOI BOOK
PUBLISHED BY ALFRED A. KNOPF

www.aaknopf.com

Originally published in Great Britain by Hodder &
Stoughton Ltd, London.

Knopf, Borzoi Books, and the colophon are registered trademarks of
Random House, Inc.

Grateful acknowledgment is made to Harvard University Press and the Trustees of
Amherst College for permission to reprint "Forbidden fruit a flavor has," an excerpt
from "He ate and drank the precious words," "Mine enemy is grown old," and
"The past is such a curious creature" from *The Poems of Emily Dickinson*,
edited by Thomas H. Johnson, copyright © 1951, 1955, 1979, 1983
by the President and Fellows of Harvard College (Cambridge, Mass.:
The Belknap Press of Harvard University Press). Reprinted by permission of
Harvard University Press and the Trustees of Amherst College.

Library of Congress Cataloging-in-Publication Data
Fesperman, Dan, [date]
The arms maker of Berlin / by Dan Fesperman. — 1st ed.
p. cm.
ISBN 978-0-307-26837-2 (alk. paper)
1. History teachers—Fiction.   2. World War, 1939–1945—Archival resources—
Fiction.   3. Weisse Rose (Resistance group)—Fiction.   4. Bonhoeffer, Dietrich,
1906–1945—Fiction.   5. Code and cipher stories.   I. Title.
PS3556.E778A89 2009
813'.54—dc22   2009003802

Manufactured in the United States of America

First American Edition

*For all those people
who dig up the secrets*

My most beautiful poem?
I didn't write it.
From the deepest depths it rose.
I kept it silent

Mein schönstes Gedicht?
Ich schrieb es nicht.
Aus tiefsten Tiefen stieg es.
Ich schwieg es.

—from the poem "Schweigen" ("Silence"),
by Mascha Kaléko

THE
ARMS MAKER
OF BERLIN

ONE

T HE BIGGEST HAZARD of studying history," Nat Turnbull
once told his wife, "is that if you spend too much time looking
backward, you'll be facing the wrong way when the forces of
the here and now roll forward to crush you."

As if to prove the point, his wife filed for divorce the following
week, catching Nat completely by surprise.

Five years later he was again facing the wrong way, so to speak,
when a pair of phone calls summoned him urgently back to the dan-
gers of the present. He was three stories underground at the time,
asleep at his desk in the stacks of the university library. An unlikely
location, perhaps, for the beginning of an adventure in which lives
would be lost, but Nat was trained to appreciate that sort of irony.

The first call arrived just as a dark dream of another era goose-
stepped across his brain. His cell phone jolted him awake, squirming in
his pocket like a frog. Opening his eyes to utter darkness, Nat realized
he must have slept past closing hour. It wasn't the first time. He kept a
flashlight for these emergencies, but it seemed to have disappeared.
No use groping for the lamp, either. Security would have cut the
power by now. Library budgets weren't what they used to be at Wightman University.

The phone twitched again as he fumbled in his pocket. He was
addled, groggy, a miner regaining consciousness after a cave-in. What
time was it? What day? What *century*? Mandatory question in his line
of work. Nat was a history professor. Specialty: Modern Germany. At
Wightman that covered everything from the Weimar Republic of 1919
onward, and while Nat was in love with the sweep and grandeur of the

whole era, neither friend nor foe was under any illusion as to his true calling. He remained as thoroughly haunted by the long shadow of the Third Reich as those Hitler-centric folks on the History Channel. In Nat's treasure hunts, *X* never marked the spot. A swastika did, or some pile of old bones. Dig at risk of contamination.

He snicked open the phone, and the blue glow offered a beacon of hope until he saw the incoming number. Gordon Wolfe, his onetime master and commander, calling at 1:04 a.m., meant Nat was about to be subjected to an angry tirade or a teary confessional, and either would likely be served in a marinade of French cognac and Kentucky bourbon. He answered with a vague sense of stage fright.

"Gordon?"

"No, it's Viv. Gordon's in jail. You have to get up here."

"Jail? What's happened?"

"They took him away. Him and some archives. They took everything."

"Gordon's archives? *All* of them? Where are you, Viv?"

"Blue Kettle Lake. Our summer place."

The Adirondacks. Of course. That was where the old Minotaur always retreated when the going got tough, and lately the going had been unbearable.

"The police handcuffed him the moment we walked in the door. You'd have thought he was John Dillinger. They're saying he stole it, that he stole everything, which is nuts."

"Stole what, Viv? Slow down. Start at the beginning."

By now the phone light had switched off. Nat, sole survivor of the European Research Collection, again sat in the darkness of carrel C-19 in the basement stacks of Hartsell Library. He had often boasted he could find his way out of here blindfolded. Tonight he might have to put up or shut up.

His nose could have told him the approximate location—musty leather bindings, chilled concrete, the chemical reek of spooled microfilm—a bouquet that probably explained why he had just been dreaming of a similar place across the Atlantic. Except there all the writing was in German and the records were haunted by so much industrialized horror that you never got comfy enough to nod off.

In his dream he had been visiting the place during wartime, a quarter century before he was born. He was descending a narrow stairway as bombs crashed overhead, and he was vaguely excited, as if on the verge of a huge discovery. Yet at each passing level the light dimmed, his dread deepened, and a grim realization took hold: The closer he got to his goal, the greater the risk that he would lose his way or be buried in rubble, forever irretrievable by family and friends.

Guilt having its say, no doubt. Work had consumed the better part of Nat's last two decades, dating back to his undergraduate years, when a dynamic professor named Gordon Wolfe had infected him with a virulent strain of historical curiosity. The affliction had now outlasted the aforementioned marriage, a procession of careless affairs, and the upbringing of a daughter who had just finished her sophomore year at Wightman. This being a party-hearty Thursday following final exams, Karen was probably seated at this very moment with her friends around a noisy table, polishing off a celebratory pitcher of beer.

Nat had canceled a dinner date to come to the library. It seemed necessary at the time. But so far the only fruits of his labor were an unscheduled nap, and now he had learned that Gordon Wolfe was in jail in upstate New York, where the old man apparently would remain until Nat could talk Gordon's wife, Vivian, down from the high ledge of hysteria. Judging from her voice, she had been perched there quite a while.

"It was some old files," Viv said. "Gordon says they were planted. That's all I could get out of him before they took him away. They bumped his head on the goddamn patrol car. We didn't even have time to take off our coats. When we turned on the light there was a pile of boxes sitting there, right on the kitchen table. Then a bunch of FBI guys came in from the living room."

"The FBI? Good Lord. What kind of files?"

"I don't know. Something from the war. Gordon can tell you. I got the idea he'd seen them before, just never at our house."

"Two boxes? Ten?"

"Four. They moved everything to the sunroom before I got a good look, and now I can't even get in there. I'm a prisoner in my own house."

"You see any labels? Any markings?"

"A few stickers. Ask Gordon. But first we've got to get him out. They haven't set bail, but I can take care of that. I want you here for the arraignment. We can ride over together, tell the judge it's all a lie."

Unless it wasn't. Frame-up or not, what in the hell was Gordon Wolfe doing at the age of eighty-four with a missing archive at his summer home in the hills? Especially if it was *the* archive, the one Gordon had forever mooned about to both students and colleagues in his less-guarded and more-imbibed moments. More than sixty years ago he had been one of the few wartime caretakers of that trove. Then, after the war ended, four boxes full of information had slipped through everyone's fingers, disappearing somewhere between the Alps of Switzerland and the towers of midtown Manhattan.

Gordon had been looking for this lost treasure ever since, and during particularly acute outbreaks of gold fever he sounded like an old prospector around a campfire. He had even brought up the subject at his long-overdue retirement party, a melancholy event six years ago when everyone but Gordon had been at a loss for words, stifled by the awkward knowledge that Wightman was nudging him not so gently into the box marked "Emeritus." What was it Gordon had said that day as he blustered on? Some bold proclamation while he waved his drink, his blocky head thrust forward like that of a reckless boxer, punch-drunk and asking for more. Now Nat remembered:

"Oh, it's out there, all right. Nobody burned it. Nobody bombed it. But somebody took it, and I wish I knew who, 'cause it's got secrets you can't find anywhere else. Not a dud among 'em. *Live* ammunition. Pick it up and it might go off in your hands. *Boom!*"

Whereupon he sloshed bourbon onto the tie of the assistant dean for students.

Gordon's mother lode was a trove of wartime gleanings from an American OSS station in Bern, Switzerland, which had been a listening post in a zone of tense but genteel neutrality. Right on Hitler's doorstep, as historians such as Nat liked to say. It was run by Allen Dulles, the genial, pipe-smoking Lothario who a few years later became one of the first chiefs of the CIA, making him the nation's ranking Cold Warrior. The missing boxes were only a fraction of the voluminous files Dulles collected during the war, of course. And much of his other work had been well documented, most notably in accounts of the German double agent Fritz Kolbe, who smuggled secret documents out of the Nazi Foreign Ministry by taping them around his thigh.

Gordon ended up working for the OSS literally by accident. Dulles arrived in Switzerland by train only hours before Vichy France shut its borders in late '41. Cut off from reinforcements, he cobbled together a staff from borrowed diplomats, marooned American bankers and students, disaffected expat Junkers, a Swiss financier's wife who was a former Boston debutante—who, conveniently, also became his mistress—and American airmen whose bombers crash-landed in Switzerland.

Gordon was one of the downed airmen, selected by Dulles mostly because of his fluency in German. It saved him from spending the rest of the war in a Swiss internment camp, although by his own account he was little more than a clerk, translating speeches and making sure Dulles never ran out of paper clips. Gordon compensated for this lack of espionage glamour by telling hair-raising tales of his missions as a ball turret gunner in a Flying Fortress on bombing runs over Germany. To drive home the point, he wore a battered leather flight jacket and walked with a limp—the result, he said, of a flak burst and a bad parachute drop.

This image of dashing-flyboy-turned-spy-clerk-turned-scholar might have followed him to the grave if not for a bit of "gotcha" journalism that had appeared only a week ago in Wightman's campus newspaper, the *Daily Wildcat*.

Gordon's B-17, it turned out, hadn't been shot down at all. It hadn't even dropped a bomb during its final flight. It flew plenty of other dangerous missions, but Gordon was making his maiden voyage as a last-minute replacement. Somewhere between England and the target city of Regensburg the pilot got lost, ran low on fuel, circled into the Alps, and finally brought the plane to rest in a Swiss meadow, where the unscathed crewmen were immediately surrounded by milk maidens and lowing cattle. Gordon's limp, the *Wildcat* said, was either the exaggerated by-product of a childhood illness—the very malady that kept him out of the infantry—or an outright affectation.

Although Gordon was retired, he was still a well-known figure around campus, not least for a series of free lectures he delivered every summer to the townsfolk, complete with colorful descriptions of his aerobatic derring-do. But there would be no speeches this summer, and a book contract that was to have been his scholarly swan song had already been canceled.

Now, if Viv was to be believed, you could add an arrest at the hand of federal agents to his roll of dishonor. And who knows, maybe the man was guilty. Because if he *had* finally tracked down the missing boxes, then Nat could well imagine him hoarding them, at least for a while. It was easy enough to guess how the old fellow would have justified it, by garrulously referring to his temporary possession as a "finder's fee."

"So can you come?" Viv was insistent.

Nat sighed. He wanted to tell her to call a lawyer. Then he could get a full night's sleep and drive up tomorrow, if at all. Let the old bastard stew away in jail, especially after everything that had happened between them. But Viv headed him off at the pass.

"Gordon won't let me call a lawyer. He said to get you instead. It was the last thing he said as they put him in the car. 'Get Nat. He'll know what to do.' "

"Since when did Gordon make sense in this kind of situation, Viv?"

"I know. But for what it's worth, he was sober. Mostly, anyway."

"We haven't spoken in years, you know. Unless you count those late-night calls he likes to make."

"I know that, too. I'm sorry. Gordon's sorry, if it makes any difference. And not just 'cause he's in trouble. He's said it a lot lately."

Sure he had. But in spite of himself, Nat experienced a tug of old loyalties. Or maybe he was still just eager to please—student to teacher, apple in hand.

"Okay. I'll come."

"Thanks, Nat. I'll never forget it. And I'm sure Gordon won't."

Yes, he would, probably within minutes. But Nat had endured that before. Besides, there were other motivations. If the boxes were what he suspected, he might get first crack at them.

"I'll leave right away," he said. "Don't wait up."

Viv hung up, and Nat found himself back in the dark, inhaling the stale, silent breath of all those books and ledgers. They, too, seemed to rest at night, the cells of a drowsing giant who might roll over at any moment and crush him with the weight of their lore. Nat believed there was more than just physical heft to these materials. They retained a spirit as well, some gusty breath from the souls of their creators. It wasn't that he believed in ghosts. It was more a reflection of how thoroughly he let such materials inhabit his mind.

But more practical matters beckoned. He was already dreading the long drive. Six hours minimum, meaning he would have to stop for breakfast, maybe a nap. Good thing he'd nodded off here. With any luck he would make it in time for the arraignment, although he realized now that Viv hadn't given him a time or place. He tapped the desktop like a blind man, groping for his things. Then the phone throbbed again. Viv with the logistics, no doubt.

"Yes?"

"Don't be alarmed."

A man's voice this time, calm and deliberate, with an odd echo as if it were bouncing off the far wall of the stacks.

"What?"

"Don't be alarmed. I'm on your floor, over by the stairwell."

So the man *was* in the stacks. Nat felt like leaping from his seat, but in what direction? For all he knew, the fellow was only a few yards away.

"Are you a campus cop?"

"No. A friend. Or that's how I hope you'll think of me."

"Me, too."

"C'mon. We need to get moving."

There was a metallic snap as the caller hung up, which made Nat flinch in his chair. Across the room, a tiny light switched on, casting a narrow white beam that scoped down the long aisle before coming to rest on Nat's right knee, where it waggled briefly.

"This way," the man said.

"Do you have a name?" Nat answered.

He was back in the role of trapped miner, only he wasn't so sure about the rescue party. His voice held steady, but he was a little scared. He considered bolting, since he probably knew these corridors better than his adversary did. But without his own light he would soon wind up facedown, or smashed against a shelf.

"We'll discuss details outside."

"Maybe I should call 9-1-1, in case a campus cop is on patrol outside. Wouldn't want him seeing us coming out of a locked door after hours and overreacting."

"It won't work."

"What won't?"

"Your phone."

He was right. Nat couldn't get a signal. For that matter, how had he gotten one to begin with? Never before had he been able to make or take a call this deep in the stacks. Library officials were content to let the place remain a cell phone dead zone, and he had only rarely heard one ringing. How had the two calls gotten through, then? And what had become of his miraculous signal? This was beginning to feel like one of the scenes he reconstructed a bit too luridly in his books. Some doomed hero of the resistance, cornered at last by the Gestapo. Fear crept a little higher in his chest, and his voice tightened.

"What is this? What are you doing?"

"Sorry for the spook act, but we're wasting time. I'll explain outside."

Assuming they made it.

"Let me get my things."

Nat groped for a pen and a sheet of paper as he rose from his chair. He scribbled blindly: "1 a.m., 5-18-07, Am being abducted."

Whoever found it would know who left the note because this was Nat's assigned carrel. Then he had another idea and laid down his cell phone. "Last call on phone has his number," he scribbled, hoping he wasn't writing over the previous message. He then added a postscript.

"Pls tell Karen Turnbull," he wrote, jotting her number. His daughter. Probably the only person on the planet other than his department head who would care enough to follow up. A sobering realization when you were about to walk off into the dark with a stranger, and not much of a comment on the life he had built.

"What's taking so long?"

"I'm making sure I've got everything."

It was partly true. Other than the note and his phone, Nat believed it was important that he not leave behind a single item. For one thing, it was his usual careful way as a researcher. For another, he had a feeling he wouldn't be returning for quite a while.

TWO

NAT'S ESCORT NUDGED HIM FORWARD through the darkness like a border collie, brisk and insistent. He knew all the back corridors and obscure stairwells. Either he was lucky or had scouted the route, and Nat didn't want to dwell on the implications of the latter.

Neither man spoke until they pushed through a fire exit into the starlight. No alarm sounded, another anomaly. But it was a relief to be outdoors, where the air smelled of mown grass and spring blossoms. Nat stared up through a canopy of new oak leaves while the sweat cooled on his back. He was weighing the odds of running when his escort produced an ID in the beam of a flashlight.

"Neil Ford, FBI."

"You might have told me."

Nat's shoulders relaxed, and he saw now that the guy was practically a kid, a buzz-cut rookie. Amazing how much menace you could project as a disembodied voice.

"Sorry. Protocol."

"You have a protocol for apprehending people from libraries?"

Neil glanced around, as if there might be someone in the hedge eavesdropping.

"There were extenuating circumstances."

"Such as?"

The agent cleared his throat.

"We should get moving."

"Where? What's this all about?"

"You're needed on an expert consultation, a matter of some

urgency. Voluntary, but we'd have to leave now. It's up at a place called Blue Kettle Lake, five hours from here."

"More like six. They must want me to review Gordon Wolfe's files."

"You already know?"

"Viv—Gordon's wife—called just before you did. How'd you find me?"

"Your daughter. She said the library was your second home. Sometimes your first."

Ouch.

"No offense, sir, but she sounded like she'd been, well, hoisting a few."

"End of exams. She's entitled. How'd you do that thing to my phone?"

"Excuse me?"

"Make the signal disappear."

"I didn't. Lost mine, too." He glanced around again. Something was making him nervous. "I would have ID'd myself right away, but I wasn't certain the line was secure. Frankly, I wasn't even sure we were alone."

"Are you sure now?"

"To my satisfaction."

"Shit."

"What?"

"I left my cell on the desk. With a note saying I'd been abducted."

"We'll take care of it."

"You better, or this place will be in an uproar. Small campus. Bad news travels fast. And make sure my daughter gets word that I'm okay."

"Like I said, we'll take care of it. I'm supposed to tell you that you'll be compensated for your services. Whatever your going rate is."

"I don't have a going rate."

"Then make one up. Think big—it's the government's tab."

"Good idea. We taking your car?"

"Have to."

"Protocol?"

Neil nodded.

"Then I can sleep on the way up. How will I get back?"

"We'll provide transportation. You should also be apprised that the Bureau has rented a car for your exclusive use while you're up there."

"Consider me apprised. Sounds like they expect this to take a while."

"A few days, tops. We can stop by your house to pick up your things."

"I should probably clear this with my department head."

"He's already signed off."

"You work fast."

"Your name was at the top of our list."

"Figures. I was Gordon's protégé."

"Was?"

"Long story."

Actually it was fairly short, but Nat didn't feel like telling it for the umpteenth time. He had once been far more than a protégé. He was Gordon Wolfe's heir apparent, anointed years ago by the great man himself, when Nat proved to be the best and brightest of several graduate assistants.

At first it was an unspoken arrangement, a natural progression. For five years Gordon and he attended conferences together, coedited research papers, and collaborated on articles for the popular press. Eventually he began fielding Gordon's cast-off requests for speeches and interviews. The old fellow's temperament didn't make it easy. But Nat persevered, mostly because the work was so damned exciting. Part sleuth and part scholar, he was always eager to track down the next lead, even when it meant forsaking his duties as husband and father.

On a snowy afternoon ten years ago he finally attained the ultimate level of trust and acceptance when Gordon took him aside in an off-campus tavern to confess that he was driven by more than just a lust for knowledge.

"Money, old son," Gordon said tipsily. "Let's face it, the swastika sells. Always has, always will. Nobody did it quite like those bastards, and everyone still wants to know why. Hell, *I* still want to know why."

Gordon had to shout to be heard above a neighboring table of undergrads, who were loudly discussing *Simplicissimus*, the prewar German satirical magazine. Or was it *The Simpsons*? Wightman wasn't exactly covered in Ivy.

"Stay the course," Gordon said, "and you'll always be assured of a paying audience."

At one level it was disillusioning. At another it was comforting—Hey, you could actually make a living at this! So Nat and the old man clanked mugs to seal the deal just as a student shouted, "Doh!" quoting Homer.

Not long after that, Nat began receiving congratulatory e-mails, indicating that Gordon had passed the word. And so it was ordained: Nat would become America's next great university authority on all aspects of Germany's wartime resistance movements, small as they were, just as Gordon had been for the previous thirty years.

Then things began to fall apart.

The biggest problem was personality. Gordon Wolfe was vain, prickly, and abrasive, a bullish temperament to match his welterweight build. He was worse when he had hoisted a few, as Neil Ford would have said, and unfortunately Gordon believed booze was a vital part of the professorial persona. His daily regimen included wine at lunch, bourbon before dinner, brandy by the fire, and, if he was restless enough, more bourbon at bedtime. By the time he realized alcohol was a mere stage prop, just like his Dunhill pipe, it might as well have been stitched into the fabric of his campus tweeds.

Yet in other ways the two men were perfectly matched. Both could disappear into their work for weeks at a time, and both gravitated to the sort of research that shook things up—digging up the goods on a Kurt Waldheim, for instance, or discovering the shameful folly about some purported hero—a "gotcha" aspect that now seemed ironic in light of what had just befallen Gordon.

They also shared a belief that scoundrels, not heroes, were the driving forces of history, and thus worthy of greater scrutiny. The pop concept of the "Greatest Generation," for example, struck them as quaintly ridiculous, albeit ingenious in its marketing. Even the self-infatuated boomers would have looked Great seated alongside Hitler and Stalin.

So, for every resistance movement or Hitler assassination attempt that had failed, Gordon and Nat wanted to know more about the weak links than the strong ones. Just as when a building collapsed no one wasted time studying the parts that *didn't* fail. Look deeply enough into the origins of some huge movement in history, they believed, and you would inevitably find a personal snub, a romantic breakup, or some kind of thwarted ambition.

Neither would have been satisfied studying an era that survived only as parchment and tombstones, or tumbledown ruins. They needed a history that could still speak through the mouths of those who had lived it or, at the very least, through interrogation transcripts and frames of old film. Nat's idea of a perfect afternoon was an interview in a musty *Bierkeller* with some aging soldier, spy, or diplomat. Meeting one of those relics was like coming upon a majestic old maple in which the sap of memory had flowed and collected to the point of bursting. Tap it at the right spot and you could capture it all. He had come to think of himself as history's version of a sugar farmer in snowy Vermont—bucket in hand and earflaps down against the cold of ignorance as he notched the old giants one by one, before the last of them withered and fell. And what better subjects than the Germans, who were themselves obsessed with the past.

Early on, Nat's hard work attracted all the right sorts of notoriety. Speaking invitations multiplied. Honors were bestowed. So was a book contract. The only colleague who wasn't impressed was Gordon Wolfe. It was one thing to groom a successor. It was quite another to be usurped before you'd departed the throne, especially when your oldest sources kept telling you what a charmer, what a sage, what an insightful and indefatigable *digger* this sober young fellow Nat Turnbull was.

Then Nat published his first book, *Dietrich Bonhoeffer and the Knights of Conscience*, a slim, scholarly volume that examined a network of Berlin resistance figures and, typically, focused on their downfall. Its appeal was narrow, but reviews were glowing. Soon afterward Nat noticed a marked coolness in Gordon, but they soldiered on.

Three years later Nat celebrated the publication of his second book, *The Gentleman Underground*. It, too, was about the doomed resistance movement, but took a stab at a wider audience with a broader perspective and a breezier style.

Gordon was notably absent from the launch party. Hurtful, but hardly ominous. Then the summer issue of the *Central European Historical Quarterly* landed in Nat's mail slot at Wightman. His book was the subject of the lead review. The critic was Gordon Wolfe. Nat could still recite the signature paragraph from memory.

"The Gentleman Underground," Gordon wrote, "is marked by faulty logic, thin research, and an overweening dependence on the clever turn of phrase. Perhaps blinded by the prospect of attaining a wider audience as a writer of 'pop history,' Dr. Turnbull has lost touch with

the core values of his profession. Or maybe he is simply one of those cynical types who believes that because the swastika sells he can pawn off any half-baked effort as serious scholarship."

The reception elsewhere was far kinder, but nothing could ease the humiliation of Gordon's public rebuke. Everyone in the field knew its larger message: The king had smothered the heir in the cradle.

In the five years since, Nat had never regained his zeal or his balance. He still threw himself deeply into research, but more in the manner of an alcoholic on a bender, drinking to forget. His projects had lost their sense of daring, and in the intervening doldrums he settled for the snug comforts of tenure, lapping at academia's daily bowl of lukewarm gruel at insular gabfests and conferences.

His personal life was equally uninspiring. With a failed marriage already in his ledger, he began settling for easy liaisons with like-minded burnouts, relationships that ended not in tumult but from lack of interest. His canceled date that night was a case in point. She was smart and attractive, a professor of economics. Nat begged off by citing a scholarly deadline, but now realized he simply hadn't been up to the chore of discussing John Maynard Keynes in order to earn an invitation back to her place.

About the only positive recent development was that he had reestablished relations with his daughter, Karen, beginning with her enrollment at Wightman. They now spoke almost daily, and their friendship had progressed to the point that she was moving into his spare bedroom for the summer, with her mother's blessing.

Gordon and he, on the other hand, had spoken only four times since the big breakup. The conversations were always via telephone, and always after midnight—calls placed by Gordon from well beyond the bounds of sobriety. The first two times a halting apology gave way to a rant. The third time he rambled on about the old days, one story after another while Nat lay in bed with the receiver tucked to one ear and a graduate assistant with striking legs nuzzled against the other. Half asleep and half aroused, Nat kept waiting for a punch line that never came.

In between he occasionally saw Viv in town, usually at the local organic grocery. She always waylaid him in the store's farthest reaches, as if it were an operation she had plotted for days—reconnoiter the produce, lurk past the omega-3 eggs, then ambush Nat at the wholegrains bakery. She invariably approached with the sympathetic expression of a kindly aunt at a funeral, and chatted for as long as he would let her.

"Don't worry," she always said. "He'll come around."

Their last such conversation had occurred only weeks ago, when she had nearly admitted defeat, and for the first time had tried to explain Gordon's behavior.

"I know it's a cliché, Nat. But I've always blamed the war for the way he is."

"The war?"

"The Gordon I knew before the war never would have written that review. And never would have let your estrangement go on this long. What makes it so hard to understand is that he still thinks of you as a son."

Another shopper reached past him for a bag. It was embarrassing having this conversation next to a bagel bin. Nat prepared to bolt, but Viv continued.

"Gordon keeps walking himself up to the precipice, up to where you're waiting on the other side, but he can't bring himself to make the leap. It's the same reason we never had children, Nat. He could never make the leap. And I blame the war."

A few days later Gordon followed up with the last of his late-night calls, a self-pitying diatribe against the history department and "all our enemies," whoever they were. But, as if finally heeding Viv's advice, he ended on a note of conciliation, promising great things yet to come if only Nat would bear with him a while longer.

"Legacy," was the word Gordon kept slurring as in "a legacy from me to you that will make things right." It was striking enough that Nat perked up his ears during the next several days for any departmental gossip, or any other hint that the old fellow had come up with something new—or old, as the case might be.

His hopes faded as the days passed. Then the newspaper story came out, shooting down Viv's theory that Gordon was traumatized by the war. The man had never even been under fire. Maybe he was just an ornery old bastard. Sometimes it was that simple, a possibility that seemed likelier still now that Gordon had been caught with a batch of stolen files. If this was the "legacy" he'd mumbled about, Nat would know soon enough.

"So what, exactly, are these files they want me to look at?" he asked Neil once they were under way. "Viv didn't seem to know much, other than it was a lot of old boxes."

The agent glanced over. The green glow of the dashboard display seemed to transform him into a shadowy young troll, hoarding treasure beneath the bridge.

"I'm not allowed to say."

"Oh, c'mon. I'll see them in a few hours anyway."

"Special Agent Clark Holland will debrief you. He's my supervisor."

Nat sighed. Then he sagged against the door to watch the streetlamps pass on the road leading out of town. He was on the verge of nodding off when Neil asked a question.

"How old are you, sir?"

"Thirty-nine."

"My brother's thirty-nine. Dangerous age."

"Possibly."

"What's the 'E' stand for?"

Although everyone called him Nat, the name in the phone book and on his office door was Dr. E. Nathaniel Turnbull.

" 'Emerson.' As in Ralph Waldo. He was a New England Unitarian, same as my mom."

True, but misleading. The full story was that his mother took a fancy to the name after reading it on the console of the delivery room television. She must have thought it sounded stout and reliable. Or maybe she confused its cachet with that of Zenith, whose slogan at the time was, "The quality goes in before the name goes on"—a reassuring thought when you're about to give birth.

Not that his gene pool offered an excess of quality. His father was a high school mathematics teacher and baseball coach, raised in northern Virginia by Southern Baptists—not the foot-washing variety, thank goodness. His mother also taught school—home economics, as it was known then—before she quit to begin producing a quartet of children in the suburbs of Philadelphia.

Nat had a younger brother and two older sisters. As children they argued over Monopoly deeds, the last slice of pie, and a wide variety of territorial rights involving couch space, the backseats of cars, and the television remote. To prove this was not mere childishness, they later argued over their parents' eulogies and worldly possessions. In some strange migratory quirk, all three of his siblings ended up in Orange County, California, where each ran an electronics store. All three lived within minutes of the freeway, and for all Nat knew all their stores offered both Emersons and Zeniths. They were enthusiastic Republicans, and he almost never spoke with them.

"You like it at Wightman?" Neil asked.

"What's not to like? Small and undistinguished. Bland campus in a bland town in the blandest part of Pennsylvania."

"The basketball team's pretty good."

"When you can get tickets. Trouble is, town and gown value hoops more than scholarship, but I guess you can't have everything when you're only charging $42,000 a year."

"Wow. That much?"

"And going up five percent in the fall."

"They treat you okay?"

"Not bad. Once you're tenured, they pretty much leave you alone."

"Well, you certainly *look* like a professor."

Nat smiled. He wasn't sure if it was a compliment, but he supposed it was true, at least for his generation of academics. No pipe and no tweed. His wardrobe was that of the perennially rumpled class—frayed chinos, wrinkled oxfords, low-cut hiking shoes, and whatever shapeless jacket was at hand. He drove a twelve-year-old Jetta with rust spots on the doors. The wall-to-wall bookshelves in his small frame house were overflowing with the latest books and journals from his field of study, although most items in his refrigerator would soon qualify for historic preservation.

There was a rugged aspect to his features—coarse sandy hair, strong jawline—and he got outdoors just enough to put some color in his cheeks. But the most intriguing thing about his looks was a slight squint, which betrayed not only inquisitiveness but an air of intensity. Some women took it as a challenge—"This one's difficult, but possibly worth it"—and concluded he must be searching for something, possibly them, only to discover far too late that what he was really after was an old piece of paper from 1938.

Males, on the other hand, often interpreted his expression to mean that he must be up to something. Maybe that was why Neil Ford was still playing things close to the vest.

Soon they hopped onto the interstate, and Nat fell asleep to the whine of tires and the prop wash of passing rigs. He didn't awaken until they exited for an all-night truck stop. You could tell from the loneliness of the road that it was quite late.

"What time is it?" he croaked.

"Four. I need coffee."

"Want me to drive?"

"Can't. It's against—"

"I understand."

The coffee smelled like hot Styrofoam, but it did the trick for both of them.

"So you know his wife well?" Neil asked.

"Viv? Pretty well. She's always been kind to me."

"Special Agent Holland said they'd been drinking. A lot."

"The drinking isn't Viv's fault. She has to, to keep up with Gordon."

That's how it had been for years. Viv either played along or spent the balance of the evening watching her husband fade from view on the wrong side of a glass. On weekdays he left her behind, but on Saturdays and Sundays she gamely kept pace. Nat had never been comfortable watching it happen, and on previous visits to Blue Kettle Lake he finished his two beers and retired early rather than witness their mutual disintegration.

"Well, from what I heard about the arrest she was pretty pissed off."

"Wouldn't you be? She says the files were planted."

"Wouldn't know about that."

"How'd you guys end up on the case?"

"Local police. They'd gotten a tip."

"Anonymous?"

"Like I said. A tip. They went to the house, saw the boxes through the window, found a key beneath the mat, and walked right in."

"No warrant? Sounds iffy."

"Not when there's probable cause. And not when the cop's best buddy is the local judge. Weird legal system they've got out in the sticks of New York. Town judges with all the power in the world. I doubt this one's even got a law degree, and the cop is his business partner. Holland said they own a gas station together, and the courthouse used to be a body shop."

"How'd they know to call you guys?"

"I gather it was pretty obvious this wasn't your average stash of paper. Although, any way you look at it, it's still just paper."

Spoken like a true bureaucrat, for whom any pile of documents was just some headache to be sorted and filed. In Nat's line of work it was the stuff of dreams, of untold enchantment, especially on the rare occasions when it still had the power to create and destroy—matter and anti-matter, rolled into one. Nat's fingertips tingled.

"And the boxes are still at the house?"

"Seemed like the best place for now. We've posted guards round the clock."

"No wonder Viv's pissed. House full of agents and her husband in jail. So I guess we're stopping there first?"

"That's the plan."

An hour later they exited the interstate for good. Nat rolled down a window to let in the cool night air, and they began the long creep into the Adirondacks. The road was virtually empty, and the woods closed in from the shoulders. Now and then their headlights caught the glowing eyes of some animal on the prowl.

Nat wondered what was about to unfold. Fireworks, probably, once Viv realized he was working for the opposition. But memories awaited him, too, and plenty were good ones. The Wolfes' summer home was comfy and rustic, the setting peaceful. To Nat it was tangible proof that even a lifetime of academia might not render you penniless at retirement, although he wasn't the only one who had always wondered how Gordon was able to afford the surrounding twenty acres. Department gossip maintained that Viv's family had carried the freight. Or maybe Gordon's book contracts were better than advertised. Not the case with Nat's, alas. Both his volumes were already out of print.

In past summers Gordon and he had often collaborated there, hashing out scholarly problems during hikes and fishing trips. The old man, in spite of his limp, could be quite the outdoorsman when the spirit moved him, stalking the trails in his leather bomber jacket.

The best part had always come when they arrived back at the house. Nat sank into the leather couch and breathed in the aroma of wood smoke and grilled trout. Then, after dinner, Viv served as moderator while Gordon and he talked shop. Until the drinks began piling up. Always the drinks.

Now those images were joined by the thought of the old boxes, looming like an oracle, awaiting only the right command before yielding their secrets. He wondered if he would be able to view them without Neil or someone else looking over his shoulder. Maybe they would even let him make copies. He had packed his camera and tripod just in case.

Nat slept again, and this time the sun woke him. They were almost there, working their way past towns with names evoking real estate scams and Indian war councils—Green Glen, Naugatuck Falls, Wopowog. Shuttered tourist cabins huddled in the woods by thawed lakes, awaiting summer.

"Your rental is parked at the house," Neil said. "Here are the keys."

When they reached the turn for the gravel road that led to Gordon's driveway, Nat borrowed Neil's cell phone to call ahead.

"Viv? Hope I didn't wake you. I'm headed up the drive."

"Thank God you're here. They've got me surrounded. I'll put some coffee on."

So they hadn't yet told her about his arrangement with the FBI. Poor Viv.

"Sounds great. Be right in."

He snapped the phone shut and braced for the worst.

THREE

Berlin

ANOTHER DREAM of Liesl, his first in years.

As always, her image fled before Kurt Bauer could hold it, chased from his eyelids by the chill martial gray of a Prussian morning. A blink, a sigh, and she was gone. Throw open the lace curtains and perhaps he would see the last wisp of her spirit, racing across the dim rooftops of Charlottenburg. And if he ever caught up to her, how would she greet him? With a smile of gratitude? A glare of accusation? Love? Forgiveness?

Downstairs, a loud voice echoed in the foyer. A door rattled shut.

Now Kurt knew what had brought on the dream. Nearly sixty-four years ago he had been awakened by the very same noises on the day he learned Liesl was gone—slammed doors, shouting messengers. All that remained to complete the sequence was the tread of slippers as his father, Reinhard, plodded upstairs to break the news. The old man had relayed it with the clacking dispassion of a stock ticker, as if he were announcing a pay cut down at his factory.

Kurt's father had just come in from the rain, having gone out to buy a newspaper, knowing that the weather would hold the bombers at bay. He had peeled off his wet woolen socks and laid them on the big tile furnace to dry. Their vapors had preceded him up the stairs, and to this day Kurt associated the smell of wet, baking wool with death. It turned his stomach like the stench of a rotting corpse. He insisted that his wife, Gerda, buy him only cotton socks, much to her puzzlement.

Like the vast city he lived in, Kurt lay down each night with a host of unwanted shadows—guilt, loss, regret, the pain of old wounds. Bleak visions poured from within like smoke from a brick chimney.

The guilt, he believed, was unwarranted. He attributed its staying power less to his own actions than to his homeland's tormented psyche. Here they pushed atonement as if it were a commodity, force-feeding it via the leftist media like some miserable brand of muesli, until you couldn't stomach another bite. At least today's young people, for all their faults, were wising up to that con. Never let them make you pay for something you hadn't bought.

The front door slammed again. Then silence, until he heard Gerda's house slippers scraping down the hall toward the kitchen.

"Who was it?" he called out, his voice a rasp.

"Repairman." Wearily, as if she had been up for hours, and maybe she had. "For the icebox. He's gone to fetch a part."

Yet another item to mend in the house of the man whose very name meant durability for millions of consumers worldwide. Not that Kurt Bauer was any stranger to irony. Try to be good and play by the rules, and what did it earn you? Heartbreak, then ruin. Admit to any imperfection and they held it against you for life. Stray beyond the lines aggressively enough, however, and not only did you get things done, you also earned accommodation, even respect.

But soon enough he would no longer have to worry about such things. At age eighty-one, Kurt Bauer had begun clearing the books, settling old accounts, and smoothing the path toward immortality, for himself and for his family's esteemed name in the world of commerce. To his surprise, most of his unfinished business still had to do with the war, even though Kurt had been only nineteen the day Hitler finally did everyone a favor by blowing his brains out.

A desire for vengeance also figured into Kurt's plans. After decades of being on the defensive about certain delicate matters, he was at last in position to strike back. Those who had tormented him the longest, and had taken away what he cherished most, would finally answer for their crimes.

Kurt would have said that love was the driving emotion behind his plans. But his brand of love was a case study in arrested development. Most people who reach his age have long ago discovered that love's deepest pain comes from watching the suffering of others—our children as they stumble, our elders as they grow feeble, or our spouses as they succumb to pain and infirmity. But Kurt had no children, his parents died suddenly while he was bustling through his twenties, and his marriage had long ago devolved into a series of bloodless jousts, drained of empathy. He still viewed love through the eyes of a young man who has suffered a signature heartbreak. For him, the idea of emotional pain still boiled down to a single name: Liesl.

As he lay in bed he rubbed a scar on his chest as if it were a battle medal that had been pinned there by a head of state. It was a comet's tail of wrinkled pink flesh, carved by hot shrapnel on the morning of Liesl's death.

After his father delivered the news, the young Kurt had refused to believe it without seeing for himself. He jumped on a bicycle and raced through the streets to the prison just as the sky began clearing in the west to open the way for more bombers. The ride took a good half hour, and his lungs were heaving as he spied the first pile of fatal rubble through a breach in the outer wall. The place was still in chaos from the raid the night before—three prisoners had reportedly escaped—and Kurt walked through the opening as boldly as if he were a guard. Workers were already picking through the debris.

Nearby, a pair of legs poked barefoot from beneath a collapsed wall. It made him light-headed with agony and fear. He wondered if he could even bear to look at her face. Why hadn't they yet dug her out? Was it Liesl? Did he have the courage to check?

A siren sounded. More bombers were approaching, black insects against the sky. The flak guns began to pound. Everyone ran for cover except Kurt, because he had resolved to see her, come what may. He pulled away a splintered doorframe, tore aside a pile of bricks, then knelt coughing in the dust as he dug blunt fingers into a mound of shattered masonry.

That was when he saw the hand, poking from beneath a few bricks just to his right. A girl's hand, covered in dust and grasping a sheaf of crumpled papers. Kurt snatched the papers, read them. They confirmed the worst possible news. This was Liesl, and these were her release documents, signed only moments before her death. She had been walking toward freedom when she was killed.

The papers fell from his hands, and he sobbed loudly just as a huge explosion emptied his lungs and threw him forward atop the bare legs. His face landed hard against something clammy and stiff. A toenail cut his cheek.

Kurt struggled to his knees, looking around wildly for assistance, for anyone who might help dig her body from this terrible grave. Glancing down, he saw the delicate feet that he had once playfully buried in the sand at the beaches of Wannsee, the slender calves he had stroked while the summer sun warmed their backs.

Hands grasped him roughly from either side, lifting him to his feet. Someone shouted an angry command, which he barely heard over the ringing in his ears.

"Get him out of here! Take him to the shelter. More planes are coming!"

Glancing at the sky, Kurt registered vaguely that the sun had come out. Oncoming bombers flashed silver, like a school of fish. They spewed wobbly lines of black dots, bombs headed for the ground. As someone yanked him away he saw that shrapnel had torn Liesl's wrist, but there was hardly any blood. She was dead, a slab of spoiling meat.

A prisoner shouted from an upper window.

"Get out of the weather, you stupid fool!"

Laughter erupted from other cells, and then a second blast blew a searing chunk of metal across the yard and into Kurt. It raked his flesh just below the sternum, marking him forever as the war's own, a stigmata of his martyrdom upon the altar of Liesl.

The old Kurt stroked the scar again as he lay in bed, feeling the puckered flesh beneath the coarse gray hairs on his sagging chest. Rescue workers had taken him for treatment even as he begged them to keep digging. Witnesses later told him Liesl had been thrown clear of the prison by one of the first bombs. Killed instantly, they said, right there on a walkway as guards led her toward the front gate.

But in the confusion of war no one was ever able to tell him where they took her body. A common grave, perhaps, because her family never came to claim her. Her parents and sister were killed that very day as well, by another bomb across town. And by the time the Red Army arrived more than a year later, the Bauers themselves had fled Berlin. They escaped south by southwest, traveling first by car, then by train, and finally by foot until they reached the Alps and the border of Switzerland, all the while cutting deals and making new plans for the future.

Ancient history, Kurt supposed. But sometimes, as with his dream moments earlier, the ache of longing from those distant days seemed brand-new, sharp enough to make him clutch his chest in pain.

Kurt swallowed a cry of agony. Then he pushed away the heavy blankets and forced himself out of bed. His bare feet were unsteady on the oak floor. Tendons flaring, he stepped stiffly toward the chilly tiles of the bathroom, then swayed a bit while he endured the interminable wait to make water. There was a burning sensation as the weak yellow stream plinked into the echoing bowl. He glanced at the mirror, the sink, the huge old tub, all of which had somehow survived not only the war but also his family's long absence in Switzerland. The house remained grand, despite everything that history had thrown its way. Like Kurt, it was a miracle of survival but in constant need of repair. Roofers last week, plumbers before that. Now the refrigerator.

But outside the house, the Bauer name had quite a different connotation. Bauer factories were still among the most profitable in Europe, and in consumer circles it was received wisdom that anything bearing the Bauer name was built to last.

Not that Kurt had much to say about it anymore. Several years ago he had turned over daily operations to his nephew, Manfred. A sixth generation of Bauers now ruled, while a seventh waited in the wings. Not bad, considering that the Bauers had now endured socialism, Nazism, anarchy, monarchy, Weimar hyperinflation, the reichsmark, the deutschmark, the euro, two world wars, and then the Cold War.

Of course, it was always easier to survive upheaval when your business provided the chemical and metallurgical building blocks of destruction. Keep coming up with ways to make killing more efficient and you would always have friends in high places and, when necessary, in plenty of foreign lands.

Even that status hadn't kept the Bauers from occasionally running afoul of various official snoops and regulators, though, especially in the years after Kurt led the family business into the nuclear marketplace. The sensitivity of that venue, plus the fickle nature of peacetime alliances, made for tricky relationships. A country that was a friend during the week you took an order might have been designated an enemy by the time you filled it. And who could say for sure where some middleman might next peddle your merchandise? Best not to ask, especially as long as export laws remained comfortably vague.

So affairs had become cumbersome at times, and even dangerous. Other nations filed complaints. Investigators came calling, wanting a peek at the Bauer books. Kurt had offered testimony when pressed, but kept his Rolodex well hidden, memorizing certain key contacts when necessary. And when that didn't work, he had resorted to baser tactics. Amazing how much it could cost to make a few paragraphs disappear from some UN report on proliferation issues.

Under those kinds of circumstances, who would ever blame an old arms maker from Berlin for deciding that there was still some tidying up left to do with regard to his standing in the world?

So, on a morning already freighted by memory and regret, Kurt cleared his throat and picked up the bedside phone. He paused to make sure Gerda was safely out of earshot, then punched in the number for an apartment across town in Kreuzberg, temporary home to a foreign fellow who, as a precaution of cover, was living well below his means among Turks and Arabs.

Kurt used a CryptoPhone for these transactions, a state-of-the-art machine. Made in Germany, of course. Three thousand euros, but worth it. Its scrambling and encryption technology meant every conversation was secure. But he played it careful, all the same. You didn't make it this far by trusting just anybody.

A man answered in German. The voice and accent were familiar.

Kurt, being the only regular caller to the number, didn't bother to say hello.

"Any news?"

"Yes. The American is in jail."

"Encouraging. So are you about to make the acquisition?"

"Nothing certain. But I feel strongly that it will be soon."

"Any sign of the girl?"

"I am told she is nearby."

"Tell your man to take care with her, even if she is a pest. Girls always get caught in the middle of these things, and it never ends well. At this point you need concern yourself only with him."

"Are you ready to arrange delivery?"

"Only when you have something to deliver."

"As I said, I expect it to be soon."

"As soon as you are proven correct, I will act. But not a moment sooner. Phone immediately when it is done."

"Of course."

Kurt hung up and glanced toward the window, past the lace, where a weak sun was trying to burn through low clouds. To his mind, his present position was enviable. Three important people now awaited his latest pronouncement—one in Washington, one in Tehran, and one in that godforsaken little outpost in the hills of New York. None were his employees, although a few of his own recent hires were already on the march as well. But for the moment all three seemed quite willing to dance to his tune. He just needed to make sure things stayed that way.

His legs ached, so he climbed stiffly back into bed and sagged against the pillow. Liesl was always on his mind after these phone calls, even when he hadn't just dreamed of her, and this morning she seemed closer than ever.

He wondered if she might still be out there, flitting between the chimneys, daring him to take a look, her eyes lit by the fires of her old causes. Nobility and rightness had always been on her side, and so had Kurt. If he slid back beneath the covers instead of going downstairs, would she favor him with another visit? Probably not. She never came at his bidding.

But he had other ways of seeking her out. Concentrate hard enough and he could place himself back in the organ loft of that medieval church in Dahlem, on the frigid afternoon just before Christmas, in 1942. He was there now, treading a creaky stair while voices murmured nervously in the old wooden pews below. Seditious talk that had thrilled even as it terrified. No one had yet seen him, and he hesitated. It would have been so easy to just wait them out and then turn for home, not yet a name on their dangerous list. Maybe his father was right about these people. Sure, the government was insane, and without a doubt the leader had flipped his mustache. But this was treason, all the same. Betrayal.

Then, peeking through the slats of the stairway, he spotted Liesl sitting in the back, her valiant face in profile, as inspiring as sunlight through the leaves of an enchanted beech. And at that moment he was sure the risks were worth it, or at least that *she* was worth it. So he continued down the steps, no longer taking care to be silent, until a face or two in the back looked up and saw him, and nodded at his arrival.

A short while later she stood and made her speech while all of them watched in admiration. Even Bonhoeffer, the pious old meddler whose martyrdom had made history, had been impressed with Liesl. You could see it in his eyes whenever he spoke to her, his instant recognition that she possessed a grace and wisdom well beyond her years.

Climbing aboard this memory, Kurt drifted deeper into his subconscious, and within seconds he, too, might as well have been out there on the clouds in a place no one could reach, not even his smug little associate in Kreuzberg.

In his mind's eye he now watched himself at age seventeen, leaning forward in the straight-backed pew while Liesl spoke. The seat was uncomfortable, built centuries earlier, and the old Kurt no longer felt the downy softness of his pillow. Instead, a knot formed in his back, the pew creaked, and he heard Liesl's voice very clearly. As he listened, the sound transported him even further back through time, another entire year, to that charmed night when he stood beneath a grand chandelier, a glass of champagne in hand, and first saw her, standing on the opposite side of the room. A starched collar chafed at his neck, but he didn't mind, because the girl whose name he didn't yet know had just opened her mouth in joy and surprise, and the sight took his breath away.

The young Kurt smiled. The old Kurt did the same. Then both Kurts listened, enraptured, as her laughter filled the room.

FOUR

V IV WRAPPED NAT UP in a huge hug the moment he came through the door. Neil had agreed to wait in the car to delay the inevitable letdown.

"You're a prince for coming."

"No, I'm not. How's Gordon?"

"Sleeping, I hope. I guess we'll find out. He doesn't even have his meds."

"Meds?" This was new.

"Digitalis, for his heart. He's old, Nat. Too old to be treated this way."

So was Viv. Her stiff gray hair was all over the place, and her eyes were red from drinking or crying, maybe both. She wore leather mocs and a white terry-cloth robe stained with bacon grease. Her weight was up, yet she still looked frail. She was a wreck.

"Tell me what happened."

She poured a mug of coffee and they sat in the kitchen. He wondered nervously when Neil would barge in. He'd asked for five minutes, but doubted he would get them.

"It was one big cock-up. Oh, Nat, what am I thinking? Let me fix you breakfast."

"Keep your seat, Viv. Just talk."

She paused, plucking at nails already torn to the quick.

"We'd been down to Sparrow Lake for dinner. A new Italian place. Dreadful. I had to drive on the way back, three guesses why. When we came through the door, well, I pretty much told you. They were in here like the Gestapo."

"FBI people?"

"Five of them. And they still haven't charged him. Left that to the local yokel, some Barney Fife who said he was arresting Gordon for theft."

"Wait. He's not in federal custody?"

"That's why the arraignment's local. But you'd never know from all the manpower. I've got an agent in the living room, one in the sunroom, and two out in the drive. They've been in the car all night, drinking coffee and running the engine. The fumes go straight up into the bedroom, but they don't care."

Neil Ford walked in, and another agent approached from the opposite direction. He was the one who spoke first.

"Dr. Turnbull? Glad you could make it." He thrust out a hand. "Special Agent Clark Holland. We've got plenty of work for you. Thanks for delivering him, Agent Ford."

Viv looked back and forth, whipsawed. She put a hand to her mouth like she'd just seen a horrible accident, and she stood uncertainly. Nat reached across the table to steady her, but she backed away, wobbly with sudden rage.

"I wanted to tell you first, Viv. They called right after you did."

"Guess you never got over being the prodigal son."

"It's not like that."

"Sure, Nat. I see *exactly* how it is."

He looked to Holland, but the agent was no help.

"If you'll excuse us, Mrs. Wolfe, I'd like a word in private with Dr. Turnbull."

"Private. My own damn house and *he* wants privacy. Well, he's all yours. I'd ask for a ride into town later, Nat, but I guess you'll be going with them."

"I'd be happy to take you. I've got my own car."

Holland shook his head.

"I'd prefer you didn't," he said.

"See? They already own you." She set off down the hall.

"Let's talk later, Viv."

"Sure, Nat," she called over her shoulder. "Whatever you fucking say."

Holland smiled uneasily and took Viv's seat.

"She'll get over it. Once she learns what you're here for."

"What *am* I here for? Agent Ford wasn't exactly forthcoming."

"The short version is that we appear to have recovered some old intelligence files that have been missing for quite some time, stuff collected by the OSS in Switzerland, from '43 to '45. We'd like you to confirm the provenance and summarize the contents."

So it was true, then. They'd found the mother lode, Gordon's long-sought treasure. And for the next few days Nat would have it all to himself. For all the awkwardness of the setup, the news was electric.

"What we're asking shouldn't take long," Holland said. "Quick and dirty."

"Slow and steady would be better. You could do quick and dirty yourselves. Have you informed the National Archives? They'll want to know right away."

"Of course. They wanted to send one of their own people, but we preferred you."

"Let me guess. Too proprietary for your tastes? These things technically belong to the CIA, you know. That's where the archives will send them."

"Like I said, speed is important. I'm sending you off to freshen up and get a bite to eat, then you can get cracking. We've booked you at a B&B if you want to shower and shave. Our treat, of course." Then he stood, ready to roll.

"Okay if I have a quick look at the boxes first?"

The agent glanced at his watch.

"I suppose. This way."

Nat's anticipation built as they strolled toward the sunroom. Four narrow boxes—gray cardboard with metal corners—were stacked on a coffee table, awash in morning sunlight. They had flip-top lids like the ones on cigarette packs.

"Do you mind?" Nat said, reaching for the nearest.

"Go ahead. They've already been dusted."

Nat saw smudges from fingerprint powder. The corners were dented, as if the boxes had been handled roughly.

"Were they stacked this way when you found them, two on top of two?"

Holland nodded.

"Then whoever put them here either didn't know how to handle this kind of material or didn't care. Meaning it definitely wasn't Gordon."

"His prints were all over them."

"Maybe the prints are old. Even if he was drunk, he'd know better. They shouldn't be stacked now, either. Or sitting in the sun."

Nat knew how fragile this stuff could be. Many records from World War II were printed on cheap stock, high in acid. Even medieval parchment was sturdier. Another few decades would turn these papers to dust. They were probably as brittle as autumn leaves already.

Holland, cowed into silence, watched as Nat reverently pulled open the lid. The smell was of rotting cellulose, and he could have sworn there was also a whiff of coal smoke and Alpine air, an essence of Bern from those distant years when so much was at stake.

He gently thumbed a few folders, checking the labels. Already he saw snatches of writing in German. Despite his weariness from the overnight ride, being in the presence of such extraordinary material had cleared his head, and in that moment it occurred to him why the FBI must be insisting on "quick and dirty."

"You're looking for something specific, aren't you?"

"You could say that."

"Care to tell me now? That way I can be thinking about it over breakfast."

Holland hesitated.

"Ever heard of a student resistance group called the White Rose?"

"Sure. They're famous. A German director made a movie about them more than a decade before *Schindler's List*, just when everybody was working up an appetite for tales of 'good Germans.' Led by Sophie Scholl, the pretty college student from Munich, and her older brother Hans, who fought on the Russian front. Cranked out a bunch of anti-Nazi pamphlets along with their friends until the Gestapo rounded everybody up. Hanged or beheaded, most of them. The Brits got hold of one of their pamphlets and dropped a few thousand copies out of a propaganda bomber, but that was about as far as their influence went. Unless you happen to believe the whole Berlin mythology."

"Berlin mythology?"

Was it his imagination, or had Holland flinched?

"There were five or six White Rose cells besides the main one in Munich. The pamphlets found their way to maybe a dozen cities, and the Nazis arrested enough suspects for at least five trials. But no records of any trials or arrests in Berlin have ever turned up. Meaning that either the paperwork was blown to smithereens or there wasn't any to begin with. And whenever you get a vacuum like that, well, people take liberties. Some of the resulting theories have been a little fanciful, to say the least."

"Fanciful?" Holland seemed to brighten.

"Tying the White Rose to Dietrich Bonhoeffer, for example, the famous resistance cleric, not to mention the subject of my first book. Bonhoeffer was involved in the bomb plot against Hitler. You know, von Stauffenberg and the exploding briefcase."

"I take it you don't believe in those connections?"

"Only in the vaguest sense. Bonhoeffer knew a White Rose contact—that's been established. And maybe there was a meeting or two in a church, like-minded friends talking things over, that sort of thing. But I've never believed in any material connection, no. And certainly the Berlin White Rose—if it even existed—never did anything of note."

"Then I suppose that's something you can keep an eye out for, this whole Berlin question. Two days should be sufficient, don't you think?"

"Possible. But—"

"Good. All I needed to hear."

"One other thing, before you send me to breakfast."

"Yes?" Holland was halfway across the living room.

"I promised I'd attend the arraignment. Vouch for Gordon's character, if necessary."

"No objections, as long as you don't get too chummy. It's at nine. We'll be there, too. But if you speak to him, use absolute discretion concerning anything we've discussed. That goes for everyone you deal with. Family, colleagues, even the waitress at the diner."

"National security, huh?"

He was expecting a laugh, or at least a smile. Holland offered neither.

A half hour later Nat emerged from the world's weakest shower to bump his head on a sloped ceiling. FBI agents had taken all the rooms with tubs and canopy beds, leaving him an attic space that would have once been called a garret. He threw open the curtains on a tiny gabled window. A few townspeople were out and about, their breath clouding in the chilly morning air. He spotted his next destination just down the block, a diner where the windows were fogged with steam.

Ten minutes later he slid into a booth while a waitress poured coffee. No sooner had he opened the menu than two of the agents took the next booth down and nodded hello. Was this how it would be from now on—watched and herded until the job was done?

They followed him to the arraignment, too, three blocks to the so-called courthouse at the end of town. It was a converted body shop, just as Neil Ford had said. Someone had whitewashed the cinder-block walls, but faint lettering underneath still boasted of tune-ups for $39.95. Wood-grain paneling was tacked over the old garage doors, and orange carpeting had been rolled onto the concrete slab. Church pews of varnished mahogany provided the seating—five rows on either side of a center aisle. Holland was already seated on the left, along with the two agents from the diner. No one had turned on the heat, so everyone was keeping their coats on. Nat took a seat near the front on the opposite side.

The judge's bench was a plain desk and a folding chair, flanked by flags. On the back wall was a calendar advertising the local Shell station, presumably the one owned by the judge and the town cop. Nat was prepared for entertainment. Gordon could be wittily combative even when sober, and who knows what he might say in this tinhorn setup.

A new arrival took a seat on Holland's side. A woman, early thirties, blond and attractive. Nat guessed she was a reporter, or had come for another case. Something about her was unmistakably arresting. It wasn't style or polish. If anything, she looked like she'd had a rougher night than Nat. Her hair stood out like Viv's, and her clothes were frumpy—brown corduroy pants, a bulky white peasant blouse, no coat. Part of the attraction was her heart-shaped face, classic features in all the right places. Full lips were set in a determined pout, smoldering or ultra-serious, depending on your interpretation. But what really set her apart was her eyes. Deep brown, bright and alert, they broadcast a beacon of needful intensity. Even in repose, she was a woman of urgency.

A door opened up front. In came Gordon, followed by a policeman who took him to a chair on Nat's side of the room. He looked pretty good, considering. Red-nosed but clear-eyed, and he had shaved. He studiously ignored Nat.

The judge followed, tall and ungainly, late fifties. He shrugged on a black robe over jeans and a plaid flannel shirt. No shave for him, and Nat could have sworn there were toast crumbs in his stubble. Just the sort of fellow you could imagine shaking his head and saying, "It's only a busted hose, but we gotta pull the engine." He sat at the desk and cleared his throat just as Viv entered from the rear and took a seat a few rows behind Nat.

"Looks like everybody's here," the judge said. "I'm Darrell Dewey, and over there by the flag is Officer Willis Turner. Welcome to the town court of Blue Kettle Lake, State of New York. We are now in session."

He glanced at some papers.

"What've we got, Willis, two cases?"

"A drunk and disorderly from guess who, along with the celebrity professor."

Dewey peered down his nose at Gordon, who smiled at the description.

"And where is our friend Mr. Wellborn—now there's a contradiction in terms. You gonna bring him out now, or wait till we're done with this one?"

"His wife brought breakfast. He's still eating."

"Well, isn't that sweet. Then let's get to it. The case of Ashford County versus Gordon Wolfe. I take it you're Professor Wolfe?"

"Yes, sir." His voice was clear, strong.

"Lawyered up?"

"Don't need to."

Dewey raised his eyebrows and looked around, as if someone might volunteer.

"You might want to reconsider. Especially since it's my understanding that certain federal authorities—your peanut gallery over there—have taken a keen interest."

"Need one even less as long as they're involved."

"Your business. And mine is to set bail. Officer Turner has requested, presumably at the urging of *others*"—he glanced theatrically toward the federal contingent—"that bail be set at half a million."

Viv gasped. Gordon smiled.

Dewey continued, "Frankly, I can't do that in good faith on a simple possession of stolen goods charge, which as far as I can tell from the paperwork is all we have at this point."

"Go ahead, Your Honor," Gordon said, looking far too confident for his own good. "Won't bother me. I don't intend to pay no matter what the amount."

"Suit yourself. But this is my courtroom, and I'm setting bail at twenty-five grand." He slammed the gavel down as if hammering a dented fender. "Willis, go see if Ed Wellborn can squeeze us into his social schedule."

The policeman went to fetch the other man while the judge fiddled with paperwork. Nat slid down the pew toward Gordon, who finally acknowledged him with a wink.

"Viv says you've made camp with the barbarians," he whispered. Not angrily, but with a twinkle in his eye.

"Not exactly. I just—"

"Don't worry, Nat. I understand completely. It's the first thing they've done right. Just do as they say. Inspect everything carefully and diligently, and tell them exactly what you find. Or more to the point, exactly what you *don't* find."

"You act like you know what they're looking for."

"More than you do, apparently."

They were on sensitive ground, especially with Holland only twenty feet away.

"Don't get nervous," Gordon said. "I won't ask you to say anything you shouldn't."

It was already their most congenial conversation in years. Maybe jail agreed with him.

"So you're not posting bail?"

"I'd just as soon stick it out in here than out there where they are."

"You need anything? Your meds, maybe?"

"Viv brought 'em over. Could sure use a drink, though."

"Can't help you there."

"Didn't think so. How 'bout some pens and paper, then? Tell Viv to send some over."

"I can take care of it."

"No. You concentrate on your work. It's the best thing you can do for me, even though Viv doesn't know it yet. The faster the better. But the most important thing is that you proceed thoroughly and professionally. The way you always do."

His first compliment in ages, and it still had the power to please.

"You sure you don't want a lawyer? I could make some calls."

"Hell, Nat, they planted those boxes. The way I figure it, they've been setting this up for quite a while. Where do you think that story in the *Daily Wildcat* came from?"

"The feds?"

"The kid that wrote that had more of my military records than you'd even get from a freedom of information request. You really think that's the work of a second-year journalism student?"

"Why bother?"

"Flush me out. Give them leverage."

"For what?"

"Except I'll be the one with the leverage. You'll see."

"For *what*, Gordon?"

"Just do your job, Nat, and your employers will be ready to deal. The sooner you finish, the sooner your old professor gets out of this chicken coop."

"Unless they move you to some federal chicken coop."

"That's the last thing they want."

"Let's go, sir." It was the cop, Willis Turner, who had arrived with the other prisoner. Gordon stood, then stooped toward Nat for a final word.

"Actually, there is one thing you can do. Tell your Mr. Holland that as long as he's going to all this trouble, maybe he should give me some protection. This place is wide open."

"Protection from what?"

"Her, for starters." He nodded toward the mystery woman in the peasant blouse, who to Nat's surprise had moved to the front row just across the aisle. "She's a damned nuisance. But it's the others that really worry me."

"What others?"

"Holland will know. Just tell him."

Typical Gordon. Playing up the drama for all it was worth, now that he was the center of attention. The cop led Gordon away before Nat could ask more, and the old man's age showed in the stiffness of his first steps. Nat thought he heard a sob from Viv in the back, but Gordon was grinning as he went out the door.

Nat turned, half expecting Holland to be glaring in disapproval. But the only person paying any attention was the young woman, who looked away quickly, as if she had been eavesdropping. Maybe she was his federal minder. He tried staring her down, but she kept her eyes averted, and he was too intimidated by her looks to introduce himself.

When he stood to leave, he was mildly disappointed that she didn't follow. Oh, well. If she really was with the FBI, he supposed they'd be meeting soon enough.

FIVE

ONLY HOLLAND and the two agents from the diner were at Gordon's house when Nat began reviewing the files. No sign of Viv or the mystery woman. Agent Neil Ford had vanished, presumably to wherever he'd come from.

"I'll leave you to your work," Holland said. "Let me know of any special needs."

"Peace and quiet should do it."

"And do you have a camera? A notebook?"

"Uh, yeah. Both."

"Sorry, but you're to lock the camera in your car until completion. Keep note taking to a minimum. Anything you write down belongs to us."

At least they couldn't confiscate his memory. Another reason to proceed slowly.

For all his eagerness, the first hours were tedious. The archive was cluttered, as such things usually are, with grunt work—German press summaries, translations of Nazi speeches from Radio Stuttgart, interoffice correspondence over matters so trivial that they had become irrelevant within days. So far, not a single mention of the White Rose.

But here and there were tantalizing glimpses of people and events that Nat knew about, and he paused to savor them. It wasn't just scholarly indulgence. It was the only responsible way to proceed, lest he miss an obscure but previously unknown connection to either White Rose activities or the Scholls.

Nat was reasonably familiar with the major players of wartime Bern—the spies, businessmen, and diplomats that Dulles and his pickup team of operatives had mingled with. In one folder he spotted a reference to a meeting between Dulles and Gero von Gaevernitz, a debonair German financier who spent the first years of the war shuttling between Bern and Berlin while piling up an impressive hoard of intelligence.

Fearing for his safety, Gaevernitz left Germany for good in late 1941 to take refuge in Bern, where he became a confidant of Dulles. They met almost daily at the spymaster's ground-floor flat at Herrengasse 23, and Gaevernitz often arranged introductions with visiting Germans willing to pass along information. Switzerland's wartime blackout made it easy for clandestine visitors, who approached a back entrance via an uphill path through terraced gardens overlooking the River Aare. As an extra precaution, Dulles talked the locals into removing the bulb from the streetlamp that illuminated his doorway.

Dulles's status was an open secret. That was the way he wanted it, calculating that the best way to join the spy game was to let it be known that he was open for business. It was one reason the British never put much stock in his product. They figured he was being played for a fool. Too bad for them. By war's end Dulles was an expert at separating fact from rumor, information from disinformation.

He brought to the job a masculine but genteel clubroom manner, puffing a pipe and sipping port during amiable hearthside chats. Considering the privations of rationing, he offered one of the best tables in town. Shucked oysters, perhaps, followed by roast leg of lamb. Nat had seen those items and more on the household cook's grocery lists, which were on file in a tattered notebook at the National Archives. The cook turned out to be jotting down other items as well, and she was promptly fired when Dulles found out she had been passing information to the Germans.

That was par for the course in wartime Bern—a crowded nest of espionage hatchlings, all crying for their daily feed, then wondering what it was they were really digesting for their masters back home. And Gordon Wolfe, even if nothing but a lowly clerk, had been stationed at the center of it all. That much soon became clear to Nat from the "GW" notations penciled at the corner of several filings. It was eerie to come across his initials, especially while knowing that at the time Gordon was roughly half Nat's current age. Hard to think of him as an ambitious young snoop after having just seen him at the courthouse, shuffling off to jail.

Nat wondered anew why Gordon seemed so eager for him to do a thorough job. And what was it that everyone really wanted him to find? Or *not* find, in Gordon's case. White Rose materials, while interesting, would hardly seem to have much impact on the here and now. And if Nat came up empty, how was that supposed to strengthen Gordon's hand with the feds? Theft was theft, whether the goods were helpful or not.

Halfway through the first box Nat still hadn't found anything even remotely connected to the White Rose, not even in the news summaries. But he had noticed a potentially important anomaly. The label on the box's spine said it contained folders 1–37. A quick count showed that only 33 folders were inside. Numbers 4, 5, 11, and 12 were missing. Was this what Gordon had meant? If so, then where was the missing material, and what was its significance?

Shortly before lunch Nat came across a few items that he figured might someday be useful in his own research. One was a lengthy and colorful account from February 1943 of a visit to Dulles by a German banker, Dieter Elsner. The poor man swallowed so much of Dulles's port that he ended up facedown in the rear garden—next to a grape arbor, appropriately enough. The cook, presumably more reliable than her turncoat predecessor, helped drag the portly fellow back indoors, where Dulles and she revived him long enough for Elsner to groggily telephone a business associate to come retrieve him.

The associate turned out to be industrialist Reinhard Bauer, whom Nat was familiar with from the man's prominent role in Germany's wartime armaments industry. He also became a player in the country's postwar economic renaissance, partly by switching from tank parts to coffeemakers. Bauer was one of those eager-to-please Hohenzollern blue bloods who had dropped the "von" from the family name to appease Hitler's mistrust of the aristocracy. But he was never enough of a gung-ho Nazi to attract the attention of war crimes investigators.

Dulles's typewritten account noted that Bauer arrived at his rear entrance within minutes of Elsner's phone call, which led the spymaster to believe that the whole evening had been a ruse to arrange an introduction. Bauer showed up impeccably dressed, even though it was

2 a.m., and before they even reached his supposedly drunken friend, Bauer was already offering to share his insights on the German rearmament effort led by Reichsminister Albert Speer. The conversation began with such promise that Dulles summoned an interpreter to the house shortly afterward to help translate, since his German and Bauer's English weren't exactly the best. Dulles then assigned the code name "Magneto" to Bauer for use in all ensuing correspondence. It was a decent find for Nat, because up to then he had never come across any evidence that Reinhard Bauer had assisted the Allies. Already the trip was worthwhile.

The odd part was that Gordon had never before mentioned the meeting or Bauer in either his published work or any of their conversations. Yet Gordon had been the summoned translator, and his initials appeared on the memo—a lonely "GW" penciled into the lower left corner.

Nat's stomach growled. It was one thirty. He had been at it for four hours, and to his surprise he was nearly done with the first box. At this rate, two days might actually be enough to complete the assignment, just as Holland had said. How disappointing.

"Hungry?"

It was one of the agents, who had been babysitting Nat from a seat in the living room.

"Yes."

"I could get us some takeout."

"Thanks, but I could use some fresh air. I'll try the diner."

"I'll get my car."

"Alone, if you don't mind."

The man nodded, but looked disappointed. Probably bored out of his mind.

"I have to check your notes before you go."

"Haven't taken any."

"Gotta search you, too."

He patted Nat down from head to toe, then pronounced him good to go.

To Nat's relief, no one followed from the house as he departed in the rented Ford. But halfway down the mountain a sedan in a turnout tucked in behind him and stayed on his tail all the way into town. It was a black Chevy, like the ones the feds were driving. He parked across the street from the diner, and the Chevy took a space half a block back. No one got out. Maybe they were just making sure he wasn't visiting Gordon.

Nat took a menu but decided he had better check in with Karen before ordering, in case news of his "disappearance" had spread. He reached for his cell phone, then cursed as he remembered it was still on his desk. The waitress directed him to a pay phone by the restroom doors and changed a few bucks into quarters so he could use it.

Sending Karen off to Wightman had been his ex-wife Susan's idea, and she had sprung it on him like a trap, by arriving unannounced on his doorstep the day of their daughter's enrollment. At the time he viewed it as a vengeful prank, payback for years of neglect. But he saw now that it was a gift he hadn't deserved, a last opportunity to make friends before youthful bitterness hardened into adulthood.

During Karen's first semester he dutifully visited each week, usually taking her to dinner. Their conversations were strained, awkward. When she inquired about taking one of his classes, he found himself subtly steering her elsewhere, and later wondered why.

It wasn't fear of favoritism, he decided, or a lack of confidence in his lectures. Nat was an engaging speaker, with a wall full of teaching awards. Then it came to him. He realized he had become the very sort of professor she would see right through and, ultimately, despise— glibly entertaining on the podium but AWOL whenever students or office hours beckoned. Sort of like the father he had been. Always leaving others—his graduate assistants, Karen's mom—to deal with the messier affairs of disputed grades, delicate egos, and the youthful need to feel loved and included.

Symptomatic of this approach was his standard preamble, the one he had been using for years to open each and every course:

Faces to the front, you sons and daughters of YouTube and Facebook. Cell phones off. BlackBerries disabled. iPods silenced. Mouths shut.

I will offer this information only once, so take heed. Henceforth we will proceed at my pace, not yours. No one is to ask me to back up, start over, or slow down. The lazy and the inattentive will be summarily abandoned, and from here onward you will need to know exactly where we are, where we've been, and where we're going. Those, after all, are the reasons we study history, correct? History plays for keeps, and so do I.

Until Karen's arrival he had always thought of his little intro as standard shock therapy for bored undergrads, a mildly clever alternative to merely handing out the syllabus. But as he sat across from her in a downtown eatery, telling her once again why it might be wiser to take Mainstream Currents in American Political Thought, he realized he would never be able to repeat those words with her in the audience. They were too much of a self-reproach, a confession of the sort of person he was becoming.

Not long afterward they achieved a breakthrough, when Karen became infected by the same sort of intellectual fever that had possessed him at her age, under Gordon's influence. For her the subject was poetry—specifically, the poems of Emily Dickinson. Hardly the first time a female undergrad had fallen under the spell of the Belle of Amherst. Then again, Nat hadn't exactly been the first male smitten by the Past.

In any event, it gave him an easy point of entry into her inner life, since he knew firsthand the excitement she was feeling. It was a little bit like watching someone fall in love. He was charmed, even a little jealous, wishing he could borrow some of her spark for his own hurtful romance with History.

By encouraging her enthusiasm he first won her gratitude, and then her trust. He ordered a poster from the Emily Dickinson Museum, which she immediately tacked up above her desk. He then sealed the deal by beginning a father-daughter parlor game of swapping Dickinson quotes whenever they met, with each of them tailoring the passage to prevailing circumstances. Thank goodness the Belle wrote a zillion poems, giving Nat gobs of material. Their exchanges became well known in the history and English departments, prompting a colleague of Nat's to remark archly, "If her life had stood a loaded gun, does that make dear old dad a vintage Luger?"

So now, standing in the diner as her number rang, he searched his memory for an appropriate stanza. About then he happened to glance out the window of the diner, just as the door was opening on the Chevy that had followed him into town. The mystery woman from the courtroom got out and headed his way. His stomach fluttered. By the time Karen answered, he was fumbling for words.

"Dad?"

"I'm here. Just give me a sec. Got to load some quarters."

"I heard about your cell phone. That was a very dramatic note you left behind."

"So the FBI called?"

"At, like, seven this morning. Just what my hangover needed."

"Sorry. I realized later I'd overreacted."

"Where did they take you?

"Up to Gordon Wolfe's summer house."

"The one with, like, fifty deer antlers in the living room?"

"That's called Adirondack style. I'd forgotten you've been there."

"I was only eleven. But even then I remember thinking he was a scary old guy."

"Not anymore. They've thrown him in jail."

"Wow. Crimes against humanity?"

"Seriously, he's in deep trouble. They found a stolen archive in his kitchen. That's why they brought me in."

"To do what?"

He quoted the stanza that had popped into his head:

" 'He ate and drank the precious words, His spirit grew robust.' "

"You're, uhhhh, appraising the archive?"

"Like, very good. Unfortunately they're only giving me two days."

"What does Professor Wolfe think of all this?"

"He's surprisingly supportive. Seems to think I can help his case. None of which I'm supposed to be discussing, by the way."

"And with a blabbermouth student, no less. Does the FBI have your cell phone?"

"They're supposed to. Why?"

"Well, about an hour after they called I got a hang-up from your number."

"Checking out my call menu, I guess. Natural-born snoops."

"Except this was some guy with an accent, wondering who I was. When I asked for his name, he hung up."

"Hmm. Could've been Sobelsky. His carrel's next to mine, and he's Polish. Maybe he was sleuthing on my behalf. I should call him."

"Better cancel your service before somebody runs up the bill."

"As if you'd know anything about that."

"No comment. When do you get back?"

"Another day or two, probably. Meaning I won't be there to help you move in. Can you get your stuff over from the dorm okay?"

"Don't worry. Dave said he'd help."

Dave, her campus boyfriend. Meaning they'd be alone in Nat's house. Great.

"I know what you're thinking, Dad. I won't be stupid."

"Just as long as Dave isn't. Say hello to your mom for me. But I wouldn't mention the moving arrangements if I were you."

"Like I said, I won't be stupid."

He smiled as they hung up. But something about the news of the hang-up didn't sit well, not with the skittish way Holland was acting— as if this really *was* some sort of big deal concerning national security. Nat would have dialed up his cell number to see who answered, but he was out of quarters.

Instead, he scanned the diner for the mystery woman. No sign. He slid back into his booth to find that his coffee was going cold. Finally he could relax, and he felt the weariness of the long night settling into the backs of his eyes. It would have been quite easy to stretch out on the banquette for a nap, and he was on the verge of nodding off when someone sat down in the opposite seat.

He opened his eyes to see the woman from the courthouse sitting directly across the table. Again he was struck by the intensity of her eyes, which gave him a jolt as potent as the coffee. Her blouse smelled like cigarettes. From that, and from the choppy hairstyle, he deduced that she was European. When she spoke, her accent confirmed it.

"Hello, Dr. Turnbull. My name is Berta Heinkel."

"Heinkel? Same as the aircraft?"

"Yes. No relation."

German name, German accent. He thought immediately of the hang-up call to Karen, but that had been a man.

"So I guess you're not one of the feds after all."

"Feds?"

"The FBI."

"No." She glanced behind her. "Will they be joining you?"

"Not if I can help it. Who are you, then?"

"A historian, like yourself. I have an interest in the materials."

She handed him a business card: Professor Doktor Berta Heinkel from the Free University of Berlin.

"How do you even know about 'the materials,' Dr. Heinkel?"

"Please, call me Berta. I was in College Park doing research. A friend at the archives told me. He said there had been an arrest and that they were bringing in an expert."

"The National Archives?"

She nodded.

"And you just dropped everything to come up here?"

"The first available flight. I rented a car at the airport."

"Wow. That's dedication."

"It's my life's work."

"Your life's work," he said, marveling at the phrase.

"I knew right away they would choose you. As their expert, I mean."

"Did you, now?"

Ingrid Bergman. That's who her eyes reminded him of, especially up close. The question was whether they were more like Ingrid's eyes in *Casablanca*—liquid and warm, brimming with promise—or in *Notorious*—burning with intent, a troubled soul who knew what she wanted and would soon have it.

"Of course. You were the natural choice. The only choice."

Such flattery. He was leaning toward *Notorious*.

"And what's your particular interest in this discovery? Which, by the way, I'm not supposed to discuss."

"You are probably also not supposed to discuss that you have not yet found what you are looking for. Yet I am sure this is true."

"Why do you say that?"

"Because what you are looking for is not there. The materials have been sanitized. Or that is what I think."

"You sound like you've been talking to Gordon Wolfe. Or maybe you just overheard us in the courtroom."

Her eyes flared, but she didn't deny it.

"I couldn't hear everything, of course. But neither of you said a word about the White Rose, yet I know that is the main object of your search, and it is mine as well."

He was amazed, and a little alarmed.

"Look, I shouldn't be having this conversation. You could be anyone."

"What do you need to know about me? I am a scholar, quite qualified. I am single, thirty-three, have lived in Berlin all my life."

"Where in Berlin?"

"Prenzlauer Berg."

"East Berlin?"

"Is that a problem?"

"Not since '89."

"I only want to help. I already know more than you ever will on this subject. Or the feds, either."

The way she said "feds" was almost comical, like some Euro sophisticate trying to play the role of Chicago gangster.

"I'll be happy to pass along your name and number to the FBI."

She shook her head disdainfully, as if such work was beneath her.

"Then why have you come here?"

"To offer my assistance to you. For afterward. When you are done with your review, you will want to know more. That is the nature of materials like these. They develop their own attraction."

Like you, he thought.

"That is when I will be able to help you. Because there is more material out there, waiting to be found. More than those four boxes."

So she knew the number of boxes. Her friend at the archives had been indiscreet, and somehow Nat wasn't surprised that the friend was a "he."

"How do you know there's more?"

"I have been studying this puzzle long enough to learn all its missing pieces."

"Just because they're missing doesn't mean they still exist. There was a war going on. Things got burned, bombed, or looted."

"Not in Switzerland."

Good point.

"So you say you want to help me. But I'm guessing what you really want is for me to help you."

"Describe it that way if you wish. I am convinced that between the two of us we can find what I'm looking for. When that happens, I will be happy to share the credit. And since you are far better known in our field, you will end up winning most of the glory. That is fine. It is not my concern. I am only interested in locating the information."

"I take it that your specialty is the White Rose?"

She nodded.

"Since I was fifteen."

"Goodness. It really *is* your life's work."

"My grandmother was a friend of a member when she was a girl. She told me all the stories. She said the friend was killed when the Berlin cell collapsed, or maybe 'imploded' is a better word. She said there were arrests, and even executions, but that all the official records were destroyed. She was determined to prove they had happened, but she was never able to travel into the West. A month after she died, the Wall came down. I took it as a sign that I was meant to continue the job for her."

So, another believer in the so-called Berlin cell. But at least this one seemed to have some firsthand information, even if a bit vague.

"Nice story. And I'd love to hear more about your grandmother's stories. But I'm afraid I still can't help you. Not yet, anyway." She nodded briskly, as if she expected nothing less from such a narrow thinker. "I do have one question, though. Any idea why Gordon Wolfe would refer to you as a 'damned nuisance'?"

For the first time Berta seemed knocked off balance, but she recovered quickly.

"I suppose it's because I approached him once as well. Several times. He, too, said no, and look where it got him. If you change your mind, my mobile number is on my card."

She gathered her handbag and briefcase and stood to leave. Nat had a vague sense of having narrowly avoided involvement in a very complicated venture. He wasn't sure whether to feel disappointed or relieved.

But like any good salesman, Berta Heinkel hadn't really finished. She had saved her best pitch for last.

"It's not just the White Rose that is of interest to them, you know."

"No?"

"No. It is the Berlin chapter in particular. Maybe they aren't willing to tell you that. But I am certain."

He shrugged and didn't say a word, although his expression probably told her all she needed to know.

"I even have a name," she said, reeling him in further. "Someone who is apparently mentioned in the materials."

"Yes?"

"Kurt Bauer, the arms merchant. Quite famous now, but he was practically a boy then, not even old enough for the army. But there will be no trace of him in those boxes, either. Unless it is some passing reference to his father."

"Reinhard Bauer?" It slipped out before he knew it.

"Yes. So you have already found it. They met, you know."

"Who did?"

"Reinhard Bauer and your colleague, Gordon Wolfe. Kurt met

Professor Wolfe, too, although they were both very young at the time."

"In Switzerland?"

"Yes. It happened because your friend was a spy, and not a very good one. At least, that's my theory. So you see? Already you know more than when I met you. Keep working with me and you will have a far better chance of getting all that you want."

The remark was stirring on several levels. Then she turned and slipped out the door, baggy blouse and all, although at that moment she couldn't have been more alluring to Nat if she'd been wearing high heels and a strapless gown. He watched her through the window all the way to her car, but she never once looked back. A virtuoso performance, he had to admit. He was breathless.

SIX

WAS IT REAL or was he dreaming?
Berta Heinkel crawled toward Nat across the bed in the half-light before dawn. She wore a short nightgown of antique silk, the kind of precious material that might once have been traded for war ration coupons or black-market Luckies. Slinky and smooth, like her skin. He stroked his fingers down her back, the perfect start to his day.

A sharp knock at the door rudely answered Nat's question. He awoke to full daylight, an empty bed, and a painful erection. The innkeeper shouted crankily through the keyhole.

"Mr. Turnbull?"

"Yes?"

"You're wanted downstairs. A Mr. Holland. He says it's urgent."

"Tell him five minutes."

The bedside clock read 6:07 a.m. He knew Holland was in a hurry for him to finish the boxes by this afternoon, but this was ridiculous, seeing as how he had worked until almost ten o'clock the night before.

The innkeeper's footsteps receded down the stairs, but their sound was soon drowned out by the brusque approach of a heavier tread. Nat barely had time to pull his trousers over the bulge in his briefs before the door flew open. In stepped Clark Holland, suit pressed, tie knotted.

"Is this really necessary?"

"Gordon Wolfe is dead. We've got work to do."

"What? Gordon's *dead*? How?"

"Heart attack, less than an hour ago. They found him on the floor of his cell. An EMT revived him for a minute or two, but that was it. Pronounced dead at 5:23 a.m."

Nat sagged onto the bed and took a deep breath. His voice emerged from high in his throat, as if someone were squeezing his windpipe.

"His medication. Viv said—"

"That wasn't the problem. He got his pills yesterday."

"Does she know yet?"

"You're going to tell her. It's our first stop. But first I need some answers."

Holland swung himself onto the room's one and only chair, facing backward. He folded his arms on the top of it while Nat absorbed the blow. Nat was sitting where Berta had just been on all fours in his dream, and he was annoyed that he still couldn't shake the image, even in the face of this terrible news. Gordon was dead. Impossible. It felt as if twenty years of his life had just been wrenched loose, thrown into a box, and abruptly carted away before he could even catalog the contents.

"I can't believe he's gone."

"How did he seem when you spoke to him yesterday?"

He wished Holland would slow down with the questions.

"Well?"

"Same as always, I guess. Only sober. In a way he was almost happy, spoiling for a fight. He looked pretty good. Or I thought he did."

"Was he especially agitated about anything?"

"He wasn't thrilled to be in jail, if that's what you mean. But I wouldn't say he was overwrought. Viv's the one I would have pegged for a breakdown. And you want *me* to tell her?"

"Did you visit him last night?"

"No."

"Or any other time since you saw him in the courtroom?"

"No. That's the only time."

"Any phone calls between you?"

"None."

"You're certain?"

"Absolutely. What are you getting at?"

"What about the girl, the German you met at the diner at lunch yesterday? Did she visit him?"

At the mention of Berta he hunched over to hide the lingering evidence of his dream.

"Doubtful. You'll have to ask her."

"Did she relay any messages between you, either oral or written?"

"As far as I know she hasn't even spoken to him."

"Answer the question."

"No."

Holland stared for a few seconds, as if waiting for Nat to break. Then he stood quickly.

"Get dressed. We're going."

"There was one thing." It had just occurred to Nat, along with a nasty stab of guilt.

"Yes?"

"Gordon told me yesterday to ask you guys for better protection. And I never did, of course. I thought it was just more of his usual dramatics."

"Protection? Against what?"

"He said you'd know."

Holland shook his head, irritated.

"He was talking nonsense. Just like this morning."

"What do you mean?"

"In his only moment of consciousness, the EMT asked what he'd had for dinner the night before. He smiled and said he'd been to the Metropolitan Club in Washington. Those were his last words. The doctor figured it was some kind of private joke. Maybe you'd know the context?"

"The Metropolitan Club? Never heard of it."

"You're certain?"

"He must have been delirious."

Yet the phrase tugged at some old memory, just out of reach. Not from his shared experiences with Gordon—they had never been to Washington together—but from somewhere. Viv might know. Ugh. Telling her was going to be an ordeal for both of them.

But it wasn't Viv he was thinking of by the time Holland and he reached the bottom of the stairs. It was Berta Heinkel. Obviously he had been impressed by her performance in the diner. But now he was upgrading his review, because she had seemed to know things about Gordon that the old man had never told him. And now he would never be able to ask.

Over the next few days he would continue to be impressed. Because, by day's end, Berta Heinkel's peculiar expertise would be in great demand. And within a week she and Nat would be seated together on a Swissair nonstop from Washington to Bern—the very place where, long ago, Gordon Wolfe had begun assembling the makings of his own destruction.

SEVEN

Berlin—December 20, 1941

D ON'T YOU HATE PARTIES like this?"
Not much of a pickup line, but the girl brightened as if
someone had finally pushed the right button. Or maybe it was
just the glow of the candles from the Christmas tree, a towering spruce
that lit up the room even more than the Biedermeier chandeliers.

"Don't I ever," she said above the roar of conversation. "It's the uniforms I hate most. Everyone showing off, even the ones who aren't in
the Wehrmacht. What good is a uniform when you're just working for
some ministry, sitting in an office all day?"

"Exactly," the boy said.

"Sometimes I think we've all gone a little mad with this war mentality. My name is Liesl, by the way. Liesl Folkerts. And you are?"

"Kurt. Kurt Bauer. And I feel exactly the same."

He didn't really. Nor did he hate the uniforms, except out of envy.
He wished he was wearing one, if only because then he might look
eighteen. If anything, he found the girl's comments bracingly scan-
dalous, the sort of remarks that might have caused a more seasoned lis-
tener to employ the precautionary tactic now known as the *Berliner
Blick*—an over-the-shoulder glance for eavesdroppers.

But at age sixteen Kurt was too young and inexperienced, not to
mention spellbound.

The girl's boldness was especially remarkable considering the setting—a Christmas party at the elegant home of Wilhelm Stuckart, second in command at the Interior Ministry. The many various uniforms
of the Reich were indeed in abundance on this icy winter evening.

Already Kurt had spotted the fussy getups of the Ministries of Interior, Armaments, Economy, and Propaganda. One Luftwaffe staff officer wore a god-awful white jacket as silly as Göring's, and with almost as many bogus ribbons. The only members of the uniformed class not strutting like peacocks were two Gestapo wraiths dressed in the black of the SS. They lurked amid the holiday greenery like tall, somber elves.

Otherwise the scene was festive enough, with a bounty and opulence rare to behold in this year of rationing and restrictions. Brisk servants toted trays of champagne and foie gras across the Oriental rugs and floors of Italian marble. A long, sturdy buffet table made of Black Forest walnut held a huge silver platter of smoked ham and an icy bed of oysters on the half shell. There were also overflowing bowls of potatoes, beans, salads, and baskets of bread, plus more chocolates and pastries than Kurt had seen in ages. He had already spotted a magnificent butter stollen for later sampling.

The pleasant surprises were not limited to the buffet. The Stuckart washroom offered real toilet paper and scented bars of genuine soap.

But the evening's most interesting fare was the talk. This was some of the best-informed gossip in Berlin. Even seemingly frivolous blab offered tasty morsels. Moments earlier Kurt had overheard two spangled women debating which hotels in occupied Paris would offer the most stylish accommodations for visiting Germans come springtime.

The hottest topic was the Americans, who had just entered the war. From what Kurt could gather, the consensus from the corridors of power on Wilhelmstrasse seemed to be that the Yanks wouldn't make much of an impact for at least a year, and by then the war would be over.

One of the few topics he *hadn't* heard discussed was why the German advance on Moscow had suddenly stalled. Too risky, he supposed. Yet here was this slip of a girl named Liesl daring to proclaim that she was sick of uniforms and then openly questioning the nation's war fever. Kurt was enchanted. Then again, he was predisposed to enchantment, having just spent ten minutes maneuvering himself into position to speak with her.

And on at least one count he genuinely agreed with her: These sorts of parties weren't to his liking. Coming here had been his father's idea. It was yet another session in Reinhard Bauer's crash course in the social dynamics of wartime commerce, a tutelage that had begun just after Kurt's sixteenth birthday. Already he had endured weeks of formal introductions, factory visits, and ministry auditions.

This week had been typical: Monday, coffee at the Bosch Works in Kleinmachnow. Tuesday, lunch at the Ministry of Armaments. Then a Wednesday train ride to the city's northwest reaches for a tour of the Rheinmetall-Borsig factory, followed by Thursday's engineering tutorial on metallurgy and Friday's luncheon with accountants at the Red-White Tennis Club, where his father was appalled to discover that the ballroom had been commandeered as a barracks for the crew of an antiaircraft battery, newly positioned on the back lawn.

To close out the week they had come to the Stuckart party, where Kurt was expected to feign a politely casual air and exude holiday cheer even as he strived to make an impression. The Stuckarts lived only a few blocks from the Bauers' home in Charlottenburg, and Kurt had sweated beneath his starched collar as they walked the darkened streets of the blacked-out city. Hard to believe that only two winters ago he had been among the crews of teen boys daubing the neighborhood curbs with luminous white paint to help people find their way in the dark. It was a Hitler Youth project, speaking of silly uniforms. Kurt's group had also helped the neighbors build sandbagged new exits from their basements, which had been converted to bomb shelters.

At least Kurt's father hadn't insisted that he wear the annoying Hitler Youth lapel pin. Kurt had left that behind in a dresser drawer. Good riddance. Nothing was more certain to mark you as a juvenile if you happened to meet some attractive young woman.

It wasn't that Kurt didn't sympathize with his father's need to display loyalty. That would always be an issue for the Bauers. Reinhard blamed himself, tutting that he had waited too late to join the Nazi Party. He had then compounded his problems by dropping the aristocratic "von" from the family name. As acts of appeasement go, it didn't exactly rank with Neville Chamberlain at Munich, but it was nearly as ineffective. Party hacks still mistrusted them as Hohenzollern blue bloods, and their peers now dimly regarded them as slumming opportunists, little better than Jews in their grasping zeal for reichsmarks.

Not so long ago, Kurt would have welcomed his status as an industrial debutante. He had once longed for the day when, like his forebears, he would be counted on to make big decisions affecting the livelihoods of thousands. But that sort of trust had been reserved

instead for his older brother, Manfred, and for years it had been Manfred who got the grooming and the testing. Manfred tagged along on
corporate retreats into the fresh air of the Hartz Mountains, and on
collegial weekend hikes into the piney depths of the Grunewald.
When war seemed imminent, Reinhard fretted over whether to press
for an officer's posting for Manfred in the Wehrmacht or to instead
finagle placement in some safer endeavor that would still offer the
badge of national service.

Then along came the blitzkrieg. Like everyone else, Reinhard
watched the grainy newsreels of hapless Poles with their lances and
horses, and then the fleeing Frenchmen in medieval helmets. He concluded that the rest of the war would also proceed in this "easy" fashion, even as patriotic obituaries soon began filling the newspapers. And
so, to Manfred's delight, Reinhard steered his elder son into the officer
corps.

He should have known better, of course. It was like putting all of
your money into a stock at its peak value. Two months after Manfred
departed for the front lines, the Wehrmacht invaded the Soviet Union.
By the time of the first snowfall it was apparent that the stock price was
falling, although up to now everyone had been too stunned to even
whisper about selling. So, with Manfred indisposed for the indetermi-
nate future, Reinhard decided he had better begin preparing Kurt, just
in case.

The boy at least had a head for math and physics, and he was also a
whiz at English. And with so many students gone off to war he had
been able to enroll in university a year ahead of schedule. But it soon
became clear to Reinhard that Kurt had been left to his own devices for
too long. He had developed an unfortunate appreciation for literature and music, plus a certain dreaminess that meshed poorly with the
no-nonsense mentality of high commerce. It was making for a rocky
transition.

Kurt, then, had walked to the party with an air of resignation, and
when a Stuckart servant held open the leather blackout curtain in the
foyer and took his overcoat, he braced himself for a trying night.

At least Erich would be there. Erich Stuckart, son of the party's
host, was an entertaining schoolmate always good for a few laughs.
Kurt immediately spotted the long, horsey face, just like his dad's.
Erich, too, wore a suit—boring pinstripes in midnight blue. It might
have made him resemble the Gestapo wraiths if not for a bright red

necktie, which Kurt saw now was pinned with a tiny gold swastika. His father's doing, no doubt, because Erich's first order of business was always devilment and drinking, an agenda that already showed in the high flush of his cheeks.

"You've escaped your father. Well done!" Erich said. "I've run my own gauntlet of government types. Dad's idea, of course. But hopefully I'm through for the duration."

"I got lucky," Kurt said. "The minute we walked in he was cornered by some state secretary for economics having a wet dream about the subject of Reichsbahn rolling stock."

"*There's* the only rolling stock *I'm* interested in. Check out the caboose on that one."

Erich tipped his glass toward a passing woman whose dress was several sizes too tight.

"This clothes-rationing business is simply the best," he said. "My mother's seamstress tells her that most women now are rehemming their skirts instead of buying new ones when the edges start to fray. A few more years of war and everything will be mid-thigh. So here's to the plucky Red Army. Long may they hold out in their rat-infested dachas."

Kurt snatched a dripping champagne glass from a passing tray.

"Nice spread you've got, speaking of rationing."

"Shellfish aren't covered, you know, so the oysters were a breeze. The ham and champagne are straight from Paris. The only problem was that everything was sitting in some warehouse west of town, with no trucks and no gasoline. Dad had to find three droopy Poles to lug it here on handcarts. They covered everything with blankets the whole way or they never would have made it through Spandau. People took one look at the sad sacks pulling the load and probably figured it was a mound of horse manure. So drink up. This could be your last bubbly for months. Or at least until your sister Traudl's wedding."

"He hasn't even asked her yet."

"Oh, he will. All the SS men are getting hitched. It's all the rage before going to the front. You better brace yourself for a lot of stupid background checks. They go back six generations, you know. All very silly."

Kurt had overheard his parents expressing worries about this very prospect. But before he could muster up any anxiety of his own, he saw the girl. She was across the room, laughing at something a woman next to her had just said. The candlelight lent her face the radiance of a flower that has just opened its petals. Eyes full of promise. Delicate features. He instinctively wanted to provide her with special care and handling and shepherd her away from this bruising hubbub. Yet the more he watched her talk, the more her movements revealed an underlying fierceness. An emphatic passion punctuated every word.

He couldn't hear a word of what she was saying. It might have been as frivolous as hemlines, or as grim as a casualty list. But did that really matter? She could probably make any topic seem vitally important. He was so riveted that he didn't notice that his father had tracked him down.

"Ah, there you are, Kurt. There is someone you need to meet, right over here. This way, then. *Kurt!* Come along!"

Erich offered a sympathetic shrug, and Kurt spent the next several minutes nodding dutifully at the remarks of a crusty old Prussian named Helmut who was supposedly doing great things with aircraft components over at the Argus Works in Reinickendorf. He exclaimed in earnest approval for the next five minutes while wishing he could tear his eyes away for another glance at the girl. Finally both men were spirited away once again by the man from Economics, who was still gushing about rolling stock.

Kurt turned to search the room. She was still there. He made a beeline back to Erich, hoping for useful intelligence. But Erich spoke first.

"Have you seen that hot little number who just arrived? My God, how perfect."

Oh, no. Had he, too, been struck by the same bolt of lightning?

"Which one?" Kurt asked apprehensively.

"The one in pink. Over there."

Erich pointed to a young woman whom Kurt's mother would have charitably described as a floozy. She had large breasts, amply displayed, and deeply rouged cheeks. She was showing far too much leg— another victim of rationing, perhaps—and was waving a cigarette as if it were a conductor's baton. Her orchestra was three attentive men in uniform, who by all appearances were just as impressed as Erich.

"Very nice. But who's that one, over there by the tree?"

Erich grudgingly shifted his gaze.

"Oh, you mean Liesl?" He smiled. "Now there's an odd one. Pretty. But an odd duck for sure."

"Odd how?" Kurt's tone was defensive.

"Give her a chat, you'll see. Just don't let your father hear what you're talking about. Or mine, either. *That* kind of odd."

Erich, like his dad, had cultivated the ability of damning by implication without offering any specifics that he might have to account for later.

"The good news is that if you happen to like her, she's one of our fellow students at the university. A year ahead of us, but still . . ."

That was all the encouragement Kurt needed to take up the chase. And now there he was, talking to her at last, and finding to his relief that along with her other powers, she also had the ability to put him immediately at ease, which was rarely the case with Kurt and pretty girls.

"Bauer, you said? Is your father the bomb maker?"

He laughed.

"I suppose he wouldn't mind that description, as long as you don't call him the bomb *thrower*, like he was some Bolshevik. But our factories don't really make bombs. Just the fuses, plus the parts for about a dozen other things. Aircraft, artillery, and, well, a bunch of stuff I'm never supposed to talk about. Not out in public, anyway."

"Sounds important. Where is he?"

"That man at the buffet table. By the oysters."

"The one who's looking around like he lost something?"

"Yes."

"You?"

"Good guess."

"Turn around, then, and move behind me. Next to the tree. I'll block his view."

So she was playful, too, not exactly common currency among German girls these days, except the silly ones who giggled at everything. A natural-born conspirator as well, which seemed like another mark in her favor despite its obvious risks—or maybe because of them. For too many days now Kurt had been walking the straight and narrow, taking care to say all the right things. It was a relief to engage in a little rebellion, especially with such an appealing comrade in arms.

"How come he's not wearing a uniform?"

"Well, he is, sort of." This had just occurred to Kurt.

"The gray suit, you mean. Captain of commerce?"

"Yes."

"Then what does that make you?"

She reached out and, thrillingly, ran her fingertips down his lapel. He was again glad he hadn't worn the pin.

"A corporal in training, I suppose."

"Ah. But groomed for promotion."

"Exactly. It's just about all I do anymore, other than school. We spend every weekend going to parties like this. Introductions. Names to remember. Lots of people I'll probably never see again. Which is why it's so nice to escape with you for a while."

"I suppose I'm another of those new names you'll never remember."

"Oh, I doubt that very much, Liesl Folkerts."

What must she have made of this soberly dressed young man who had taken such an intense and immediate interest in her? To look at him—the clipped haircut, the noncommittal face, the correct-to-the-point-of-stiff posture—Kurt Bauer certainly seemed like a very conventional boy, which was hardly her type. But perhaps she also sensed that what he longed for most, even though he never could have articulated it—not yet, anyway—was to be freewheeling and spontaneous, even a little careless.

And as she already knew firsthand, these times were not well suited for the freewheeling, and certainly not for the careless. Unless you had the right sort of patch on your sleeve, or official title to your name, doing as you pleased was almost guaranteed to land you in trouble. Or so her father always told her, every time she spoke her mind.

All that Kurt knew for sure about himself was that in addition to the usual adolescent yearnings of libido, curiosity, and optimism, more-complicated emotions were often straining to be accounted for. Perhaps this was why he reacted so viscerally to Liesl Folkerts. Not only had her looks arrested him, but she had also tuned in right away to his thwarted inner voice, so accurately that she seemed to be humming along with it, perfectly in key.

As he watched her speak, he again thought of her as a newly opened blossom. The brilliance of her beauty, like that of all flowers, would doubtless fade over time. But he decided then and there that in some ways she would never wilt. Not her. And that kind of enduring spirit was worth taking risks for.

"Oh, there's Ludwig," she said, breaking his concentration. Liesl nodded toward the foyer, where a resplendent young man in an officer's dress uniform had just entered. Her expression was now somber—or was it admiring? Kurt's heart sank.

"I really need to talk to him."

"Please do," he said, feeling stung as he stood aside. But she didn't depart.

"It will keep until later. I want news from him. He's been at the front, you know, fighting the Russians. I'm desperate to hear how things are really going, but that's not something you just go up and ask out of the blue, with everyone listening."

So even Liesl had her limits. But he wondered about the nature of her interest.

"Do you know someone at the front, someone close to you?"

He braced for word of a boyfriend, perhaps even a fiancé.

"My older brother has been there for months. Same unit as Ludwig, and we haven't had a letter since October."

"My brother, Manfred, is in Russia, too. He's down near the Caucasus."

"It's crazy, isn't it? The way they're strung out all over Europe, and all over the east. I worry we've bitten off more than we can chew. But look at everyone, carrying on like it's all but decided."

"Oh, I'm sure they worry, too. I know my father does."

"You're right. I shouldn't be so judgmental. It's just that people are so timid now. They hide behind their laughter and won't speak their mind. So when someone finally does, it can sound like treason by comparison, which only makes everyone clam up more. Are we no longer allowed to express doubt?"

"It doesn't seem to stop you."

He said it with a smile, which she returned.

"That's only because I stay in practice. If I stopped I'm not sure I'd ever be able to start again. I'd be too scared."

"And where do you go to stay in practice? To the Tiergarten, maybe, to declaim from a park bench?"

"Actually, there is a place. Very informal and comfortable, among friends. With a minister presiding, so even your parents would approve."

"Yes?"

He sensed an opening. Some venue to which he might invite himself along without seeming presumptuous. Better still, maybe she would invite him, even though he was mildly alarmed by the idea of a minister who sanctioned loose talk of doubt and dissent.

"Have you heard of the Reverend Bonhoeffer?"

He had, but only in passing. The associations were vaguely negative, and he couldn't help notice that even Liesl had checked her flanks before uttering the name.

"Isn't he pretty outspoken?"

"I know he doesn't have the best of reputations in some circles. But he's very devout, very gentle, and he travels abroad for the Foreign Ministry, so it's not like he isn't doing his part for the country."

"I hadn't heard that."

"All he wants is for Germans to do things for the right reasons. Mostly what we talk about is how to appeal to people's better nature."

"It sounds like a good thing, then. And you do this where? In his church?"

"Oh, no. He's not allowed to preach anymore, and they closed his seminary years ago. He has us over to his home. Nothing official. Just a small group of students, on Sunday afternoons when he's not out of the country and has time for us. We're getting together tomorrow, in fact."

She hesitated, and Kurt held his breath. To his relief, she plunged forward.

"You could come, too. If you liked."

Hardly the sort of company his father wanted him to keep, but that only made the invitation more appealing. Kurt experienced a stab of nostalgia for the sorts of gatherings he had attended around the time of his sixteenth birthday but had given up after his father diverted him onto the narrow-gauge rails of the business world. A more relaxed and Bohemian world of books and music and ideas. It had great appeal.

"Yes," he said. "I'd like that."

His answer came in the nick of time, because shortly afterward his father again tracked him down. The next time he looked around for Liesl, she was deep in conversation with two elderly women, and it would have been rude to interrupt.

But they did have a final exchange of sorts, just as stirring in its way. It occurred not long after Erich's mother, a fusty and traditional sort who seemed to enjoy bossing the servants around, loudly announced the commencement of Christmas carols. Erich's sister struck up a tune on the piano, and the crowd joined in—sparsely at first, then in full voice.

The third and final song, which drew the evening to a close— making Kurt suspect that had been Mrs. Stuckart's true purpose—was predictable enough. It was "Stille Nacht," or "Silent Night." Considering the venue, it wasn't surprising that everyone, as if by rote, concluded with a secular third verse that had grown popular during the war.

Silent Night, Holy Night
All is calm, all is bright
Adolf Hitler is Germany's Star
Showing greatness and glory afar
Guiding our nation aright.
Guiding our nation aright.

Kurt searched out Liesl halfway through the verse and found her engaged in perhaps her boldest action of the evening.

Her lips were still. She wasn't singing a word.

His heart leaped at this daring display, even as he feared for her. It emboldened him just enough to halt his own singing, although he did turn so his father wouldn't see. He nodded just enough to catch her eye, and when she nodded solemnly back he felt the color rise in his cheeks, a holiday red.

When he noticed one of the Gestapo fellows glaring from across the room, it was all he could do not to join in for the final line. But he managed, barely, on the strength of a single inspiring thought:

Tomorrow he would see her again.

EIGHT

Berlin—January 20, 1942

To KURT BAUER, the Folkertses' house was a place of enchantment, and not just because Liesl lived there. Its pitched roof, gabled windows, and wooden shutters oozed Alpine charm, while the neighboring Grunewald provided a hushed backdrop of dark pines and fairy-tale beeches. Add a dusting of snow and a curl of chimney smoke, and you had the very essence of cozy German *Gemütlichkeit.*

That was the tableau Kurt came upon that morning as he pedaled his bicycle down a powdery trail with a pair of wooden skis strapped on the back.

It had been exactly a month since he had met Liesl, and already he had become a regular at her address on tiny Alsbacherweg, visiting at least four times a week. The route was happily familiar by now. He would haul his bicycle to his neighborhood U-Bahn station for the ride south to her stop at Krumme Lanke, where he would then pedal the final half mile to her doorstep in a rising bubble of anticipation. At times he went out of his way to pass by, even if it meant a detour of half an hour, simply so he could ping the bell on his handlebar to say hello, while taking a special thrill whenever Liesl flicked back the curtain of her upper window to wave.

Today he was expected. Neither Liesl nor he had classes this afternoon, and they were planning to ski the new snowfall on the mazelike trails of the Grunewald for as long as daylight permitted. Kurt had prepared for the outing as if for a minor expedition, using ration cards to buy bread and cheese, then tossing into his rucksack his last bar of Christmas chocolate, a vacuum flask of spiced cider, a first aid kit from his days in a *Wandervogel* youth group, and a flashlight for finding their way home after dark.

He needed a break like this. His father's agenda of corporate visits had only gotten more hectic. In addition, his family was now preoccupied with the future prospects of Kurt's sister, who on the previous weekend had accepted the marriage proposal of her SS boyfriend, Bruno Scharf.

His affairs at the university were also in turmoil. One of his favorite professors had just been arrested, or so rumor had it. The only official word was an ominous notice tacked to the classroom door, which said that Professor Doktor Schlösser would be "absent until further notice" due to sudden health problems.

That left Liesl as his only source of joy, although she more than made up for the rest. And today he would have her all to himself. No parents, no friends, and, best of all, no discussion groups to get everyone's emotions in a lather. The last was Kurt's only source of discomfort in this new romance. Not because he disapproved of Liesl's views but because he cringed at the thought of their two social circles ever intersecting in some intimate setting. It was bound to happen, he supposed. But whenever he imagined, say, Erich Stuckart breaking bread alongside some of the earnest young men he had met at Dietrich Bonhoeffer's house, he envisioned either a shouting match, a fistfight, or an arrest—and sometimes all three.

Liesl's crowd had taken some getting used to. For much of that first evening at Bonhoeffer's Kurt had said as little as possible, content to let Liesl conclude that he was shy around strangers. The truth was that he was a bit shocked by some of the talk, and while he wasn't inclined to disagree, he hadn't yet been up to the task of joining in.

Bonhoeffer himself had seemed welcoming enough. For someone who supposedly posed such a threat to national security, he was mild and kindly, even docile.

The music playing on his phonograph was another matter entirely. A choral selection in English, it was unlike anything Kurt had ever heard—strange, moaning voices of such high passion that the hair on his neck stood up. Soloists burst through hailstorms of rhythmic clapping like shots of adrenaline, evoking cats in heat or women in childbirth. It was one thing to experience the soaring emotion of opera, where all the power was channeled and focused, but in these recordings the energy was raw and untrammeled. Unnerving, but admittedly exhilarating. Kurt supposed that the propagandists who always railed against jazz and swing would have had a field day with this stuff, and he amused himself by imagining Goebbels flailing his arms in rage over this very record.

"Who is singing?" he shyly asked Liesl.

"It's a Negro spiritual." Her smile made it clear that she approved. "Pastor Bonhoeffer has a lot of them. He collected them while he was living in New York."

"Herr Bonhoeffer lived in America?"

Was it wise to be playing such music from a country that was now their enemy? Especially on a Sunday, when "quiet rules" were in effect on every street. What if the neighbors overheard?

Liesl must have noted his uncertainty, but instead of criticizing she sought to reassure.

"Don't worry, it was years ago. But isn't it silly, the idea that something like music could corrupt you, especially when it's so full of life?"

Then she squeezed his hand, and as far as Kurt was concerned the matter was settled.

He was less certain about some of the other people in attendance. A few were downright strident, even boastful in their dissent. The most abrasive was a fellow named Dieter Büssler, who loudly told a coarse joke about why the golden angel on the Victory Column had recently been moved to a higher pedestal—to keep Goebbels from getting up her skirts. Dieter struck him as all talk, just the sort of fellow who might get everybody in trouble and then be among the first to run.

Others he liked immediately, such as the quiet-spoken Christoph Klemm. Christoph, too, told irreverent jokes, but his were more sophisticated, and cleverly refrained from mentioning their targets by name, as with the one that clearly referred to Gandhi and Hitler: "What's the difference between Germany and India? In India, one man starves for millions. In Germany, millions starve for one man."

Kurt laughed louder than was warranted, partly out of nerves. It was a bit like being back in grammar school and having the boy at the next desk show you a naughty drawing of the teacher. It intrigued him to realize there must be more of this racy material out there, in parlors and living rooms far beyond the sedate comfort of his parents' house. But he sensed that he had best enter this new realm carefully, and should closely guard its secrets.

When his mother asked later how the evening had gone, he sanitized the description, making it as bland as possible. He didn't dare mention Bonhoeffer's name.

"But you were there for hours. What did you do?"

"Oh, you know, the usual sorts of things. Listened to music. Chatted with the girls. Nothing that exciting."

But it *had* been exciting, he realized, an exhilarating blend of sudden love and a fascination with the forbidden. The two ingredients now seemed inextricably bound, as if neither would be quite as exciting without the other.

Liesl was putting on her skis when he arrived, and within seconds they were darting through the trees, scooting downhill on a trail that cut between the small woodland lakes of Krumme Lanke and Schlachtensee and then led straight into the densest part of the forest.

The sky was a metallic gray, and the raw air burned his cheeks. In only minutes it felt like they were miles from civilization. Long brown furrows cut the snow where wild boars had rooted for acorns the night before. The only sound apart from their breathing and the hiss of their skis was the wind soughing in the pines. It kicked up a crystal mist of blown snow.

Pausing for their first rest, Liesl bent forward awkwardly on her skis and nuzzled him with flushed cheeks. They kissed, and were so swept up that afterward they nearly tripped while disentangling their crossed skis, which of course made them laugh, a bright call of joy through the forest gloom. Kurt felt strong enough to ski all the way to the North Sea.

"I used to wonder why these woods always made me so cheerful," Liesl said, as they got back under way. "Then one day I realized it was partly because of the bark on the pines, the way it is colored. Do you see what I mean?"

He did, now that she mentioned it. Most of the bark was a deep brown, but on every tree the southern exposure was a lighter shade, almost golden.

"It makes it look like the sun is shining," Kurt said.

"Even on a day like this. The perfect illusion for the German winter."

For Kurt, Liesl had a similar brightening effect, except her radiance was no mere illusion. He pulled to a stop and leaned forward for another kiss.

Their plan was to have lunch around noon, but the skiing was so good and the daylight so fleeting that they kept going, pausing only for an occasional nip of the hot, sweet cider. Then, just as the lowering sun finally peeped through the clouds, Liesl cried out in dismay.

"What's wrong?"

"My left binding. It's broken."

They stopped for a look. It wasn't promising, and in resting they realized that the air was growing colder. Kurt got out the first aid tape and tried to rig a binding sturdy enough to get them home, but it snapped within a few yards.

"What now?" she said.

For a change, it was his turn to set the tone, and he relished the opportunity. He scanned the sky, the trees, and a nearby crossing to assess their probable location and their best options.

"We must be pretty close to the Wannsee by now. If we head south-west, we could have a bite to eat down on the beach, then walk to the S-Bahn stop. If it gets dark, I have my flashlight."

"I like that idea. Lead the way."

"You use my skis. I'll carry yours."

He half expected her to object, but she seemed touched by his gal-lantry. She slid along up front while Kurt kept pace at a brisk march, and sure enough they soon emerged from the trees at the south end of a strip of snow-covered sand along the waterfront. It was Europe's largest inland beach, and on hot summer days it was packed with sun-bathers and umbrellas. Today, with an icy west wind blowing in off the water, the strand was empty.

"It's quite romantic," Liesl said. "A perfect place to watch the sun-set."

They ate their late lunch in companionable silence while seated on a large stone lapped by small waves. They saved the chocolate for last. Neither had eaten any sweets for more than a week. Kurt exulted in his weariness, feeling that the day had been a huge success. He cupped his hands around the last cup of warm cider and leaned toward Liesl's lips as she snuggled closer.

Then his attention was drawn to the whine of an engine coming from across the water. A small boat was headed their way, its running lights already burning in the deepening shadows of 4 p.m. Whoever was at the helm was watching through a big pair of binoculars.

"Not the police, I hope," Liesl said with a note of worry.

"We are trespassing, I suppose, even though we came onto the beach south of the fence. But it's not like they charge admission this time of year. Still . . ."

He stood up and squinted across the water. A voice called out from the boat.

"Kurt? Is that Kurt Bauer?"

"Yes. Hello, Erich!"

"Erich Stuckart?" Liesl asked.

"His family has a villa just across the way. They're probably visiting for the day."

She tightened her grip on Kurt's arm.

"He's always seemed nice enough. Although I can't say I'm a fan of his father's."

Erich swung the wheel around just before he would have run aground. He throttled back on the engine, and the boat settled into a gentle rocking motion a few yards offshore.

"And Liesl Folkerts, too, I see!" He said it with an air of revelation, reminding Kurt uneasily of what Erich had said about her at the party. "Skiing on the beach, are you? Can't say I've ever heard that recommended. Of course, boating's not the sanest activity on a day like this, either. I've got little tracks of ice on my cheeks from the tears the wind caused. All very masochistic. I could hitch you up to the stern and pull you across the Wannsee if you liked?"

That coaxed a laugh out of Liesl, and Kurt relaxed.

"Her bindings broke, so we came down for a rest," he explained. "We were just about to walk over to the Wannsee Bahnhof."

"The Nikolassee stop would be closer from here, but even that's about a mile through the woods. Why don't I give you a lift farther across the water, to shorten the walk?"

"That's kind of you," Liesl said.

"No problem. I'll just beach this crate, and you can climb over the side."

He gently maneuvered the boat into place, just close enough for Liesl to make it aboard without soaking her feet. Kurt handed over the rucksack and both pairs of skis, then joined Erich at the helm, where his friend pulled a leather-covered flask from inside his coat.

"A little fuel for the trip back," Erich said. "Part of Dad's secret stash of cognac from the Paris pushcart express. Not that you should breathe a word of it to him, of course."

"My lips are sealed. So what brought you to the villa today?"

"The whole family's here. My dad had some big appointment nearby, so he decided we'd all make a day of it. Unfortunately it's boring as hell. Nothing to do but sit there staring at the boar heads lined up on the wall. And it's cold as a cave, or will be till he gets the fireplace going."

"So you decided to warm up with a little dash across the waves?"

"Yes. I'm brilliant that way, aren't I?"

Erich flashed his goofball horsey smile, gritting his teeth into the biting wind as he revved the engine back to full power. They headed down the shoreline. New tears were already streaming from the corners of his eyes.

"You know," he shouted above the noise, turning so that Liesl could hear as well, "if you two were interested, it would sure help warm the place up if you could stop by for a while. By now they should have a fire going, and afterward I could give you a lift home in my dad's car. He's got the ministry ration allotment, so gas isn't a problem. It would be quicker than taking the S-Bahn."

Kurt sensed potential trouble in the arrangement and was on the verge of saying no. But when he glanced at Liesl she nodded. Perhaps she was more tired than he had realized.

"I'd like that," she said. "And thank you."

"Splendid! Then let's change course. Hold on!"

He turned the wheel sharply to starboard, and they leaned into the sweeping curve, heading west toward what remained of the dusk, a faint glow in the bare treetops along the far shore. So much for keeping his two worlds apart, although Kurt supposed they were bound to have collided sooner or later.

"I heard yesterday that congratulations are in order for your sister," Erich shouted. "When's the wedding?"

"No date yet. Depends on when he's posted to the front, I guess."

Liesl gave him a look, and Kurt felt like a fool.

"Wedding?" she said. "Traudl's getting married and you haven't told me?"

"Well, it's not really a sure thing until the background check is finished."

"Nonsense," Erich said. "He was probably just afraid you wouldn't approve of his new in-laws. Bruno's an SS man. Spit-polished and shiny, with all the lightning bolts. Very fearsome. Except to Traudl, of course."

Leave it to Erich, even in jest, to zero in on the real reason Kurt had kept the news from Liesl. He didn't dare look at her.

"Well, I'm sure that if he's all right for Traudl," she said awkwardly, "then he's probably a fine young man."

Later, when Kurt would look back on the progression of the whole disastrous evening, he would decide that this was where events had begun to veer off course. Not only did it wreck their earlier sense of ease, it primed them for what turned out to be their most fractious disagreement.

"So what was your dad's urgent business?" Kurt asked, hoping to change the subject.

"See that big white villa on the far shoreline, dead ahead?"

"The one with the huge lawn?"

"That's it. Normally it's some sort of guesthouse for visiting security police, but this morning there was a big powwow there. Or *boring* powwow, I should say. Invitation only—not that anyone would have wanted to crash it. Especially since the host was the even more boring Reinhard Heydrich. Talk about someone who loves to hear himself speak. My dad said he hardly shut up the entire morning."

Heydrich was the chief of the Reich Main Security Office, which made him boss of both the Sicherheitsdienst, or SD, and the Gestapo secret police. Rarely, if ever, did anyone toss around his name as lightly as Erich just had. Liesl shifted uncomfortably at Kurt's side.

"I don't know about boring," she said, "but he's certainly dangerous. Supposedly he's the reason Professor Schlösser's been detained. Another faculty member complained to Heydrich's office about something Schlösser said in a lecture. Three days later he disappeared."

"Yes. He can be meddlesome that way."

"That's putting it mildly."

Erich glanced back at her, then broke into an awkward grin.

"I suppose you're right. I'm too used to hearing about him from my dad's perspective. To him, Heydrich's just a power-crazy bureaucrat nosing into everyone else's business."

"What was the meeting about?"

"Jews, of course. My poor father had to go because the minister wouldn't. Frick is such a milquetoast. My dad doubts he'll even last out the war. But maybe it was all for the best, because Frick doesn't know his ass from a hole in the ground where the Jews are concerned, and ever since the Nuremberg laws everyone assumes that my father is some kind of expert. He's not, of course. He just knows how to write an airtight law."

"Airtight," Liesl said. "That's one way of putting it."

Her face was stony, which made Kurt nervous. His earlier fears were right on the mark. Mixing these two in close quarters was volatile. And while Kurt sympathized with Liesl's views, he believed there was a proper time and place for expressing them, and this wasn't one of them.

"So you think my dad's too hard on the Jews?" Erich said it with an amused air, which Kurt knew would only provoke her. "Believe me, he did them all a great favor by keeping their big noses out of certain places. The best thing a Jew can do right now is lay low, and with those laws in place they *have* to play it safe."

"Next you'll be telling me that all that cold weather in Russia is actually good for our boys at the front, because bullets don't hurt as much when you're numb."

"Very good!"

Erich laughed, apparently oblivious to just how close he was to pushing her into an explosion. To him this was all in good fun. For all of Kurt's love and admiration for Liesl's boldness, there were times when he wished that she, too, wouldn't take things so seriously.

For whatever reason—Erich's laughter, perhaps, which may have showed Liesl the folly of arguing further with a buffoon—she lowered the volume of her next remark, which Kurt recognized as one of Bonhoeffer's statements from the previous Sunday.

"The Apostles were all Jews, you know. And if they had all just decided to 'lay low,' as you put it, then none of us in Germany would ever have become Christians."

Erich smiled again.

"My father's bosses wouldn't necessarily see Christianity as a good thing, you know. I'm not even sure my father would, sorry to say." Then, after the briefest of pauses, "So what are your plans for later, you two? Because I've been thinking, maybe it would be easier for everyone if you both just stayed for dinner. As long as Liesl didn't hound my father too much about the Jews, of course."

That was Erich all over, careening from glib to serious and back again in the blink of an eye, as recklessly as he piloted the boat. Nothing seemed to matter very much to him apart from girls, a stiff drink or two, and a roaring good time.

Kurt should have said no right away. The only thing that stopped him was the thought of his father, who would have dearly wanted him to say yes. Currying favor in the Stuckart household was high on the Bauer agenda, mostly because Erich wasn't the only person who thought so little of the current Interior Minister, Wilhelm Frick. Stuckart was the real power behind that throne.

So Kurt paused, and the lapse proved fatal.

"We'd love to," Liesl said. "As long as I can phone my parents from your villa to let them know I'll be late. It will be interesting to hear what your father has to say."

Her answer seemed to surprise both young men, although Erich recovered quickly.

"Splendid," he said. "And my mother will be thrilled. She hasn't seen Kurt in ages. As for my father, well, if he can endure four hours of Heydrich, then he can damn well put up with whatever any of us has to say."

Erich pulled out his flask for another quick swallow, and roared with laughter into the icy breeze. Kurt's stomach began tying itself into knots.

THE WANNSEE WATERFRONT had become quite the enclave for Nazi bigwigs over the past several years. Goebbels had a place there. So did his undersecretary, Hermann Esser. Economics Minister Walther Funk was another neighbor, as was Hitler's physician, Dr. Theodor Morell. The Reich Bride School had set up shop nearby. And it was only fitting that Stuckart had a villa, too, since his Nuremberg laws had helped free up some of the properties from previous owners at such reasonable prices.

The size and scale of the Stuckart place was fairly modest, but inside the decor was that of a Bavarian hunting lodge. Just as Erich had said, the heads of trophy animals stared down from the walls of the vaulted main room—elk and boar mostly, a procession of antlers and tusks that seemed fearsome and predatory, especially when you were already worried sick that your girlfriend would wander heedlessly into a field of fire.

Erich's mother answered the door and took their coats while Erich introduced Liesl and announced that they were all staying for dinner.

"My apologies that none of our servants are here," she said. "I'm afraid that we only brought a cook, and even at that I must apologize in advance for what will be a very simple dinner."

She hustled down a hallway with their things. Erich's father must have already returned—Kurt spotted a brochure on a side table promoting the villa where the meeting had been held. The cover featured a handsome black-and-white photo of a grand room with polished wood floors and a splendid view of the lake. The sales pitch referred to its "completely refurbished guest rooms, a music room and billiards room, a large meeting room and conservatory, a terrace looking onto the Wannsee, central heating, hot and cold running water, and all comforts."

Not exactly a terrible place to have to spend a morning, he thought, no matter what Erich said.

They gathered by the fire along with Erich's two older sisters and an elderly uncle. The flames were roaring by then. Liesl warmed her hands, her expression unreadable. She had been very quiet since they arrived. Soon afterward Erich's father joined them. Presumably he had changed out of his work clothes. He wore a tweed hunting jacket and heavy wool pants, and he smelled of pipe smoke.

"Good to see you, Kurt," he said heartily. "I could have used your father with me today. Lots of questions about railway logistics and hauling capacities. All quite baffling to me, really. I'm afraid none of us was quite up to the challenge."

"I can ask him to phone you, if you'd like."

"Please do. I'd like to tap his expertise on some of these matters."

Liesl gave him a cold look, which only went to show how little she understood about the business world, he supposed.

Stuckart offered everyone a drink, and to Kurt's relief Liesl accepted. Maybe things would be all right after all. He wondered idly where Erich had put the flask of cognac.

The "simple" dinner was anything but. There was venison roast and cold duckling, served on Dresden china with the finest silver. Somehow the Stuckarts had even found green beans, perhaps from the larder, along with shredded winter greens and mounds of potatoes dripping with fresh dairy butter. For dessert, a red berry compote, Rote Grütze, served the traditional way, with vanilla sauce. Each course came with a different bottle of wine fetched from the villa's cellar. Conversation was cordial and blessedly dull, and by the time everyone had moved on to coffee Kurt was feeling unguarded enough to believe the worst of the danger had passed.

Liesl, in fact, was looking quite healthy and inviting after their strenuous day in all that fresh air. She seemed refreshed, too, as she sipped from the china cup.

"Thank you for the lovely dinner," she told Erich's mother. "I can't tell you how luxurious it is to taste real coffee again."

"Yes," Stuckart's father chimed in from the head of the table. "I simply can't stomach any more of that fake stuff. Roasted barley mostly, but I'm told some brands even have ground-up *acorns*! Like we've been reduced to boars, rooting through the forest. What is it I heard you calling it the other day, Erich? 'Nigger sweat' or something?" He chuckled. "That sums it up pretty well, I'd say."

Liesl set her cup down with an unnerving rattle, although only Kurt seemed to notice. When Mrs. Stuckart offered a refill, she shook her head.

Talk then turned to the war, as it always did. As was also customary, the women mostly stayed out of the conversation, speaking in asides to each other about other matters. Except for Liesl, who leaned forward and followed closely as the elder Stuckart led the way.

"Field Marshal Leeb has been removed from command of Army Group North," he said. "The word just came down today."

"Isn't he the third one to lose his job?" Erich asked.

"All since the first of December. But Kuchler has taken his place. A good commander. He'll buck them up for sure. It may take some doing, maybe even a little more juggling of commanders, but the Führer will have us back on the right track in the east. By the time the spring thaw is here, we'll be ready to go back on the offensive. Winter in wartime is always about waiting things out, anyway."

"Did you hear about that poor man, von Reichenau?" Mrs. Stuckart asked, in a rare interjection.

"Old news, dear," Stuckart said, indulging her with a smile. "He was appointed weeks ago. The new commander of Army Group South."

"Yes, I know. But he just dropped dead of a heart attack. Right there at his headquarters."

That wiped the smile off her husband's face.

"You're certain of this?"

"Lotte heard it from his wife only this morning. And he was so young, too, as these things go. A terrible tragedy."

Everyone was still digesting that bit of news when Liesl spoke up.

"I am afraid that the war in the east is lost," she announced. "I have heard that almost anyone who is realistic now believes there is virtually no way that we can win."

The response was shocked silence. Kurt stared at his saucer. The fire popped, and a log dropped with a thud and a shower of sparks.

Mrs. Stuckart glanced uneasily around the table, as if gauging how much the comment had upset everyone. She dabbed her mouth gingerly with a napkin. Even the glib Erich managed only a cough.

Kurt felt compelled to speak up, to somehow try to limit the damage. It was bad enough that the Interior Ministry's second in command was sitting right there. He, at least, was probably used to hearing such candor from others in government during guarded moments, so maybe he would overlook it as a mistake of youth. But you never knew when someone else—even one of Erich's sisters, for example—might feel compelled to pass along a defeatist remark to the wrong kind of policeman.

Everyone there had probably heard the story of Karlrobert Kreiten, the talented young concert pianist who had remarked to a friend of his mother's that Hitler was "a madman" for ordering the invasion of the Soviet Union. His mother's friend turned him in the next day, and he was now awaiting trial in Plötzensee Prison.

"It is easy to be discouraged these days," Kurt said haltingly, "but we are all doing what we can. Liesl does volunteer work for wounded soldiers, you know. She collects cloth for bandages, and reads to them in hospitals in Berlin. The very ones who have been serving on the eastern front. I can see how that kind of experience, day after day, wouldn't leave you feeling very hopeful."

No response, not even from Liesl. Kurt sensed his fruitless words drifting up through the chimney and off into the night sky.

Stuckart then rose from the table, his big frame suddenly menacing. He stepped over to the fireplace to toss on another log, levering it into place with an iron poker. Then he addressed Kurt without looking back toward the table.

"Speaking of the front, young Kurt. Erich will soon be turning eighteen and reporting for officer's training. What about you?"

"Of course. As soon as I am eighteen."

"When is your birthday?"

Liesl took his hand beneath the table and squeezed it.

"Late October, but I am still sixteen. I skipped a grade to enter university early."

"Next October is a long way off. By then the conscription laws may have changed. You may be eligible earlier than you think, especially if, as your friend believes, we continue to fare so poorly in battle. As that date approaches, I urge you to try and be as judicious as possible in what you say out in public. You should also take care in the company you keep. Because when the time comes for your father to secure a favorable appointment on your behalf, all sorts of things will be weighed and measured."

Kurt knew at that moment that if he did not somehow speak up on her behalf she would be deeply disappointed. But with almost everyone at the table seemingly imploring him to be on his guard, he was unable to come up with the right words. Instead, he simply nodded and said evenly, "Yes, sir."

Liesl gently released his hand and looked down at her lap.

"More coffee for you, my dear?" Mrs. Stuckart asked.

She shook her head, saying nothing.

A few moments later, Erich cleared his throat and began talking about his foolhardy boat trip. Within seconds both his parents were chiding him companionably, as if nothing untoward had occurred, and not long afterward they all rose and placed their napkins on the table. Erich offered to drive Kurt and Liesl home.

Because of the blackout, the car's headlights were covered in dark felt with tiny slits, meaning even the reckless Erich had to go slowly. To make matters worse, the roads were icing, and they poked along at an agonizing pace in awkward silence. After dropping them off at Liesl's house, Erich sped away, the car fishtailing so much that he nearly struck a tree.

For a moment neither Liesl nor Kurt made a move. They just stood on the sidewalk, holding their skis, as if trying to fathom what came next.

"Well, I suppose you tried," she said finally, wearily. "But I can't say that you tried very hard."

"And you," he said, suddenly aggrieved, "tried much *too* hard! It is one thing to express your deepest feelings at Dr. Bonhoeffer's house.

But at the villa of someone who is practically a cabinet minister? Liesl, what were you thinking?"

"It was a harmless remark. And only an opinion."

"Nothing is harmless to these people if they don't agree with it. What you said may be true, but it won't do your cause much good if people in power decide to silence you."

"It *may* be true? *My* cause? Is it not your cause as well? Or is your only cause to unbutton my blouse and then run away at the first sign that someone disapproves of me? What does it matter if you are 'silenced' if you have nothing to say to begin with?"

"Of course I share your cause. Of course! I only want you to be more careful."

"Your kind of careful is the way of cowards."

"That's not true!"

"Yes, it is. Why, you can't even speak the truth to me."

"That is simply not so!"

"Then why didn't you tell me Traudl was engaged? The single biggest event in your family, maybe all year, but I don't hear about it because, what? You think I'll disapprove? Erich was right, wasn't he?"

His silence told her all she needed to know.

"You are too careful in this way, Kurt. Too busy hiding pieces of yourself because you think it will please me, or worse, please some awful person in a red armband. You think you are doing it to build a safe foundation for your future, but can't you see that the time for real action is now—or there might not even be a future?"

This kind of talk scared him even more, but he tried not to show it. So they went on in this fashion several minutes longer, fighting their way to a stalemate, until gradually their remarks began to lose some of their heat. But just as Kurt started to think they had weathered the storm, he made what would turn out to be a fatal error. Concerned that her parents might overhear them, he glanced nervously toward the windows of the Folkertses' house, and Liesl saw the worry in his eyes.

"Look at you!" she said, her fury renewed. "Scared that my parents might have their ears to the keyhole. Even now you can't stop worrying that someone will disapprove instead of trying to get to the heart of this trouble between us, this terrible split."

He was alarmed by her words, and the worst was yet to come. When he reached out a chilled hand to take hers, she slapped it away.

Then her eyes flared, as brightly as if she had struck a match in the darkness.

"This can never work!" she said. "Never! I kept waiting, kept thinking you would come around, and that your better instincts would prevail. But you are becoming exactly what your father wants—just another person to say yes to whoever he needs to please."

"That's not true. I—"

"I can't see you anymore, Kurt. I don't *want* to see you anymore. Not with all of the growing up you still have to do. Because some people never grow up, or not in a way that allows them to develop the courage of their convictions. And I am afraid that you are one of those people. I am sorry, Kurt. Good-bye."

He felt like she had kicked him in the stomach, and he was momentarily incapable of answering as she turned to go. Instead of protesting, or pleading, or running after her, he just stood there in the snow, rooted to the spot, mutely confirming every terrible thing she had just said.

He would think of plenty of suitable answers later, of course, such as, "I'm only sixteen. Give me time to grow into this." Or, "Please, don't mistake foolhardiness for courage. If we don't fight battles only of our own choosing, then they will pick us off, one by one, on the grounds of their choosing."

But by then he was alone on the U-Bahn, staring gloomily at his skis and his dripping bicycle. When she slammed the door to the house he was still stranded on the sidewalk, a strangled cry of protest dead on his lips, with no company to console him except the moon, the forest, and the chill darkness of a winter night in Berlin.

NINE

ELIVERING THE NEWS of Gordon's death to Viv turned out to be worse than an ordeal. It was a fiasco.

The first bad sign was Willis Turner's police cruiser parked in the Wolfes' driveway. Turner emerged from the driver's side as Nat and Holland hopped out of the FBI Suburban. The fat policeman waved a sheet of paper at them while nodding toward the end of the dirt lane, where two New York State Police cruisers were just arriving, blue lights ablaze.

"Is this your idea of breaking it to her gently?" Nat asked Holland.

"I've got no idea what these clowns are up to. You better get in there."

Nat hustled up the steps to where Viv was already throwing open the door. A breakfast cigarette burned between her lips. She looked primed for an outburst of foul temper as she surveyed the onslaught.

"What the hell do they want now? And why are you leading the charge?"

"I didn't bring them." He steered her back inside and shut the door behind them.

"But I've got bad news, Viv. About Gordon."

Nat felt her sag as anger gave way to fear. He settled her into a chair at the kitchen table, then sat down beside her and took her hand.

"How bad?"

"It's his heart."

The cigarette fell from her lips.

"Where'd they take him?"

"I'm afraid he didn't make it, Viv. They found him this morning, passed out on the floor. He regained consciousness for a few seconds, then they lost him."

She sighed loudly and shuddered into a sob. He squeezed her hand. An odd little sound escaped her lips, like the moan of a leaking balloon. Then her face twisted, and she sobbed a second time before somehow regaining control. At exactly that moment Willis Turner and Clark Holland burst through the door, arguing at full volume.

"This is a court order!" Turner shouted, still waving the sheet of paper. "These archives are material evidence in the investigation of a suspicious death!"

"The court run by your grease monkey crony? That's fucking worthless!"

"Not when it's backed by the enforcement power of the New York State Police."

Two troopers in sunglasses loomed into view, followed by a third, who toted a rifle.

Nat and Viv were still holding hands. Neither could believe what was taking place.

"The death is suspicious?" she asked, whispering as if they were watching a movie.

"I suspect it's just a pretext. He wants the boxes."

"Why?"

"Who knows? The way this town works, maybe he's selling them on eBay."

They giggled in spite of the moment, or perhaps because of it, and the release of tension restored enough of Viv's composure for her to take command.

"Gentlemen!" she shouted, rising to her feet. "Don't you think your behavior is a little inappropriate? Haven't you done enough for one day? Out of my house, immediately!"

By then the first two troopers had collected the boxes from the sunroom and were lugging them out the door, one under each arm, like burglars with small televisions.

Holland seemed to realize that for the moment he was defeated, and either good sense or good breeding prompted him to nod respectfully and lower his voice.

"Sorry for the scene, Mrs. Wolfe. I was just delivering Mr. Turnbull to break the bad news. I'll see that the others depart immediately."

Turner was happy to oblige now that the goods were being loaded into the trunk of his cruiser. But he couldn't quite hide a smirk of triumph even as he offered condolences.

"My respects, ma'am." He dared to tip his hat. Then he nodded at Nat. "Mr. Turnbull? A word outside, if you don't mind."

Holland shot Nat a warning glance, and Viv again squeezed his hand. Even now, Nat was drawn irresistibly toward the departing archives, but there was no way he was going to leave Viv in the lurch like this. Then she dropped his hand.

"You'd better go see what he wants," she said. "Heaven knows, that's what Gordon would have wanted. But come back later, Nat. I'll be needing you."

Then she nodded her assent, which was benediction enough for Nat. Holland frowned as Nat scooted out the door to find Turner waiting by the cruiser, arms crossed.

"Holland will head straight to federal court, you know," Nat said. "Albany, I'm guessing. They'll be back before the close of business with a search and seizure order."

"Maybe," replied Turner. "But among the many conveniences this town has footed the bill for in recent years is a mighty fine copy machine. I figure I can get the better part of it duplicated in the next six, seven hours, especially if you're there to help show me the good stuff."

Nat had expected something like this. The state cops were ready to roll, engines idling for an armed escort into town, and now Turner was proposing to hire away the FBI's handpicked expert. The feds sure had underestimated this dumb-looking prick.

"What's your interest in this?" Nat asked.

"Like I said. Evidence."

"Is there really anything suspicious about Gordon's death?"

"How am I supposed to know until I've examined the evidence?"

"Who's paying you, some collector?"

"Just doing my job as the town's peace officer, Mr. Turnbull. The only person being asked to moonlight is you. You on board or not?"

"One condition. No, two."

"Name 'em."

"I get copies of your copies. In fact, I've got a digital camera back at my room that will go twice as fast as your machine. Then I can burn everything onto a CD for you."

Turner mulled that over for a second, as if deciding whether he was being conned.

"Fair enough. What else?"

"I need an assistant. With two cameras we can move twice as fast."

"That German gal?"

"You know her?"

"This is a small place, Mr. Turnbull. If I didn't know just about everybody, I wouldn't be doing my job."

"One other thing. After the arrest the FBI said something about you being tipped off."

"That's right."

"What kind of tip?"

"I'm not at liberty to say."

"You're as bad as them."

"I've met your conditions. Take it or leave it."

He took it. Not that he wasn't still wary of his new business partner. What was Turner's real agenda, and who was he working for? But the man did have the boxes, and for the moment that was enough. Nat nodded and opened the door to the cruiser just as Holland emerged from the house.

"That material is still classified," the agent warned. "You could go to jail for this."

"While working under a court order at the behest of an officer of the law? I don't think so. And I can finish the evaluation you wanted while you're waiting to regain custody. Besides, you guys won't decide what parts remain classified. That's the CIA's job."

"I don't get involved in those squabbles."

"So it's already a squabble? Interesting."

Holland frowned and said nothing more.

BERTA DIDN'T NEED to be asked twice, or even nicely, to join the unlikely new team. When Turner and Nat pulled up at the courthouse she was already waiting outside with her backpack and camera. Nat had retrieved his own. He had also done the necessary math.

The four narrow boxes held about two linear feet of material, which meant about four thousand pages. Both of them moving at top speed might need eight hours to photograph everything, and the feds might return with a court order in as little as four. Something had to give. Nat had already been through half the material, and he could sort out the stuff that wasn't worth copying. The rest they could cull on the fly. It would be close.

Berta said little as they set up tripods on a long table beneath a fluorescent light. They opened the boxes and got to work, quickly easing into a rhythm and stopping only to change batteries. Turner made a run for coffee and kept an eye out for the feds.

Nat cringed at the way they were manhandling the pages. A professional archivist would have read them the riot act. But at the rate the CIA was declassifying material these days, some of this stuff might not again see the light for years. Even at that, he swore loudly when Turner placed a sweating Big Gulp cola only inches from a memo personally signed by Allen Dulles.

When Berta left for a bathroom break, Turner leaned across her tripod for a closer look and said, "Pardon me, Professor, 'cause you're the expert. But from what I've seen so far, this stuff looks pretty routine. Mind telling me what all the fuss is about?"

"That's what I'd like to know. Maybe your patron could offer some hints."

Turner grinned slyly.

"Like I said. I'm just gathering evidence in an investigation."

"Whatever you say."

"But these boxes aren't the first bit of funny business we've had up at the Wolfes' place this spring."

"No?"

"There was a break-in, 'bout a week ago. A few doodads missing, but not much else. Just enough to let 'em know someone had been poking around. When I was filling out the paperwork, the missus said their place in Wightman had also been burgled."

"When?"

"Gordon hushed her up before she could say. But apparently we're not the only ones around here who think this is hot stuff. Our friend Mr. Holland asked me last night if I'd noted the presence of any foreign nationals."

"You mean like her?" Nat nodded toward the ladies' room.

"Males."

"Nationality?"

" 'Middle Eastern origin' was all I could get out of 'em."

"Middle Eastern? In a hunt for American files from Switzerland about a bunch of old Nazis?"

"That was pretty much my reaction."

On second thought, Nat could certainly think of a few Israelis who might have a keen interest in acquiring some of this information. Nazi hunters, mostly, although that job description was dying out along with the Nazis themselves.

Also, Bern had been a popular wartime crossing point for all kinds of contacts—Italians, Yugoslavs, French, Bulgarians, Rumanians, and even a few shady travelers from Arab lands. He supposed anything was possible.

"So what did you tell him?" Nat asked.

"No trace. But I've put in calls to every inn and B&B within a twenty-mile radius, so we'll see what turns up."

He was about to ask Turner more, but Berta returned, and the lawman flashed him a warning look that said the discussion was over. Not American enough for him, Nat supposed. Just as well. There was work to be done.

By 4 p.m., with stomachs growling, they were only a folder or two from completion when Turner announced from the window, "Here they come!" Nat heard the rumble of engines and the slamming of doors. That was when an even bigger problem occurred to him.

"The cameras," he said, looking over at Berta in horror. "They've probably got an order to seize any duplications."

"Hand me your flash drive," Berta said. He tossed it as voices approached. There was a sharp knock at the door, and Turner looked over in panic. Nat then watched in astonishment as Berta placed the first of the tiny memory chips onto her tongue like a communion wafer, paused, and then gulped hard, as if swallowing an oversized pill. Then she repeated the process with her own as a second knock sounded.

"Here," she mumbled, looking a bit queasy. "Load fresh drives into the cameras. Give them something to confiscate."

"Can't hold 'em off any longer," Turner said.

Nat and Berta shoved in the new flash drives just as Holland barged in the door. Four other agents trailed in his wake. One was a woman Nat hadn't seen before.

"Gentlemen, take everything you see, and look for whatever you don't," he said. "Officer Turner, since you're such a stickler for paper-work, here are my marching orders. You three are damned lucky you're not under arrest, given the presence of those tripods and cameras. But if you'll hand them over along with any memory cards, I'll be willing to call it even. Then I'm afraid all three of you are going to have to be searched. Thoroughly."

The woman agent took Berta into the restroom for that chore. Turner complained loudly about having to strip, but Nat figured he might as well get it over with and complied as quickly as possible. Within a minute or two they were dressed again, and Holland kicked them out so his people could finish the job.

Berta came out the door with the hint of a smile and excused herself to a snack bar next door. From the sound of it, the feds seemed to be taking a greater-than-usual joy in rifling through Turner's office. The cop moaned as he listened to the groaning of nails, presumably as the paneling was being peeled back from the studs.

Berta didn't come out of the snack bar until the feds had packed up and driven away. Her face was flushed, but when she held out the palm of her right hand there sat both flash drives.

"Like coughing up a poker chip," Turner said. "I'm impressed."

"It wasn't so hard. I was bulimic once."

She said it as matter-of-factly as if mentioning she'd once had the measles. Somehow Nat wasn't surprised, but he wondered about her use of the past tense. Berta Heinkel already struck him as a particularly complex specimen of the Tortured German Soul, and what else but a sort of mania could have driven her to pursue such a narrow strain of knowledge for so many years? Perhaps the bulimia was just another aspect of that kind of personality. And it was all the more reason she would try to hide all her soft curves beneath such baggy clothes. But Nat knew from years of experience with college students that something deeper and more complicated was often behind an eating disorder as serious as bulimia. A family crisis, perhaps, or some catastrophic event at a critical age.

"Better let me hang on to those," he said. Fortunately she handed them over.

"All this talk of bulimia's making me hungry," Turner said with his usual tact.

"Me, too," Berta answered, unfazed. "I could use something a little more filling."

First they used Nat's laptop to copy the contents of the flash drives onto CD-ROMS, one set for each of them. He then stopped by the B&B to hide the copies in his room, while Berta put hers in her rental car. At last they walked to the diner.

Now that the excitement was over, Nat was drained, and all he could think about was Gordon's death, looming out there like a void. They said little during the meal. Nat and Willis Turner plowed through a platter of the meat loaf special. Neither of them could help noticing that Berta ate only about half of a chef's salad. By the time they were done it was well after sundown.

"Where does your investigation stand, now that you've got all your, um, evidence?" Nat asked.

Turner shrugged.

"Damn near finished, I guess. The doc didn't seem to think it was anything out of the ordinary."

"Poor Gordon. Not to mention Viv. Shit. What time is it?"

"Half nine." Berta offered.

"A German's way of saying eight thirty," Nat explained to the puzzled Turner. "I've got an appointment to keep. See you guys later."

Berta wasn't quite ready to say good-bye. She followed him to his car, which was still parked outside the inn, and after he climbed into the driver's seat she hung on to the open door like a teenager angling for an invitation home.

"My offer is still good," she said, "and those folders are still missing. You saw that stuff we were going through today. Junk. You need my help."

"Maybe. I have to let this sink in first."

"I understand. With Gordon Wolfe gone, you've lost that guiding voice in your head. The one that always tells you what to do next. I understand that completely."

"Who's your guiding voice?"

She gave him a smile but said nothing more. Then she pushed his door shut and backed away. He watched in the side mirror as she walked slowly down the street. A complicated woman on a private crusade. Maybe he did need her help, but he wasn't yet sure it would be worth the extra baggage.

Of course, there might also be fringe benefits. But he was trying not to think about those.

TEN

THERE WERE NO LIGHTS on at the Wolfes' house, but a full
moon was rising over the treetops. Now that the FBI was
gone, the place had the weary air of a sacked castle.

Nat smelled wood smoke as he got out of the car. Had Viv lit a fire?
On a mild spring night the mere idea seemed oppressive. Yet that was
the scene he found inside: Viv hunched forward on the living room
couch, face aglow before the hearth. She had on the same flannel
nightgown she'd worn that morning. A half-empty bottle of Gordon's
favorite cognac, Pierre Ferrand, sat before her on the coffee table. A
cigarette smoldered in her right hand.

She looked up, saw Nick, then patted the spot beside her on the
couch.

"Have a seat."

"I thought you hated cognac?"

"I hate fires, too. They were always another excuse for him to get
drunk. I guess it's my idea of a tribute. Or maybe I thought it would
help me commune with his soul."

"Any luck?"

"My vision's a little blurred. That's a start."

But her speech was crisp. Either she was taking it slow or Gordon
had previously made a dent in the bottle.

"Pour me one of those," he said, as much to prevent her from finishing it as to keep her company.

The first sip explained her craving. The pleasant blend of heat and
grape instantly reproduced the essence of a firelit winter evening with
Gordon Wolfe. By the second swallow Nat wouldn't have been sur-

prised to see the old fellow step from the shadows to began regaling them with some favored tale.

Viv's thoughts must have been on a similar track, judging from her next remark.

"He told me once that he visited the bunker, you know. In Berlin, after the war."

"Hitler's bunker?"

She nodded.

"With Dulles himself. Just the two of them. A Russian officer gave them a tour. The furniture was still intact, right down to the blood-stained couch where he'd shot himself."

"You're kidding? How come I've never heard this? Gordon never told anybody."

"He told me."

"Yeah, but . . ."

"You mean, how come he never used it to show off? Or impress people in the department? Or get laid at some conference?"

"I don't think Gordon ever did too much of that."

"Maybe not after you met him. But there were a lot of things he never talked about, considering what a blowhard he could be about other stuff."

So Gordon had toured the Führerbunker with Dulles. If true, it was quite an exalted excursion for someone who, by his own account, had been the lowliest of clerks.

"The doctor thinks it might have been an overdose," Viv said.

"Hitler's suicide?"

"Gordon's death. He thinks Gordon might have been trying to make up for the doses he had already missed. Playing catch-up with his digitalis. It's been known to happen."

"How many pills were left?"

"Plenty. But I don't know how many there were to begin with. Any way you add it up, the FBI killed him. They didn't need to lock him up. It was pure spite."

Nat didn't know how to respond, so he let it go and waited for the smooth current of cognac to carry her further downstream.

"That fellow Holland was around this evening looking for you," she said a while later. "Said you were looking over the documents with a Swiss girl."

"She's German."

"Same difference. Can't trust 'em, either way."

Now where had that come from?

"Speaking of people you can't trust," Nat said, "I was talking to Turner, the local cop. He mentioned a break-in here a few weeks back."

She nodded.

"The man's an idiot, but he's right. Gordon was all in a tizzy till he decided nothing important was gone. They hit our house in Wightman, too."

"The same people?"

"That's what Gordon figured."

"How come?"

"He never said. But he seemed pretty certain. That reminds me. He left something for you. First thing he checked after the break-in. He kept it hidden under the insulation."

"What is it?"

"Some box. He wouldn't say what was in it. But after the break-in he showed me where he kept it. Said if anything ever happened to him, he wanted you to have it. Said you were the only one who'd know what to do with it."

"Something to do with his work?"

Nat tried not to sound too excited. Who knew, maybe it was the four missing folders. Quest begun, quest ended. Just like that.

"He didn't say. You want it now?"

"Might as well."

She smiled.

"Figured you'd say that. Peas in a pod on that kind of thing." She stood slowly and unsteadily. "Trouble is, this is my third drink. I can't make it up those hideaway steps without breaking my neck. If you'll do the climbing, I'll talk you through it. Come on, I'll get a flashlight."

She fetched one from the kitchen, and they went down the hall to a cooler part of the house, where the night air coursed through screened windows. Nat pulled a lanyard from the ceiling to lower a folding staircase, which creaked as he climbed. He poked his head into stale air the temperature of midsummer as Viv handed the flashlight up to him. The beam fell first on a cardboard box with the title of Nat's first book printed on the side. It was a publisher's shipment of twenty-four copies—a significant number, considering that fewer than a thousand were ever printed. Nat opened a flap and got another surprise. Only four copies remained, meaning Gordon must have handed out quite a few.

"Found it yet?" Viv called out.

"No. You said it's beneath the insulation?"

"Just to the left of the opening, between the first two joists."

The insulation was foil-covered and fleecy pink. Nat rolled back the nearest strip like a blanket from a doll's bed, and there it was—a square wooden container twice the size of a cigar box. It was heavier than he expected and smelled of machine oil. Emblazoned on top in German script was the name of a gun shop in Zurich: "W. Glaser, Löwenstrasse 42." That alone might have meaning, he supposed.

"Got it!" he shouted down the steps. "Gangway."

The contents slid and rattled as he descended. Definitely something besides paper in there. They went back to the couch to open the box by firelight. It felt like a séance, with Gordon's spirit watching over their shoulders. Nat suppressed a shiver.

"Here goes."

He pried open a rusty hasp and lifted the hinged top. The first visible item was the peaked cap of a German officer, with a patent leather brim and gray wool top, plus the customary emblem featuring a silver eagle perched on a swastika.

"What do you think?" he asked. "War trophy?"

Viv knitted her brow.

"No idea."

"Why would he want me to have it?"

Collectors of Nazi memorabilia gave Nat the creeps, and Gordon had known that.

"Do you think he picked it up in the bunker?" she asked.

"Maybe. No note. No name on the hatband, either. Just a size, in centimeters."

He set it aside on the couch. Four other items remained.

The largest was a small bottle of brown glass, girdled by a tightly folded sheet of paper attached with a rubber band. The band broke the instant Nat tried to remove it, and he carefully slipped off the paper. The bottle was about three quarters full. He shook it. Some sort of powder.

"This look familiar?"

Viv shook her head.

The paper, coming apart at the folds, was a memo dated September

1945, four months after the end of the war, addressed to "BB-8." The sender was "GW," presumably Gordon Wolfe, at a time when he would have still been based with U.S. occupation forces in Berlin while clerking for Dulles. It had a numbered series of instructions, one through four. Nat read the first one:

> 1. There is enclosed a bottle of secret ink powder which you requested in connection with your North Africa–Near East operation. This ink is secure against any known enemy censorship or ink-developing technique. The powder is shaving talcum with the secret ink ingredient mixed in it. For cover, it could actually be used as shaving talcum if necessary.

The next three instructions told how to mix the powder with water or distilled spirits—vodka and gin were recommended—to make the ink, and then how to use it.

Nat wondered anew if Gordon's duties hadn't been more important than the man had let on. He was also intrigued by the idea of Gordon being in touch with a "North Africa–Near East" intelligence operative, especially in light of what Willis Turner had told him about the FBI's hunt for visitors of Middle Eastern origin. There was certainly no other connection that Nat knew of between Gordon and that screwed-up part of the world.

"Secret ink?" Viv said, peering at the memo. "That's a new one."

"Maybe I'm supposed to use it."

"It's what Gordon should have used to write that damn review of your book."

"Thanks for saying so."

"What's next?"

"Looks like an OSS lapel pin, stuck on his ID card. Dated October 5, 1943."

"The day he joined. A month after they crash-landed."

"Wow. Dulles moved fast."

"They were pretty shorthanded in Bern."

He picked up the next item in the box.

"Know anything about this matchbook? It's from the Hotel Jurgens in Bern. Is that where he lived?"

"No. He had an apartment, down by the river. Never heard of that place."

He set it aside. The last item was a key, wrapped with a rubber band along with a white business card and a plastic swipe card with a black metal stripe. All three looked relatively new. The business card was for Matt Boland, manager of U-Store-Em Self Storage in Baltimore.

"Must fit a storage locker," Nat said, his interest growing. Another possible resting place for the four missing folders. Assuming, of course, that the FBI was right in claiming that Gordon had stolen them to begin with. "What do you make of all this?"

Viv frowned and put aside her drink. Then she lit another cigarette and inhaled with what seemed to be an extra degree of vehemence. Something about the assortment of objects was making her uneasy. She narrowed her eyes and picked up the business card.

"Baltimore," she said. "I lived there during the war."

"I didn't know that."

"Worked on the Liberty ships. A regular Rosie Riveter. Had an apartment in a row house on Brady Avenue in Fairfield. Rough little area. Most of the neighborhood still had dirt streets. Gordon and I stayed there a few months after he came home, in early '46, and this address is practically right around the corner. Otherwise? No idea."

They stared at the card a while longer. Viv picked up the German hat.

"Maybe my metric conversions aren't so great, but I'd say this is Gordon's size."

He waited for more, but she was silent, frowning.

So what did they have here? Clues to a riddle? Cryptic signposts that would lead to the "legacy" Gordon had alluded to in his last rambling phone call? That would certainly fit with Gordon's fondness for the elliptical, the coy. Or maybe it was nothing but trivial memorabilia, meaningful only to Gordon. One last cosmic prank played by the teacher on his eager, gullible student. The first step in finding the correct answer seemed obvious enough: See if the key still fit anything in Baltimore. As for the rest, who could say?

"Another thing," he said. "While I was up in the attic I saw a box of my first book."

She smiled.

"He ordered it the day it was released. He gave them out as little favors to visiting colleagues, or people who hosted him for lectures. He was quite proud of you."

"He never told me."

"He wouldn't have. He was just too damn stubborn. Or maybe afraid is a better word."

"Afraid?"

"Didn't you ever notice the way he inched up to the line with so many people, trying to be their friend, only to back away at the last second? Like the risk just wasn't worth it. Even with me, in a way."

"Not with you."

"Oh, yes. After the war, anyway. I know you don't believe me when I say he came back a changed man, but he really did. I figured maybe he'd seen one of his buddies blown to pieces in one of those flying coffins. But, well, you read the piece in the *Daily Wildcat*."

"Then maybe it wasn't the war. Maybe it was just his true nature emerging as he grew up. It happens, Viv. When people aren't kids anymore, they no longer have to try and please everybody. Maybe that's just the way he was."

She stared at him a few seconds, seemingly on the verge of tears.

"That's probably the cruelest thing you've ever said, Nat. I guess you've earned the right. But spare me that kind of honesty in the future, if you don't mind."

"I'm sorry."

"No. It's me. Maybe it's too early to be poking around in all this stuff. Besides, you never knew him like I did. That's the real pity. No one did. All the little things he'd let slip out from time to time, like the story about the bunker. It never happened when he was being a professional. In his work he was always so guarded. Even with you."

"I understand."

"I don't think you do. When he signed on with the OSS he took an oath of secrecy, and that meant something. I met some of the others at reunions. They're the same."

"Maybe so."

Although Nat had his doubts. Oath or not, once you became a historian your goals were the exact opposite of a spy's. You no longer kept secrets; you brought them to light. Gordon had preached that as passionately as anyone.

"Or maybe . . ." Viv said, hesitating. "Maybe it was a woman. I've always wondered."

"You can't really believe that?"

"We weren't married yet when the war started, even though we had talked about it. Of course we made all sorts of promises when he left.

'Don't sit under the apple tree' and all that. But it wasn't like he was in a trench somewhere, especially once he landed in Switzerland. Wine, women, and song, from what I've read."

"Weren't you able to tell from his letters home?"

"He couldn't send any. Or get any, either. Not with the borders closed. After his plane went down I didn't even know he was alive until the Red Cross told his parents he'd landed in Switzerland. We were pretty much cut off for more than a year."

"Did you ever ask after he got back? About a woman, I mean."

She shook her head.

"Too afraid he'd tell me, I guess. But I did find something once. A book."

"Some kind of journal?"

"No. A novel. He said it was a Swiss murder mystery. It was in German, so who knows what it really was?"

"That's your evidence?"

"There was a flower inside, pressed between the pages. And a girl's name was on the inside cover."

Hardly on the level of lipstick on the collar. Viv was probably overreacting based on Gordon's later infidelities.

"He probably picked it up in a secondhand shop when he was bored out of his mind. The girl could have been a previous owner."

"That's what he said. But explain the flower."

"A bookmark. He was reading in a field, or a park, and never got back to it. I'll give it a look if you want. Put your mind at ease that it wasn't some sappy romance."

"I never saw it again. For all I know, he threw it away."

Hardly an act of the lovelorn. But Nat held his tongue. On this, of all nights, Viv was entitled to give free rein to her emotions.

"My advice to you, Nat, is that if you ever have an important question to ask someone you love, then ask it. Don't wait for the right moment. 'Cause one day you wake up and you're all out of moments."

There were tears on her cheeks. She leaned closer and Nat held on, feeling her muffled sobs. When she pulled away her face was splotchy, but she managed a weak smile.

"Maybe you'll get to the bottom of all this. You and the FBI, looking for those missing folders."

"Did Holland tell you about that?"

"Only because he thought I might know something. As if I'd tell *him*. No chance, after the nasty things he said about Gordon. But I'd tell you, of course."

"And?"

She shook her head.

"No idea. All I know for sure is that the old Gordon has been dead much longer than the one you knew. Maybe that's what you'll find hiding in those folders—the old Gordon."

"I'll let you know."

She nodded and picked up the glass of cognac. Then she thought better of it and set it back down. When she next spoke, all the energy was drained from her voice.

"Help me to bed, will you? I'm kind of tired."

Viv took his arm and wobbled toward the bedroom. He tucked her in, the way he had once tucked Karen in as a child. She shut her eyes and took his hand. For a harrowing moment he was convinced she had decided to die, and would do so then and there. But within seconds she was sound asleep.

Her other hand still held a cigarette with a drooping column of ash. Nat gently took it from her fingers and stubbed it out. Yes, Gordon was a drunk, but Nat wondered how many times the old fellow must have kept Viv from burning down the house. Like most enduring couples, they had developed an unspoken symbiosis. How long would Viv last now that Gordon's half of the survival equation was missing? He made a mental note to check up on her when he could. It was the least he could do for Gordon.

He walked quietly back to the living room and again looked over the items from Gordon's strange bequest. Mere trivia? Nat doubted it. Especially after hearing of Gordon's trip to the Hitler bunker. The items had the feel of encoded knowledge, a gift from one historian to another, and Nat felt the first stirrings of an excitement that he hadn't experienced in ages. Gordon, who in life had done so much to damage his zeal, was now reawakening it in death. Already Nat felt fiercely proprietary about these objects. Maybe he shouldn't tell Berta about them, or anyone else. It was, in other words, the usual dilemma of the treasure hunter. Who else could be trusted with the map?

He tucked the box under his arm and strolled out into the night, too restless to simply drive back into town. Moonlight illuminated the trailhead that Gordon and he had walked so many times before, and visibility was so good that Nat decided to enjoy the smells and sounds of the night forest before heading back. It would feel good to stretch his legs after such a strange and exhausting day.

Only a few feet in, he picked up a scent that was strangely out of place—a faint trace of aftershave or cologne. Maybe Willis Turner's warning of a stranger from the Middle East was preying on his mind, because when he sniffed again the smell was gone. Nat scanned the path to the front and rear. Empty. He chased the thought from his mind and continued. He didn't intend to walk far. No sense turning his ankle in the dark with so much work to be done.

After about a quarter mile, and just as he was hitting his stride, he stopped to turn back. As he did, he heard a muffled disturbance in the brush perhaps twenty yards behind. He listened intently, but there was nothing more. He started back slowly, then picked up the pace. If someone had been pursuing him, now he was in pursuit, so why not catch the quarry? Halfway to the trailhead he heard someone stumble. Ten yards before he reached the driveway a dark silhouette stepped into his path, blocking the way.

"Did you find it?" a man's voice called out.

It was Holland. Still keeping tabs. Nat paused to let his pulse slow down.

"Find what?"

"Whatever you were looking for down there on the trail."

"I was taking a walk."

"Alone?"

"Except for you."

"You're sure?"

"Why, did you see somebody? I was stretching my legs, that's all. It's been a long day."

"Thanks to you."

"What do you want?" Nat was getting irritated with talking uphill to a shadow.

"We examined the memory chips from your cameras. They were clean. Not a single shot."

"Guess we were in too much of a hurry when we took them out. Must have erased everything by mistake."

"Or maybe you had another pair of chips, which you hid somewhere."

"Care to search me?"

"Not really. Like you said, it's been a long day. Besides, if anybody knows how to handle that kind of information, maybe even put it to good use, it's someone like you, a professional historian."

Uh-oh. It sounded like Holland wanted to make a deal.

"Provided that I do what?"

"We'd like you to keep working for us. Just in a slightly different capacity. Come up to the driveway. We'll talk while you give me a ride to my car."

Nat slid past him at the top of the trail. No scent of any aftershave, just the odors of sweat and the wool of his suit. Holland hadn't even taken off his jacket. Nat unlocked the car and tried to look casual as he put Gordon's old box on the floor in the back.

"What's in the box?"

"Notes for a culogy. Plus a guest list from Viv for a memorial service."

To Nat's relief, Holland didn't pursue the matter further. He started the engine and put the car in gear before the agent could change his mind.

"I take it you didn't find anything significant in the last of the boxes," Holland said.

"Only those gaps, which I'd mentioned to you earlier."

"The four missing folders?"

"If they're numbered correctly."

"Can't say I'm surprised. All the more reason we still need your help. Oh, and here are your cameras. Figured you'll need them."

"If I agree to work for you, I'll have to be able to proceed in my own way."

"As long as your methods are legal."

"Of course. What would I receive for my trouble?"

"Same rate you're already getting. Plus expenses, within reason. Logistical help, if necessary. And first dibs on the recovered materials, once we're finished with them."

"Meaning after they're declassified, which might be never."

"It won't be never. Of course, if you find them, you'll certainly get a peek then. And chances are we'd be grateful enough to arrange for some sort of limited premature use."

"Sounds wonderfully vague. The sort of agreement you might welsh on in seconds."

"Are you in or not?"

"You're going to have to tell me more. What is this all about?"

There was a long pause, no sound but the growl of the engine in low gear and the pop of gravel against the wheel wells. They reached Holland's Suburban at the bottom of the lane, where a driver waited patiently in the dark. Nat stopped the car.

"First," Holland said, "there are a few things you should know about Gordon Wolfe. None of them fit for the eulogy, I'm afraid. To begin with, he was a thief."

"He said the boxes were planted."

"Which means he was also a liar. Worse, he was a blackmailer. Had been for years. Decades. Quarterly payments to a numbered Swiss account. Puts all this nice mountain acreage of his in a new light, don't you think?"

"And you know this how?"

"From the man he was blackmailing."

"Let me guess. One of the surviving members of the Bauer family in Berlin?"

Holland gave him a long, probing look, and Nat realized he might have goofed.

"It's not that hard to figure, from what you've already told me and what I've already seen," he said, hoping he wouldn't have to bring Berta's name into it. "And I'm guessing you think the incriminating material is in the missing folders. But you must also believe there are clues to their whereabouts in the rest of the material. The kind of clues that only a historian might notice."

"That's why we want you to continue. Start tracking down any leads you can come up with, either from the materials here or from your own sources. Or, hell, from whatever you know about Gordon. You knew him for twenty years."

"Why worry now that the blackmailer is dead?"

"As long as the information's still out there, the subject might still be vulnerable."

"And why's that so important to you?"

"Because the subject is important. And we want to keep him happy. We've been seeking his cooperation for quite some time."

"I'm presuming you mean Kurt Bauer."

Holland said nothing.

"He must be what, in his eighties by now?"

Holland sighed.

"Eighty-one."

"So he probably doesn't even run the family business anymore."

"It's not a commercial issue. Unless you're talking about the buying and selling of information, of contacts."

"What kind of information?"

"I've already said more than I should have. Let's just say he was once a very big player in a very important field, one that has our utmost attention at the moment. If we help him, then he'll help us. Unfortunately, the competition is just as interested, and it's winner take all."

"Who's the competition?"

"A smart fellow like you could probably go online and answer all these questions in about ten minutes, or I wouldn't have said a word of this to begin with. Just don't dig any deeper in the wrong places. Stick to the 1940s and everything will be fine between us."

"When did Gordon start blackmailing him?"

"See? Already digging in the wrong place."

"Well, I thought Viv might like to know."

"You're not to discuss this with his wife. For all we know she's part of it."

"I haven't exactly noticed you arresting her."

"We're keeping an eye on things."

"On her?"

"We're doing our job. Now you do yours. Just find it. We'll take care of the rest. And I expect daily progress reports. You can reach me anytime at this number."

He put a card on the seat between them. Then he handed over a folded sheet of paper.

"Take this, too. It's a letter of introduction, signed by me. Sometimes it opens doors. Other times it slams them, so use it sparingly."

Holland unlatched the door, but Nat had one more question.

"Are you sure Gordon's death was an accident?"

"Why do you ask?"

"You didn't answer the question."

"Maybe we don't know the answer yet."

"Well, if it wasn't, who's to say they won't try the same thing with me?"

"Don't worry. We'll be keeping an eye on you. You won't always see us, but we'll be around."

"How come that only bothers me more?"

"Look, I won't sugarcoat it. The competition isn't exactly known for playing by the rules. But let's not make this worse than it is."

"Speaking of which, what's up with this Middle Eastern fellow you're looking for? Is he with the competition?"

"Who told you about him?"

"Willis Turner."

Holland snorted.

"Now there's a piece of work. He's freelancing for someone. Him and that sleazeball judge. Guarantee it."

"Who?"

"We don't know yet. But you should regard him and anyone else who crosses your path as competition."

Too bad Nat had already copied the documents for Turner, but a deal was a deal. And Nat couldn't rat out the cop without admitting to having his own set of copies. Holland obviously suspected as much, but it would be foolhardy to come out and say so.

"Sounds like a pretty crowded field of people who are looking for this," Nat said. "Some unspecified foreign government, which may or may not include this loose character from the Middle East, plus whoever Willis Turner is working for, and now me."

"Don't forget your German. Actually, maybe you should forget her."

"Why? She might be a big help."

"We don't know her background. Neither do you."

"Historian. Ph.D. from the Free University of Berlin. She's a pro, too, you know."

"So she says. Growing up in East Berlin isn't exactly a point in her favor."

"Still fighting the Cold War?"

"They had some pretty strong and unsavory Middle Eastern connections on their side of the Wall. Especially among students."

"She was *fifteen* when the Wall came down."

"Just saying. Forewarned is forearmed."

"I'll keep that in mind."

"Try not to share too much. Keep her at arm's length."

It was a little disturbing hearing the agent say exactly what he had been thinking only moments ago, while looking through Gordon's little treasure box.

"Sharing is the way it works," he said, trying to convince himself as much as Holland. "It's the only way you make progress as a team."

"Slept with her yet?"

"None of your business. But no."

"I expect that's about to change."

"Are you guys experts on relationships now?"

"You'll see."

Holland smiled and slipped out of the car. Nat waited for the Suburban to drive off, so the agent wouldn't be tempted to follow. Then Nat, too, headed down the mountain. Ten minutes later, weary and dazed from the long and emotional day, he slowly climbed the stairs to his garret.

He opened the door to find Berta Heinkel waiting on the bed in the dark.

She was awake, eyes glimmering in the moonlight. Just as in his dream, she wore a short nightgown of white silk. Sleek and smooth, like her skin.

So much for keeping her at arm's length.

ELEVEN

NAT SWITCHED on the light to make sure his eyes weren't deceiving him. In the instant glare from the overhead bulb Berta threw an arm across her face and pulled up the sheets.

"I tried to reach you," she said through her fingers. "I was scared. There was nowhere else to go, so I came here."

"Scared of what?"

"Someone had searched my room. I think they were looking for the memory chips."

"You sure it wasn't just the innkeeper tidying up? These B&Bs are pretty finicky."

"They'd picked the lock. Things were missing from my suitcase."

Nat saw her suitcase now, lying open on the floor. The nightgown wasn't the only silky item. She had packed well for this kind of scene. He was tempted to sit on the bed, then thought better of it and opted for the chair, still clutching the wooden box. Maybe it was that Berta's ambition made him wary, or that Gordon had called her a damned nuisance and then dropped dead. Or maybe it was that he would have enjoyed nothing better right now than to snuggle up next to her on the bed.

Her eyes had adjusted to the light and she looked better than ever. Shoulders bare, except for the white silk straps. Hair in suggestive disarray.

"You're good at this, aren't you?" he said.

"Good at what?"

"Manipulating people."

He had expected to get a rise out of her, but she took it in stride.

"I can be. When there's something I want badly enough. But not with you."

"How do you see that?"

"Because we both want the same thing. You might just as easily manipulate me."

He smiled, admiring her skill.

"Holland returned our cameras, by the way. I don't know if you were able to tell yet from our work this afternoon, but you were right about the boxes. Four folders are missing. The feds have asked me to find the missing items. On their tab. Interested?"

She nodded, but surprised him by showing no sign of excitement.

"Where do you think we should start?" she asked.

The sheet slipped farther down her torso, showing some cleavage. Healthy tone to her skin for this early in the spring, yet no hint of a tan line. Of course, topless sunbathing wasn't exactly taboo in Europe. Nat cleared his throat, hoping to also clear his head.

"I was thinking Baltimore." He figured that would get a reaction, but her face remained blank. He opened the old box in a way that kept her from seeing the contents, and pulled out the key. "This fits a storage locker there. It's our first stop."

"All right. Are they paying my way, too?"

"Long as I'm in charge."

"Good. I've maxed out my credit cards. We'd better get some sleep. Shall you take the floor, or I?"

Well, he supposed that answered one question.

"Throw me a pillow."

She nodded and complied, somehow managing to make the toss without letting the sheet drop a stitch farther. Then she lay back down and shut her eyes. Oh, definitely no manipulation going on here, he thought, smiling to himself as he turned out the light.

As he tried to get comfortable in the dark, he wondered anew what it was that drove her. Scholarly zeal, of course. All the best historians were competitive. But there had to be something more. He was about to drift off when she spoke up from the bed.

"I have some names I can share. Old contacts of Gordon Wolfe's and Kurt Bauer's, people who might have once handled the records, or have some leads."

Throwing him a bone. It was a start.

"Living or dead?"

"Living. In Bern and Berlin. We can visit them, now that we have a budget."

"Great. But with any luck the trail will end in Baltimore."

Her silence told him she thought otherwise, which troubled him because it suggested she knew more than she was letting on. He had better check out her credentials, first chance he got. Until then, or until she opened up more, perhaps "arm's length" was indeed the best policy. Funny how sensible that sounded down there on the cold, hard floor.

TWELVE

Nat's great hopes for Baltimore died with the swipe of a card, the turn of a key, and the opening of an iron door. There before him on the concrete floor, looking lost and forlorn in the five-by-five storage locker, was a single item, barely bigger than a fist. It was wrapped in bubble plastic and smothered in tape. Definitely not the missing folders.

Berta said nothing, but Nat sensed an I-told-you-so chill.

At least they hadn't wasted much time getting there. He had planned on using Sunday to drive Viv back to Wightman for a Wednesday memorial service. She instead decided to wait on her sister, which freed Berta and him to catch a midday flight from Albany to Baltimore. They drove straight to Fairfield, rattling down its potholed lanes among the rail yards and chemical plants of an industrial waterfront. Fittingly, they wound up briefly on Tate Street, where Viv and Gordon had lived after the war. Only one house remained on the block, and it was boarded up. The trail ended at a fenced compound with a "U-Store-Em" sign out front. Nat bounded from the car, but his excitement was short-lived.

"Well, let's see what it is," he said, trying to keep the disappointment out of his voice.

He slit the tape with a car key and unwrapped the plastic. Inside was an old book with a red cloth cover and a German title, *Der Unsichtbare Henker* (*The Invisible Hangman*), by Wolf Schwertenbach. Was this the crime novel that had made Viv so jealous? He doubted Viv had been familiar with the author, but Nat certainly was. Wolf Schwertenbach was the pen name of the late Paul Meyer, a Swiss diplomat who during the war opened a secret back channel between the Swiss and German intelligence agencies. He was also an OSS source who met Dulles several times. But none of that seemed to explain why Gordon had gone to the trouble of putting the book into storage.

The publication date was 1933, although this was a 1937 printing. Nat checked inside the front jacket. Sure enough, a girl's name was penned in cursive in an upper corner, just as Viv had said. "Sabine Keller."

"Noir pulp by a hack diplomat," Berta said. "Not even a first edition. You might get five euros for it. Shall we go?"

"Hold on."

Nat flipped carefully through the brittle pages. No hidden note. No scribbles in the margins. No cryptic inscriptions from the famed author. But on page 186 he found the very wildflower Viv must have seen. Crushed yellow blossom, bent stem. Nothing special, like edelweiss. Just a buttercup plucked from a field. He left it in place, feeling that somehow Gordon would have preferred that.

"Shall we go?" Berta repeated.

"Let's see who's on duty."

They walked to a small office. A big fellow with a buzz cut and a weight lifter's build looked up from a cramped desk behind the counter.

"Would you be Matt Boland?" Nat asked, using the name from the business card.

"That's me." He seemed surprised to actually be speaking with a customer.

"Do you keep records of customer visits?"

Boland shook his head.

"For some people that's half the point. You're not a cop, are you?"

"I'm here for a friend. So you have no way of knowing when somebody would have last visited locker 207?" Nat held up the key and swipe card.

"If that key belongs to you, wouldn't you know?"

"It was a colleague's. He died yesterday."

"Sorry."

"His name was Gordon Wolfe. Ring a bell?"

"Can't say it does."

"Have you got the paperwork for 207?"

"How do I know you didn't steal that key?"

Nat pulled out the FBI letter of introduction and placed it on the counter.

"Maybe this'll help."

"You said you weren't cops."

"We're not. Let's just say we're working on contract."

"Is this some kind of terrorist thing?" Boland was getting into the spirit of things.

"Something like that."

"Cool. Why didn't you say so?"

Boland crossed the room to a set of gray drawers, where he retrieved a yellow invoice.

"What'd you say the name was?"

"Gordon Wolfe."

"Wrong guy."

"With an address in Wightman, Pennsylvania? 819 Boyd Circle?"

Boland glanced down.

"Yeah. Home phone?"

Nat rattled it off, and for good measure recited the number for Gordon's cell.

"Three for three. In that case, who the heck is 'Gordon Bernhard'?"

"Bernhard?"

"That's what it says."

"Hold on a second. I'll be right back."

Berta sighed with impatience while Nat went to the car. He returned with one of Gordon's books that Viv had given him that morning and opened it to the author photo.

"Is this the man who called himself Gordon Bernhard?"

"Absolutely. He was in here a couple weeks ago." Boland stepped to a wall calendar, where he ran his finger across a row of days. "May seventh, to be exact. The Monday from hell. We had a power outage later that afternoon, which always screws things up and gripes out the customers. Mr. Bernhard needed a new swipe card. He was probably the only customer that day who wasn't screaming at me."

The timing put Gordon's visit only a few days after the gotcha story broke in the *Daily Wildcat*, the one that had sent him heading for the hills.

"Have you got a surveillance camera with a view of 207?"

"We've got cameras covering every part of the building. Want to check it for the seventh? It's a digital system, stored on a hard drive."

Boland called up the log on a PC. The door of 207 showed up at a great angle from camera 4. Boland easily found the right day, slid the time bar back to the approximate hour of Gordon's visit, and scanned forward on high speed until a blurry figure darted in and out of the frame. Then he backed up, slowed down, and there it was, a black-and-white image of Gordon Wolfe from behind, as if they were peeping over his shoulder from the ceiling. He was empty-handed, except for the key. He turned the lock, went inside 207, and shut the door behind him. The time signature read 1:12 p.m.

"So by this time he'd already stopped by for the new swipe card?" Nat asked.

"Correct. Said his old one wasn't working."

That meant Gordon had put the new swipe card in the box in the attic during the past week. He had certainly been attending to a lot of old business lately. Tidying up. Getting ready for something.

Boland scrolled ahead. Gordon reemerged at 1:38, still empty-handed.

"What the hell?" Nat said. Had Gordon just spent twenty-six minutes visiting a taped-up novel? "Any way to slow that down?"

"Sure."

Boland scrolled back. This time Gordon exited in slow motion.

"Hold it! Back it up to when he opens the door, then freeze it. There, do you see it?"

Just behind Gordon's right leg was the right edge of a box, the size of the ones found at the Wolfes' summer home. By now even Berta was riveted.

"He left without them," he said. "He must have come back later."

"Couldn't have," Boland chimed in. "Like I said, we lost power right after that. The swipe card system went down, so I had to let people in manually the rest of the day. I'd have seen him."

"I guess he could have come back some other day," Nat said. "But if not, then he was right about one thing. Somebody planted those boxes at his house. Could you rerun his exit one more time?"

Boland nodded, and they watched again.

"Something's funny," Nat said. "Have you got any shots from farther down the hall?"

"Sure. Camera 5."

"Let's see 'em. Arrival and departure."

Boland complied. Gordon arrived at the bottom of the screen at 1:12 and walked slowly up the hall, staying on camera for eleven steps. At 1:38 he reappeared in the opposite direction, but with an altered gait. He paused halfway to hitch up his pants.

"Does it look to you like he's limping?"

"Yes," Berta said. Now she was leaning forward intently. "Run it again."

Boland wrinkled his nose at the sound of her accent. She obviously didn't fit his idea of who should be working for the FBI. But he did as she asked.

"Maybe he stiffened up while he was on the floor, looking at everything," Nat said.

"No," Berta said. "It's something else."

They watched again.

"It's like his pants were bothering him," Nat said.

Then it came to him, a bolt straight from memory.

"Holy shit," he whispered. "It's just like George Wood."

"You're right," Berta said in amazement.

"Woody who?" Boland asked. By now he was as engrossed as they were.

"George Wood," Nat said, unable to resist the urge to teach. "Code name for an old German spy named Fritz Kolbe. During the war he smuggled documents out of the Foreign Ministry by taping them to his thigh and carrying them all the way to Switzerland by train. All Gordon had to do was make it to the parking lot."

"But why not just take them out in a briefcase?" Berta asked.

"Maybe he knew someone was watching him. Either way, if he hid them up at the summer house, I suppose the FBI will find them soon enough."

"No!"

"Afraid so. Holland said they'd be making a thorough search as soon as Viv left. They'll take the place apart board by board before they come up empty."

"Scheise!"

"Hey, I thought you were working *for* the FBI," Boland said warily.

"Like I said, contract employees. If an agent comes up with the goods first, we'd, uh, lose our commission."

"Oh."

"Gordon's rental agreement—how old is it?"

Boland checked the invoice.

"Wow. Way before my time. Nineteen seventy-eight."

"Place looks newer."

"They've modernized a few times, but this was one of the first self-storage joints in the city. He must have been one of the original customers."

Seventy-eight, Nat thought. Probably around the time bulldozers started knocking down the neighborhood to make way for industry. He had a feeling those boxes had been sitting around Fairfield, one way or another, for quite a while.

THEIR NEXT STOP was the National Archives, right down the road in College Park. They had two days to search for leads before returning to Wightman, so Nat had booked a pair of rooms at a Holiday Inn. An impatient message from Holland was waiting at the front desk when they checked in: "Where are you? Please call."

Berta took her key and announced curtly that she would be eating room service and retiring early. Hot and cold, this strange woman. Or maybe just cold, now that she had secured Nat's cooperation. Just as well, considering his first order of business. Holland could wait. It was time to check up on Berta's credentials.

He quickly found her name on the Web site of the history department at Berlin's Free University. The thumbnail bio matched what she had told him. Several published papers were referenced. Most concerned the Berlin activities of the White Rose. A slender thread of scholarship, even by the eccentric standards of historians. Berta's grandmother must have told her some great tales to get her this hooked.

Surprisingly, there were almost no other online traces of Berta or her work. No quotes in the media. No speeches or seminars. It told him two things: She didn't crave attention, and she kept to herself.

Next, he Googled Kurt Bauer. Holland was right. It took about ten minutes to figure out why the FBI must be interested in helping the man.

Nat was already familiar with the family's industrial dynasty. The Bauers were a sort of junior version of the Krupps—not as rich or colorful but nearly as well connected—by virtue of their long-standing ability to produce weapons for emperors and despots the world over. Kurt entered the picture during the postwar years, when he took over management of the company in his early twenties, an impressively callow age for an arms merchant. The company's rise from the ashes was a prototype of West Germany's "economic miracle," which had been nurtured by the Western Allies as a hedge against communism.

Today most people knew the Bauer name from coffeemakers, televisions, and aircraft components. But it was the company's dealings in a more arcane line of products that had attracted the FBI's interest. Or so Nat concluded from a series of hits on Web sites tracking nuclear proliferation.

In the 1970s a shipment of Bauer jet nozzles was used to help enrich uranium for South Africa's nuclear bomb program. In the '80s and '90s, Bauer plants provided isostatic presses, vacuum furnaces, and specialized tubing to shady middlemen, who in turn funneled the parts to Libya, Israel, and Iraq.

Most of the Web sites had an axe to grind, and several tried to imply that Kurt was an unreconstructed Nazi. It didn't take a professional historian to see that their case was half-baked. Kurt's dad, Reinhard, had certainly been a card-carrying member, and he had employed slave labor in his wartime factories. But even Reinhard joined the Party late, which suggested opportunism more than zeal. It was the same reason he later tried to curry favor with Dulles—because it was good for business. If the man were alive today he would probably be working for an outfit like Halliburton, cutting deals with dictators and then helping to engineer their downfall. Whatever paid the bills.

Other critics tried to damn Kurt by association with his older brother, Manfred, who had served with a Wehrmacht unit implicated in some atrocities on the eastern front. But Manfred was killed at Stalingrad, and Kurt himself had been too young for the army during most of the war. According to the sketchy biographical record on the Internet, the Bauer family fled to Switzerland when Kurt was eighteen. That must have been when he met Gordon, if Berta's information was credible. Maybe the archives had the answer.

It was in more recent decades that the Bauer nuclear dealings had become most interesting. In the late '90s the company supposedly helped ship heavy water to North Korea and Pakistan. That transaction linked Bauer for the first time to A. Q. Khan, the father of Pakistan's A-bomb program and an infamous supplier of nuclear know-how to several rogue nations. The Bauer-Khan partnership continued through further transactions in parts and technology, according to the proliferation Web sites. Each deal was more damning, but Bauer's role became progressively harder to pin down. As a result, investigators for the German government hadn't yet laid a glove on him.

They came close in 2004, after centrifuge components in Bauer crates were seized aboard a German freighter en route from Dubai to Libya. Bauer again managed to wriggle off the hook, but a few months later he retired as chairman of the family companies. His timing suggested he had brokered a deal to avoid further scrutiny, and one of the more strident Web sites commented: "Of all the Western industrialists tainted by tawdry connections to this ruthless field of endeavor, Kurt Bauer may well be the one with the most intimate knowledge of its innermost secrets and nefarious web of contacts."

Melodramatic, perhaps, but it certainly explained the FBI's current interest in currying favor with the man. Bauer's Rolodex alone would be a valuable weapon in trying to dismantle the black market in nuclear materials, much less the man's insider knowledge. The flip side was that any nation aspiring to build a bomb would also covet the information, and that seemed to narrow the possibilities for Holland's "competition" to Iran or Syria, especially since the FBI was seeking a Middle Easterner. Probably Iran, given the current state of play.

Sobering news, to say the least. Competing with historians who might retaliate with a nasty review was one thing. Going up against an Iranian spy was quite another, especially if Nat ventured abroad, where Holland would be less able to protect him.

He realized his palms were sweating on the keyboard. Calm down, he told himself. You're working for people who know all about this stuff. Surely they would warn him if things got too hazardous, right? It seemed like an appropriate time to check in with Holland. The agent picked up on the first ring.

"You should have told me the competition was Iran," Nat said.

"Is this your idea of a progress report?"

"So you're not denying it."

"Sorry, I'm not hearing you well. Maybe I should call back."

"I thought you'd at least be impressed that I'm doing my home-work."

"Point taken. I assume the storage locker was a dry hole."

Nat mentioned his theory that Gordon had smuggled the folders out in his pants. He suggested that Holland have someone scan the surveillance video from that day forward to check for a return visit—by Gordon or anyone else.

"Good idea."

"Where are you now? What's all the hammering?"

"Gordon's summer house. We did a top-to-bottom. They're nail-ing the paneling back in place."

Ouch. Yet another grievance for Viv.

"Find anything?"

"A box of your books, actually."

"The one in the attic?"

"How'd you know?"

"I, uh, Viv told me."

"Sounds like you did some poking around the other night. I also recall you leaving the house with a box."

"Like I told you. A guest list, a few keepsakes."

"Don't remember you mentioning any keepsakes."

"You're right. This connection is terrible."

"Whatever you say, Turnbull."

"I need a favor."

"Try me."

"I want someone to keep an eye on my daughter. She moved into my house today for the summer. She got a hang-up call from my cell phone, the one I left in the library. Guy with a foreign accent."

"Relax. We're a step ahead of you. We've got her covered."

"So you're saying it had already occurred to you that she was in danger?"

"I'm saying you have no reason to worry. We're on it."

"If you're 'on it,' then how come you didn't get my cell phone back? You were going to go pick it up when the doors opened."

"Our man was the first one in the library the next morning. It was already gone."

"Meaning someone else must have been there when Neil Ford came for me."

"Draw your own conclusions."

"Why do I get the idea you're downplaying the danger?"

"Am I?"

"This Middle Eastern character, for one."

"He's our concern, not yours. And do me a favor. Get yourself a new cell phone. You need to be accessible 24/7."

"Tomorrow, if there's time. I'll be at the archives all day."

"Happy hunting, then. I'll await your call."

Not exactly reassuring. Nat needed to know that Karen was okay. He tried her cell and got a recording. Then he called his house. When she didn't pick up after three rings, he began to panic. She answered on the fourth.

"Karen?"

"There you are. I was worried about you."

Likewise, he almost said. But he didn't want to upset her.

"I guess you heard about Gordon."

"News of the day here. I'm sorry, Dad. It must be horrible for you. Especially after the way he was outed in the *Wildcat*."

"Not how he wanted to go out, that's for sure."

"How's Mrs. Wolfe?"

"About like you'd expect. I offered her a ride to Wightman, but her sister was driving down."

"Where are you, then?"

"College Park. Via an afternoon in Baltimore."

He told her about the odd visit to the storage locker. He didn't mention Berta.

"So you're saying he really was, like, a thief?"

"Looks that way."

"Then maybe his little divorce from you was, like, a favor. I'm sorry. I shouldn't be trashing him. This must be hard."

"Well, at least he left me with something to do. I may be on this for a while. The FBI wants me to follow up, see if I can find the material that's still missing. Apparently the stakes are a little higher than I'd thought. Not that you should breathe a word of this to anyone, especially strangers."

"Which reminds me. I got another one of those funny hang-ups from your cell. Same guy. You really should, like, cancel the number. I mean, he could cost you a fortune."

The news made him angry. Where the hell were Holland's people? He tried to keep his voice calm for Karen.

"Well, at least you've got Dave to keep you company."

"Dave drove home to Cleveland. So don't worry, you can rest easy."

"Actually, I was kind of hoping he'd stick around."

"What's wrong, Dad?"

"I don't like it that you're there alone. Have you thought about visiting your mom until I'm back? Especially if I have to go off for a while?"

"Already trying to get rid of me?"

"No. It's not like that at all."

"You sure? I mean, you haven't really been a full-time dad in like, what, five years?"

"No. Truthfully. I've been looking forward to this all semester. Just do me a favor. Lock the dead bolt till I'm back, and keep an eye out for anybody who might be paying a little too much attention to you or to the house. If they're in an unmarked black Chevy, it's probably just some federal people, making sure my stuff isn't disturbed. Anybody else, let me know right away."

"You're making this sound dangerous."

"I'm probably overreacting. But if I stay on this job much longer, maybe we'll have to make other arrangements. Just for a while. Look, I'll be back Tuesday night, so sit tight until then. And I hope you can go to the memorial service on Wednesday. I have to speak, so I'll need the moral support. I might not be showing up alone, by the way. There's this, uh, German researcher traveling with me."

He was grateful she couldn't see him blush.

"I'm guessing from your tone of voice that the German is a woman. And maybe even kind of hot?"

"Not hot. Just obsessed. Worse than me, even."

"A perfect match."

"Easy. Risky business, dating colleagues."

"Risk is what makes it interesting."

"You're too young for us to be having this conversation."

"But not too young to give you advice, especially when I'm the one with the boyfriends and you're all alone."

He was about to ask why "boyfriend" was plural when he heard her flipping pages. The ever present *Complete Poems of Emily Dickinson,* no doubt. Karen's Holy Bible.

"Why do I have the feeling you're about to quote some verse?"

"Because I am? Here it is. Poem 1377. From her 'Life' series."

There was a pregnant pause.

"Well. Are you going to read it?"

"Too embarrassing." She giggled. "Besides, it will be more effective if you look it up later. It's the perfect message to sleep on, especially if your German is there with you."

"Separate rooms. And she's not *my* German."

"Well, read it anyway. And don't worry, I won't talk to any strangers."

He tried to laugh. But it was far too easy to imagine her alone in the house. She'd be standing in the kitchen with the curtains open and a single light on, visible to anyone in the backyard. Those old mullioned windows, which you could unlock simply by smashing a single pane. He resisted the urge to phone Holland, lest the man conclude he had gone batty. Rest easy, he told himself. The feds are on the job.

Just before climbing into bed he fired up his laptop to track down the poem. He was hoping vainly for a bit of daughterly encouragement, or maybe a little solace over the death of a friend. But, no, Karen had of course become fixated on Berta.

Even so, he had to smile at the poem's ring of truth. It was obvious that Karen knew him all too well in spite of their years of estrangement, and as he scanned the words he imagined her reading them aloud, embarrassed or not, in a tone of amused irony:

> *Forbidden fruit a flavor has*
> *That lawful Orchards mocks—*
> *How luscious lies within the Pod*
> *The Pea that Duty locks—*

Forbidden fruit, indeed. This assignment had it by the bushel, and not just in the form of Berta Heinkel.

For one thing, Nat couldn't help but wonder if he was about to play one of those hidden roles in a momentous affair—the sort of obscure but significant action he always enjoyed unearthing years later. It was quite a temptation for a historian, this idea of a cameo upon the stage of his own discipline.

But it did seem to violate some unwritten rule of the profession. And he, as well as anyone, knew how often such actions, no matter how well-meaning, produced unintended consequences. He was also aware of the typical fate of influential minor players. The reason history tended to forget them was that they were so often erased by the very forces they set in motion. Blotted out, like the names in a classified document.

Nat folded up his laptop and slid beneath the sheets, but he didn't fall asleep for hours.

THIRTEEN

THE VOICE of Gordon Wolfe spoke from the printed page, and Nat was stunned by its disclosure. Now the voice was laughing, the old man enjoying a postmortem chuckle over the little joke he'd played only moments before his death.

"Sly old bastard," Nat muttered to himself. "So *this* is what you meant."

The occasion called for a celebratory shot of Gordon's bourbon. Alas, food and drink were forbidden in the vast reading room of the National Archives. But no rules could keep out the ghosts, which always flourished in this haunted chamber despite a picture-window view onto a sunny suburban forest.

The document before him was an OSS employment form that Gordon had filled out on October 5, 1943. To Nat's surprise, it included code names, countersigns, and secret ID numbers, hardly what you'd expect to find on a job application for a clerk or translator. The line that had just spoken to Nat was on the "Agent's Check List," an item that asked the applicant to provide a "Question and Answer by which agent may identify himself to collaborators."

Gordon had offered this: "Q. Where did you have dinner the last evening you were in Washington, D.C.? A: The Metropolitan Club." It was an eerie echo of his jailhouse exchange with the paramedic two mornings ago. Faced with death, the stricken Gordon Wolfe had journeyed back in time to his first day on the job as a spy.

For Nat, this was the thrilling beauty of research—an addictive power to commune with the dead. Better than a Ouija board, this stuff.

"See this?" he whispered, sliding the paper toward Berta.

She read it, nodded, then turned back to her own work. It was already apparent that only a reference to the White Rose or Kurt Bauer would get a rise out of her. Well, tough luck, because Nat was determined to build a new dossier on Gordon as part of their quest.

Nat was no stranger to declassified OSS archives, but his previous work had focused on OSS contacts with the German resistance. This time he was venturing into less-familiar territory, so he had sought out archivist Bill Staley, a genial old gnome who had been guiding prospectors into these shadowy mine shafts for decades. Staley knew not only where the gold was but also who had buried it, and with what brand of shovel.

"Young Turnbull," Staley said, greeting him in the reference room. "Welcome back."

Nat turned to introduce Berta, but she was gone. The latest in a series of antisocial moments since their arrival downstairs.

"Sorry to hear about Gordon. I saw his obituary in this morning's *Post*."

The *New York Times* had also run a story. Mercifully, neither mentioned Gordon's alleged thievery or the fact that he had died in jail, although the *Times* did refer to the brouhaha over his embellished military record. Holland must have worked overtime to keep a lid on things, and Nat wondered why.

Surely if Berta's source at the archives had heard about the arrest, then Staley must have, too. But the man's face betrayed no hint of recognition, only the doleful mien of someone who has endured yet another death of a valued contemporary. The ranks were thinning fast for the wartime crowd.

"I'm here because of Gordon," Nat said. "I'm looking for materials from his OSS days." Realizing that sounded awkward with the man not even buried, he added, "I'm speaking at his memorial service. Thought I might fill in a few blanks."

"I don't know much about his work in Bern. Mostly clerical, I think. Only person to ever show any interest was some college kid about a year ago. Foreign exchange student. Not sure if she came up with anything. Wouldn't have anything to do with me once I pointed her in the right direction."

Probably Berta. No wonder she was laying low. It would also

explain her lack of enthusiasm for this track of research. But why hadn't she shared her results—or lack of them—rather than letting him waste time covering the same ground?

Staley first checked the finding aids, thick volumes cross-referenced by name, place, and subject. None listed a single mention of "Wolfe, Gordon."

"Could he have had a code name?" Nat asked.

"Doubt it. But we can check the OSS master list."

That search also came up empty. Nat was on the verge of moving to the next topic when Staley raised a finger.

"We got a new batch of declassified material a few weeks ago. Those always yield a few new identities. It's still indexed under CIA numbers, but I'd be happy to check."

"Lead the way."

That was where they struck gold, taking even Staley by surprise. On a list of seven previously undisclosed code names, "Icarus" turned up next to Gordon's name.

"I'll be damned," Nat said. "Wonder why they took so long to declassify that?"

"Bottom of the pile?"

"You really think it's that simple?"

"No." Staley smiled. "But it's what they'd want me to say."

With the new point of reference, fresh leads were suddenly abundant, including the Icarus personnel file. It, too, was part of the new batch of material, meaning that probably few, if any, historians had seen it.

Nat and Berta filled out requests for the materials they wanted, and a young librarian hauled out a pair of squeaking pushcarts piled with narrow gray boxes, just like the four that had turned up in Gordon's summer home. Berta and he set up their cameras and tripods on adjoining desks and hunkered down.

The Icarus file held Gordon's employment form, the one with the reference to the Metropolitan Club. A stack of attached memos offered the flavor of Gordon's earliest assignments.

Routine stuff, mostly. Dulles sent him to meet with a shadowy young émigré from France who was offering information in exchange for passage to the United States. Gordon's report concluded the fellow was a con man.

"Agreed," Dulles scribbled in the margin, initialing it with his trademark "AWD."

Some assignments came to Icarus via Zurich operative Frederick Loofbourow, an interesting fellow in his own right. A U.S. commercial attaché on leave from an executive job with Standard Oil, Loofbourow was right out of the Dulles mold of gentleman spy, with posh digs on the Zurich waterfront.

Nat then came across a memo dated October 29, 1943, which stopped him cold. By that time, Nat knew, Dulles had been preoccupied with his new star source—German diplomat Fritz Kolbe, alias George Wood, the fellow who had taped all those stolen documents around his thigh. Thanks to Kolbe, for example, Dulles knew well in advance about the ill-fated July 20 plot to assassinate Adolf Hitler. To clear the board for meetings with Kolbe, Dulles pawned off some of his lesser sources to other operatives, including Icarus. And one of those sources was Reinhold von Bauer, Kurt Bauer's father.

"Henceforth, 543 to handle Magneto," Nat read. He recognized Bauer's code name from the stolen files he had reviewed for the FBI.

Gordon, as operative 543, didn't seem impressed by what Magneto had to offer.

"Magneto continues to insist on relocation to Switzerland," Gordon wrote. "I repeated your insistence that he is far more valuable to us in Berlin. Claims family is under pressure from personal circumstances, but would not elaborate. Said his son can also help us. Told him I would await your advisement."

"Cannot meet him at present," Dulles replied. "Stick to your guns. AWD."

A promising lead. But when Nat turned the page the trail went cold. Staring up at him was a canary-colored sheet of cardboard with the words "Withdrawal Notice, Access Restricted." Below, in smaller print, was the usual boilerplate: "Now Filed in CIA Job No. 79-003317B. Four items have been withdrawn because they contain security classified information or otherwise restricted information."

The withdrawal was dated three weeks ago, the very day the rest of these materials had become public. Someone had gotten cold feet at the last second. Holland? Although the FBI and the CIA still weren't exactly pals, maybe the Agency had asked for some last-minute sanitizing. And that made Nat think of Steve Wallace, a CIA archivist he had met years ago at a history seminar. Wallace, a decent source if used sparingly, never revealed classified information. But he sometimes nudged you in the direction of other materials, already public, that gave you what you needed. Nat opened his laptop to shoot Wallace an e-mail. Then he showed Berta the withdrawal notice.

"I'm finding those, too," she said with a frown. "But look at this."

She handed him a tattered clothbound notebook with the letters "H-P" inked on the spine. It was a Dulles logbook, stuffed with detailed alphabetical listings for his sources and contributors. "Magneto" had his own page of dated, typewritten notations.

Nat had been through that very logbook years earlier. But at the time he hadn't known Magneto's identity. No one else would have either, unless they'd had access to the information in the stolen boxes that had turned up at Gordon's.

Nat read the first paragraph, which included a boldfaced addition:

> **Source Magneto is a German businessman with excellent connections in France, Germany, and Switzerland. Resourceful, intelligent, hitherto reliable. Source's son connected with the German underground.**

"And look on the very next page," Berta said.

It was headed "Magneto II." It began with a physical description from an interesting source:

> **Would put his height at 5'11", full head of hair clipped short and brown. Typical Prussian features, well built although reduced by recent privations. Eyes wide apart, blue-gray, frank in expression. Unworldly but has acquired ease in conversation through his recent travels. Shape of head oval, ears medium but stand out slightly from head. (Icarus, 05/24/44)**

"You think Magneto II is Kurt?" Nat said.

"Has to be."

The logbook contained only two other citations for Magneto II. The first, a bit ominous in its abruptness, was dated only three months before Germany surrendered:

> **Relationship terminated. (02/10/45)**

The last entry was dated five months after the surrender. Dulles wrote it the week he departed occupied Germany to return for good to the United States:

Magneto II file to storage. To be transferred to 109. (10/8/45)

Nat didn't need to look up code number 109. It belonged to William "Wild Bill" Donovan, chief of the OSS. Whatever information the agency had collected on Kurt Bauer, someone had decided it needed special handling by the nation's reigning spymaster once the war was over. Unless, of course, the file never made it to Donovan.

"I'm betting that a Magneto II dossier is one of the four missing folders," Nat said.

"My thoughts, too."

"We should make copies," he said. "But we'll need a permission tab."

"I'll get one," Berta said.

Nat turned next to Gordon's expense filings. There were a few surprises. The first was that he had stayed at the Bellevue Palace during his first three nights in Bern. It was the city's finest hotel. Yet another indicator that Dulles had expected great things. During his first week of employment Gordon bought a bicycle license and a monthly rail pass, which gave him some mobility. In January 1944 he moved up to the next level, so to speak, by purchasing a 1937 Ford Tudor sedan for 3,500 Swiss francs and splitting a monthly gasoline ration with two other operatives. He also bought one of the requisite tools of the World War II spy trade, a Minox miniature camera.

But it was the last page that produced the most astonishing item. In December 1944 Gordon bought a Walther .38-caliber pistol and ammunition, for 201.65. The seller was the W. Glaser Waffen Shop, Löwenstrasse 42, Zurich. Nat recognized the name and address from the box Gordon had left him. Where was the gun now, he wondered? And why had Gordon needed one in peaceful old Bern?

Oddly, that was the final expense report in the file, even though Gordon had kept on working for Dulles for another five months of the war, plus several months afterward in occupied Germany. Had the other vouchers been lost? Removed? Moments later Nat happened upon another possible explanation, in a Loofbourow memo from April 30, 1945, the date of Adolf Hitler's suicide: "543 has been moved to

Mrs. Carroll's house on Seestrasse. In light of Fleece, I see no further need for his immediate services."

Was Fleece a source or an operation? Or perhaps something else altogether? Nat looked around for Berta to ask if she had seen any such reference, but she was still getting authorization to make copies. He checked the finding aids with Staley, who had never come across the term. There was no reference anywhere to "Fleece."

He did find another mention of the "Mrs. Carroll" on Seestrasse, in a message from Dulles to Loofbourow from several years earlier: "Go ahead and rent the space in Zurich from Mrs. Carroll for use in case an agent is 'traveling black.' "

In other words, the address was a safe house. Meaning they had put Gordon under wraps during the final days of the war. Strange. Switzerland hadn't been a place where lives were often at risk.

Nat's thoughts were interrupted by a woman's shout from across the room.

"Come back here! Turn around!"

He looked up to see one of the librarians pursuing Berta, who was walking briskly toward the exit. The librarian, a tall woman with long arms toned by years of hauling boxes, broke into a run and clapped a hand on Berta's shoulder. The reading room, normally cloaked in contemplative silence, was instantly abuzz.

"I knew it was you!" the librarian shouted. Nat stood up just as Berta looked toward him, face forlorn. She ducked a shoulder to free herself, but the woman held on.

"Security!" the librarian shouted. "Someone call a guard!"

"Don't touch me!" Berta shouted, yanking back as the woman held firm. Nat bounded toward them. The librarian's fingers were making white marks on Berta's skin. Researchers in every corner stood to get a better view. Others drifted closer like kids toward a schoolyard brawl. Forget the dead voices of history—this was live action.

A security guard hustled into view, keys and handcuffs jangling.

"This one's a thief," the librarian said, finally releasing her grip. "Caught her in the act a few weeks ago, and now she's back. Please escort her from the building, but search her first. Strip her if you have to."

"Hold it, now," Nat said. "I can vouch for her."

"Should I call PG County police?" the guard asked, ignoring Nat.

"Not if she's clean. Just take her card and kick her out. In fact, take her card now."

Berta grudgingly handed over her ID and looked sheepishly toward Nat as the librarian read aloud the name.

" 'Christa Larkin.' No wonder you got in. The real name's Berta something, isn't it?"

So that's why she had been keeping her head down. Yet even now her expression was more defiant than shamed.

"I'll meet you out front," she said to Nat. He nodded, dumbfounded.

"Not out front," the librarian said. "You're leaving the property entirely."

Nat wanted to challenge that, but the crowd of gawkers had grown, so he watched in silence as the guard led Berta away. Nat waited for the crowd to break up before following the librarian back to the service counter. The Icarus personnel file was still in his right hand.

"Could I have a word?" he said in a low voice. The tall woman abruptly looked up.

"Aren't you Dr. Turnbull? I'm surprised you're keeping such disreputable company."

"Look," Nat whispered—heads were already turning—"I don't know what went on before, but I can assure you she wasn't here today to steal anything."

"Sure she wasn't. Why else use a fake ID. Last time she tried to take an entire folder."

"Maybe it got mixed in with her papers."

"It was stuffed beneath her blouse, tucked in her jeans. She would have made it, too, if the guard downstairs hadn't been staring at her boobs. He saw the green cardboard between her buttons."

"A whole folder?" Her words had knocked the wind out of him.

"Just like the one you're holding. In fact—"

Her mouth dropped open.

"This one?" he asked.

"For 'Icarus.' Yes. It had just been declassified."

No wonder Berta had been so dismissive of his findings. She'd already seen them. But why steal a file that you could copy? To sell it? Possibly. Or maybe she wanted to make sure no one else ever saw it.

"I should probably take that off your hands, sir," the librarian said.

"I, uh, need to make some copies first," he said weakly. Fortunately she nodded.

He headed to his desk before she could change her mind. It now seemed important to get as much done today as possible. By tomorrow who knows what sort of orders would have come down from the archival overlords. He was now guilty by association.

As it turned out, though, the only item of interest for the rest of the day came not in a folder but in an e-mail message from CIA archivist Steve Wallace, who replied to Nat's earlier request:

"Hi, Nat. Job No. 79-003317B currently too hot to touch. Sorry. As for the four items which I understand you have already seen, I may soon have further info, but only if you're willing to swap. Watch this space."

So Steve knew all about the boxes found in the Adirondacks and wanted to arrange a quid pro quo. Nat could live with that. It sounded like there might be high-level disagreement over the handling of these materials, and he wondered why.

HE FOUND BERTA WAITING in the shade of the bus shelter on Adelphi Drive, well off the premises. She began talking before Nat was even within twenty yards. Perhaps she saw the look in his eye, the one that said this had better be damned good or you're finished.

"It was all a stupid mistake. I was in too much of a hurry that day. I was desperate."

"Obviously."

"My camera was broken, the copy machines were tied up, the place was closing in ten minutes, and I had to catch a flight. I didn't even have a chance to see if anything was worth copying. My grant was running out and the whole trip was crashing. It was stupid, all right? I was going to mail it back once I made copies. But it wasn't like there was anything worthwhile. You saw how I reacted when you showed me. I couldn't care less."

"Finished?"

She nodded.

"Of course you couldn't care less, because you'd already seen it. And if it's so unimportant, then why did you try to make sure no one else would ever see it?"

"It wasn't like that. I told you."

"Yes, but you're a liar."

Her face creased and she began to cry. He had expected that, but was nonetheless unprepared. Because all of it—her embarrassment, her shame, and now her sorrow—seemed genuine. Maybe her lame explanation was at least partially true. He'd certainly heard sillier tales of misconduct. Researchers did strange things while caught in the grip of gold fever, especially when facing the cruel limitations of closing hours and dwindling grants. Even so, pulling a stunt like that at the National Archives was on another level. It was a place where you were monitored not only by tigress librarians but also by surveillance cameras. You weren't even allowed to wear a sweater or overcoat, or bring in a bag or briefcase. Every piece of paper from the outside was stamped and inspected upon entering *and* leaving. Berta's actions bordered on professional insanity.

"If you don't believe me, I understand." She wiped away the tears. "It was the stupidest thing I've ever done."

"How'd you get the new ID?"

She fumbled in her bag and showed him a fake New Jersey driver's license. Christa Larkin, of Hackensack.

"When I came here last week I went to the security station and had them make me a new ID, like I was visiting for the first time. Then all I had to do was avoid that bitch who'd nailed me before."

Nat would have liked to check the date of her new archives ID to at least verify that part of her story, but the librarian had confiscated it.

"You've seen how obsessive I get," she said. "It always rubs people the wrong way."

"I know. It's a disease. I've had it myself."

"Let me know if you ever find a cure."

For the first time in days she offered the beginnings of a smile, then quickly shut it down, receding back into the role of uber-Berta.

"Well, I do know this," Nat said. "Another screwup like this and we're finished."

"I'll prove myself. And I am still in good standing with the archives we'll need to check in Bern and Berlin."

"Whoa now. We're getting ahead of ourselves."

"Not really, no. Look, I'll show you."

He half expected her to produce a stolen document from her blouse. Instead, she retrieved her camera and found an image for him.

"It's a memo, newly declassified, from a Swiss source to the OSS. He was feeding them information on the local flatfoots."

The "flatfoots" were the Swiss operatives who kept tabs on Allied and Axis spies. By war's end, the Swiss had arrested more than a thousand people on espionage charges. The memo Berta had found— to Loofbourow in Zurich in December 1944—said that operative Icarus and source Magneto II had drawn increased Swiss scrutiny due to a recent flurry of clandestine meetings. Their local shadows were then mentioned by name in hopes that 110 (Dulles) could persuade the Swiss to back off, especially with the war winding down. So there it was, further evidence linking Gordon Wolfe and Kurt Bauer. The names of the Swiss operatives were Gustav Molden and Lutz Visser.

"Molden's and Visser's surveillance reports might be in the State Archives in Bern," Berta said. "I have a source there. And Molden is alive."

"How do you know?"

"Well, I had to do *something* while I was waiting. So I went online with a wireless connection and found a Gustav Molden, age eighty-eight. He lives within blocks of where he was working during the war. The age is right, and he's the only Gustav Molden in Bern."

Yes, she was beyond help all right. Banished to a bus bench and she had kept right on working. And with impressive results, no less.

"Switzerland, then. Okay, I can buy that. But why Berlin?"

"Martin Göllner."

"Never heard of him."

"Remember when I said in the Adirondacks that I had a few names for you? He's one of them. He was Gestapo, a junior investigator. During the war he interrogated Kurt Bauer. I'd like to know what was said, wouldn't you?"

Nat spent all of five seconds deliberating.

"I'll finish up here tomorrow," he said, "while you pursue more overseas leads. The memorial service is in Wightman on Wednesday. Can you leave that night for Bern?"

"Do I look like I have anything else to do?"

"Maybe we should we try reaching Molden and Göllner, set up an interview."

She shook her head.

"A call could scare them off. We should just show up."

Obviously she, too, had experience in tracking ghosts. Best to sneak up on them whenever possible, an approach that Gordon Wolfe had always favored.

Nat then heard a faint echo of Gordon's voice inside his head, laughing lightly and offering encouragement. Death had done wonders for the old boy's disposition. He hadn't sounded this welcoming in ages.

FOURTEEN

Berlin—Thursday, December 10, 1942

KURT BAUER NO LONGER RODE his bicycle past Liesl's house each and every day, pinging his bell in hopes she would appear at the window. Fifteen tries without a response finally convinced him he was a making a lovesick fool of himself, and as weeks turned to months he avoided her side of town altogether, not even venturing into the Grunewald.

But one evening toward sunset eleven months later, with the anniversary of their breakup approaching, he found himself exiting the Krumme Lanke U-Bahn stop with his bicycle. As if drawn by a homing beacon, he began pedaling hypnotically toward the quaint little house on Alsbacherweg. He had no clear plan in mind. He knew only that he had to return to the scene. So on he rode even as his hands grew numb.

Pale light cast long shadows across the small lawn, and he braked to a stop as if facing a shrine. Looking up to her window, he flexed his left thumb to flick the tiny bell. Once, twice, a third time. Then he waited, breath huffing like steam from an idling locomotive.

Was it his imagination, or had the curtain twitched? He watched until his eyes hurt from the cold, but nothing budged. Finally he turned and pedaled away, slower now, but still with a sense of mission. He crossed the frozen ground of leafy woodland trails for twenty minutes until he reached the sand beach of the Wannsee.

Kurt stared across the chop toward the far horizon, where a pale band of orange lined the treetops in the last light of dusk. You couldn't see the Stuckart villa from here, so he settled for the nearest familiar landmark—the conference house where Erich's father had gone that day for the big meeting. Kurt now viewed it as a symbol of his failure—

of that terrible moment when his nerve had faltered and Liesl's had exceeded the bounds of common sense. So many things he should have done differently.

Fortunately no harm had come to Liesl as the result of her reckless remarks, although the elder Stuckart had looked into the matter further the following morning. He had then passed along his findings to Reinhard Bauer, father to father. Kurt's dad took him aside that night after dinner.

"Herr Stuckart told me of this foolishness with that Folkerts girl you're seeing. Are you sure you're quite sane, spending time with people like her?"

"What of it?" Kurt answered, not wanting to admit she had rejected him.

"What *of* it? Well, seeing as how you only seem capable of thinking of yourself, go ahead and forget for a moment what this could have meant for your family, or for our future livelihood. Do you realize what can happen to people who say things like that, and, in turn, to all of their friends?"

Kurt stared at the floor, unwilling to even nod. The pain Liesl had inflicted still hurt more than anything his father could dish out.

"Well, do you?"

"Yes," Kurt said without looking up.

"They line you up and shoot you, or drop you from a gallows. Or maybe they lop off your head. Not that you get to choose. And first, of course, they take you down to the cellar on Prinz-Albrecht-Strasse, where they do God knows what so that you'll tell them whatever they want to hear. That is why I want you to stay away from people like the Folkerts girl, who, by the way, according to Stuckart's sources, also spends her Sunday afternoons meeting with friends at that renegade Pastor Bonhoeffer's house. Or did you, perhaps, already know this?"

Kurt kept his head down.

"As I suspected. You are even more foolish than I thought. That is why I'm making this more than a request or a plea. It is an order. Understand? You will no longer see this girl. For the sake of all of us."

Kurt looked up abruptly.

"You needn't worry," he said in disgust. "She refuses to see me anymore."

His father's look of relief was infuriating, and Kurt was only enraged further by the hypocrisy of his father's next words.

"She was right, of course. That's why it was so dangerous for her to say it. The war is lost. Any fool can see it."

Then, as if to make it clear he wasn't faulting the current leadership, or the German national character, Reinhard Bauer proceeded to analyze the situation from the point of view of an industrialist. Perhaps he saw it as another opportunity to further his son's education, because he then took out pencil and paper and began toting up precise columns of numbers. Production quotas and available raw materials. Shortages across the board. Here was the reason Germany could no longer win, he said. Because they could no longer outproduce the American and Russian makers of guns, planes, and ammo.

"Do you remember all those men who came here from America during the Olympic Games?" he asked.

Kurt nodded, holding his tongue. The Bauer companies had thrown a reception in 1936 for a delegation of manufacturing tycoons from the American heartland. At the time, Berlin had been putting its best face forward for a skeptical world. Every street was clean. Bums and ne'er-do-wells were swept from view. The Americans, to a man, had spoken enviously of the orderly nature of the new regime. No unions, no strikers, and no one stirring up the rabble. Everything worked, and everything ran on time. FDR could learn a thing or two from Hitler, they gushed.

But now those same men were working overtime to make sure Berlin was reduced to cinders, so of course defeat was inevitable.

"What that means, Kurt, is that if you really want to go running around with young girls who insist on speaking their mind, then all you have to do is wait. Because it will only be a matter of years, or even months, before the fighting will end. Understand?"

"Perfectly."

He then stormed upstairs to his books and phonograph records, and refused to accompany his father to a reception at the home of a Siemens executive.

As the months passed, Kurt kept expecting the pain to fade. He had always recovered quickly from such things before. But he couldn't shake his deep sense of loss over Liesl. Nor did it help that he sometimes glimpsed her at the university. Once he called out her name, but she didn't even glance back. Now, with winter returning, the pain of estrangement was as fresh as ever.

Other aspects of his life, on the other hand, were only getting more complicated. His biggest worry was that he might soon be a soldier. He had just turned seventeen. As Erich's father had predicted, there was talk of lowering the age of conscription. With an entire army surrounded at Stalingrad, it seemed likely any day.

In addition, a pall of worry had fallen over the Bauer household. Manfred hadn't been heard from in weeks on the eastern front, and there was a new cloud over his sister Traudl's prospects for marriage. Two grim fellows from the SS Racial Office had visited ages ago to collect family genealogical information. They were supposed to have completed their background check in three months. But it had now been eleven months, and the case was still on hold due to unspecified complications. Reinhard refused to discuss it, and Kurt's mother grew deathly silent every time Traudl brought it up. The would-be bride, at least, was making the most of the delay, by hoarding enough fabric coupons for their seamstress to make the grandest possible dress. And she never had to fret about the safety of her prospective groom. Bruno Scharf had been posted to the coast of France, and his letters spoke glowingly of a farmhouse billet with fresh eggs and a cellar full of wine.

But the strangest and most troubling development had come to Kurt's attention that very morning, when his father had again taken him aside for a chat. Reinhard had returned the previous night from a visit to some of their suppliers in Switzerland, where the family had a factory near Bern.

Kurt shut the door behind him as his father instructed, figuring he was about to be subjected to a rehash of Reinhard's efforts to ensure speedier and more bountiful deliveries. It soon became clear that something more momentous was in the works. At first the elder Bauer did nothing but pace. When he finally came to rest in his desk chair, his face was ashen.

"Kurt, the things I am about to tell you must not pass beyond these walls. Not to anyone, under any circumstances. Not even your mother is to know. Is that understood?"

"Yes, sir."

"You must promise."

"I promise."

Reinhard took a deep breath and planted his hands on his knees.

"Do you remember a man I once brought to the house to introduce to your brother, an investment banker, Gero von Gaevernitz?"

"Vaguely. Wasn't his father some kind of professor?"

"Yes. Years earlier, but correct."

An indistinct image of a handsome—even dashing—fellow in a double-breasted suit with short, wavy hair came fleetingly to mind. His mother had been charmed by the man, but he remembered little else. In those carefree days Kurt hadn't been expected to pay attention to such callers, so he hadn't.

"Well, he's in Switzerland now, and I am afraid he is not a supporter of our current government. But he is nonetheless a useful man among the Germans there, and last night I met with him. Or, rather, I met with one of his representatives."

"He is in business there?"

"No. Well, yes. It's rather more complicated than that. I suppose the polite term for his new line of work would be that he is an information broker. He collects bits and pieces, makes introductions for his clients, that sort of thing."

"Who are his clients?"

Reinhard cleared his throat and smoothed a wrinkle on his trousers.

"The Americans, mostly. Or exclusively, perhaps."

Kurt was shocked.

"So he is in the intelligence business. A spy. And you met with him?"

"With his representative."

"Does that really make a difference?"

"No. Not if anyone here ever found out."

"Then why tell me?"

"Because I plan to see him again, next time I go back. This time it will be Gero himself. And at some point, if you're not sent off to war, I'm hoping that you may also have a chance to meet him. Assuming, of course, that I can arrange a travel pass, so that you can accompany me across the border."

For a man who had been so appalled by Liesl's mere words, this news was beyond astounding.

"Dad, what exactly are you saying?"

"That I have begun planning for our future. The family's. The company's. And, frankly, the Fatherland's. These people running our country now . . ." He paused, fully aware that he had entered uncharted waters. "Well, I think we all know they're not going to survive much longer. When the war ends, they'll be gone. The Allies will insist. And when that happens, we're going to want—need—friends among the Allies. People we can talk to, and who might be willing to trust us. The Russians? Forget it, unless you're a Bolshevik. The Americans are our hope. Those men you met during the Olympic Games, people like them. And people like Gaevernitz, who, by the way, is a dual citizen. He's American, too."

"I didn't know that."

"He wasn't exactly advertising it back then. But it's why he fled the country, about a year ago."

"And he's spying now for the Americans?"

Kurt's father winced at the word, but he nodded.

"My long-term goal is to meet with Gero's boss, although some elaborate arrangements may be required. If I do, I will try to reach some sort of understanding. For later."

"What sort of elaborate arrangements?"

"Middlemen. Secure locations. Evidently these things are quite complex. They have to be, I suppose, because the Gestapo and the Abwehr have people all over Bern as well. You see them in rail stations, hotel lobbies. All types from all sides, right there together. It takes some getting used to, I must say. You can't just meet people out in the open."

"And when you have this meeting, what sort of things will you tell them that a spy would want to know?"

Another wince.

"I can assure you it would be nothing you would ever be ashamed of, or that would place anyone's life in danger. Just my impressions on how things are going here. Information on industrial production. What we have lots of, what we lack. Morale, the state of our workforce. Transportation issues."

"Why are you telling me this?"

"In case something happens to me. If I was unable to return across the border, or was detained, then you will know where you must try to go, and who you must contact."

"Gaevernitz?"

"Or his boss, in Bern. An American named Allen Dulles. He arrived only a month ago, but he is reputed to be the personal representative of President Roosevelt. He has taken up residence in the city center, at 23 Herrengasse. I want you to remember that address. Can you?"

"23 Herrengasse. Allen Dulles."

"Very good. But repeat it to no one. Not as long as you are on German soil, and certainly never to anyone in Berlin."

"Of course."

"And, Kurt?"

"Yes."

"You should also know that I have been contemplating this kind of action for quite a while. It is one reason I was so appalled last year when I heard about the remarks made by that Folkerts girl. Now that I have chosen this path, we must remain above suspicion in every possible way. So I certainly hope that you have had no further contact with her."

"No, sir," he said dolefully. "I have not seen her at all."

"And what about her circle of friends? I'm told the Gestapo has put a guard outside that fellow Bonhoeffer's house, so I doubt anyone in his right mind goes there anymore."

Kurt was aghast, but tried not to show it.

"No. She's the only reason I ever saw any of them."

"Good. Because this is not a game, Kurt, especially with the war going so badly. Many Germans will be trying to arrange the same sort of accommodations, and the authorities know it. Take great care in what you say and who you are seen with. Mere words are no longer worth taking a risk for. Mere words will not bring an end to our current disastrous situation. Actions, on the other hand, can make a difference, and may help build a better future. That is why I have made my choice. It is why you must be prepared to fill my shoes, if necessary. For the sake of our family."

"I understand."

"Very good. All right, then. You may go."

So where had he gone? Straight back to Liesl's. Exactly the place his father wanted him to avoid. And as Kurt stood on the Wannsee beach, gazing at the white villa across the water, he now realized why his father's chat had prompted him to come here. Defiant or not, it was a triumph of action over words. Because now he was certain that action, not talk, was the only possible means of winning Liesl back. He must do something bold, something to convince her that he was mature, and courageous. As he stared across the waves he decided on his approach. He would take the first risky step that weekend.

His father was right. There was indeed a surveillance man hanging around outside Bonhoeffer's house when Kurt pedaled down the narrow lane that Sunday afternoon. The man was brazen, stationed beneath a telephone pole just across the street. His black trench coat and dark hat made it painfully obvious who he was working for. Perhaps that's the way the Gestapo wanted it, planting the fellow like a scarecrow to keep everyone away.

Kurt pedaled past him until the pavement ended, then turned onto a dirt path that cut into the forest at the end of the street. Screened by the trees, he circled back to the right, behind the Bonhoeffer home. He leaned his bike against a tree and set off on foot, working his way toward the rear garden, where he ducked through a hedge and between bare rosebushes to the home's rear door. He knocked lightly.

An elderly woman in an apron, who must have been Bonhoeffer's mother, answered, not seeming at all surprised to receive a visitor at the back door. She invited him inside without asking his name, and then called upstairs to her son. The pastor appeared a few seconds later with a quizzical expression, but he immediately recognized Kurt.

"Come up to my study," he said.

The room was small and spartan. Bookshelves took up an entire wall, and there was a dark wooden desk in the corner. A stack of foolscap, a fountain pen, and an inkwell indicated that Kurt had interrupted the pastor's writing.

"Sorry to disturb you," he said.

"Quite all right. It gets a bit desolate here on Sunday afternoons anymore. The rest of my family often goes out walking, so I take advantage of the solitude. I take it you must have noticed my little friend out front?"

"Yes."

"Of course, you realize that if he saw you going around to the back, that will only make him more suspicious."

"I hadn't thought of that."

"Don't worry. He's usually pretty bored by this time of day. He doesn't even come every day anymore, although he is always here on Sundays. I suppose one of my neighbors must have gotten nervous about all the students who were coming here and mentioned it to the authorities."

"Do you really think that's what happened?" He didn't have the guts to tell Bonhoeffer about Stuckart.

"I only know for sure that one Sunday there he was, with a camera and a notebook. So, sadly, I felt I had no choice but to advise your friends to stop coming. But, of course, by then you had already stopped coming."

Kurt realized the timing made him look suspicious.

"I can assure you that I never—"

"It's quite all right. I never thought you did. I had already attributed your absence to girl trouble."

Kurt blushed.

"You're right," he said. "It was Liesl's decision."

"I gathered as much. Especially from the way she defended you to the others. Almost like she was feeling sorry for you."

"Defended me?"

"Some of them concluded from your absence that you were to blame for the man out front. But don't worry. She set them straight."

"It must be hard getting used to things like that." He nodded toward the front window.

"Oh, that's pretty mild, actually. Here, let me show you something."

Bonhoeffer reached up to a shelf and plucked a postcard from between two thick volumes. He handed it to Kurt.

"I came across it in a bookstall in 1936. The 'CC' stands for the Confessing Church, of course. A reference to my seminary, the one the Nazis shut down."

It was a short poem, quite nasty:

> *After the end of the Olympiade*
> *We'll bash the CC to marmalade.*
> *Then once we've chucked out the Jews,*
> *The CC we will terminate, too.*

Suddenly there was a loud blast of static from below. Hitler's amplified voice shouted up the stairwell. More promises of death and damnation for the enemy. A roaring crowd. It was only the radio, but Kurt felt wobbly all the same.

"Excuse me, will you?" Bonhoeffer said.

He disappeared for a moment. The volume of the broadcast dropped to a dull murmur just as he returned.

"My apologies. My mother likes to turn up his speeches."

"She does?"

"Only so the neighbors will know we're listening." He shrugged. "She thinks she is teaching a lesson to whoever informed on us. Or maybe she only wants my little shadow out there to write it down in his notebook."

"He looks like such a fool when he speaks," Kurt said, blushing immediately. He wasn't sure where the remark came from, and at some level he supposed he was only trying to ingratiate himself with this calm man who might be able to help him.

Bonhoeffer studied his face. Kurt hoped the pastor didn't think he had been trying to bait him into an inflammatory response.

"He does twitch and flail about," Bonhoeffer said. "But whatever you think of his words, or of the terrible things he does, when he is up there on that podium he speaks with a genuine passion, and that is one reason he is able to connect with so many people. I am not saying I admire him, far from it. But we in the church would be more effective in spreading the word of God if we, too, exhibited some genuine passion, instead of being so didactic and precise.

"When I spent a summer in New York, years ago, I often attended a Baptist church among the Negroes of Harlem. And I have to say, no one ever fell asleep in their pews. Maybe you would have made fun of all their shouting and carrying on, but to me it was quite rapturous. If we pastors had spoken straight from our hearts instead of from our minds, maybe we would have gotten through to more people before it was too late. Instead, we droned on like chemistry professors while that little man with the mustache played the pantomime fool and lured away most of our flock."

Kurt sensed the opening he had been seeking.

"But it seems too late to change that now. Haven't we passed the moment when mere words are enough?"

Bonhoeffer gave him a long look before speaking again.

"Is that why you are here? To seek my counsel on how to best take direct action? Because I may actually be able to offer some advice. But first you must tell me something: Which cause are you here to fight for? The opposition to that man on the radio? Or the cause of winning back the affections of Liesl Folkerts?"

An outright lie would never have worked, so Kurt decided on a half-truth.

"Both. With someone like her, you can't just strive for the one or the other. You have to prove yourself to Liesl in the way that you live, not just in the way you talk."

In a moment of serendipity, Kurt then recalled something Bonhoeffer had said during his first visit to the house.

"It is like when you spoke of the difference between a cheap grace—one that comes easily and is all talk—and a costly grace, one where you are willing to make true sacrifice and take real risks."

It seemed to clinch the deal, because the next thing Bonhoeffer reached for was a pamphlet that would forever change Kurt's life, and Liesl's too. Bonhoeffer gave it to him without a word. Simply holding it in his hands seemed like a provocative act, especially when he read the first sentence: "Nothing is so unworthy of a civilized nation as to allow itself to be 'governed' without any opposition by an irresponsible clique that has yielded to basest instincts. It is certainly the case today that every honest German is ashamed of his government."

"Well?" Bonhoeffer asked. "What do you think of that? Mere words, perhaps, but a real action to print and distribute them, don't you think?"

It was all Kurt could do not to immediately hand it back, and it took an effort to keep his hands from trembling.

"Yes," he said. "It is quite an action."

"Tell me," Bonhoeffer said, "have you seen one of these before?"

"No. What is it?"

"It was printed last summer by a small group of university students in Munich. Some of them were soldiers, on leave from the front. One is a young girl, a student much like Liesl. They call themselves the White Rose, and since then they have printed three more flyers, growing bolder with every one. By the third leaflet they were calling openly for the defeat of National Socialism, and even advocating sabotage."

"Sabotage?"

"Of Party rallies, newspapers." He paused, his eyes boring straight into Kurt's. "Even armaments factories. In the fourth pamphlet they dared to state, 'Every word out of Hitler's mouth is a lie.' Now their work has begun making its way to Berlin. The flyer in your hand was carried into the city only last week by a volunteer. I would be happy to let you keep it, but, well, with our friend out front there, perhaps that wouldn't be such a good idea."

"Yes, of course. Here."

Bonhoeffer took it from his fingers and slid it back onto the shelf, well out of sight. Kurt sagged in relief. How could such work be going on right under the government's nose? It was both thrilling and terrifying.

"Definitely not 'easy grace,' associating with some movement like that, don't you think?"

"Absolutely."

Bonhoeffer stepped slowly to the window, where he stared across the street for a moment before turning around to again look Kurt in the eye. He seemed to have arrived at a conclusion. Or maybe he had only paused to give Kurt time to reconsider.

"I am going to tell you something in strictest confidence," he said, "because it involves both Liesl and this concept of costly grace. Do you think you are strong enough to confront both, simultaneously?"

Kurt nodded, but a nod wasn't enough.

"If that is a yes, then please say so."

"Yes."

"Very well. Because if you choose to take this step, there will be no turning back. Not only for your own sake, but for Liesl's. This Tuesday, at four o'clock in the afternoon, several people will be meeting at Saint Anne's Church in Dahlem. Do you know it?"

Kurt shook his head.

"Speak up, Kurt. This is not a time for timid silence."

"No. I don't know it."

"It is Martin Niemoller's church. You are familiar with his name, I would imagine."

"Yes."

Niemoller had helped found the Confessing Church along with Bonhoeffer.

"He no longer preaches there, of course. He has been in a concentration camp for nearly six years. His wife still lives next door in the parsonage, but it will probably be too risky for her to attend on Tuesday."

"I see."

"No. I'm not sure you do. This meeting is for the purpose of organizing a Berlin chapter of the White Rose. And your friend Liesl is one of the leaders. In fact, she was the one who brought me their pamphlets, at no small risk to herself. She picked up an entire box of them from the train station last week, and she is part of the effort to make sure that thousands more will be printed and distributed. If you attend this meeting on Tuesday, perhaps you will impress her with your fortitude. But in the eyes of the government you will officially be making yourself a party to these efforts. You will be seen as an active resister, an enemy of the state."

"Who else will be there?"

"Perhaps only a handful. Perhaps more." He shrugged. "One never really knows who will have the courage until the moment presents itself."

"Will you be there?"

"No."

Kurt raised his eyebrows.

"My presence would only make it more likely to attract unwanted attention. You see, I have been banned from preaching, or even teaching. For me, simply to enter a church is seen as a provocation, as terrible as that sounds. I would also be jeopardizing other activities of mine in which, frankly, the stakes are even graver. It is probably indiscreet of me to say even that. I just didn't want you believing that I was choosing the course of 'easy grace,' not out of vanity but because it would certainly not be setting the right example."

Kurt found it hard to imagine what could involve graver stakes than advocating the downfall of the government, and he wasn't sure he would have wanted Bonhoeffer to tell him.

"If you decide to attend," Bonhoeffer continued, "then you should gather in the pews beneath the organ loft. Quite a lot of people go there to pray, even at odd hours, so the authorities are accustomed to people coming and going in small groups. The building is historic, so secular organizations meet there as well. If anyone else asks why you are there, tell them you have come for a history discussion. Early Christian settlements in Dahlemdorf."

He then placed a hand companionably on Kurt's shoulder and walked him downstairs. The sun was low in the sky, and soon it would be dark, but the man in the black coat was still at his post, smoking a cigarette. It now seemed more important than ever that Kurt not be seen.

"I'll leave by the front door and go for a walk," Bonhoeffer said, turning from the window. "That should distract him long enough for you to make a clean exit from out back. Good luck, and God be with you."

"With you as well. And thank you."

"No. Thank you."

Kurt was fearful, he was excited, and he was already wondering what in the hell sort of foolishness he had just gotten into. Dahlem on a Tuesday, right next door to Niemoller's house? Possibly with snoops just like the man across the street posted on every corner? Madness.

Then he thought of Liesl, her face turned toward his for a tender kiss, in contrast to the lonely agony of the past eleven months. And that was enough. Whatever the risk, Kurt was ready for it.

On Tuesday he would see her again.

FIFTEEN

Berlin—Tuesday, December 15, 1942

KURT ARRIVED at the church a half hour early. There was still enough light to show that every street corner was empty, which made him feel better. Nonetheless, he circled behind the building to approach the entrance through the cemetery, figuring it was the least likely path to be watched. The route took him by Niemoller's house. Its gables and turrets loomed like a fortress.

The seven-hundred-year-old church was built of red brick, with a wooden belfry and steeple. He pulled back the heavy door and called out.

"Hello?"

No answer. He must be the first arrival.

Inside it was chilly and smelled of candle wax and musty hymnals. His footsteps echoed loudly, although the sanctuary was small and intimate. Medieval frescoes were faintly visible on plastered walls, but otherwise the place was unadorned. A placard up front explained that the altarpiece and other valuables had been moved to a safer location until the war was over. To protect them from what, Kurt wondered—Allied bombers or looting Nazis?

He checked every pew for anyone who might be hiding, then he sat, glancing at his watch every few minutes while he tried not to dwell on his father's warning from months ago: "They line you up and shoot you, or drop you from a gallows. Or maybe they lop off your head."

It was still only 3:40, so he decided to check out the organ loft. Someone might be hiding there, too, he supposed. What would he say if he came upon a Gestapo man? Or maybe the police were outside, after all, holding off until the entire group was assembled, waiting to arrest them all. And he, of course, would be remembered as the early bird, the most eager one in the bunch. What a catch, too. The son of a prominent industrialist. All of his father's careful and dangerous work to prepare for their future would be down the drain, washed away by a foolish act of love.

Kurt fairly tiptoed up the creaking stairway to the narrow loft. He had decided on using Bonhoeffer's cover story, if necessary: He was just looking around, soaking up the history. He knew nothing about any four o'clock meeting.

But the loft, too, was empty, and he took a seat on a choir pew. It was nice up there, more secure, a concealed position that gave him an upper hand. The feeling was reinforced the moment he heard the door opening downstairs. Two voices whispered in conversation, a man's and a woman's. Kurt leaned forward just enough to recognize two students from the regular gatherings at Bonhoeffer's. Neither was Liesl. They didn't see him, and he was fine with that.

A threesome of young men arrived next, closely followed by a young woman and two more males. Among them, he recognized the blustering Dieter Büssler and the likable Christoph Klemm. But still no Liesl.

Other than the creaking of the pews everyone was quiet, and they conversed in whispers. Such mice, these people. Where was all the boldness they had displayed so cavalierly at Bonhoeffer's? Perhaps they were overwhelmed by the prospect of what they were about to do. And who was he to talk, up there in the loft, where he began to feel sheepish. It would be embarrassing to reveal himself now. He was on the verge of resolving to stay there for the duration when the door opened again and a new voice rose to his ears.

It was Liesl, speaking in a normal tone to a woman she had arrived with.

"What a nice turnout!" she said, as if they had gathered for tea and refreshment. "And I see that Helmut is here, so perhaps we should begin. It is only right that he do the honors, seeing as how he took the greatest risk by arranging this meeting."

A pew creaked as she sat. Kurt stood as if hypnotized. He stepped gingerly toward the stairs and began descending as quietly as possible. Halfway down a step groaned, and there was startled movement in the pews below. But that was hardly a concern, because now he could see Liesl in profile through the slatted sides of the stairway. She was quiet, serene, not at all alarmed or turning toward him like the others.

"Hello?" a male voice inquired nervously. It was Dieter, whom Kurt had already pegged as the likeliest to betray them.

"It's all right," Kurt said, trying to keep his voice as strong and steady as Liesl's. "I arrived early, so I waited in the loft. I wanted to make sure no one was up there to spy on us."

"Good idea," said the fellow Liesl had called Helmut. He now stood up front.

Kurt took a seat on the row behind Liesl, but not before she turned and offered an astonished grin, cheeks flushed. Already the risk was worthwhile. She reached back across the pew and squeezed his hand.

Helmut spoke.

"Many thanks to everyone for having the courage to be here. I chose this location for a reason, and not because I wanted to put anyone in danger. In fact, the Nazis prefer that such places be used for secular purposes, so I suppose that in that sense we are simply being obedient citizens."

There was some nervous laughter.

"You cannot enter this building without first seeing the house of Dr. Niemoller. And I wanted you to see that house as a reminder of the possible consequences for your actions here tonight. Those of you who choose to go forward with us must realize that there will be no turning back. The gate will lock behind us. So while I ask for your utmost secrecy no matter what you may decide, I also will understand completely if you cannot accompany us further, even if that means that you must leave now, before even revealing your name."

He paused. No one stood, and no one said a word. Kurt watched the back of Liesl's head. She was the only one who didn't turn to look questioningly at everyone else.

"Very well, then. In that case I will begin by telling you my full name, because I know there has already been discussion among some of you over whether that is a wise idea. My opinion is that if we are taking such a big step, then we should commit ourselves fully from the beginning, so I will set the tone. I am Helmut Hartert. Like most of you here I am a student at the Berlin University. I agreed to call this meeting after conferring with some of our like-minded colleagues in Munich. Two of them are here with us tonight to help pass the torch—

Falk Harnack, who is now posted to an army unit in Chemnitz, and Jörg Strasser, who made the dangerous journey by train with a boxful of the daring pamphlets that you have already heard so much about. Falk is here without the benefit of either a pass or travel papers, so special thanks to him. He's demonstrating just the sort of commitment that we'll be wanting from all of you in the months to come.

"I also want to thank Liesl Folkerts for making sure that Jörg had safe passage through the train station to his uncle's house. Believe me, if you knew how many policemen were there that day, checking papers, you would realize this was no simple feat."

Kurt swelled with pride for her, and was more convinced than ever that he had done the right thing by coming here.

"Now," Hartert said, "shall we all introduce ourselves?"

There were nine others—four women and five men. Kurt stood first. He spoke his name loudly and clearly, wondering how many of them realized the significance—and the inherent risk—of the presence of a Bauer. Each of the others then stood in turn, announcing a name and then sitting back down. Except Dieter Büssler, of course, who felt compelled to give a short speech.

"We all know why we are here, and I hope that everyone noticed on the way in that to get to this church from Dr. Niemoller's house, you have to pass among the tombstones of the dead." That meant Dieter had also taken the coward's path through the cemetery. Kurt suppressed a smile. "They are Germany's fallen. Some from disease and from old age, some from the fields of Verdun, and some from the ruins of Stalingrad. We must show that we are worthy of their sacrifice as we prepare to walk our own valley of death in support of our beliefs."

Perhaps Dieter expected applause, because he waited a moment too long before sitting. Instead, there was an awkward cough. No one seemed to know what to say next.

Then Liesl rose.

"Those are admirable sentiments, Dieter. Of course, we are also hoping most fondly that not a single one of us will lose his life in this venture." Relieved laughter. "Nor should that be even a part of our intent. We do not seek martyrdom, because surely we do this for the living, and, for some of us, also for the glory of God. It is our enemies who celebrate death, not us. Why act for our future unless we can also hope to have a productive role in it?"

Dieter looked suitably chastened, so Liesl softened the blow.

"But we do thank you for the passion of your words and the nobility of your intent."

She then smiled sympathetically at Dieter, warmly enough to almost make Kurt wish he had delivered the blowhard soliloquy.

With equilibrium restored, Falk Harnack announced to general approval that two of the original members of the White Rose in Munich had promised that they would soon travel to Berlin to offer support.

"Dr. Bonhoeffer has endorsed this idea as well," he said, "although, as you know, it is best if he doesn't appear at gatherings such as this, due to the ban on his teaching, and also because he is so often under surveillance."

Other White Rose cells, he said, had sprung to life in Hamburg, Cologne, Stuttgart, Freiberg, and Saarbrücken. Batches of pamphlets had even crossed into Austria and been seen on the streets of Vienna. Then, to set the tone for the job ahead, he read aloud each of the four pamphlets that had been published to date.

Even in his buoyant mood, Kurt went a little weak in the knees as he listened to the damning words. He found himself wondering anew if he had searched thoroughly enough for intruders in the loft.

Helmut Hartert stood again.

"There are some here who wish to distribute these pamphlets that Jörg has brought from Munich, and that is fine. But I also believe strongly that we should write our own. One concern that I have expressed to Jörg and Falk is that the anti-military tone will not go over so well in a city where you see a wounded veteran or a war widow almost every time you board the S-Bahn. We must strike the proper tone for our own city, with help and contributions from all of you, of course.

"In the meantime, I have secured a small printing press. All that remains now, besides the writing, is the procurement of supplies. Ink and writing paper are our greatest needs, and we urgently need volunteers to provide them. The most difficult of these tasks will be the acquisition of paper. Not only due to rationing but because the authorities have become very suspicious of anyone seeking large amounts of paper who isn't associated with an officially sanctioned publishing concern. So, then, any takers?"

Liesl glanced back at him, and Kurt knew exactly what she was thinking. While they had been seeing each other the previous year, he had acquired paper for her by stealing it from a secretary's desk at his father's office. He had boasted at the time that there was plenty more where that came from, and now she was counting on him to rise to the occasion.

"I can do it," he blurted. "I can get the paper."

The others looked at him in surprise. He felt burdened almost the second the words left his mouth, but there was no taking them back.

The meeting ended not long afterward. He experienced a brief feeling of panic as the door opened, half expecting a blast of bright lights and a loud voice hailing them over a megaphone, announcing that they were all under arrest.

Instead, night had fallen. All was quiet. No one lurked on the corners, in the churchyard, or even among the tombstones.

Liesl took his hand before he had a chance to speak, and they strolled off toward the entrance to the Dahlem-Dorf U-Bahn station.

"Would you like to come over to my house, to have dinner with my parents and me?"

"Yes, I'd like that very much."

He would have to come up with a cover story for his parents, of course, but he supposed that was going to be a fact of life from here on out. His father must never know.

"Welcome to your new life as an adult," she said. "I am so glad to see you have grown into it. And as happy as I am for our organization, I am even happier for myself. I've missed you."

It was about then that Kurt noticed the stout young woman walking just behind them. Up to now she hadn't made a sound. Kurt had already forgotten her name. Liesl turned and introduced her.

"Kurt, this is Hannelore Nierendorf. Hannelore, please meet Kurt Bauer."

She reminded him of someone, but he didn't realize who until he noticed the sign for the U-Bahn looming just ahead. The thought of the subway tunnel jogged his memory. Hannelore was a dead ringer for "Frau Knoterich," the cartoon image of a plump, gossipy chatterbox that had begun appearing on subway propaganda posters, which inveighed against rumormongering. Her costar was the skinny "Herr Bramsig," a doom-and-gloom pessimist.

Hannelore offered a muted "Guten Abend" and a cold stare. Either she wasn't pleased to meet him or this was the expression she showed everyone, but Liesl seemed oblivious to either possibility.

"She will also be joining us for dinner, but of course we will not be able to discuss this evening's matters around my parents."

Well, that was too bad. He had hoped to have Liesl all to himself once the meal was over. But there would be plenty of time for that in the days to come, and with that thought he felt restored, renewed. Life, for all its new risks, again seemed full of possibility. Or it did until Hannelore brought him back to earth with a gruff question.

"Where do you think you will find paper? It won't be easy, you know. You can't just go out and buy it, even if you have enough coupons."

"My father's offices. That's where I'll start."

"Remember, he's a Bauer," Liesl offered. "The armaments family."

"Ah, then no wonder you have joined us, with so much to atone for."

"That's not what I meant," Liesl said. "It's his father's business, not Kurt's."

The admonishment temporarily silenced Frau Knoterich. Kurt decided he could handle Hannelore's presence just fine as long as Liesl was around.

When she again squeezed his hand, he even stopped thinking about what he had just learned at the church: that from here on out, he would be risking his life every time he met these people; that Liesl, the love of his life, was also the gravest threat to his future.

He shoved all that to the back of his mind and walked briskly forward, smiling grandly.

SIXTEEN

Berta's head rested against Nat's shoulder as their flight crept up on a Zurich sunrise. She had been asleep for three hours, close enough for Nat to smell her hair. Shampoo and cigarettes, the same blend that had scented his pillow when she'd tossed it to him on the floor of the B&B. It had triggered a few dreams he would rather keep to himself.

Was she flirting now, wanting something, or just being human? He chalked it up to the cramped seating—the Bureau wouldn't spring for business class—and also to her gratitude. No matter how much she knew about Bauer and the White Rose, she needed his reputation and credentials. Nat could open doors that had been slammed in her face. He was sympathetic to this need. Without Gordon to shepherd him through the early years, he, too, might have grown frustrated enough to do something stupid like stealing a document. Not that he wasn't still wary of her. But as long as she kept coming up with new leads, they were better off working in tandem.

He hated long flights, but after the ordeal of the memorial service he had welcomed the idea of eight hours of enforced boredom. The muffled roar of the engines, the headset chatter of the in-flight movie—all of it helped him decompress. Grief wasn't the problem. Viv's tears, and his own, had been cathartic. The harder part had been enduring the hypocritical maundering from the podium and the unseemly congratulatory tone of his peers, who kept reassuring him with smug nods and arch asides that he had at last inherited the mantle of succession.

The day's bright spot was Karen, who remained at his side throughout. She comforted him after his mess of a speech, which he rushed ungracefully and finished in tears. At the reception she helped ward off the supplicants who seemed intent on paying tribute. He supposed part of her reaction was simply a young person's discomfort over a proximate death. She was also still a little spooked by the two hang-up calls she had received from Nat's stolen cell phone, one of them only hours before Gordon's passing—as if some angel of death had tuned in to her wavelength on its way north.

But she seemed most disturbed by the realization that this was the eventual fate of all aging scholars—done in by their passions, then relegated to postmortem dissection by tipsy peers at a dreary gathering around cold cuts and a punch bowl. Nat noticed her watching sympathetically as poor Viv was cornered repeatedly by the same colleagues who only weeks ago had been gloating over Gordon's takedown in the *Daily Wildcat*.

"Is this all there is?" Karen asked, and he knew she didn't mean the buffet.

"His work will be remembered," Nat said, patting her arm, although he, too, worried for Gordon's legacy. Soon the old man might be better known as a thief and a blackmailer, or even as some sort of blundering spy. Worst of all, Nat's work for the FBI might play a big role in the revision.

"He never had children, did he?" Karen asked.

"No. I guess that's one way I've already outdone him."

He smiled, keeping it light, but she seemed grateful all the same. It had been nice, having her stay in his house the night before and knowing she would still be there in the morning, bleary-eyed by the toaster as they ushered in the new day. It made him feel like he had finally been readmitted to the fraternity of Fatherhood. After years of associate membership, he again had full rights and privileges, even if those included compulsive worry and constant concern.

He saw her look toward Viv with a tear in her eye.

"She'd love to see you if you could drop by while I'm away," he said. "It would do her good."

"Sure. But you're the one I'm worried about."

"Me? I'll be okay."

"Mom said it was hard enough when you lost him the first time, after the bad review. Now he's gone for good, and you never won him back."

"You keep forgetting the benefits of my field of endeavor. I'm a historian. I may find him yet, out there in some lost archive. With his help, even."

"All that old stuff worries me," she said. "Sometimes it's more dangerous than it's worth."

"Let me guess. You came across some warning from the Belle."

She nodded, but didn't return his smile. This was serious.

"I'll bet you can recite it from memory."

She nodded again, solemnly, then obliged him, keeping her voice low so no one else would hear. It gave her words more impact, as if the poet herself were speaking through his daughter, a resurrected Cassandra:

> The Past is such a curious Creature
> To look her in the Face
> A transport may receipt us,
> Or a disgrace—
>
> Unarmed if any meet her
> I charge him fly
> Her faded Ammunition
> Might yet reply.

"That's good," Nat replied. "A little too good."

"I thought so, too. Be careful."

You, too, he wanted to say. But didn't, for fear of alarming her. He hoped Holland's men were still on the job.

THE JOLT OF JET WHEELS against the tarmac brought Berta's head upright.

"Zurich?"

He nodded. Her scent lingered on his shoulder. They were finally in Europe, the place where all the old things hide best.

"Assuming they didn't lose our luggage, we should make the 8:40 train to Bern," he said. "What's our plan of action?"

Berta had begun courting her archival source by telephone, hoping to finagle a look at the Swiss surveillance reports from the war years. She proposed to go see him right away, and Nat agreed. He would check them in at the hotel and stash their bags while she visited the archives. Then they would reconvene at the Bahnhof at 11:30 to pay a joint visit to the doorstep of Gustav Molden, the Swiss flatfoot who had been assigned to Gordon during the war.

In the meantime, Nat would get his bearings with a brisk walk through the medieval heart of the city. He wanted to shake off the jet lag, stop for a double espresso. Then he would begin collecting images to go with all the names and facts jammed in his head.

It was his favorite way of making old documents come to life, and the best part was that central Bern looked much as it had sixty-four years ago. That made it easier to imagine the young Gordon Wolfe slouching along the arcaded sidewalks, hands stuffed in the pockets of his leather bomber jacket as he headed to a meeting with Dulles, the pipe-smoking spymaster in a rumpled overcoat.

It was Nat's imaginative powers that had eventually given him an edge over Gordon as a historian. In fact, Gordon's envy of those powers had contributed to their falling-out. Nat could make the old characters from the archives live and breathe. It was one reason he enjoyed his craft. The more vividly he began to see an era, the easier it was to tease out its secrets.

They easily made the 8:40 train, and upon arrival Berta set out for the State Archives while Nat secured their rooms. Earlier he had decided that, like Gordon, they would stay at the Bellevue, the posh hotel on a bluff above the River Aare. During the war it was a notorious den of spies, which to Nat made it the perfect starting point. Pricey, but the FBI was paying.

Bern was named for a bear, as if the city had crawled out of a crease in the Alps to lie down on its horseshoe bend. Its bluffs sheltered a medieval grid of narrow arcaded streets marked by grand clock towers and cathedrals and lined by timbered buildings along bustling market squares. While the arcades gave the city much of its charm, they also lent a certain hooded aspect, a shadowy sense of concealment.

Nat set out for the town center. He tried seeing the place through Gordon's eyes by thinking back to an item he had found in the archives, a Dulles memo to his mistress and Girl Friday, Mary Bancroft, which described how he had taken their newest operative out for an introductory stroll.

Gave 543 the grand tour. Christened him Icarus, seeing as how he literally fell to us from the sky. He finds it quite a lark being here in Shangri-la and comes across as a sharp tack. A Princeton man, and his German is first rate. We'll start him slow and see how well he learns to walk—or fly, as the case may be with our Icarus. Let's hope he doesn't emulate all of his namesake's destiny. The sun is very hot in our business.

Dulles described their progress stop by stop, and Nat followed their route. He proceeded with an odd sense that at any moment he might spot them up ahead or catch a whiff of pipe smoke. Reaching the Nydegg Bridge, he gazed down at the green river, swollen by spring melt, and then crossed to the city's famed bear pit, where shaggy beasts loped in the sunlight, craning their necks toward the moms and children at the rim.

I told Icarus those bears were like us, hemmed in by every border, unable to roam. Yet see how everyone approves of their presence and smiles down on them? He, too, would receive such favorable treatment, so long as he lived by their rules and didn't stray. Try breaking free and they would hunt you down. So work hard, but behave.

Nat followed their trail to the Cathedral of Bern, or Münster, where the young spy and his master had inspected the magnificent central portico, a profusion of painted characters carved against a colorful tableau. The Archangel Michael stands tall with his sword as he fights a demon worthy of the Axis Powers. On either side are teeming mobs—to the left, robed in white, the Chosen; to the right, naked and wretched, the Damned.

That will be us up there someday, I told him, cast among the winners or losers. Your work may well decide which.

From there they proceeded to the Dulles bachelor digs on Herrengasse, eluding a flatfoot by detouring to the back entrance through a small park behind the Münster, with its sweeping view of the river. Today a small orchestra was playing in the gazebo, just as Swiss musicians had played throughout the war. Shangri-la indeed, Nat thought, when you could stroll to your boss's house to the tempo of a Strauss waltz.

With dusk falling, Dulles had prepared a crackling fire to ward off the October chill. He then brought out the port, sherry, and brandy. They must have talked tradecraft, because two days later Dulles sent Icarus a typewritten checklist, 1 through 9, headlined "The Technique of Intelligence."

Some high notes from our discussion, he scribbled in the margin.

Most of it was standard fare: *3—Assume that every phone call is over-*

heard, and so on. But the last item seemed just as appropriate for a prowling historian as for a budding spy, not only for its wisdom but for its strong sense of foreboding:

9—Be skeptical of everything, everybody. Don't let pride of discovery blind you as to worth of individual or info.

Nat checked his flanks, half expecting to notice several people watching from behind newspapers and hat brims. But his untrained eye saw only shoppers on their way to market.

Before heading to the Bahnhof he pulled from his pocket the faded old matchbook Gordon had left in the wooden gun box. Nat had brought all of the strange items with him, partly out of superstition. The matchbook advertised the Hotel Jurgens on Aarbergergasse. Not a single match had been used. Obviously a keepsake, but why? There had been no reference to the place in his tourist guidebook, which made Nat wonder if it still existed. But when he turned the corner a few minutes later, there it was—middle of the block with a modest sign over the entrance.

He stepped into the small lobby, barely big enough for a couch and an easy chair. The place wasn't particularly modern. Yet, at least on this floor, it was clean and well kept. He figured it for one of those hotels where the floors squeaked, the radiators whined, and the windows stuck, but you always had clean linens and ample heat for the rawest winter night. No one was at the desk, but when he cleared his throat a chambermaid poked her head out of the office. She held a stack of towels.

"Is the manager in?"

"Nein. No. Back soon, one hour. But the rooms, they are not free."

Her way of saying there were no vacancies, probably. He wasn't sure what he would have asked the manager anyway. He supposed he had naively believed that in some strange way he would know right off what to do, but this time his intuitive powers failed him. Not a single vibe. Maybe jet lag was to blame. Or maybe there was nothing to find.

He glanced again around the lobby, and when it became clear that he was making the maid uncomfortable he said good-bye. Halfway down the block he turned, feeling he must be missing something. But before he could determine what it was, his new cell phone rang. He had bought one in Wightman that would also work in Europe.

"Success," Berta said. "Karsten has arranged for a viewing." A male. Of course. "He'll have Molden's and Visser's surveillance reports ready for us at 3 p.m. Since I'm done early, why don't I meet you at Molden's house? Maybe you should go up first to break the ice. It's a nice sunny day. We could invite him to lunch."

"You should be there, too, when he opens the door. With an old fellow it never hurts to show a pretty face."

Molden seemed grateful for the company and invited them in. He certainly wasn't dressed for visitors—droopy brown sweater frayed at the elbows, wool pants dotted with lint, white socks, house slippers. A bald spot like a tonsure gave him a monkish air, and his apartment smelled of dust and old cheese. On the other hand, a state-of-the-art sound system blared a Debussy prelude, and his coffee table brimmed with new magazines.

"So you want to talk about my work during the war?" he asked, smiling wistfully. "Now those were enjoyable days. Bern was the spy capital of Europe, you know. And my job kept me out of the army. No marching through the mountain snow for me, thank God. With my luck the Germans would have invaded the day I arrived at the frontier."

He placed a hand on the small of Berta's back as he spoke, having warmed to her right away, as Nat had predicted. It was easy to see why. Rather than suiting up in her usual ensemble, Berta had worn a button-up silk blouse the color of fresh cream. It was tucked tightly enough into a trim pair of black slacks to show every contour.

When they suggested lunch, Molden steered them toward a café in the sunny Bärenplatz, only blocks away. They took a table bordering the square, where vendors sold vegetables and cheeses beneath colorful awnings. Molden and Nat ordered tall glasses of lager and platters of *Rösti*—fried potatoes piled high with melted cheese and two eggs, sunny-side up. Berta got mineral water and a salad.

"What were conditions like during the war?" Nat asked, still hungry for atmospherics.

"Well, there were all the shortages. The bumpkins in the hills didn't have much beyond their kitchen gardens and their cows. Cheese on the table, morning, noon, and night. But here? Not so bad. And there was a strong sense that we were the last light left on in the whole house of Europe. Everyone else had rolled up their awnings and put things under lock and key. Hiding under the bed until the last bomb fell."

"While you fellows partied on."

"The ones with expense accounts did, anyway. I mean, look at

Dulles. The man had *gout*. All of us laughed about that. But for a young fellow like me, it was a strange way to come of age. Working in a trade where nobody was who he said he was and everyone had something to hide."

Berta sighed and gave Nat a look that said, "Enough small talk—this fellow could drop dead at any moment." Nat reluctantly took out his notebook.

"Something tells me you're going to ask next about that slippery American I followed for two years."

"How'd you know?"

"Well, he was one of only three people I was assigned to, and he was the only American. Plus he damn near cost me my job. Him and that fucking German. No offense to you, my Liebchen." He winked at Berta.

"You may say whatever you wish about my countrymen from that era," Berta said. "But to which one in particular are you referring? Kurt Bauer?"

"All in good time," he said, sipping his lager. It left a foam mustache on his gray stubble. "First I must tell you about my adventures with Icarus."

"You called him that, too?" Nat said.

"We knew his real name, of course. Gordon Wolfe. He made it easy to find out, the way he operated. Sloppy and reckless, at least at first. Always in a hurry."

No wonder Dulles had sent the laundry list of advice.

"Give me an example."

"Well, the thing with the phone, for starters. Back then Swiss phones didn't cut off when you hung up. That made it possible for the central exchange to plug in to almost any room, using the phone as a microphone. The only way to stop it was to unplug the phone between calls. Dulles discovered this right away, of course. But not Icarus."

Molden told a few more tales like that. Slipups and bumbles that made his job easy. But with experience, Icarus became increasingly elusive. Berta, who seemed impatient with the talk of tradecraft, tried to move the conversation forward by mentioning the name of Kurt Bauer's Swiss shadow.

"Your colleague Lutz Visser," she said. "Did you work with him much?"

Molden flicked his hand dismissively, as if to shoo a fly.

"Visser is dead. And good riddance. An overbearing liar. Spinning so many stories about every German he tailed that toward the end they just put him on a few Belgians and let him say whatever he pleased."

"What kind of stories?"

"You are interested in lies? I thought you were historians."

"Sometimes even a lie contains a grain of truth."

Molden shook his head in irritation.

"What did Visser say about Kurt Bauer?"

"Same sort of claptrap he said about every German. That Bauer was mixing with Gestapo bad guys. Cooking up plots. Hell, he was a boy, barely eighteen. Not that youth ever kept any Germans from behaving badly. Bauer was lost here, mooning about with nothing to do. Probably left a girlfriend behind, that's what I always said."

"How did you happen to get a look at him?" Nat asked.

"Easy. He met with Icarus. Several times." Another swallow of beer. Another mustache. Then he laughed. "Bauer didn't like our man Icarus one bit, I can tell you that! But of course Visser only took that as a sign that Bauer must be up to no good."

"And you're certain he was wrong?" Berta asked.

"Oh, as you say, there is often a grain of truth. The Gestapo contact, for example. You couldn't be a German in Bern without having the Gestapo look you up, especially if you were as prominent as Bauer. Naturally they wanted to know his whereabouts. But by that late in the war I would say he was the one with more influence in that relationship."

"How so?" Nat asked.

"Well, this was late '44. Even the Gestapo knew the war was lost. Their people here were well beyond the orbit of Berlin, and they weren't interested in fighting to the last man no matter what the Führer said. A few began placing their bets on the Americans. Some of them probably figured Bauer would be a good middleman for meeting Dulles. But people like the Bauers were already too preoccupied with looking out for themselves."

"Of course they were," Berta said. "And the Bauers came out of it quite well."

"People like them always do, and with good reason. They're more interested in making money than ideology. So you see? Visser was a lying shit."

"But even you said Bauer didn't like Icarus," Berta said. From her aggressive posture, you could tell she wasn't thrilled with Molden's conclusion that Bauer was an okay guy.

"This is true. And the feeling was mutual. You saw it in their body language whenever they met. Shoulders turned away from each other. Never face-to-face, unless it was confrontational. Visser wasn't exaggerating that part."

"Bauer must not have been that much of an opportunist," Nat said, "if he couldn't even bring himself to butter up a small player like Icarus."

"He felt he had been pawned off. He wanted an audience with the big boss and thought if he sulked enough they might let him see Dulles himself. When that didn't work he tried making big promises to the errand boy."

"What kind of promises?"

Molden shrugged.

"I don't know for sure. I only have theories. Offering to spy on his Gestapo contacts, perhaps. Or his Nazi friends. Stuckart was also in Bern by then, you know."

"Wilhelm Stuckart?"

"Wilhelm's son, Erich. He arrived in late '44, toward the end of summer. He and Bauer were school chums."

Well, this was news. Wilhelm Stuckart was a high official in the Nazi Interior Ministry, best known for cowriting the Nuremberg laws, which codified German anti-Semitism. He was also one of fifteen muckety-mucks who attended the Wannsee Conference in 1942, where the murderous Reinhard Heydrich laid out the basis for the "Final Solution" of the Jewish Question. Stuckart was convicted of war crimes at Nuremberg but got out of prison in 1949. He died four years later in a suspicious car accident.

Nat hadn't even known Stuckart had a family. But Berta seemed to know all about Erich. Nat could see it in her eyes. Perhaps it was one of her jealously guarded secrets. She was watching Molden carefully, as if worried about what might spill out next.

"What was Erich Stuckart doing in Bern?" Nat asked.

"Same thing as Bauer. Trying to cut deals for his family. Leaving messages for Dulles and anyone else who would see him. Visser, of course, claimed Stuckart had bigger plans, and was hatching them with Bauer."

"Did Icarus know about Stuckart?" Berta asked.

"Who can say for sure?"

Nat sensed that at times Molden was still covering for past short-comings. Maybe he had been a lousy spy. To watch him now, tucking into his *Rösti*, Nat could easily imagine him wearying of the chase on a nice spring day, opting instead for a *Bier* and *Schnitzel* at some establishment like this.

"Even if Icarus had known about Stuckart," Molden continued, "why should he have cared? There were other operatives assigned to the likes of Stuckart. And by then, of course, Icarus had far bigger concerns in Adelboden."

"Adelboden?" Nat asked.

It was a town in the Alps, about an hour south of Bern. By the end of the war, its hotels had been overflowing with interned American airmen who hadn't been lucky enough to get jobs like Gordon's.

"Yes, Adelboden. Did you not know about Icarus and his little Fräulein, his pretty little waitress?"

"I'll be damned."

"You knew this?" Berta said. Her tone was accusatory.

"Not really. But there was a memo in the archives from Gordon to Dulles, 'The Case of the Pretty Waitress.' All about some Swiss damsel in distress in Adelboden. I copied it, but I didn't think it meant much at the time."

"Oh, she was quite important to him," Molden said. His smile was a leer.

"Wasn't she charged with something?" Nat asked.

"The security police believed she was helping American airmen escape. She supplied them with civilian clothes, and on her holidays she drove them to Luzern, where they made their way across the border into France."

"Do you remember a name? The memo seemed to make a point of not mentioning it."

"Good for Icarus. Purposely keeping her out of the official record. Yes, I remember her well, and in the end we all agreed she was a pretty good egg. She did all right for herself with tips, of course, but she never charged a penny for taking anyone to the border. That's one reason the charges were dropped. Of course, it didn't hurt that Icarus intervened. He got some American lawyer to take her case."

"And her name?" Nat prompted again.

"Sorry. It was Keller. Sabine Keller."

"You're joking."

"You know of her?"

"Not really. But I have seen the name."

Amazing, Nat thought. Sabine Keller. The signature in the book Gordon had put under lock and key. Even Berta looked startled. Nat now recalled the most striking thing about the "pretty waitress" memo—its affectionate tone. Gordon had not only given her the benefit of the doubt, he had taken her side. Quite a contrast to his dismissive reaction to other sob stories. No pity for anyone until the pretty waitress came along, toting her Swiss murder mystery with a wildflower tucked between the pages.

"At first we were a little surprised when Icarus started spending so much time down there," Molden said.

"You were surprised by love?" Berta asked, oddly animated. "The oldest and strongest emotion in the world? How could that have surprised you?"

Such an unlikely question, coming from her. Nat wondered what could have triggered it. Molden also seemed taken aback, but he recovered with a shrug and a sip of beer.

"Then maybe it is true what they say about us Swiss, that we are a cold and precise people, a nation of watchmakers. Whether or not he was in love, I cannot say for sure. But it certainly made my life easier, because my bosses didn't care in the least about the doings of some mooning young couple. So it was always a breeze for me when Icarus went courting. I had some nice outings, down there in Adelboden."

"When did all this take place?" Nat asked. "The memo was from July of '44."

"He really wasn't down there much until November. But by Christmas, well, I am surprised he kept his job. A shame, really, because by then he had gotten quite good. Bad for the Americans, but good for me." He raised his glass in tribute.

"So is that how Icarus almost cost you your job? Some minder found you lazing in an Alpine café?"

"Oh, no. He disappeared on me. I lost him completely."

"For how long?"

"For the rest of the war. He went down to Adelboden one night just after the New Year, walked into her door, and, poof, I never saw him again."

"So this was in January of '45?"

"Yes."

It was the same time Gordon had disappeared from OSS account books and official correspondence. His name hadn't resurfaced until late April, in Loofbourow's cryptic memo alluding to Gordon's presence in a Zurich safe house, due to someone or something called "Fleece." Eight days later, the war in Europe ended.

During the same blackout period, Kurt Bauer had been terminated as an OSS source. And Erich Stuckart had also been in the neighborhood at the time. Bauer's file had then been sent straight to the top of the OSS—or would have been if it hadn't disappeared, perhaps courtesy of Gordon.

"Any theories on where he went?" Nat asked.

"I argued at the time that he must have decided to escape. Along with his girlfriend, of course. She certainly would have known how to help him pull it off."

"Except Gordon kept working for Dulles. In Germany, during the occupation."

"So I heard, as did my bosses. That's when they nearly fired me. They were convinced I must have missed something major."

"And what do you think?"

"Maybe I did. Like I said, he was good by then."

"Did the name Fleece ever come up? Either as a code name or an operation?"

Molden shook his head.

"No. Is that what he was up to?"

"I don't know."

They sat in silence a moment, the three of them drifting with their thoughts. Sensing that the conversation had nearly run its course, Nat took a shot in the dark.

"Tell me, Herr Molden, in all the time you followed him, did Icarus have any favorite mail drops? Any secret places where he liked to stash things?"

Berta moved forward in her chair, and Molden seemed to sense the sudden tension. He swiveled his eyes from Nat to Berta, then broke into a broad grin. He milked the moment by swallowing the last of his beer.

"You're looking for something, aren't you?" he said. "Is that what this whole thing is about, something Icarus left behind? Is this some sort of treasure hunt?"

Berta narrowed her eyes, but Nat didn't mind. Maybe the old fellow had been a decent operative, after all, if he was this perceptive.

"Might be," he allowed. "So?"

"No place special, I'm afraid. The one mail drop I knew of was in an old church, a small chapel that burned down maybe twenty years later. So that wouldn't help you."

"What about a place called the Hotel Jurgens?"

Berta perked up at this new reference and shot Nat another accusatory glance. Well, too bad, because she was certainly still holding back items.

"Dulles used to house some of the American airmen at the Jurgens, but I never saw Icarus go there. The crewmen stayed there the night before catching trains into Germany for prisoner exchanges. As far as I know, it was never a mail drop. But I'm surprised at you two, especially since you think that the Swiss know nothing about love."

"What do you mean?" Nat asked.

"Well, the woman, of course! This Sabine Keller. If you'd seen the two of them together, you'd know that anyplace Icarus would choose for stashing something would somehow be connected to her."

It made sense, especially in light of the book. But who knew if Sabine Keller was even alive, much less her whereabouts.

"Do you know what became of her?"

"No idea. Because she disappeared, too, you see. Around the same time as Icarus. Except in her case, she never turned up again."

Interesting, Nat thought, and definitely worth following up.

They were startled suddenly by a loud noise from a nearby table. Two couples of middle-aged Americans in shorts and polo shirts had burst into laughter, enjoying a joke at a waiter's expense. Nat had overheard them earlier, groaning about sore feet and tram routes, and now they were even drawing stares from the neighboring café.

"Americans have become the new Germans," Molden said with a frown. "Blustering their way around town, asking loudly for menus in English. The swagger of conquerors."

Or maybe just the nature of noisy tourists, Nat thought, especially ones with plenty of money. Like the Japanese family at the next table, shooting video of everything that moved. Or that man standing in the square, snapping pictures of their café. In fact, he seemed to be aiming his lens at their table. Or had been, until Nat started watching. Now he was lowering his head and walking briskly away.

"That man," Nat said. "Do you know him?"

Molden followed his stare.

"What, you mean that Arab fellow?"

"Arab?"

"Well, that was my impression. But I suppose he could be Turkish or Greek. All I know is that he's been watching this place quite a while. I kept expecting him to ask for a table. Maybe it's just my old training, noticing him like that. Funny how those habits never really leave you."

"Maybe," Nat said, keeping an eye on the side street where the man had disappeared. "Or maybe you still know tradecraft when you see it."

Molden's smile faded. He shoved his plate away and put his napkin on the table.

"This business you're pursuing. I won't pretend I know what it's all about, but maybe it would be best if you left me out of it from here on. I do thank you for the lunch, though."

From then until they dropped him off at his apartment, Molden was wary and watchful. Exactly how he must have carried himself during the war, Nat figured. Back when nobody was who he said he was and everyone had something to hide.

Back when Bern was the spy capital of Europe.

SEVENTEEN

WHAT NAT NEVER COULD HAVE KNOWN or learned, no matter how many old documents and code names he dug up, was what took place when Gordon Wolfe met Sabine Keller.

Nor could he ever have known that Gordon's final conscious thoughts, only seconds after the old man wryly offered his OSS countersign to the jailhouse doctor, were of that very moment sixty-four years earlier when he first laid eyes on Sabine.

Such are the limitations of history, and also of espionage, because even the masterful Allen Dulles had no inkling of what befell his young flyboy operative on that July afternoon.

Gordon saw her before she saw him. She was sprawled in tall grass on an Alpine riverbank in the valley town of Adelboden. He had come looking for her in response to a written plea from an American airman, a lieutenant who appreciated her efforts on behalf of his compatriots and thought she was getting a raw deal from the Swiss. Not much of an assignment, really, but they sent Gordon because he knew the ways of these flyboys.

He checked first at the hotel where she worked—and where the lieutenant was billeted. The proprietor said she was on break, but he could probably find her eating lunch down by the river.

Moments later, that was indeed where he spotted her. She was reading, as luck would have it, a Wolf Schwertenbach novel with a red cover. Her feet tucked beneath her. Her hair was pulled to one side, and her head was tilted down toward the book to expose a fine, graceful neck.

On his way into town, Gordon had stopped at a café for a pint of lager. He did it to steel himself, because this wasn't going to be pleasant business. His instructions were to tell her she was on her own, that the Americans could do nothing for her. But the beer had put him in a mellow mood, and the sun was so warm that he had taken off his leather jacket and slung it across his shoulder. And so he approached her casually, almost jauntily. Anyone watching might even have suspected he was her lover, coming to surprise her.

She must have heard his footsteps swishing through the high grass, because she turned suddenly and, sensing his buoyant mood, smiled up at him with the fullness of her beauty. Her light brown curls were golden in the summer sun.

"Fräulein Keller?" he asked, his voice nearly catching in his throat.

"Ja. Bist du der Amerikaner?" Immediately employing the familiar verb, which further disarmed him.

"Ja."

"I speak English, too, if you prefer. Is it bad news that you bring me?"

Maybe it was her smile, or her expression of benign resignation, as if she were quite content to let him decide her future. Whatever the reason, Gordon changed his mind on the spot and decided to hell with orders.

"No. It's not. I can't guarantee anything, of course, but I'll do what I can."

She nodded, as if that outcome, too, was all in the natural course of things. It only endeared her to him more. He extended a hand to help her stand. But first she plucked a small yellow flower and pressed it into the book to mark her place, which he saw was page 186.

Her face came up to his shoulder, and her hair smelled of grass and sunlight and wildflowers. He knew instinctively that if he were to embrace her, her body would fold neatly into his, a perfect fit. After all the whores and hangers-on he had encountered here—and occasionally sampled—Gordon Wolfe knew then and there that he had come home. The realization frightened him, considering all that he had left behind in the States, and the important promises he had made. This was just a fairy-tale episode in a land of myth, right? Another freak happenstance in this magic bubble of neutrality.

He shook his head to clear the cobwebs, and she must have wondered why. Perhaps she attributed it to the beer on his breath. But she did not let go of his hand, because she, too, had fallen under the spell of the encounter. So together they walked back up the riverbank to the hotel where she worked, to begin seeing what he could do about straightening out her future. Because now it was his future as well. Of that he was certain.

EIGHTEEN

ORDERING THE SECOND BOTTLE of wine was a mistake. Nat realized that the moment Berta suggested they take the rest of it upstairs to her room. And not just any room, but a big one with a fine view, low lighting, and a soft queen-size bed at the luxurious Bellevue Palace. The sort of room that might have had a thumb tab for "Seduction" in the leather-bound guide to its amenities.

When reserving their accommodations earlier, Nat had chalked up his extravagance to his quirky urge to follow in Gordon's footsteps. He also liked the idea of taking advantage of the FBI's generosity. But as he swayed against Berta's shoulder in the rising elevator he wondered if ulterior motives had also been in play. Because when the waiter began hovering with their bill as the night turned cool on the hotel terrace, it became all too easy to assent to Berta's request that they head someplace warmer. That was when he decided the second bottle was overkill.

Not that he and Berta hadn't earned the right to celebrate. Her contact at the Swiss Archives paid off nicely, letting them copy every surveillance report from Molden and Visser. Who knows what treasures might lie in wait in the details? While that alone wasn't earthshattering progress, between it and their lunch with Molden they believed they were forming a clearer picture of the Gordon Wolfe–Kurt Bauer backstory. Even if that didn't lead directly to the missing files, they realized over dinner that it might lead to something equally valuable—the information that had prompted Gordon's blackmail to begin with. Why worry about finding Gordon's stash of copied secrets if you could unearth the secrets themselves?

They reached that triumphant conclusion just before Berta suggested that they enjoy the rest of the wine upstairs. She said it in an offhand tone, but Nat was immediately wary and excited, especially after having seen her in action that afternoon.

In dealing with the clerk named Karsten at the Swiss Archives, Nat had instinctively assumed the role of asexual, disinterested colleague while Berta set the tone. She went to work on the poor dupe with unwavering eye contact and a series of small touches to his forearm, his shoulder, and his knee as they sat side by side, reviewing a microfilm index. The fellow responded by letting them stay an hour past closing time to make copies. By the end of their session he was helping slide documents into place beneath their cameras.

So be on your guard, Nat told himself, as the elevator door opened to their floor. Yet he couldn't suppress a thrill—as well as another characteristic response—when she tucked her arm under his as they strolled to her door.

Berta immediately threw open the window, with its bluff-top view of the River Aare. She leaned exultantly into the cool night. Fresh mountain air, from the peaks of the Berner Oberland.

"Look at that!" she said, holding out her glass for a refill. "If the morning isn't hazy, we'll be able to see the Eiger and the Jungfrau."

Was she saying they would both be waking up here? Nat's room was across the hall, with a view of an air shaft. He tried shoving his imagination onto another track by thinking of Gordon and wondering what the young airman's first impression of this hotel must have been. Had he, too, been with an attractive young woman?

"You're thinking of him, aren't you?" Berta said. "Him and his waitress. You're very spiritual in that way. In fact, I've never met such a spiritual historian. It's almost like you believe these places are haunted."

"Not haunted. But there's something of him here. I do believe that. Nothing I could ever pin down, but it's in the air."

"And what's your reading on this 'presence' of his, for lack of a better word?"

"Optimism. Deliverance. I'd wager those were his strongest emotions."

"Why?"

"Have you ever seen the ball turret of a B-17? The gunner is practically in a fetal position, hanging out the belly of the plane for eight hours a pop. Air temperature at twenty below for most of the way. Flak and fighter planes coming at you from everywhere. Then, poof, his plane ducks out of the battle, lands in a Swiss meadow, and a few days later Allen Dulles offers him a job, asking if he'd like to play at being a spy, all expenses paid. Then on his first night in Bern he walks into a room just like this—hell, for all we know, this *was* the room—and instead of being crammed into a ball turret while being strafed by Messerschmitts he's lying down on a big feather bed."

"With a nice local whore."

"Possibly. Either way, he must have been thinking he was the luckiest man in the world."

"And what about you? Are you feeling lucky?"

She brushed a stray hair from his forehead. It was all the prompting he needed. He touched her face and drew her close, an effortless movement that brought her lips to his, open and willing. Subsequent events took care of themselves, or as much as they needed to once a man and a woman are in the proper state of mind and have consumed nearly two bottles of Neuchatel Blanc before retiring to a swank room where "Do Not Disturb" is printed in three different languages.

Afterward, Nat poured himself another glass, even though the wine had lost its chill on the bedside table. He felt more attuned than ever to Gordon's mood upon arrival in Bern—the sudden sense of new possibilities, the hint of exotic risk. All of it familiar, if for different reasons. He also thought he had a clearer read now on Berta, and he turned to her with a question.

"What, or who, were you thinking of when you made that comment to Molden about the powerful force of love? And don't worry, I'm not expecting you to say me."

"My Oma," she said, using the German word.

"Your *grandmother*?"

"Don't look so surprised." She seemed a little offended. "It's still love, any way you look at it."

"How disappointing. You sure it wasn't some ex-boyfriend?"

"Oh, I've always had men in my life. But I've only known one grandmother, and she was with me every day for fifteen years. Living in the same small apartment, worrying about the same nosy neighbors. She was there when my mom and dad couldn't be."

"A nice old Hausfrau?"

"Only because the government wouldn't let her work. She was

quite the agitator in her day, a formidable woman. Of course, I thought it was my role to keep her out of trouble so the authorities wouldn't take her away. Or maybe it was just because I was such a good little Communist and wanted her to be one, too."

"*You*, a good little Communist?"

"Oh, goodness, yes." She laughed. "Chapter leader of the Young Pioneers. Marched in every May Day parade. Read everything I could find about Rosa Luxemburg. When I think back, I don't know how she put up with me."

Berta seemed to get a little dreamy, then a little nostalgic. Enough to make Nat believe she really *had* been talking about her grand-mother.

"She taught me so much, really. How to spot informants, or other people you couldn't rely on. How to look for the truth when everyone else wanted to surround you with lies."

"Your guardian against the Stasi?"

Nat said it whimsically, but Berta turned somber.

"Something like that," she said, lowering her head.

He felt awkward, figuring he had killed the mood.

"And she, uh, got you hooked on this White Rose business?"

"Yes. She was sure that her friends from the war—the ones who didn't make it—had been betrayed. And Bauer was one of only three or four people who could have betrayed them."

"So he's your prime suspect?"

"Oh, no. There are several. He just happens to be the one I've focused on lately."

"Have you tried talking to him?"

"Only by mail. I've asked nicely several times, but he has always said no."

Keep going, he thought. Tell me more. As helpful as it was to finally hear more about her motives, he wanted substance, too. Names. Details. But she must have noticed he was hanging on every word, because she quickly changed course.

"I should have known you'd think I was talking about a man when I mentioned love."

"Well, it's not like that would have been unusual. Love does tend to work that way."

She shrugged. Her neck and shoulders were beautiful, perfectly smooth.

"This idea of finding a mate for life has never been so vital to me. Nothing personal, but when men are so readily available, after a while all you worry about is when to choose and when to reject."

"You make it all so romantic."

She smiled, and slid closer on the bed.

"You asked, so I told you. It is the way I choose to live my life. I research what I want, fuck who I want, stay where I please, when I please, and I set my own hours each and every day. And if sometimes I choose to mix business with pleasure"—she stroked a fingertip down the inside of his thigh—"well, that is what works best anyway when things are going well. Don't you think?"

"I suppose."

"Is there another woman in your life?" she asked. "A woman you're serious about?"

"Not at the moment."

"It would be quite all right with me if there was. I'm never exclusive in these matters. It's part of what makes me attractive. Men sense my availability, but also that I will only be temporary. Safe, but a little dangerous, too. A very enticing combination, don't you think?" Her fingertips again skimmed his thigh, a tickle of nails. She began just above the knee and ended just below the spot where he hoped she would keep going, now that it was standing at attention. Instead, she doubled back and continued to slide her fingers back and forth, silk on leather, while speaking in a warm, low monotone, her Prussian vowels suggesting the darker possibilities of a dominatrix. She could have commanded, "Show me your papers," and it would have thrilled him to the marrow.

"I like that word, 'enticing,' " she said. "It sounds exactly like what it means. The little hiss in the middle, like a whispered invitation. There is no German word quite that good for seduction. 'Seduce.' That is also a fine word. Although maybe with a dart of poison, too. Don't you think?"

"Poison doesn't sound very safe. And 'safe' definitely isn't a word I associate with you."

"Good. Because love is never safe. Lust, even less so. As for how well either of them mixes with this business we are pursuing, I suppose we will find out."

But he was no longer interested in talking about their goals, or her linguistic preferences. Nor was she, apparently, because those were the last words they spoke for the next fifteen minutes.

Peace and darkness then descended upon the room. She spoiled the mood a bit by pulling a pack of cigarettes from the bedside table, but, this being Europe, Nat decided he could endure the smoke. At least the window was still open, and the clouds of her exhaust lent a period feel to the scene. They might have been hiding in a seedy room above a rail station at some wartime crossroads, traveling under false names with forged papers, on the run from the secret police. It was a nice fantasy to languish in, and he carried it into his dreams.

Then, as always happened to Nat on transatlantic trips, he found himself wide awake. The red digital display on the bedside clock said 3:19. It was his usual onset of Euro jet lag, and he knew from experience there wouldn't be much more sleep until dawn. Berta, back on her home turf, still slept peacefully. He propped on an elbow to watch her, mildly aroused as he checked for any sign that she might soon join him in the waking world.

He thought of the verse Karen had offered, the one about forbidden fruit. Its taste was indeed sweet. What would his daughter make of him now, having succumbed so readily? Nat pictured her thumbing through the *Complete Poems* at top speed, searching for something appropriately salacious and disrespectful to sum him up. What time was it in the States? A little after 9 p.m. Good timing for a phone call, but the circumstances weren't exactly optimal.

Looking again at Berta, he wondered about her love for her grandmother as the supposed motivator of her zealous research. According to the Wolfe-Turnbull school of historical thought, Berta's explanation remained incomplete. Even assuming that her Oma had practically raised her and had taught her how to deal with Stasi bad guys, such generalities felt insufficient. There had to be some single big moment involved—a rescue, a failure, a near-death experience; take your pick. Nothing less would explain why a young woman as smart and pretty as Berta Heinkel had become such a single-minded vagabond in so narrow a field of research. And for fifteen years, no less.

Or was he misreading her? Maybe she had latched on to the topic only recently but had peddled the tale of lifetime obsession to win his allegiance. Other colleagues had certainly tried more underhanded tactics.

It was useless to just lie there, so he pulled on his trousers and went to the sink for a glass of water. Maybe he would go for a walk. He threw open the bathroom window for another look at the night. With the streets empty you could hear the river surging through a massive sluice gate. A lone car poked across the bridge.

What he really needed was a drink, something stronger than the dregs of the wine. He shuffled to the console cabinet and plunged into the minibar for a bourbon. Then he opened the refrigerator, hoping to retrieve some ice before the light awakened Berta. He shut the door, but not before the glow illuminated the edge of a manila folder atop the fridge, just beneath the shelf for the television. So far, Berta hadn't shared the contents of either her briefcase or her camera. This might be a rare opportunity for a sneak peek.

He made sure she was still asleep. Then he took the folder, a pen, and a sheet of hotel stationery, slipped into the bathroom, and gently shut the door behind him. He turned on the light, flipped down the lid of the toilet and took a seat. Not exactly optimum conditions for research, but it would do.

The tab on the folder said "Plötzensee," which he knew was a prison in Berlin during the war. The Nazis had often used it for political prisoners.

Inside was a typewritten sheet of names atop a stack of eight-by-ten photos in black and white. There were seven names on the list, next to two columns of dates. The first column was headed "Date of Incarceration." The second, "Final Disposition."

Was this, perhaps, a roster of members of the Berlin White Rose who had been arrested? If so, it was new ground indeed. No other historian had yet come up with this many names associated with the Berlin group.

The most interesting name was the first one: Kurt Bauer. Incarcerated March 20, 1943. Released September 3, 1943. Five and a half months in prison hardly seemed like evidence of betrayal, unless he had spilled his guts during interrogation. Even then, considering the Gestapo's torture tactics, it certainly would have been forgivable for a teenage boy to break under pressure. More damning, perhaps, was that Bauer was the only one of the seven to be released.

The other six had also been incarcerated on March 20. Three of them—Dieter Büssler, Christoph Klemm, and Ulrich Lindner—were listed as "executed" on August 19, 1943. The fourth, Liesl Folkerts, was listed as "killed" on September 4, the day after Bauer's release. The fifth, Hannelore Nierendorf, was listed as "escaped," also on September 4. The sixth, Klara Waldhorst, was also executed, on September 12.

From his previous research, Nat knew of only three names besides Bauer's that had been associated with the Berlin cell up to now— Helmut Hartert, Falk Harnack, and Jörg Strasser—and none of them was on this list.

Hartert was the only one of the three who was a Berliner. He had survived the war and, to Nat's knowledge, had never been arrested. Harnack had communicated with the Berlin group as an emissary from the original Munich cell. He had apparently also visited Dietrich Bonhoeffer, the dissident cleric at the center of both of Nat's books. Harnack had been arrested in a roundup of the Munich members, tried, and then released. Strasser, whose only apparent role was to transport a batch of White Rose leaflets to Berlin, had been questioned by the Munich Gestapo and released.

Nat supposed that any of those three might just as easily have betrayed the Berlin members as Bauer.

But when he reappraised this new information, Nat saw that the most intriguing name belonged to Hannelore Nierendorf, who had escaped. Might she still be alive? He aimed to find out. But he would have to do so without tipping off Berta, or else she would realize he had been rummaging through her papers. For all he knew, Berta had already interviewed the woman. He hurriedly copied the information onto the stationery.

There were no other documents in the folder, so he turned to the photos. The first, judging by the scenery, had been taken fairly recently. It was of an old man in a baggy dark overcoat clutching a small bouquet of flowers. His face seemed vaguely familiar, and he stood on a wide sidewalk before a high brick wall. There was some sort of historical marker in the background. Nat squinted to make out the lettering: "Gedenkstatte Plötzensee."

Of course. The site of the infamous old prison was now a national memorial site. He then realized who the man was: Kurt Bauer. Nat had seen contemporary photos on the Internet.

Had Berta snapped it? If so, then she had probably followed him to the site, which struck Nat as a bit creepy. Maybe it happened the day she asked Bauer for an interview. But hadn't Berta just told him that she had only tried contacting Bauer by mail? Nat turned over the photo. Berta had scribbled a date: "4 May 2007." Less than a month ago.

The next photo was also of Bauer and was also taken at Plötzensee. Same overcoat, different lighting, different flowers and, on the back, a different date. "4 April 2007."

There were three more shots of the elderly Bauer at Plötzensee. In two he glared at the camera as if he had recognized the person taking his picture. In each he held a bouquet. They had all been snapped on the fourth day of a different month the previous year.

Nat rechecked the roster of names. Every death except Liesl Folkerts' had occurred on August 19 or September 12. Liesl died on September 4. Could she have been Bauer's old flame? Judging from the flowers, Nat would bet on it. But why wasn't she listed as "executed," like all the others? The alignment of dates suggested she may have been shot while trying to escape with Hannelore Nierendorf. Perhaps Bauer had even been involved in the plot, since he had been released the day before and would have been in a position to help.

Interesting, all of it.

Berta's doggedness in snapping the intrusive photos, on the other hand, was troubling, even by Nat's standards. And the Plötzensee shots were only part of the story. There were seven more glossies in the file, and six were of Bauer. None was dated, but each looked recent: Bauer climbing into a limo outside an upscale town house; Bauer delivering a speech to a roomful of suits; Bauer at a posh restaurant; Bauer on a park bench reading an edition of *Frankfurter Allgemeine Zeitung;* Bauer again in a limo, this time while stopped at a traffic light; and finally, Bauer awaiting a flight at Tegel Airport in Berlin. Judging from the fuzzy images in the foreground, each photo had been shot through a long lens. The one at the airport had been snapped through a pane of glass. All of them had presumably been taken without his knowledge or consent.

The seventh photo was also an eight-by-ten, but Nat didn't recognize the subject. It was another old man, around Bauer's age, holding a newspaper as he stood on a front porch in his bathrobe. Somewhere in Europe, probably Germany, judging by the style of door and windows. Wooded neighborhood. No date, and no writing on the back. Another member of the Bauer family, perhaps? Or maybe a White Rose survivor?

Nat took a deep breath and wondered what to do next. Then he nearly jumped out of his skin as Berta called out from the bed.

"Are you all right in there?"

"Yes," he replied through the door. "The, uh, dinner was a little rich, I guess. Plus all the wine."

"Not to mention the excitement afterward."

He heard Berta climbing out of bed, so he stood, grabbed a towel, and draped it around the folder and the sheet of paper. He then ran the tap for a second and shut off the light. When he opened the door he was holding the papers beneath the towel while awkwardly pretending to dry his hands. Luckily, Berta wanted a glass of water, and she brushed past him to get to the sink. Once he heard the tap running, he stepped to the TV console and hurriedly slid the folder back into place. Then he tucked the sheet of stationery into his pants pocket, pulled off his trousers, and got back into bed.

"You drank a bourbon?" she called out.

Shit. He had left the mini-bottle on the floor, along with his empty glass.

"Hair of the dog. As a precaution."

"Already? Too early. It will never work."

She emerged shortly afterward, naked and sleek in the dimness. A half hour ago the sight would have been arousing. But not after what he had seen in the folder. He shut his eyes, feigning sleep. She slid in beside him and was soon breathing evenly, but Nat remained awake. He couldn't shake the image of Berta stalking the old man, capturing him unawares from behind trees and hedges and from her car. If the man had refused her request for an interview, her behavior amounted to little more than harassment, not to mention a waste of time.

The power of love? This looked more like the power of obsession. Nat tried to sleep. The next thing he knew, he was awakening to full sunlight. The clock said it was nearly seven. He dressed quietly to keep from waking Berta and crept into the hall.

The door to his room was ajar, and a maid's cart was parked outside. They certainly started early around here. He entered to find a man in a hotel jacket stooped at the end of the bed, fussily tucking in the linens. But Nat hadn't slept here, so why did the bed need making?

The man straightened quickly and brushed past him toward the door, moving briskly, face averted.

"Just finishing, sir." An accent, not local.

He looked around in a panic for his things. The box of Gordon's keepsakes was still in his bag, thank goodness, tucked between a pair of shirts. His laptop was still here, too, but the screen was up and the drawer of the disk drive was open. The bastard had copied his files—all the electronic versions of his documents, his sources, notes from the Molden interview, and everything they had photographed yesterday at the Swiss Archives. Nat ran into the hallway, colliding sharply with the laundry cart, but the man was gone. He heard elevator doors opening around the corner at the far end of the hall, so he sprinted in that direction. Then there was a faint ping, like a bell in a boxing ring, and he heard the doors shutting. By the time he rounded the corner the row of display lights showed that the car was just reaching the lobby.

Round one to the opposition, whoever he was. And last night's bout, he now realized, had gone to Berta by technical knockout. She had maneuvered Nat into a corner of his desires and knocked him senseless. He had been stupid to drop his guard. For all he knew, she might even be working with the fellow who had just disappeared.

Even more worrisome, the next round would be staged in Berlin—Berta's home, Bauer's home, and, to Nat, a city of almost spectral power, haunted by millions.

He had better start being more careful, and soon.

NINETEEN

THE GOOD NEWS WAS that Nat and Berta reached Berlin without further incident.

The bad news was that Erich Stuckart was dead, according to the microfilmed obituary that Nat had just rolled onto the screen: killed at age twenty-eight in an auto accident in March 1954, only four months after the same fate befell his father. If you believed the conspiracy theories that said the elder Stuckart had been assassinated by vengeful Jews, then maybe Erich had been rubbed out as well.

"Too bad," Nat said. "He'd have been perfect."

Berta didn't seem particularly disappointed, which made Nat suspect she had already been down this trail. He wondered if she had ever searched for the whereabouts of Hannelore Nierendorf, too, and he was tempted to ask. But then he would have had to explain how he'd discovered the name, and that would have ended their partnership. He had already checked the Berlin phone book and found no such listing, although she could have married or moved elsewhere. It irked him that Berta probably knew for sure.

She sat to his left. They had been in the Bundesarchiv for three hours after arriving at Tegel on a morning flight, and neither had yet been willing to let the other out of sight. Nat figured his own wariness was justified, but what was bugging her?

The new dynamic had been evident since breakfast, when they discussed their lodging arrangements for Berlin. Nat had assumed she would suggest they stay at her apartment. Instead, she insisted on a hotel.

"My place is way up in Prenzlauer Berg. We'd spend half our time getting to and from the archives."

"I just figured you'd want to get back home. Open the mail. Spread out a little."

"It will be better this way. More efficient."

They wound up at a small hotel just off the Ku-Damm, a location only marginally more convenient than Prenzlauer Berg.

"One room or two?" the clerk asked.

Nat looked at Berta, then back at the clerk.

"Two."

Neither said a word as they rode the elevator. The silence continued through most of their U-Bahn trip to Krumme Lanke, the nearest stop to the Bundesarchiv. The ride put Nat in a contemplative mood, and he shared his thoughts as they approached their stop.

"This used to be the stop for the Berlin Document Center, back when the Americans ran it. Remember that old dump?"

"Yes. SS files and Nazi Party records. I guess they've all been moved."

"Just as well. That building gave me the creeps. Like a big bunker in the woods. I felt like I was stirring up evil spirits every time I walked in. They've turned it into condos, you know. Amazing anyone could actually live there."

"Why? It's a nice location. Right by the Grunewald and near all the lakes."

"Nice? One of the old air shafts is by a playground now. You can jump off the swing set and look down to the place where they probably sorted Heydrich's mail."

"They've turned that part into an underground parking garage."

"I know. The tenants use it, with their baby seats and their BMWs."

"So?"

"Well, wouldn't you feel a little haunted, waking up there every morning?"

"I wouldn't be German if I wasn't haunted. But all the ghosts are up here." She tapped her head. "Like a microchip implanted at birth."

"Not for me," he said. "In Berlin they're everywhere, especially when I'm really wrapped up in my work. I know it's not rational."

"Well, *that* part I can understand, at least."

She smiled, and he returned it. Finally, some warmth.

The train doors opened and they climbed the stairs, emerging into sunlight.

Then along came the moment that, for Nat, changed the complexion of the day. Perhaps it was prompted by the conversation they had just had, or because his mind seemed to be racing in a million directions at once, trying to arrange all that he'd learned into some semblance of order. But for whatever reason he sensed an unsettling presence, a sudden shadow across his thoughts. Except this time the feeling was almost benevolent, as if someone were wishing him well. And he wasn't in a gloomy archive or at the site of some atrocity. He was simply standing at the entrance to the Krumme Lanke U-Bahn station, awash in sunshine.

"What is it?" Berta asked. "Are you all right?"

He blinked as if emerging from a dream.

"You just had one of them, didn't you? One of your little hauntings?"

He shrugged. She smiled.

"These spirits, do they ever tell you things?"

"No. And they're not spirits. I don't believe in ghosts. But they do seem to arrive with some sort of intent. To help or to hinder."

"And this one?"

He faced away from her so she wouldn't see him blush.

"She seemed to think we were doing fine."

"She?"

"You asked. That's how it felt."

But hours later, as they sat in the Bundesarchiv, Nat questioned the accuracy of his reaction, because they were getting nowhere. The Erich Stuckart lead had literally reached a dead end, and the files on Erich's father, Wilhelm, had offered nothing useful.

"I guess our next stop is Martin Göllner," he said. "Your Gestapo man."

"He lives under a different name now. Hans Mannheim. His apartment is in Moabit."

"You're certain that he once interrogated Bauer?"

"In late '43, just as the White Rose was collapsing all over the country."

"And you know this how?"

"A Gestapo rota sheet that I came across a few months ago. But there was no transcript of the interrogation. It was either destroyed by bombing or looted by the Russians."

"Or stolen." By someone like you, he thought but didn't say. "This Göllner. Or Mannheim, I guess I should say. Hasn't he already blown you off once?"

"Last month. I was a little aggressive."

"Imagine that."

"At least I'm not the one seeing ghosts."

"They're not *ghosts*. It's a gut feeling." He wished he'd never told her. "And right now my gut feeling is that it's 2 p.m. and I'm starved. Let's try the café across the street."

"Sure. Maybe your spirit will pick up the tab."

THE CAFÉ ZEN WAS A GREEK PLACE in the German style, meaning the dishes were bland, and most of them tasted the same. Nat ordered a gyro, and had eaten about half and spilled about a quarter when his cell rang. He answered guiltily, figuring it was Holland, whom he still owed a call from the day before.

"Dr. Turnbull?"

"Speaking."

"Willis Turner, in Blue Kettle Lake. What's your ten-twenty?"

"Berlin."

"Wow. Good signal."

"Aren't you up kind of early?"

"It's eight thirty, and I had an important question. That German gal you were working with, any idea how to get ahold of her?"

"Maybe. Why?" He gave her a glance and took another messy bite of gyro.

"I'm beginning to think Gordon Wolfe really was murdered, and as of now she's my only suspect."

The meat caught in his throat. He looked away from Berta and swallowed hard, while trying to maintain a normal tone of voice.

"How could that be possible?"

"I'm not at liberty to say. It might be nothing. But there are some things that don't add up, so how 'bout letting me know if you happen to run into her?"

"Sure."

"Oh, and you had asked about that anonymous tip, the one on the boxes?"

"Yes?"

"The call came from a little B&B just up the highway. Their only guest that night was a Christa Larkin of New Jersey. Ring any bells?"

"Sounds familiar, but—"

He stopped, remembering now. It was Berta's alias, the one on her fake ID at the National Archives.

"You still there?"

"Yeah."

"And?"

"Drawing a blank. Sorry."

"Well, let me know if it comes to you later. And Dr. Turnbull?"

"Yes?"

"If you do happen to see Berta Heinkel, keep your distance. I'm guessing she's more dangerous than she looks."

"Good advice."

They hung up.

"Who was it?"

"University business. Excuse me a second. Need to use the men's room."

He crossed the floor and shoved open the door. He splashed his face and toweled off while he stared at the fool in the mirror. Don't panic, he told himself, and don't jump to conclusions. For one thing, how could Berta have gotten into the jail, much less found a way to induce a heart attack? Both possibilities seemed so unlikely that he began to calm down. And it wasn't as if Turner was the world's smartest lawman.

But the call reinforced something that had already been preying on his mind: Before he took another single step alongside Berta Heinkel, he had better check further into her background. He had felt that way to some degree ever since finding such scant evidence online. Now those feelings had real urgency. Fortunately, he was in exactly the right place to follow up. But first he would have to act as if nothing had happened, which wouldn't be easy. When he went back to the table he stared at his plate, tongue-tied, and when Berta touched his arm he flinched.

"Easy. It's me, not a ghost. We'd better get going. Göllner's not getting any younger, and enough people have died on us already."

"Funny how that keeps happening."

"What do you mean?"

He looked her in the eye, wondering if she was actually capable of such a thing.

"Nothing. Let's go."

GÖLLNER'S, or rather Mannheim's, neighborhood in Moabit had seen better days. His building, just across the street from a small, scruffy park, looked like a place where the tenants were barely hanging on. Peeling paint. Smudged windows. Pigeons on the eaves and windowsills. You had to be buzzed in for entry, so they waited until an old Turkish man in a skullcap came out the door, and they slipped inside. The nameplates on the dented mailbox told them Mannheim was on the fifth floor. The stairwell smelled of disinfectant and rot. The walls were sprayed with graffiti.

Nat knocked at Mannheim's door. Berta waited on the landing of the floor below, explaining that she hadn't gotten such a great reception on her previous visit. The brassy commotion of a Bavarian oompah band—music you rarely heard in Berlin—emanated from a stereo system across the hall. It sounded like Oktoberfest in full swing.

"Who is it?" A man's voice, scratchy but strong. Nat addressed him in German.

"My name is Professor Doctor Nathaniel Turnbull. I am here to see Hans Mannheim."

An eye appeared at the peephole. A lock slid back, and the door opened to the limit of a security chain. A stooped old fellow with pale blue eyes silently assessed Nat. He wore a black wool overcoat and thick house slippers, and even with the stoop he was well over six feet. The steamy smell of boiled sausage and potatoes emerged through the crack.

"Your credentials, please."

"Chairman of the Department of History," Nat said, handing over his passport and campus ID. A lie, but he knew from experience that big titles often carried weight with ex-Nazis.

Mannheim-Göllner handed everything back.

"My apologies, Professor Doctor, but I don't wish to address matters of the past."

"Perfectly understandable, considering what you must have lived through in 1945 and beyond. But it's not your past, per se, that interests me. Not even as it relates to an old friend of yours, Martin Göllner."

Mannheim flinched, but didn't shut the door. If anything he seemed more interested.

"I'm not familiar with this Göllner fellow you speak of."

"That's fine, because I'm seeking information on others. People who have not yet been held accountable to the degree that Mr. Göllner has."

"All the same. How did you learn of his name?"

"Research. But no one else seems to know, and I don't intend on telling anyone."

Mannheim squinted at him for several more seconds. Then he shut the door, slipped off the chain, and opened the door wide.

"You have three minutes to make your case."

And Nat was betting the old Prussian wouldn't need a watch to keep track. The fellow ushered him in. Nat glanced around at a small kitchen and the remains of a late lunch. The living room window was propped open to let in the raw air. His host took a seat on the couch and gestured toward a straight-backed wooden chair directly opposite. It was small and wobbly, very uncomfortable, which of course put Nat at a disadvantage. Just like old times on Prinz-Albrecht-Strasse, he thought.

"My apologies if I interrupted your mealtime."

"State your business. You now have two minutes, twenty seconds."

"Kurt Bauer, the industrialist. You interviewed him once, when he was young."

"Seventeen. And, yes, it was an interview, just as you say. Not an interrogation. He came to us voluntarily. I tell you that for free, only because it should be established before we proceed any further."

"Absolutely."

"However, at the present time I don't have the proper materials at my disposal for discussing the matter fully."

"Proper materials?"

"The interview transcript."

"It was my understanding the transcript no longer exists."

"Correct. The original and all official copies were destroyed in early '45. You have only your air force to blame."

"In that case, I'm willing to settle for your best recollection."

"Then your work habits must be very sloppy. Perhaps I shouldn't speak with you."

"But under the circumstances . . ."

"Wouldn't you *prefer* a transcript?"

"Of course, but you said—"

"What I *said* was that the original and all official copies were destroyed. But in those days careful employees kept unofficial copies anytime a case was politically sensitive."

"Such as a case involving the son of a prominent arms merchant, for example."

"Exactly."

"Wise of you." Not to mention potentially helpful for Göllner after the war, especially if he ever wanted to ask a favor from some prominent German who might have left behind a dirty little secret. "I'll be glad to wait while you retrieve it."

"That is not so easily accomplished. It is in a secure location. And, as you might imagine, there are expenses involved with retrieval. You would need to defray the cost."

"Within reason, of course."

"Ten thousand euros, payable tomorrow."

Nat rocked back in the undersized chair, nearly toppling it.

"I said within reason."

"I can assure you that is quite a bargain, Professor Doktor. This was not just any interrogation. As a result of it, three people lost their lives. Besides, I have cut the rate considerably, a measure necessitated by my rather desperate circumstances. I can assure you that a previous buyer paid far more, although at that time even a few packs of cigarettes or a bar of chocolate was considered something of real value."

"Previous buyer?"

"Does that aspect interest you as well?"

"A little. Maybe even fifty euros worth."

"A hundred."

"Eighty."

"A hundred. Last offer."

Nat grimaced and reached for his wallet. He plucked out two fifty-euro notes and held one of them forward, just out of Göllner's reach.

"I need a name for the first fifty. Details of the transaction get you the second fifty."

Göllner fidgeted and narrowed his eyes.

"There isn't a name, as such. Those fellows never gave them. They worked in codes and aliases, a bunch of cocky young boys playing at spies, like *Emil and the Detectives*."

The skin prickled at the back of Nat's neck. He knew exactly where this was going, and he waved the euro note like a flag of victory.

"Fifty for the code name. Fifty more for the particulars."

"Icarus."

A wrinkled hand snatched the bill with surprising speed, but Nat didn't mind at all. He was too preoccupied imagining the young Gordon Wolfe trooping between the fallen bricks of bombed-out Berlin to track down stray rats like Göllner.

"Icarus was an American, correct?"

Göllner nodded.

"Describe him." Nat handed over the second fifty.

"He walked with a limp. A war wound. Wore a bomber jacket. One of those bastards who'd blown this place to cinders. He was working for the OSS, part of their 'White German' operation. I know more about him, too, but that will also cost you."

Nat wondered what that meant, but he didn't have enough cash on hand to find out. Not yet, anyway. Besides, the transcript was more important. He was quite familiar with the White German operation. It was a Dulles pet project during the occupation, and his staff had begun laying the groundwork in Switzerland. Its object was to identify German clergymen, professors, businessmen, politicians, and scientists who were untainted enough to form a core leadership for a new non-communist Germany. If you happened to be versed in the nascent fields of rocketry or nuclear physics, your chances of inclusion were even better, even if a little cleaning was required first.

"There was no way I was going to make the grade," Göllner said, "but Icarus said his handlers wanted to know if Bauer did. So I gave him what I had."

"Sold it, you mean."

Göllner shrugged.

"It was a seller's market. Between them and the Russians, everyone was choosing from their lists of favorite Germans, and of course both sides enjoyed pissing on their rivals' choices. Meaning sometimes they had to clean the piss off a few of their own."

"And you think Icarus was cleaning the piss off Bauer?"

"Of course."

"So you sold him the copy but still kept another one for yourself."

"In case the Russians ever came calling."

"Did they?"

"No. But now you're here. I'm just as happy to do business with another American."

"This first transaction, where did it take place?"

"This very room."

The hairs on his neck rose again. Who needed spirits when you had this kind of proximity? The scuffed floor, the plaster walls, the view of the park through the old window—they were probably virtually the same as when Gordon had come. Even Nat's chair was old enough that Gordon might have used it.

"It was a respectable building then," Göllner said. "No Turks. Just a lot of Germans without enough to eat. War widows. People who knew how to earn an honest living."

Yes, an honest living. Like interrogating people to within an inch of their lives and then turning a profit from the transcripts, selling dirt on your countrymen for ten thousand euros a pop. Nat wondered how many other transcripts Göllner had peddled.

"What did Icarus pay for this document?"

"The most valuable thing he had to offer. A new identity."

"That's how you became Hans Mannheim?"

"There were a lot of people looking for that fellow named Göllner. Some of them were fairly important. I decided Göllner would be better off dead, figuratively speaking, so Icarus agreed to make him go away."

"And what did Icarus say, once he'd seen the transcript?"

"No more. Not until I have received full payment for the transcript."

"How soon can you have it?"

"Tomorrow. Sixteen hundred hours. And do not try to follow me to it. I am old, but I still remember my training, and I still have friends."

"Sixteen hundred hours, then. I'll be here."

"One other thing. Two of you came in downstairs. Who's the other one?"

Now how the hell did he know that?

"A colleague. She's waiting on the landing."

"If it's that obnoxious hippie woman from the Free University, then

I know how you found out my name. Bring her with you tomorrow. I have been avoiding her for two years, but now there is some information I want from her. It's mandatory, part of my price. People have been poking around here lately, and I think she may be responsible."

"What kind of people?"

"Tomorrow. Just bring her."

Berta was waiting just outside the door. The music from next door was still loud enough that she couldn't have overheard their conversation, even with her ear to the keyhole. Just as well. He had already decided not to tell her about Gordon's visit in 1945.

"Success?" she asked.

He glanced back, wondering if Göllner was watching through the peephole.

"Outside."

Nat checked the building entrance for a security camera but didn't find one. Maybe Göllner had been watching from his window.

"Well?" she asked.

"He'll have a copy of the transcript tomorrow at four. He wants ten thousand euros."

"Greedy bastard!"

"If it's everything he claims, it will be worth it. He says three people lost their lives as a result. I'm assuming he was referring to members of the Berlin White Rose."

"Only three?"

"Isn't that enough for you?"

Then he realized what she meant. Her Plötzensee fact sheet listed four fatalities. But one had simply been listed as "killed." Göllner must have been referring to the executions. Of course, Nat couldn't make that point, nor could Berta make hers, without either of them revealing their deception.

"Where will we get ten thousand euros?" she asked.

"I'm betting he'll settle for half as a down payment."

"But even five thousand is a lot. For me, anyway."

"I'll take out a cash advance on my plastic. It'll probably max out my credit cards, so you're welcome to chip in. Especially if you want to share the material."

Her mouth dropped in surprise.

"You're as bad as him," she said. "I'll have to check with my bank."

"Maybe we should take care of that now, separately. We could probably use an afternoon off from each other. We can meet tonight back at the hotel. Deal?"

Berta gave him a searching look, but nodded. She seemed a little hurt, and it bothered him until he recalled what Willis Turner had said. She turned on her heel and strolled away without a further word. Nat watched her for a block. Then he turned in the opposite direction, rounded the nearest corner, and hailed a cab.

"The Free University in Dahlem," he said. "History Department, on Koserstrasse."

It was time to find out more about the real Berta Heinkel.

TWENTY

Professor Christian Hermann was an old acquaintance of Nat's. They crossed paths at least once a year at some conference or another, and Hermann was always good for a beer and a few witty stories of his travels in Eastern Europe, where he had made a name for himself by plumbing state archives for captured Nazi documents. Some of his discoveries had been under lock and key for decades behind the Iron Curtain.

Hermann's longtime obsession, however, was his search for the last original manuscript of Hitler's sequel to *Mein Kampf.* Most people didn't even know Hitler wrote a sequel, nor would they want to read it. But Hermann had been captivated by the idea of finding the *Zweites Buch* ever since learning that the first manuscript, discovered in 1958, was a collation of typescript and carbon copies, meaning that a second must also exist.

He had been searching for fourteen years. His operative theory was that it had ended up at the Berghof, Hitler's mountaintop getaway, and that an American GI must have walked off with it when the troops looted the place in the spring of '45. This meant he often sought out U.S. veterans, and Nat had helped arrange introductions to plenty of skeptical old men. As a result, Hermann was always willing to lend a hand, and when Nat phoned from the taxi the professor urged him to come by at once.

"You'll have to press the buzzer downstairs. Classes are out, and I'm the only one here. Considering it's a Friday you were lucky to catch me at all."

The history department was in a frumpy stucco building in a leafy suburb. Nat scanned the dozens of posters in the foyer advertising upcoming symposia. No one could talk a subject to death like the Germans, leaving you in a funk of earnestness that could linger for days. He was disheartened to see that the topic of the Third Reich wasn't mentioned on a single item. He had first noted this trend in the wake of 1995, following a six-year orgy of fiftieth-anniversary commemorations of the war. Having dutifully immersed themselves, the Germans then seemed to shake off the era like a wet dog taking shelter from the storm. And by then, of course, a hot new topic had come along—the deadly legacy of the Stasi, and East Germany's security state—fresh corpses, more readily exhumed, not to mention that West Germans could participate in the discussion guilt free.

The buzzer sounded. Nat took the stairs. Christian Hermann was waiting with a cold pilsner.

"Turnbull! A perfect surprise. The department head is away, so we can drink all we like as long as we hide the empties. But you should have given me more warning. I'm preparing for a trip to Riga in the morning, so I can't even treat you to dinner."

"I'm lucky to be here at all, considering the weird little errand I'm on. It's for a law enforcement client, so it's not exactly pure research."

Hermann frowned. He would never consider taking a government assignment. Hardly surprising for someone who studied his country's most notorious regime.

"I'm not sure what my department head would find more objectionable. These beers or the idea that I'm helping a representative of George W. Bush."

"That's not where I need your help. I want advice on one of your colleagues."

"From the Free University?"

"Yes. Berta Heinkel."

Hermann raised his eyebrows and set his beer down on a student's paper.

"My God. Are you mixed up with her romantically or professionally?"

"The latter."

"They sometimes go together. That's why I asked."

"Which one usually produces worse results?"

"Ha! Good question. Although without firsthand experience I cannot say for sure."

"How is she regarded professionally?"

"If you had asked me two years ago, I would have given her the highest marks. She is intelligent, a strong researcher. And dogged, very determined. Sound, too. Never sloppy in her methods. Or didn't used to be. She was also teaching then, and students liked her."

"What happened?"

"That's what we'd all like to know. Frankly, I think she began to get a little obsessed. All of this White Rose business, do you know about it?"

"Oh, yes."

"I hope that's not why you're in Berlin. The further mythologizing of Hans and Sophie Scholl, student angel pamphleteers of Munich? Pardon my disrespect, but what a crock. Admirable, yes, but let's not kid ourselves about their zero impact."

"You're preaching to the choir, Christian. But my impression was that Berta has been on this White Rose hunt for ages, not just a few years."

"It was always her specialty. But only in the last year or two did she let it take over her life. She began missing appointments, blowing off meetings. There was some kind of eating disorder, too. A colleague used to find her vomiting in the women's room."

"Jesus."

"Her teaching declined. They replaced her at midterm in two courses. Her research suffered, too. Anything that didn't have to do with the Berlin White Rose, poof, it might as well not have existed. Some colleagues suspected drugs, but I think her only addiction was this quest, because that was also when the complaints began to come in."

"Complaints?"

"Of harassment, stalking even. Kurt Bauer, the big industrialist, I'm sure you've heard of his company. Your shaver probably has his name on it."

"Or my latest shipment of heavy water."

Hermann laughed.

"Yes, that too." Then he eyed Nat carefully. "Government work, you said?"

"Let's just say I have an understanding with regard to reimbursement and a rough arrangement on how to share any results."

"Your government has never liked Kurt. Mine's not keen on him, either. His dabbling in nuclear materials made everyone nervous. Although I gather Pakistan quite likes him. Is this what concerns you, or are your interests confined to your usual area?"

"I'm afraid it's nothing I can discuss, Christian."

"But you're working with Berta, which must also mean the White Rose. Interesting."

"You said there were complaints. From Bauer himself?"

"His lawyers. People like Bauer never file their own complaints. A court issued some sort of restraining order."

"You're kidding."

"An exclusion zone, one hundred meters."

That would explain Berta's interest in long-lens photography.

"Did it stop her?"

"His lawyers said it didn't, although at least she no longer rang his doorbell or staked out his parking space. But he wasn't the only one who took her to court."

"There were others?"

"A White Rose survivor in Duisberg, some old Gestapo people, even a few Americans who served with the occupation forces. Come on, you really haven't heard about this?"

"It's not like she'd be eager to tell me."

"No, I mean from your colleagues at Wightman. One of her targets was Gordon Wolfe, your very own . . . well, whatever you'd call him after he, uh . . ."

"He was my mentor. It's still okay to say it. We made our peace, just before he died."

"Died? Gordon's dead?"

"A week ago. His heart."

"I had no idea. My condolences."

"Thanks. But Gordon was one of the complainants?"

"Oh, yes. He said she had followed him for days at a time."

"Good Lord."

"Yes. Not very smart, making people think we're a bunch of lunatics here. Still, she might have weathered the storm if it hadn't been for the Stasi file."

"The *what*?"

Hermann nodded glumly.

"I am afraid so. Berta was an informant."

Nat's heart sank. In latter-day Germany there were few things more damning, or more fatal professionally, than being outed as an informant for the East German secret police. It was a catastrophe, the sort of revelation that might explain a lot—bulimia, stalking, obsession—all her possible pathologies. But even then Nat couldn't quite believe it.

"How is that possible? She was fifteen when the Wall came down."

"I know. That's what made her case so remarkable."

"The good Pioneer," Nat mumbled.

"Excuse me?"

"She told me about her childhood. Laughed about what a good little Commie she was."

"Apparently that included spying on her parents."

"She informed on her *family?*"

"With the best of intentions, of course. Or that was her defense. Trying to reform them, protect them from the authorities. You know, there is a summary of it around here somewhere. One of the department gossips, Professor Schneider, finagled a look at the report and did a synopsis, which she distributed to all our mail slots."

"How sweet of her."

"Yes. Heaven help anyone who gets in Schneider's way. I think Berta bedded one of her boyfriends. Now where did I put that thing?"

Hermann yanked open a drawer. Papers flew out like cloth snakes from a clown jar.

"Ah. There it is."

It was crumpled, and stained with coffee rings, but Nat spotted Berta's name.

"Yes," Hermann said, reading it over. "Mostly family members. Schneider did us the service of listing them, although she was of course polite enough to substitute initials for the forenames. 'To protect their identity,' she said. Here, take a look."

Nat checked the names first:

F. Heinkel, father.
J. Heinkel, mother.
H. Heinkel, grandmother.
L. Hartz, family friend.

"Apparently she never reported anything major," Hermann said.
" 'Daddy criticized Chairman Honecker at dinner.' That sort of rot.

The lovely Frau Schneider claimed Berta's grandmother suffered genuine repercussions, but she never dug up the details. Not for lack of trying, I'm sure."

"Berta said she was quite fond of her grandmother."

"All the more reason to keep her on the straight and narrow, then. Love does strange things to people, Turnbull, especially in the German state of mind."

"Spoken like a true German."

Hermann smiled crookedly.

"It is my patriotic duty as a historian to speak poorly of our national character."

"Pretty easy to do so in Berta's case. How did this come to light?"

"An anonymous letter to the department chair. A photocopy of her file was enclosed."

"You think Bauer sent it?"

"It's what everyone suspects. But she already knew the file existed. She told Schneider she had gone to see it herself, a year earlier."

"Isn't that about the time she went off the deep end?"

"Yes. I suppose she realized it would eventually become public."

Maybe, Nat thought. Or maybe the file's contents, rather than its mere existence, sent her into a spiral.

"Can I copy this?"

"Keep it. I should have thrown it away ages ago."

Nat could request the whole file if he wanted. Stasi records were stored right across town. But there was no guarantee he would be allowed to see it. Bauer certainly shouldn't have qualified, but people like him always found a way around the rules. Even if Nat got permission, he would have to wait weeks, even months. More to the point, it was a sideshow. Gordon Wolfe and Kurt Bauer were still the main event.

"So tell me, Turnbull. How on earth did you get mixed up with Berta Heinkel?"

"By reading her credentials on your goddamned Web site, for one thing."

"Oh, dear. We should fix that. Although officially she is still employed. You know how slowly these things go, and the chairman has managed to keep everything out of the papers. Of course, that will change once the firing becomes final. They've scheduled disciplinary hearings, but she has petitioned for delays. Health reasons, she claimed."

"Mental, no doubt."

Hermann laughed, spluttering beer onto his shirt front.

"Sorry. I know it isn't funny. In fact, it has pretty much ruined her. She lost her office, even her apartment. One of those nice renovations in Prenzlauer Berg. Last I heard, she had moved in with a friend."

No wonder she had insisted on a hotel. She must be financing everything with maxed-out plastic. He felt bad for asking her to chip in on the payment to Göllner.

"Well, I guess it's a good thing I stopped by."

"You don't look it."

"I didn't say I was happy. But I needed to know."

"That's always our downfall, isn't it? Our need to know?"

Hermann clinked his bottle to Nat's and they downed the dregs, appropriately bitter.

"I must pack," Hermann said. "I am taking my wife to dinner. A peace offering. I had to cancel our weekend in Tuscany to make this trip to Riga."

"Let me guess. A fresh lead on the *Zweites Buch*?"

"Like I said. Our downfall. Can I drop you somewhere?"

"No, thanks. I walked from the U-Bahn. Frankly, right now I could use the air."

It was dark when they left the building. Nat watched the taillights of Hermann's Opel disappear. A breeze carried the scent of pine needles, and the streets and sidewalks were empty. He supposed he should call Holland with an update, but he decided that first he would call Karen.

So much to tell her, especially about Berta, which he knew was her main subject of interest anyway. Karen would want poetry, of course, as part of his presentation. But somehow even the brooding lines of Dickinson weren't nearly broad or flexible enough to enfold Berta's dark complexities. How, indeed, could he explain to an impressionable girl of eighteen the ways in which a surveillance state could swallow your entire childhood?

He was punching in the number when he heard footsteps approaching from behind. Something about their urgency made him reconsider the call. No sense being overheard.

Nat kept walking, but the footsteps drew nearer. He glanced over his shoulder, expecting to see a jogger. Instead, it was a thin figure in a leather jacket. No reason to panic, but he walked faster. The footsteps did, too, moving closer. Nat broke into a trot, feeling silly yet frightened. Scuffing soles told him his pursuer was still gaining.

Nat lengthened his stride and lowered his head, going all out. By then he could hear labored breathing—closing, closing. A hand fell on his shoulder, and he cried out as the grip spun him around. They lost balance. Nat landed on his rump, his pursuer atop him. They grappled clumsily. Nat, in a panic, saw a stubbled face, dark eyes leering eagerly, the sharp scent of sweat and cologne. He tried rolling free, but a huge hand pinned his chest, and a second thrust forward with a flash of metal lit by the streetlamp.

He wrenched sideways just enough to avoid a blow to the chest, but the blade tore his sleeve and sliced open his forearm, a line of heat. The attacker again raised the knife just as light exploded from a nearby hedge with a bright yellow flash and an unearthly bark—once, twice. His attacker cried out and fell away onto the sidewalk, gurgling as if he were choking. Nat scuttled crablike into the dewy grass, palms against pine needles.

Just as a sense of deliverance was sinking in, another set of hands clamped his shoulders, and a gruff voice whispered in Berliner German, "Don't make a move," while a second man gripped his forearms and pulled him roughly to his feet.

"What's happening?"

"Quiet! Stay still!" The grip around his arms tightened.

Both men were dressed in dark clothes. Two more rushed forward from the shadows, one of them holstering a pistol in his jacket. All four wore gloves. Down on the sidewalk, his attacker lay still in a spreading pool of blood.

Seemingly from nowhere, a black Mercedes pulled to the curb with its lights off, followed closely by a second. The man behind him briskly patted Nat down from head to toe. The doors of the first car opened and the driver rasped, "Put him in. Let's go."

"Will someone just tell me what the hell's going on?" Nat shouted.

The man behind him clamped a gloved palm over Nat's mouth.

"Not another word!" he whispered harshly. "Get in the car. No struggling unless you want to end up like the other one." He twisted Nat's arm to show he meant business.

"Ow! Easy!"

They shoved him onto the backseat and piled in after him.

"Where are you taking me? Are you the police?"

"No questions."

The driver started the engine, still no headlights. Nat twisted around for a view through the smoked windows and saw the body being loaded into the second car while someone else sluiced water onto the sidewalk to wash away the blood.

The whole thing had lasted no more than a minute or two, and the manpower and hardware employed were, in themselves, impressive— eight men in dark clothes and gloves, two unmarked cars, a gun with a silencer. Result: one man dead, a second captured, both wiped from the scene like fingerprints from a doorknob.

The car pulled away smoothly. He was flanked on both sides, and there were two men up front. No one said a word. By now Nat assumed that the initial assailant must have been a member of Holland's "competition," meaning he was from Iran or Syria. If so, then who were these people? And why the need for so much tidiness? More to the point, who would be capable of orchestrating it?

The answer seemed obvious. The same sort of fellow who could illegally obtain a Stasi file, of course. Kurt Bauer. No wonder the scene had unfolded with such industrial precision. Build a better shaver. Construct a neater abduction. It was all in the engineering.

After a block the driver switched on the headlights. The other car wasn't following. Maybe Nat was going to be all right. He took a deep breath and realized he was shaking.

"Can someone tell me where we're going?"

"Take care of him!" the driver barked, and before Nat could respond a hood came down over his head. A drawstring was cinched tight at the neck, and the darkness was complete. When he reached up to loosen it, someone slapped his hands away.

"Cuffs!" the driver said.

They wrenched his wrists behind him and tightly clamped a pair of handcuffs on them.

"C'mon! What is this?"

No one answered.

His breath was warm against the heavy fabric, which smelled of panic and old sweat. Nothing like the stench of fear to set your mind at ease. He thought of Karen, and how he should have called her earlier, and he wondered how long before he would talk to her again, if ever. She might even be meeting the same fate. Maybe these people were rounding up everyone, everywhere. If only he had stayed in contact with Holland, perhaps none of this would have happened. Fear and panic made him shout again.

"Where are you taking me!" He was embarrassed by the strangled tone, so he repeated it, this time trying to master his emotions. "I said, where are you taking me?"

Still nothing. Just the maddening hum of German engineering in full trim as the Mercedes leaned into a curve, purring like a great cat that has eaten its fill. He spent a few seconds trying to calm down, wondering how he might free himself. Fat chance, with all these people around him. For a while he tried to keep track of their course, but he had already lost count of the turns, and the hood kept him from even detecting the strobe of passing streetlamps. His arm stung, and blood was seeping onto his torn sleeve.

The driver swung the wheel sharply left, and the engine echoed as if they had just entered a tunnel. Nat's stomach told him they were plunging downhill, below street level. The springs sagged as they hit a speed bump and went deeper into a series of right turns—three, four, five, then more for at least a minute longer until they stopped.

By then they must have been several stories underground, and when a door opened he detected the bunkerlike smell of damp concrete. The engine shut off. More doors opened. Whatever they were planning to do, he sensed it was about to happen.

"Get him out," a voice said sternly from outside the car. "Quickly."

Maybe they would take off the hood and all would be revealed. Bauer himself would be there, seated in a big swivel chair like some caricature of a tycoon gone mad. He would puff a cigar and scold Nat for reckless research. Then he would hand over a folder of forged documents, his version of setting the record straight, and the thugs would unlock the cuffs and send Nat on his way, chastened but intact.

But no. The hood stayed on. His assailants gripped him tightly as they climbed from the car.

"Bring him here," the voice commanded. "This is where we get rid of him."

Not at all what he wanted to hear. Yet, for all his dread and panic and thundering pulse, part of him wasn't a bit surprised. Hadn't he predicted as much for years, in class after class, albeit with a glibness totally inappropriate to the current moment? And as the men yanked him forward, Nat's own words returned to him like a prophetic taunt:

"History plays for keeps, and so do I."

TWENTY-ONE

Berlin—February 18, 1943

THE SHRILL CRY of a police whistle pursued them down Uhlandstrasse. Thank God for the blackout, or they would have been easy prey as they ran down the sidewalk.

"There's a U-Bahn station coming up," Kurt hissed in the dark. Liesl and Hannelore were barely keeping pace. They rounded the corner and half stumbled down the steps of the station as the whistle sounded again.

"Hurry!" Liesl shouted.

Hannelore, predictably, had fallen farther behind, but when they reached the platform Kurt saw that luck was with them. A train lay waiting, rumbling like an animal ready to pounce. They clambered aboard just as a harsh voice shouted from the stairway.

"Halt! Polizei!"

Luckily, the subway driver either didn't hear or was more worried about his timetable, because the doors jolted shut and the train lurched forward. With a rising moan it was soon hurtling into the tunnel. Kurt saw a fleeting image of a huffing policeman arriving on the platform with two black-clad Gestapo officers in his wake. Then, darkness, and the empty clatter of the tracks. He exhaled loudly and sagged forward in his seat. Sweat dripped from his nose onto the slatted wooden floor. His body stank, but so did everyone else's these days. Between the ban on weekday bathing and the shortage of decent soap, every railcar smelled like a sweatshop.

Kurt looked across the aisle. Hannelore had of course taken the seat next to Liesl. Lately, Kurt and Hannelore seemed to be competing every day for Liesl's time and attention. But at the moment he was angrier at Hannelore's slowness.

The occasion for their close call was the fourth meeting of the Berlin White Rose. It was supposed to have been the first meeting to produce tangible results. Kurt had finally been able to steal a boxful of paper from his father's offices. Eight full reams—four thousand sheets in all. Given the regime's mania over seditious literature, a cache like that was as valuable as diamonds.

White Rose pamphlets out of Munich had been spreading across the country in recent weeks, and the local Gestapo was in a frenzy to keep the material out of Berlin. Anti-Nazi graffiti that appeared by night was gone by morning. Their group had decided that only an explosion of locally produced pamphlets could overcome such diligence.

Helmut Hartert had drafted their first message and was standing by with his printing press. The fourth meeting had been called to vote on the final wording. Then Kurt was supposed to hand over the paper so that the printing could begin.

He had lugged his precious cargo up five flights of stairs to the site—an empty loft above an exclusive dress shop. Christoph Klemm had chosen the place after a week of scouting. The shop, owned by his uncle, had been shuttered by the Propaganda Ministry after Goebbels deemed luxury items an affront to the long-suffering troops.

It was a relief to get rid of the paper, especially after the risks Kurt had taken to acquire it—swiping his father's keys from a pants pocket long enough to make a wax impression, getting a set of copies made by a shady old Bolshevik in a Kreuzberg tenement, dodging the night watchman and his snarling dog, lugging the damn box through the dark along the rat-infested wharves of the Hohenzollern Canal, and, finally, hauling the dangerous cargo to the meeting aboard the S-Bahn.

But now it had come to nothing. The meeting had been under way for only half an hour when the excitable Dieter, posted as a rooftop lookout, cried out from above:

"Polizei! Five of them, and they're coming up!"

Fortunately, Christoph had devised elaborate contingency plans for just such an emergency, although the box of precious paper had to be abandoned. They climbed to the roof to make a breathtaking crossing of the back alley to a neighboring building, on a span of stout but wobbly beams. To Kurt, the blackness below seemed bottomless, especially with the cold wind rushing up his trouser legs. He was surprised no one fell.

Christoph then pulled in the planks behind them while everyone clambered down the stairs of the rear building. This allowed them to emerge into the streets one block over from where the cops were still trudging upstairs and shouting orders.

They scattered in twos and threes, but even then the police had nearly caught his threesome. Thank goodness Kurt had removed everything from the box of paper that might have identified its source. With his sister's wedding still on hold, his father was already nervous enough about official scrutiny without being linked to this.

Kurt looked across the subway car to offer Liesl a smile, but she didn't notice. She seemed badly shaken. Her eyes were huge, as if the night's drama had come as a complete shock. He fought back a surge of anger. "What did you expect?" he wanted to shout. "This is not a game. This is exactly what we bargained for!"

Just as quickly the thought disappeared, and he wanted to hold and protect her. But he couldn't, of course, with Hannelore in the way. Liesl leaned across the aisle to speak. Hannelore and he bent forward to listen. Their three heads nearly touched.

"What do you think happened tonight?" Liesl whispered. "Were we betrayed?"

"No one in our group has the guts to betray us," Hannelore said scornfully.

No one but her, she meant. She had often criticized their timid progress.

"Dieter said something to me just before the meeting, about one of the neighbors acting suspicious," Liesl said. "He said someone from next door was prowling around outside. Maybe they heard us and thought we were thieves, looting the dress shop."

"Dieter," Kurt said with disdain. "He should have told everyone."

Hannelore nodded. Dieter was one of the few subjects they agreed on.

They broke their huddle and sat up again, beginning to relax. That was when Kurt noticed a propaganda poster just above Hannelore's seat. It featured the ubiquitous duo of loose-lipped troublemakers, Frau Knoterich and Herr Bramsig. The Frau's uncanny resemblance

to Hannelore, along with his giddiness over their narrow escape, pro-
voked a sudden burst of nervous laughter.

"How can you possibly find this funny?" Hannelore whispered.
"We barely made it."

The heads of a few passengers turned their way.

"Sorry. It's just that—" No, he'd better not.

"Well?" A challenging tone, as irritating as ever, so he took the
plunge.

"It's the poster above your head. I couldn't help but note the resemblance."

Hannelore turned to look. Unfortunately, so did Liesl. As if that
weren't bad enough, a foul-smelling old man seated near Kurt began
laughing in a succession of wheezes.

"You're right!" the fellow exclaimed. "She *is* Frau Knoterich. It's
her doppelgänger!"

Liesl must have also been giddy, because to Kurt's amazement she,
too, laughed.

Hannelore was outraged, but the reddening of her cheeks only
sharpened the resemblance, which sent the old man into a fresh gale of
laughter. As the subway pulled into the next stop she stood angrily and
flung open the doors.

"You two," she said loudly, "can just ride home with all the Nazis!"

The other riders turned away in shocked silence as she disappeared
across the platform. The old man stood nervously and shuffled to
another seat. When the car was under way again, no one spoke, which
made the two-minute ride to the next stop seem more like ten. Liesl
and Kurt scampered out of the car, and to their relief no one followed.
As soon as the train departed they burst into laughter and fell into each
other's arms.

"My God, but that was close," Liesl said. "Of all things for you to
think of at a time like that. Frau Knoterich! What made it worse was
that the old guy next to you looked like Herr Bramsig. I felt terrible for
Hannelore, but I couldn't help myself."

"Oh, she'll get over it."

"Yes, but will she get over you?"

"So you've noticed she doesn't like me?"

"And also that the feeling is mutual. Even at the meetings you never
agree. What's wrong with you two? Don't we all want the same thing?"

Yes, Kurt thought. We all want Liesl. And for now, at least, he had her to himself.

Twenty minutes later they reached their bicycles and pedaled off to Liesl's house. On arrival Kurt discovered more good fortune. Liesl's parents were still away, visiting friends. Liesl's sister was gone, too. A night that had careened so close to disaster suddenly seemed full of promise. Such were the fortunes of wartime, Kurt supposed. Nothing was certain. Luck was all.

When Liesl turned on the light, yet another pleasant surprise was revealed.

"Look!" she cried. "Chocolate!"

It was true. An entire bar, perhaps half a pound, poking from butcher paper with only a corner missing. You could already smell it, like something from another era.

"My mother said she'd have a surprise for us, but this is amazing."

"I haven't had any chocolate since . . ." Kurt paused.

"Since when?" she asked.

He had been about to say, "since December," when his father and he had attended yet another holiday party at the Stuckarts' house. But he didn't want her to know that he still kept in touch with Erich. Did she really expect him to give up everything from his past life? Besides, if he changed his habits too much, people would get suspicious. He was sneaking around enough as it was. Tonight his parents thought he was seeing a mindless Heinz Ruhmann comedy at the Ufa-Palast, on a date with Heidi Falken, whom he hadn't spoken to in ages.

"Oh, I don't know. A long time."

"Mmmm," she said, taking the tiniest of bites. "Here."

She broke off another piece and held it out. He opened his mouth, and she placed it on his tongue. Kurt licked a bit of melted chocolate from her fingertips, and she smiled. He was about to follow up with a kiss, but she abruptly backed away and refolded the butcher paper.

"We should save it. We can divide it when everyone else is home."

Her voice was quieter, and he could tell she was still a little fragile. Understandable. One stumble and they would have all been sitting in Gestapo interrogation cells by now, down in the basement on Prinz-Albrecht-Strasse.

"How 'bout some music?" he said, flipping on the radio.

Maybe that would calm her down. With any luck the stations wouldn't be playing the nationalist dreck that had recently dominated the airwaves. Three days of national mourning had followed the announcement two weeks ago of the German surrender at Stalingrad, and ever since then the radio had played little more than dirges and marching songs. And of course there was never any jazz or swing, not the real stuff, just the counterfeit local version that had been approved for public consumption. Lately everyone seemed too cowed to show any joy, lest some officious snoop decide you weren't "supporting the troops" in a suitably serious manner.

But there was no music tonight, only a familiar hectoring voice backed by an obliging crowd. It was Goebbels, shouting something about the new plan for victory in the east.

"So much for that idea," Kurt said, reaching for the Off switch.

"No, wait. I want to hear it. We need to know what he's up to. Please."

Well, that would certainly end his chances for the evening, Kurt thought. Nothing quite like the venom of the Cripple to get a girl out of the mood. He sighed and took a seat, sagging onto the Folkertses' leather couch, which smelled like her father's pipe tobacco. At least the chocolate was good. The taste lingered sweetly on his tongue.

"Did you hear that?" she hooted scornfully. "He said we should all try to emulate Frederick the Great, right after saying that by the end of the Third Silesian War he was fifty-one years old, had no teeth, suffered from gout, and was tortured by a thousand pains. Well, that should really inspire the masses."

The problem was that the masses *did* sound inspired—over the radio, anyway. Kurt wondered who was in the audience. Handpicked Party loyalists, perhaps, although there sure were a lot of them. As if in answer to Kurt's question, Goebbels began describing the crowd gathered at his feet.

I see before me a cross-section of the whole German people in the best sense of the word! In front of me are rows of wounded German soldiers from the eastern front, missing legs and arms—

"Then how are they clapping?" Liesl said derisively.

Behind them are armaments workers from Berlin tank factories—

"Good God," Kurt said. "This must have been what they were talking about the other day at the office. An order came in to send at least a hundred workers to the Sportspalast tonight. That's them you're hearing—Bauer employees, screaming their lungs out. Too bad they didn't send some of the Poles instead. They'd have eaten him alive."

"Your dad's using captured Poles?"

"Czechs, too. A whole boxcar arrived just the other day. Jews, mostly. Sticks and bones. Some didn't even make it off the train, and they smelled like an outhouse. I wonder where they sleep at night, because it's not like we have anyplace handy."

"Where *do* they go?"

"A government compound, I guess. Some sort of barracks. Who knows?"

"It's probably horrible. You should find out. Do something about it."

"Liesl, not even my dad can tell Speer and Sauckel what to do with guest workers."

" 'Guest workers.' You make it sound like they're glad to be invited."

"How do you know they aren't? Have you seen the newsreels from Warsaw? There's nothing left of the place."

She shook her head, but said nothing more, apparently unwilling to argue the point. Or maybe she was just exhausted, because she sagged against him on the leather cushions. The warmth and pressure of her body produced an immediate reaction. An erection stiffened against his trousers.

"Listen to him now," she said.

The Cripple had raised his voice to a tumult. Kurt could easily picture the wiry man's emphatic gestures, elbows thrust out at right angles as he waved his forefinger like the barrel of a Luger. It might have all been silly and melodramatic if not for the crowd, which was lapping it up, roaring a huge "Ja!" at every command. He was exhorting them with a series of questions now, appealing to their deepest need for vengeance.

I ask you, do you want total war? If necessary, do you want a war more total and radical than anything that we can even imagine today?

"Ja!"

Even Kurt almost shivered. But given what they had endured earlier that evening, the worst moment came a few seconds later.

Do you agree that those who harm the war effort should lose their heads?

"Ja!"

They sounded like they meant it. Liesl pressed closer and turned her face to his.

"I'm scared, Kurt. And the worst part is, I'm not sure I will ever stop being scared. Not after tonight."

"It will be better in the morning," he said, stroking her hair. "It always is. We'll go for a walk in the Grunewald. Enjoy some of that fake sunshine you see on the tree bark."

She shook her head, as if that was no good at all.

"Sometimes I think we'll never even survive the year. Not just us. Everyone. Either the police will take us away or some bomb will blow us all to pieces."

His arms were around her now, and her face rose to his.

"Tell me that if they ever come for me you will do everything you can to save me," she said. "Promise me."

"Of course I will. I promise."

"And that should be true for your family as well. Your sister. Your mother and father. We must all do everything in our power to save each other from the madmen. No matter what happens, no matter what the risk."

Her eyes pleaded, on the verge of tears. Her emotions had reached a peak, and they were alone. No parents. No Hannelore. Just the two of them pressed together on the soft leather couch in the dim glow of a single lamp. He kissed her, and she responded with urgency. And when, a few moments later, he slipped his hands beneath her sweater she didn't resist as she had in the past. Instead, she pulled his shirttail from his trousers and slid her own hands up his back, pressing closer.

Kurt was not particularly experienced in these matters. The closest he had come before to sexual conquest had been in the backseat of Erich's car with a girl from their school who was said to be available to all comers, although she had only let Kurt briefly slide his hands to the tops of her thighs.

But at that moment with Liesl experience was no longer necessary, because matters took on a momentum of their own. They moved as if racing against time, one step leading to the next until his pants were off, and then her undergarments. Then he was climbing atop her, groping for position. Her hand guided him into place as she stared up at him, the vow they had made still evident in her eyes. Life or death, and this was their choice.

His movements were a little awkward at first. And just when it was seeming perfectly natural and comfortable, it ended all too quickly. But that, too, was okay, because she smiled and ran a finger down his chest, then softly kissed his lips, his nose, his eyelids. It was almost holy, a consecration of their promise.

"I am glad," she whispered. "Glad that we did this."

The radio had moved on to a marching song, with a drumbeat like the tramping of a thousand boots. They lay still, as if to let this army pass by their hiding place, and when the song was over she said again, "I am glad we did this."

"I am, too."

Outside, the sound of laughter. Cheerful voices were approaching up the sidewalk.

"My parents!" she cried.

She grabbed her clothes and ran for the bathroom. Kurt buttoned his shirt and pulled up his trousers. Whoever it was had stopped, even though the chatter continued. Of course. They had gone out with neighbors and were now saying good-bye. It gave him just enough time to cram his shirttail in and buckle his belt. His socks were still on, and he jammed his shoes on just as the door opened. Liesl's father gave him a puzzled look.

"Where is Liesl?"

"She's, uh, in the back. She should be right out."

Liesl's mother smiled and said hello, although her father still seemed wary. He had clearly been brought up short by the idea that Kurt and Liesl had been here alone. Thank goodness everyone stank these days, enough to cover all the telltale smells. And thank goodness the lights were low, so that they couldn't see the flush of his face.

"Hi, Mom. Hi, Dad." Liesl appeared, smiling, hair combed. "How was your evening?"

"Ah, too much wine," her mother said, "but that's a nice problem for a change."

She was obviously too jolly to notice anything untoward, although Liesl's father was now looking everywhere, eyes darting, as if studying the evidence.

"Kurt and I just got back," Liesl said. "But he can only stay long enough for a bite of chocolate. We both took a little nibble right when we came in."

"That's what it's here for, so please do. Just don't ask me how much I paid for it while your father is in the room."

This finally coaxed a smile from the man, and Kurt breathed easier. Two close calls in one night. But the earlier episode made this one feel like a lark.

Liesl walked him outside, and rose on her toes to kiss him good-bye. Such a momentous day, and now the perfect ending—an embrace beneath the sheltering pines. He searched her face in the glow from the window. Was there a touch of regret? Perhaps. But there was also an unmistakable freshness, the excitement of new territory, a look that said there would be more time together just like this and no one could stop them.

The thought kept him content all the way home, even as he pedaled into a wintry headwind. There was a nervous moment when a pair of cops stopped him on Kantstrasse. But they were only checking identity papers, and by the time he reached Charlottenburg he was even toying with the idea of another raid on the office paper supply.

It was well past eleven o'clock, and Kurt expected he would have some explaining to do. Instead, he threw open the door to find everyone in the parlor, gathered in a tight circle that had the air of an emergency. His sister, Traudl, was sobbing, his father ashen. His mother's head was bowed, and her hands were folded in her lap.

"What's wrong?"

Reinhard shook his head.

"Everything," he said. "The SS people were here. From the Racial Office."

His father handed him a sheet of paper. It was some sort of genealogical chart with the words "Bauer Family" printed beneath a swastika.

"Your great-great-grandmother," his father explained. "On your mother's side."

Reinhard didn't say it disapprovingly, but Kurt's mother looked away in shame and wiped a tear from her eye, as if she had forfeited the right to let them fall.

"Tainted," she whispered. "My blood is tainted."

Kurt found it halfway across the page:

"Anna Goldfarb, Jew."

Born in Breslau, East Prussia, in 1826. She had married Karl Becker—his mother's maiden name was Becker—whose lineage otherwise contained nothing but Aryan heritage, all the way back to 1800. But none of that mattered now.

"What does this mean?" Kurt asked.

"What do you think?" Traudl shrieked. "The wedding is off! My life is ruined!"

She ran from the room and up the stairs. Her bedroom door slammed.

"What does this mean?" he asked again.

"I don't know yet," his father said. "But it's serious. We could lose everything."

"They can't. We're too vital to the war effort. Speer won't let them."

"Everything," his father repeated. "The worst part is, I saw it coming. Once they didn't answer after three months I knew they must have found something, but I wouldn't admit it to myself. I think that's one reason I started checking possibilities in Bern."

"Bern?" Kurt's mother asked. "In Switzerland?"

Kurt and his father exchanged glances.

"It's complicated," Reinhard said. "And meaningless. Now I'll never get another pass to travel."

Kurt was sorry to hear that. He had grudgingly warmed to the idea of contacting the Americans. And to his surprise his father had been making progress. Only a week ago Reinhard had returned from Bern to confide pridefully that he had been granted a personal audience with the much-heralded Mr. Dulles. The American had even assigned his father a code name, Magneto. Useless now, of course, if the family lost its factories.

And what of Liesl? Surely she wouldn't object to this Jewish connection, but her parents might. Even if they didn't, Kurt might now be sent away, or imprisoned. Would they sew a Star of David onto his clothes just for this? Worse still, what if the authorities now decided to dig further into their activities? Surely they would discover not only his connections to Bonhoeffer but also everything about the local cell of the White Rose. His father was right. This meant disaster.

Kurt was too agitated to sit and watch his parents stare blankly at the floor, so he went upstairs. Perhaps something could be done to stave off events, given all their connections. He stepped into the bathroom and splashed his face. Then he looked in the mirror, studying his features, searching for some sign of his Jewish blood. Could you tell? He turned in profile, wondering if he had become so inured to all the propaganda that he was now imagining things about the set of his eyes, the shape of his nose. Perhaps later tonight there would be a knock at the door, and his family would be transported to one of the resettlement camps that no one ever discussed. Board a train at Grunewald station, one of those long ones that always left full and returned empty. A one-way ticket east.

And what had he been doing up to now to stop such diabolical measures? Hardly anything, really. Risking his neck to steal paper, or to cast votes on the wording of a pamphlet. What good was a pamphlet in times like these? Once again, he had fallen back on the relative safety of mere words. "Easy grace," as Bonhoeffer had put it. There must be some stronger action he could take, not just for his family but for Liesl and him as well. He recalled her words from an hour ago: "We must all do everything in our power."

Then an idea occurred to him, striking in its simplicity: a one-man job, a bold operation with no need to rely on weak vessels like Dieter or unstable temperaments like Hannelore's. Lots of planning would be necessary, of course. But surely he could manage.

Then the doubts began leaking in. Costly sacrifices and trade-offs would be required, and none of them would come easily. Blood might even be spilled, perhaps by people he admired and respected. The price was too high. His conscience would never be able to bear the burden. He sighed, temporarily defeated.

Then he considered the consequences of doing nothing, and realized that the cost was even greater. This was what war demanded of people, he supposed. It thrust upon you unclean decisions with unclean results. The best you could hope for was to minimize the damage, to act before others decided matters for you.

So, with a dizzying sense of destiny buzzing in his temples, Kurt resolved to act while he still could, if only because this new idea offered the one possibility that most heartened and excited him: guaranteed survival for Liesl and him, as well as for his family and its business empire. Not only for the duration of the war but on into peacetime. Surely that would be enough to justify almost anything, especially when the alternative was doom for them all.

Fifteen days, he told himself. That would be his deadline. Fifteen days to either carry out this bold plan or come up with another course of action. Either way, he was now grimly certain that the coming weeks would define him as a man from that point onward.

Kurt stared defiantly into the mirror, as if daring himself to raise an objection.

TWENTY-TWO

Berlin—March 5, 1943

JUST BEFORE 10 A.M. on a blustery Friday in late winter, Kurt Bauer strolled nervously into the shadow of the city's most dreaded building.

The structure itself wasn't imposing. Five stories of stone with a mansard roof, it had once been a hotel, then an art school. Its elegant rows of high windows suggested a place of light and enlightenment. Its current name suggested otherwise: the Reich Main Security Office, home to the Gestapo and the SS.

Kurt had already approached the entrance once, only to have his nerve fail him. On his second try he again veered away, heading north toward the Brandenburg Gate while taking deep breaths of the chill morning air. After fifteen days of thought and planning, he had finally settled on a risky course of action, and by day's end he hoped to have secured a safe future for his family and, more important, for Liesl and him.

But first he had to go through with it.

He had set out from Charlottenburg at sunrise, hoping to steel his resolve by making the four-mile journey on foot. It was bitterly cold, and even with gloves on he kept his hands shoved deep in his pockets. The sights along the way did little to put him in the right mood. Half the shops on the Ku-Damm were shuttered. Charlottenburger Chaussee, normally a grand, sun-washed promenade, was cast in eternal twilight by a canopy of camouflage netting, a ruse to hide the street grid from daylight bomber attacks. Even the Tiergarten was a mess. Its trees had been hacked away for firewood, and its expansive lawns were cross-stitched by trenches, dug as emergency shelter from bombs. Two soldiers stood begging on a street corner, their greatcoats still muddy from the eastern front. A third, missing a leg, slept on a park bench. Had the poor man even survived the night? Kurt didn't have the heart to check.

The most depressing sight of all, at least to Kurt, was the brooding Kaiser Wilhelm Memorial Church. Normally its high steeple and Romanesque towers evoked stateliness and strength, but this morning they only reminded him of the aborted rendezvous that should have occurred there a week earlier.

It was to have been a pivotal moment for the Berlin chapter of the White Rose. Hans Scholl, one of the White Rose founders in Munich, had been due to meet Falk Harnack, the young soldier who had been present for the Berlin chapter's formative meeting. Harnack was then supposed to escort Scholl to Bonhoeffer's house for a meeting that would connect the White Rose movement to the heart of the German resistance.

News of this scary but welcome development had made Kurt rethink his plan of action. Considering the predicament his family was in, he hadn't felt like risking his life for mere pamphlets anymore. But if bolder action was in the offing, maybe he would hold off on his one-man operation. His father had even mentioned rumors of an assassination plot against Hitler, with help coming from high inside the German officer corps. With the war going so badly, it was the one act that might spare the country further destruction, and in turn spare his family.

But Scholl never showed up. Harnack nervously smoked a few cigarettes in the dark, passed word of the aborted rendezvous to Bonhoeffer and to the other White Rose members, and then returned empty-handed to his army unit in Chemnitz.

By the following afternoon the reason became painfully clear. News spread that the Scholls had been arrested a week earlier. They had been taken to Munich Gestapo headquarters for questioning, and four days later they were executed by guillotine.

Further details were sketchy, but apparently the roundup of White Rose members in Munich was continuing. Some of the arrested members had ties to Harnack, and to Helmut Hartert, who had organized the Berlin cell. If they talked, then every Berlin member would soon be at risk.

The cell met hastily to discuss what to do. One member, Renate

Fensel, had already dropped out after their earlier near escape. That left eight of them, not counting Harnack, who was still serving in the army. Everyone agreed that it would be best to lay low for a while—everyone, that is, except Hannelore, who urged immediate action.

"They'll have us all in the net soon anyway," she said. "We might as well fight back."

She proposed that they do something to grab the public's attention. Throw a firebomb at Goebbels's headquarters, or toss one at his Wannsee villa. The others looked at her like she was crazy, even Liesl, and every morning since then Kurt had opened the morning newspaper expecting to see Hannelore's name splashed across the front. If they were lucky, maybe she would be shot in the act and never have a chance to reveal their names.

At his family's home in Charlottenburg, meanwhile, things were even worse than before. His brother, Manfred, had been reported missing during the retreat from Stalingrad. His mother barely ate, and his sister wouldn't leave the house. She moped around with a copy of Goethe's *The Sorrows of Young Werther*, the novel that had once inspired thousands of lovesick German boys to leap to their deaths.

The only bright spot was that his father had somehow wangled a travel permit for another trip to Switzerland. But even that turned out badly when he failed to secure a second meeting with Dulles. The Americans seemed to be losing interest.

So, on the day after the most recent White Rose meeting, Kurt decided to carry out his one-man plan after all. Now he just had to steel up the nerve to go through with it.

He circled the Brandenburg Gate and set course once again for the Reich Main Security Office. Glancing toward Pariser Platz, he spotted the hulking antiaircraft battery atop I. G. Farben headquarters. It reminded him of his father, who had boasted just the other day of government plans to put a similar battery atop the Bauer offices in Spandau. Amazing that the old man could still play the role of proud patriot after everything that had happened. Perhaps that was all his father had left. Unless Kurt acted now.

Five blocks later he began his third approach, and this time he kept going. He pushed through the heavy doors past a pair of sentries into a bustling lobby. At the security station next to the stairway, flanked by two more sentries, he was greeted by an officious-looking fellow seated at a big desk.

"Yes, young man?"

Kurt spoke quickly. Pause now and he might never get the words out.

"I have important information to report."

"As does everyone who comes through that door." The man sounded bored. He looked down at his desk and began flipping through a magazine. "Your name?"

"Kurt Bauer."

"Fill this out."

Without looking up, the man shoved forward an official-looking form. Kurt stood straighter, cleared his throat, and spoke louder.

"I am the son of Reinhard Bauer, of the Bauer Armament Works."

The fellow stopped turning pages and looked up for a reappraisal, no doubt taking note of Kurt's fine wool overcoat, the dark kid gloves, and the white shirt with its starched collar. He shut his magazine.

"What is the nature of this report?"

"Firsthand information concerning the activities of a local resistance organization."

The fellow cocked his head.

"Firsthand, you said?"

"I know who is distributing those pamphlets from the group known as the White Rose. All of that and more. But I am putting you on notice that in exchange for this information I expect to receive certain considerations. For myself and for my family."

It was the last part of this sales pitch that had been hardest to plan. Informing on friends was terrible enough. Kurt had justified it to himself on the grounds that their names would soon be known anyway, due to the recent arrests. But to demand a favor from the Gestapo took more fortitude than anything he had yet attempted. For all he knew, they might laugh in his face, then take him out back to be shot.

Yet now that he was actually speaking, he heard in his voice the tone that his father usually reserved for balky clerks and secretaries, or shop foremen who weren't pulling their weight. Maybe all that training to prepare him for the business world was finally paying off. Already he sensed that this clerk wasn't accustomed to dealing with the likes of a Bauer, so Kurt pressed his advantage.

"I don't wish to speak to just anyone. Nor will I tolerate a lengthy wait. Well? What do you plan to do about it?"

"I know just the person," the man said, nodding briskly as he raised a finger. His manner was transformed. An observer might have figured him for a deskman in a posh hotel, attending to a valued guest. "Excuse me while I phone him for you."

AT THAT MOMENT, Martin Göllner was in a staff room upstairs, hoping that no one smelled the coffee he was brewing. It was his first real coffee in months, and he didn't wish to share. It had been delivered an hour earlier, a bribe from an old Jew who had been outed by a neighbor after the neighbor grew tired of the Jew's barking dog. Not that the bribe did any good. The Jew was now locked in a cell downstairs, awaiting questioning. He would be pumped for any information on the whereabouts of friends and relatives, and by tomorrow afternoon he would be riding an eastbound train. But it was the nosy neighbor that Göllner wanted to throttle, because now there was a lot of extra paperwork to take care of, when what Göllner really wanted was a day off.

Such petty motives were typical for him lately. His caseload was drowning in trivia—shrewish wives denouncing unfaithful husbands, unfaithful husbands denouncing troublesome mistresses, troublesome mistresses denouncing shrewish wives. The circle never stopped. And don't get him started on all the disputes between neighbors, or students and teachers, or employees and bosses. Most of it came from the nattering rabble of the *Mittelstand*, cooped up during the bombing raids in overcrowded basements where everything smelled of mud and rat dung. No wonder they were at one another's throats.

The problem for Göllner was that once any complaint, no matter how small, became official, it had to be investigated. Because the only thing worse to his bosses than letting a political malcontent or an undiscovered Jew run free was letting uncleared casework pile up on their desks. The joke of it was that most of these busybody informants believed that his office was all-powerful. Everyone imagined a vast network of spies, all of them super-Nazis of SS rank. The reality was that the Gestapo relied heavily on the rabble for its tips. Berlin had become a city of tattletales, a gossip mill with eyes and ears in every building.

Göllner, like most of his coworkers, had been a cop before the war. He had walked a beat for a year and served a mere two months as a gumshoe before the new hierarchy took over. But he was bright, and he knew when to keep his mouth shut, so he was promoted quickly

through the ranks. He now had an SD uniform to go with the imposing title of Sturmbandführer. Currently he straddled two desks in
Berlin's district operations, reporting to the head of Subsection A,
which looked into matters of political opposition and sabotage, and
also to the head of Subsection B, which kept a lookout for Jews and
renegade clerics.

At the moment his only productive paid informant was a Catholic
priest who was so desperate to hang on to his job that he sent Göllner
weekly summaries of his parishioners' confessions. Hilarious stuff,
mostly. But worthy of an arrest or two when things got slow.

The coffee was finally brewed, and so far no one had noticed. Göllner picked up the pot just as his phone rang next door. His secretary
shouted for him.

"Coming!" he answered. He carried the pot with him, supposing
that now he would have to share it with her. By the time he picked up
the receiver she was already pouring herself a cup, and her mug was
bigger than Göllner's.

"Yes?"

It was Brinkmann, the toad from the lobby. Yet another visitor was
seeking an audience, although for a change Brinkmann was on his best
behavior. When Göllner heard the visitor's name, he understood why.
His senses went on full alert.

"Send him up immediately," he said. "In fact, you are to escort him
personally. Have one of the sentries sit in for you. Take Mr. Bauer to
interview room 7-A and lock the door. Tell no one else who he is."

"Yes, sir."

"You'd better leave him with some water, a full pitcher with a glass.
And ask first if he needs to use the toilet. We'll go carefully with this
one."

He needed to speak with his boss. They weren't accustomed to this
type of visitor. The rich and the privileged almost never brought their
complaints through the front door. They tended to either settle matters between themselves or go straight to the top. In fact, wasn't Reinhard Bauer supposedly a pal of Wilhelm Stuckart's? Göllner had seen
them in the papers, photographed together along with Speer. Then
why was the man's son here, strolling in off the street like some street
cleaner from Moabit?

Göllner sighed. This would be interesting, but potentially tricky.
He picked up the phone and dialed the number for his boss.

THE DOOR SHUT as the obsequious little clerk from downstairs departed. Kurt poured himself a glass of water and took stock. The windowless room was chilly, so he kept his coat on. Framed photos of Hitler and Kaltenbrunner, the new boss here, faced him from the opposite wall. He wondered how long they had waited before taking down Heydrich's picture after the assassination in Prague the year before. He drummed a finger on the table, then stopped, thinking someone might be listening at the door. He didn't want to let them know how nervous he was. Despite the chill he had begun to sweat, so he took off his coat and folded it across the back of another chair. At least they had let him take a pee.

After about fifteen minutes, the door opened. Kurt rose instinctively, just as he had been taught to do when one of his elders entered a room. The man was surprisingly young, and didn't cut a particularly impressive figure. In fact, what he mostly looked like was a dull drone, a cop, someone to whom you might report a bike theft or a vandalized window. The man paused in the doorway, as if also taking stock. Then he entered, followed by a stenographer. The two of them sat down across the table, side by side.

"I am Sturmbandführer Martin Göllner. Before we begin, I have been instructed to ask for some identification. As I am sure you can understand, it isn't every day that someone walks in claiming to be the son of Reinhard Bauer."

Kurt obliged him, and watched the man read. He didn't seem to be in a hurry. Kurt had a feeling this would take a while, and a knot that had already formed in his stomach did a slow tumble and turned into a cramp. He bent at the waist and emitted a sigh.

"Very well," Göllner said, handing back his papers. "We may begin."

Kurt had given a lot of thought to what to say first. His father's recent lessons on how to do business had come to mind. He must take the initiative, set the tone. No matter how threatened he felt, he figured he could maintain some leverage as long as he didn't give up his choicest information too easily. He also needed to make it seem that he had more backing and clout than he really did. So he started out boldly.

"I am here on behalf of my family. I wish to offer important information concerning state security and morale, but only in return for certain assurances that my family's patriotic role in the war effort will be allowed to continue. I also want assurances that those closest to me will not be harmed, although I am quite willing to be punished for my own indiscretions."

He hadn't planned on adding the part about punishment, but somehow in his momentum the words spilled out. Perhaps he was already ashamed of what he was doing. If Göllner was impressed, he did a good job of hiding it. He merely glanced at the stenographer to make sure she was getting everything. Then he answered in a monotone.

"All of that is quite interesting, Mr. Bauer. What is it you wish to tell us?"

"First I must have your assurances."

Göllner was clearly not pleased to be answered in this manner. He frowned and jotted something in a small notebook while the stenographer kept her pencil poised in the air.

"Very well. But tell me first, does your father know you have come here?"

"I am here with his blessing."

"So he is aware at this very moment that you are here? Answer carefully."

"No. He is not."

Göllner again wrote in his notebook. A drop of sweat slid down Kurt's back.

Kurt spent the next few minutes outlining his family's current state of affairs. He mentioned his brother's war service as well. He took special pains when describing the canceled marriage and the background check by the Racial Office.

"I wish to make it clear that, up to now, no one in my family ever knew that this particular ancestor had been a member of such an undesirable faith," he said.

He noted a shift in Göllner's expression, perhaps even a hint of relish, and he worried that he might have done something wrong. Had he been able to read the man's mind, he would have realized that Martin Göllner was sighing inwardly in relief that this boy was seeking "assurances" on such a trivial matter. These SS ancestry checks were a huge pain in the ass, not to mention a colossal waste of manpower. Although marriages were sometimes halted as a result, nothing further ever came of them, especially not when the so-called taint had occurred so long ago. But it was just as well that Bauer didn't know that. Once again, it was a case of the Gestapo's reputation preceding it, its presumed thoroughness in enforcing every little matter. All this fretting by the Bauers was foolish, unless of course some ranking minister—Stuckart, for example—took a personal interest in seeing that the family was punished. But that, too, seemed unlikely when you considered that the Bauers were supplying every Panzer division.

Göllner let the boy prattle on. He could then act like he was doing the family a big favor. He wouldn't even need clearance from a higher-up to offer a "deal."

"There is also the matter of a certain young lady who must be protected in all these proceedings," Kurt continued. "She is not a member of my family, although I like to believe there is a chance that she may be fairly soon. She has been the victim of overzealous friends, one in particular, and as a result she has been goaded into participating in reckless behavior. If you take steps to prevent this friend from further influencing her, then I am sure she will respond quite reasonably."

"Look, Mr. Bauer. I can't guarantee that she won't be punished, not until I hear what it is she has done. But in any investigation there is always the possibility for leniency. So why don't we proceed on that assumption, and also on the assumption that no harm will come to your family or its business interests. That way you have already accomplished half of what you came here for. But now you must begin offering me something in return, unless you would prefer this to become a very lengthy and awkward process, in which your father and no doubt many other persons above me would have to become closely involved. Understood?"

"Yes, understood."

Kurt poured himself more water, swallowing twice to wet his lips.

"And, of course, you must also understand that whether or not I can live up to these terms depends greatly on what it is you give me. Its quality and quantity. Both matter. Details, meaning names first and foremost, are of vital importance. Certainly you must see that my generosity can extend only as far as yours?"

"Yes, sir."

"Very well, then. Begin."

Göllner nodded to the stenographer, who flipped back a page of her notebook. Then he lit a cigarette, inhaled slowly, and sagged back comfortably in his chair.

Kurt began. And, as requested, he was very generous indeed.

TWENTY-THREE

Berlin—March 20, 1943

THE GESTAPO OFFICERS ANNOUNCED their arrival at the birthday party of Dieter Büssler with a prim knock at the door, as if already apologizing for bringing arrest warrants instead of gifts.

Their decorum was oddly appropriate, because in a sense they *were* invited guests. Kurt Bauer had tipped them off to the party's details. No need to smash windows or batter down a door when you could catch the entire membership of the local White Rose gathered at a punch bowl.

Kurt had worked out the logistics for the raid with Martin Göllner during a four-hour conversation, a chat that proceeded more like contract negotiations between rival lawyers than an interrogation. At the time Kurt had been relieved by the air of civility. Later he wondered if it hadn't placed him at even more of a disadvantage, because in the end he was no match for Göllner in the subtle art of give-and-take.

Göllner emerged from the confrontation with the names, roles, and contact information of every local member of the White Rose. Kurt came away with a few lukewarm assurances that had strings attached. The biggest of those—a promise to let his family hold on to its business empire—had never been in doubt to begin with, as Göllner well knew.

Would the Gestapo have discovered the White Rose names anyway, through interrogations elsewhere? Göllner implied as much to Kurt, but later told his superiors that he doubted it. The Munich interrogations of Falk Harnack and Jörg Strasser hadn't yielded a word about White Rose activity in Berlin, although the two men would certainly be asked about it now, if only to double-check Kurt's offerings.

For Göllner the most sensitive issue was Kurt's insistence on serving a prison sentence along with his friends. No doubt the boy wanted to convince the others that he hadn't been the rat aboard their sinking ship. He also wanted to assuage his guilt and impress his girlfriend. But incarcerating any Bauer would be a hard sell with Göllner's superiors. He got them to go along only after convincing them that he could leverage the results of the family's racial background check against Kurt's father, Reinhard.

On the Saturday morning before the fateful birthday party, Göllner worked out the final details with Reinhard himself, face-to-face. Before telephoning to arrange the meeting, Göllner allowed Kurt to warn his father in advance. That meant he had to tell his father about everything, which turned out to be harder than telling Göllner. Reinhard was furious about his son's foolish White Rose activities, not to mention the boy's defiance in continuing to see Liesl against his wishes. But once he got over his anger he earnestly got down to the business of trying to work out the best possible deal for Kurt and the family.

The meeting was at the office of Göllner's supervisor, on Prinz-Albrecht-Strasse. Göllner relinquished the last of his precious coffee in order to display the proper hospitality. He assured the industrialist that for the good of the family—indeed, for the good of the country—his son Kurt would have to spend several months in Plötzensee Prison. Reinhard grimly assented.

The only other sticking point was the matter of Kurt's girlfriend, Liesl Folkerts. Reinhard had no interest at all in protecting her, but Kurt wanted her freedom ensured. The complication was that she had already come to the Gestapo's attention, from a nosy old charwoman who overheard Liesl telling a crude joke about Hitler at a charity sale of used clothing. As if that weren't enough, a second woman had then witnessed her pressing a wool scarf on an elderly shopper while saying, "Please, take it. It's not as if the government is going to help you."

One of Göllner's colleagues had begun building a dossier on the girl, a body of evidence that now had to be set aside in favor of the arrangement worked out with the younger Bauer. In exchange for this accommodation, Kurt agreed to enter the army three weeks after his release. The gesture was largely symbolic, as he would have been due to report on his eighteenth birthday anyway. Still, families as prominent as the Bauers had been finding ever more creative ways to keep their sons out of the military.

For Göllner, then, the hard part was done. The dirty work would be left to the four officers who carried out the raid. He would then help interrogate the suspects, although he figured they would have little to offer beyond what Kurt had already told them.

For Kurt Bauer, on the other hand, the worst was yet to come. He prepared for the birthday party as if for a funeral, keeping mostly to his room and moping the way his sister had after her broken engagement. He exited the house only once in the preceding days, to shop for a birthday present for Dieter. He found himself putting a lot of thought into it and wound up using nearly all of the family's monthly clothing coupons to purchase a fine woolen scarf. Maybe it would keep Dieter warm in prison, he thought, little knowing the boy's neck would need far more protection than a strip of cashmere.

Göllner had assured him the raid would be carried out with as little fuss as possible, but Kurt wasn't convinced. When the evening arrived, he rode his bicycle to Liesl's house to escort her there. He pinged the bell in hopes that he wouldn't have to face her parents, but her father came to the door and beckoned him inside. Everyone was all smiles. By now Liesl's parents thought of him as a polite and humble gentleman. He smiled thinly and said little. At least they wouldn't have to witness the awful moment of their daughter's arrest.

As they mounted their bikes, it occurred to him that the Gestapo might already have them under surveillance. He imagined officers hiding in the trees, watching with binoculars.

"Kurt, what's wrong?" Liesl asked. "You're so quiet. Has something happened?"

He blinked in confusion, wondering what to say.

"It's my sister, Traudl," he stammered. "She's still so upset."

Liesl laid a hand across his.

"I really do think your family is going to be okay. Cheer up. Tomorrow is the first day of spring. I even saw a crocus yesterday. Even the war can't stop them."

She squeezed his hand. He nodded grimly, and for a fleeting moment he considered telling her everything. They could escape through the forest, pedal to a train station to flee south toward

Switzerland, crossing the Alps to safety. Just Liesl and him, enduring like the crocuses. But he knew she would never come, not if he told her. She would be furious, lost forever. Worse, she would try to warn everyone, and the evening would turn dangerous, even deadly. Pursuit and gunshots, shrill whistles and snarling dogs. They pedaled away in silence. By the time they reached Dieter's house his mouth was so dry that he could barely swallow.

It was the first time he had met Dieter's parents. Mrs. Büssler was like her son, showy and boastful in speech, reserved and cautious in manner, as if harboring a deep insecurity. Mr. Büssler was a quiet man with a pipe who seemed resigned to a secondary role in the household. As soon as the guests arrived he retreated to a back room with his newspaper.

Nearly everyone was there—seven of them in all, just as Kurt had promised Göllner. Helmut Hartert had recently been called into military service, and presumably would be dealt with elsewhere. Harnack was still with his army unit in Chemnitz. The idea that everything might go off without a hitch was both exciting and horrifying. In the ensuing small talk Kurt hardly knew what he was saying, and every few minutes he checked his watch, not knowing when and how the Gestapo would announce its presence.

After an hour, Dieter's mother brought out a rather sad-looking ham that they must have been saving for a special occasion, plus bowls of potatoes and creamed spinach. She poured a jug of homemade wine into the punch. Kurt drank freely of it, and by the end of his third glass everyone began to seem cheerful and relaxed, so much so that he allowed himself to fancy that maybe Göllner had gotten the date wrong, or fouled up the address. Better still, maybe his father had somehow engineered a last-minute reprieve, using his connections to put a stop to this nonsense. They were only students, after all. Surely a man of such value to the war effort had enough clout to prevent the arrests of a handful of upper-class children? What were a few pamphlets when stacked against the might of the Bauer war machine? Kurt took his empty glass for another refill, his cheeks flushed with false hope. He even managed a smile for Hannelore when he noticed her watching him.

Then came the first knock. It sounded normal, even gentle, and at first only Kurt heard it. Perhaps it was a neighbor, or a family friend bearing gifts.

The second knock was firmer, but still not what you would call insistent. But when Dieter's mother threw open the door, four men in black SS uniforms entered, three with guns drawn. The first one carried some sort of official-looking paper, and he spoke sternly as everyone else went silent. Liesl eased to Kurt's side and took his hand.

"Frau Büssler, I am here to inform you that all of these young people are under arrest for crimes against the state."

Someone dropped a glass.

"No!" Liesl cried.

"Stay calm," Kurt whispered, finally able to muster some bravery now that he knew roughly what was coming next.

Dieter's mother clapped a hand to her mouth. His father had appeared in the hallway, pipe in hand, too stunned to speak.

Christoph Klemm, always the boldest in the bunch, charged toward a window. One of the officers struck him on the head with a sidearm. There was a sickening crack, and Christoph slumped to the floor.

The group's commander looked too thin for his uniform. It was baggy at the shoulders and the waist, and his belt had been tightened a few extra notches to hold up his bunched trousers. Maybe he, too, wasn't getting enough to eat, or perhaps the fittest members of his unit had been sent to the front. Kurt felt oddly offended that they were being arrested by such a second-rate bunch. Or maybe he already knew he would vividly remember every detail of this moment—the shocked faces and deathly silence, the way that the shred of ham he had eaten seemed to be twisting in his stomach like a parasite.

"This needn't be difficult," the officer said. "All of you place your hands on your head and line up against the opposite wall."

"Are you going to shoot us?" Dieter asked, almost in a shriek.

"Shut up, Dieter." It was Christoph, rising unsteadily. His lower lip was bleeding, and a lump was visible below his right ear. He swayed a bit, still woozy.

Everyone moved toward the wall, Kurt following numbly as they crowded together, elbows bumping like antlers above their heads, a meek herd. Thinking about this moment in the abstract had been bad enough. Now, with the menacing black uniforms and Dieter's mother sobbing uncontrollably, it was worse than he had imagined. Nor did it help that he suddenly found himself wondering whether his family could have toughed it out, even if he had taken no action. He was angry at himself. The heat boiled up in his cheeks, and he clenched his fists. Liesl noticed and whispered in alarm.

"Don't try anything, Kurt. It's not worth it. Maybe it will be nothing."

"Quiet!" the commander shouted.

Kurt stared back at her, mute with rage and self-loathing. A hand shoved him roughly, and he fought down an impulse to strike back. It wasn't that he feared retaliation. His real worry was that if he resisted, the commander would single him out, here and now, and reveal his duplicity to all. Then his efforts really would have gone for nothing.

There was a sudden sound of a body collapsing to the floor. Kurt glanced over his shoulder to see Christoph in a heap.

"Stay away from him," the commander said mildly to Dieter's mother, who had stepped forward in concern. Then, to his men: "Take him out to the truck."

Hannelore turned abruptly and spat at one of the soldiers, who shoved her hard against the wall. She cried out in pain and anger. Kurt caught her eye, and for a second he was certain she could read his every thought, so he blushed and looked away.

An officer emerged from the hallway, shouldering roughly past Dieter's father and holding aloft a small stack of White Rose pamphlets.

"These were beneath the boy's mattress."

Had Dieter really been so stupid? Hannelore shook her head and cursed under her breath. Shortly afterward the officers led them outside, where a military truck had pulled to the curb with its tailgate down and its canvas flaps open in the back.

"Climb aboard, one at a time," the commander said. "Slowly and orderly, while keeping your hands above your head."

Neighbors had gathered on the sidewalk. There was concern in their faces, but also shame. Guilt by proximity. You could almost sense them calculating what this might mean for their own prospects in the future.

Two soldiers with rifles climbed into the truck and closed the tailgate and the canvas flaps, plunging everyone into darkness. The truck pulled away. Kurt peered through the slit between the flaps and saw a passing tram. The only light visible was from the blue sparks in the overhead wires.

They were seated three to a side in the bed of the truck, with Christoph curled in the middle like a sack of flour.

"Where are we going?" someone asked.

No one answered.

The ride continued for twenty minutes. When they finally stopped, bright lights were switched on and someone shouted an order. It sounded as if a gate was being opened. The truck bumped forward. Kurt saw a brick wall topped by barbed wire.

"I know where we are," Hannelore whispered. "Plötzensee Prison."

Kurt had known this was their destination, but somehow it didn't make the arrival any easier to bear. Liesl took his hand in the dark, and for the first time in days he was able to muster some courage. He even allowed himself to begin thinking about their future. Maybe this would be the low point, he told himself. In four months, perhaps five, the worst would be over. Make it through this ordeal and he would still have Liesl, trusting him, touching him. And surely they would still be together years later as well. If so, then it would all be worth it.

The truck stopped again. A guard threw down the tailgate and pulled back the flaps. They were staring at an open door leading into a brick cellblock.

His life in prison had begun.

THE FIRST LETTER from Liesl arrived a week later, five handwritten pages smuggled between their cells by a guard bribed with ration coupons from her family. It was Kurt's first moment of joy and color in a drab world that had shrunk to the dimensions of his five-by-nine cell.

Kurt had entered a sort of hibernation. It hadn't even occurred to him to try to communicate with the others—not that he would have been inclined to do so except in Liesl's case. The less they knew of his guilty thoughts, the better.

So he passed the time reading books sent by his parents. He was mildly amused when his sister forwarded her worn copy of *The Sorrows of Young Werther*, which he was able to read with a certain detachment, taking comfort in the knowledge that he, unlike Werther, might still win his true love in the end.

At other times he stared longingly out his small, high window for hours on end. The view across the prison's outer wall was of the Hohenzollern Canal, the waterway leading to the loading docks of the biggest Bauer factory. Sometimes he smelled the smoke from the factory as it drifted on the afternoon breeze. At least that meant it was still functioning—no sure thing judging from the frequency of the bombing raids. Almost every night now the sky filled with the beams of searchlights. Whenever the pounding of the explosions and the flak bursts finally stopped, there was always plenty of chatter from the other cells. Some of it was in foreign tongues, usually French or Polish. Kurt never tried answering, even when the words were in German.

Liesl, on the other hand, had obviously been working diligently to establish connections to all their friends. This was clear from the surprising wealth of information in her letter. Some of the news was hard to take.

> Dearest Kurt,
>
> I suppose by now that you, too, have suffered the awful and degrading experience of interrogation at the hands of our captors. Yesterday I was made to stand for five hours in the middle of a room while a guard watched through the door. I pissed into my clothes and nearly fainted. The only break they allowed was for a glass of water, but even then I was not permitted to sit down, and of course this only caused me to piss again. Afterward they did not let me wash or change clothes, so as you can imagine I am quite impossible to be around. Even the guard seems to grimace as he passes my door.
>
> Unfortunately, I am told that they wish to speak with me again this afternoon, so who knows what the hours ahead will bring. I am told they have been similarly harsh and determined in their efforts with all of us, but suffice it to say that so far I have been steadfast in my refusal to speak at all about any activities other than my own, for which I have willingly assumed full responsibility as a matter of conscience. In my lowest moments I try to remember the words of Dr. Bonhoeffer. Truly, no easy grace remains for us now, so we must summon all of our faith and fortitude. I am confident that you are doing the same, and I wish you strength even as I send my love.
>
> I am afraid that some of the others are of the opinion that Dieter must be to blame for our fate. They cite his carelessness in having kept the pamphlets at his house. Some of them have also remarked on the ease with which the officers entered his house, and the strange way that

his father behaved that evening, as if he was ashamed to have anything to do with us. I suppose they see that as evidence he was already aware of what was to come. Perhaps they are right, but I have tried to keep an open mind. I have always found Dieter to be a sweet boy even though he is impulsive and has never been a careful planner. It is difficult to accept that he would have been a party to this without having revealed it through some false word or gesture. We shall see, I suppose.

Have you heard yet from your family, and your poor sister? One of my first thoughts after the terrible night of the raid was that this event would only make things worse for them, at a time when they can least afford it. Please send them my love, and, if possible, reassure me that they, too, have not been dragged into this awful abyss.

With all the idle hours now at my disposal, I confess to experiencing many moments of weakness when I try to imagine what will become of us. I do take some hope from the days that have already passed. The students who were arrested in Munich were tried and executed in only a day or two, and I believe that many of them were several years older than us. Perhaps the thinking here is that they will offer us a second chance. Or maybe I am being terribly naive in my wishful thinking, and their only intention is to drag out the process as long as possible. One of the others seems to think that we will be here for weeks, or even months, based on things that he has heard from his parents. It is the uncertainty which is hardest to take. My lowest moments seem to come when I dare to dream that we might still have a future.

All right, I must finish. The guard has promised to pick up this letter in the next hour just before the shift changes. Please stay strong, my darling.

All my love,
Liesl

As the days passed, Liesl's notes continued, and Kurt always answered. He, of course, had not been interrogated since their imprisonment. But to cover for himself he wove elaborate descriptions of tough treatment and steadfast resistance, tales that were so deeply imagined that at times he almost believed them.

Word trickled in from the others. By the end of the second week he had received letters from everyone except Hannelore, although the only one he bothered to answer was Christoph, whom he had always admired.

Even poor Dieter sent him a message. It was obvious from his aggrieved and defensive tone that he had picked up on the suspicions of the others, and his shrillness only served to make him seem guilty. Kurt thought it best to say nothing at all on the subject, figuring that the whisper campaign and Dieter himself would do the job for him.

The third week brought devastating news from the outside. Dietrich Bonhoeffer had been arrested. Details were sketchy, and Kurt agonized that his own revelations might have somehow led to it. It might have been easier to take if Bonhoeffer had been jailed at Plötzensee, where he could have joined their network of secret correspondence. Instead, the authorities took him to Tegel Prison, just across town.

But events within Plötzensee soon reminded them that they had plenty to fear regarding their own prospects. On the evening of May 13, nearly eight weeks after their arrival, Kurt heard a stir of activity outdoors. He looked out the window to see a single file of prisoners casting long shadows as guards led them into a low building between the cellblock and the outer wall. He counted thirteen in all. It was just before 7 p.m.

For the next half hour, a series of barked commands issued from the windows of the low building. Some were followed by muffled cries, others by a great slamming thud, which echoed across the yard. Finally there was a brief period of silence, followed by a frantic spell of hammering. When that stopped, the door of the building opened and two guards emerged, carrying a wooden coffin. Two more guards followed with a second coffin. Thirteen bodies came out in all.

The next morning he got the full story from a guard, who seemed to relish explaining what all the fuss had been about. The low building was the Plötzensee death chamber. The sickening thunks had come from the slamming blade of a guillotine. The prisoners that weren't beheaded had been hanged from hooks along a rear wall. The thirteen victims were members of a resistance cell known as the Red Orchestra, for its ties to the Soviets.

The next few months brought further killings. The peak came on August 5, when nineteen more members of the Red Orchestra filed into the death house. But the worst was yet to come. In mid-August, the news arrived in a note from Liesl: Their trials had begun. Kurt had to pretend that he knew all about it and that he, too, was going into the dock. But he could only imagine how horrible it was as he read the descriptions from the others, as each was led into the so-called People's Court for trial and sentencing.

The worst and most vivid account was Christoph's.

> *Our judge was Roland Freisler, the devil himself in his awful red robes. He wore a perched crown hat and saluted like a madman, as if pointing to the thunderclouds and awaiting their command. He hardly listened to a word I said. He just screamed and sneered and berated me at every turn. When the end came he shouted the verdict of guilty, and then his sentence, screaming to the gallery, "This beet must be uprooted and replanted! Yank him from the ground, then bury him in it!" That is his way of saying I am to be hanged ten days from now, on the 29th of August, along with Ulrich and Dieter, who I am ashamed to admit that I have sorely misjudged in this affair.*
>
> *What is the word from you, and have you been to court yet? I await your news with equal measures of dread and compassion. I am determined to carry myself with dignity and defiance to the very end, and I am confident that you will do the same.*
> *Your loyal friend,*
> *Christoph*

Kurt crumpled the note in anguish. In the following days word arrived that Klara and Hannelore had also been sentenced to hang, but not until September 5. Kurt considered writing that he, too, had been sentenced to death, to keep the others from assuming the worst. But if he did, Liesl would know later that he had lied to the others. Before he could think up what to say, the news arrived that Liesl had inexplicably—to everyone else, at least—been sentenced merely to five years in jail. The official explanation was that she was the youngest of the three girls. That gave Kurt the out that he had been seeking, because at seventeen he was the youngest of the males, and the Nazis had generally avoided executing underage suspects, as long as you weren't a Jew. The beheading at Plötzensee the previous year of a seventeen-year-old boy—yet another pamphleteer—had led to a rare public outcry against the government.

Liesl, while overjoyed to hear his life had been spared, seemed to suspect that his family's prominence must have had something to do with it. She concluded that this must have worked to protect her as well, because in her next note she asked, "Is there nothing your father can do for the others, or, at the very least, for Hannelore?"

He decided that the safest bet was to play along, so he replied, "With regret and no small measure of shame, I must reveal that my father has expended all of his possible influence, and I can assure you that even that did not come without many sacrifices, in light of what the government now knows about my family."

Executions at Plötzensee always began at 7 p.m. On the day that Christoph, Ulrich, and Dieter were to be killed, Kurt lay on his bed waiting in dread for the groan of the downstairs door and the tramp of feet toward the death chamber. They were right on schedule. He couldn't bear to watch, and when he heard Christoph's voice, wavering yet loud, yell, "Our memory will outlive our killers!" he shut his eyes tightly and sobbed in shame. Then he clamped his thin pillow around his ears, pressing hard and humming like a boy afraid of thunder, so that he wouldn't hear the shouted orders, the muffled cries, or the hammering of the coffin lids.

His humming wasn't loud enough, so he began singing like a madman—old tunes from kindergarten, Christmas carols, whatever came to mind. And when he opened his eyes much later and dropped the pillow, which was soaked in tears and sweat, he saw that it had grown dark outside. His untouched dinner sat cold on a tray the guards had brought. The only sound was the twitter of a nightingale, tuning up for the evening. A half hour later an air raid siren wailed into action, and he listened for the distant drone of approaching bombers. On came the flak guns and the bomb bursts, and for a change he welcomed them. The searchlights seemed to sweep the sky clear of all the ill spirits that had been set loose from the death chamber.

For the next several days he ignored contact with everyone, even Liesl. At noon on September 3 he finally wrote her. He had just penned the salutation when there was a knock at the door. Guards never knocked, so he wondered who it could be.

"It's Göllner. Your time is up."

For a harrowing moment Kurt was convinced that their deal was off and that he was about to be led downstairs to the death chamber, where he would find Liesl already hanging by a hook. Instead, Göllner entered with a sheaf of documents.

"These are your release papers. Come downstairs. All you have to do is sign."

He sagged in relief, not least because it meant he would not have to endure the executions of Klara and Hannelore. In his mounting guilt he had even begun to admire Hannelore's reckless defiance.

"And Liesl?" he asked. "She is being released, too?"

"There has been a slight delay where she is concerned. Nothing to worry about."

"What do you mean?"

"That's why they sent me. To explain, so there will be no fuss. She will be coming out later, perhaps at midnight. Some sort of glitch with the paperwork. But, as I said, not to worry. You will have three weeks to spend with your lady love before going off to the army. Maybe she will volunteer for the nursing corps and you will see her at the front."

Kurt wanted to punch him, but knew better.

"Come on. Your father is waiting."

He stepped out the door of his cell with a feeling of immense relief. Then he saw a face watching from a small window in the opposite door. What if the neighboring prisoners had overheard Göllner? If Hannelore found out, she might still poison the well for him. He kept his head down and his eyes to the floor. Now that he was on the verge of freedom, he found himself reverting to old resentments.

Kurt's father greeted him with a huge hug. It was the first time he had ever seen tears in the man's eyes, and it moved him deeply. But he reverted to his skittishness as they crossed the prison yard toward the front gate. He could feel the eyes of the other prisoners on his back. Fortunately, no one called out his name. He hoped that Hannelore, Klara, and Liesl had cells facing in another direction, because surely they would misunderstand. Or, worse, they would understand all too clearly.

But he cheered himself with the reminder that by tomorrow at this time Liesl also would be free. She would have no choice but to write it off as some strange act of mercy or political influence. Hannelore might argue otherwise, but she would soon be dead. Not the best of circumstances for beginning the rest of their lives, but certainly preferable to the ghastly alternative.

The thought made him glance over his shoulder as he approached the gate. His last sight inside the prison was of the low brick chamber of death, with its guillotine and its hangman's hooks. He shivered, and then stepped into freedom. Tomorrow he would begin putting all of this behind him.

Instead, of course, the bombers came once again that very night, and by morning Kurt was back on the scene, kneeling in the rubble, clawing at the smoldering bricks until he found her legs, and then her hand, still curled around the document that was supposed to have set her free.

TWENTY-FOUR

THEY SHOVED NAT through a door and onto an elevator. He was still hooded, but each extra second without a gunshot or a blow to the head made him dare to hope that something other than the worst lay ahead. Why go to the trouble to take him into this building unless something besides an execution awaited?

They stepped off the elevator into a hallway with lights so bright they even penetrated the gloom of the hood. His escorts maintained their silence. He wasn't sure how many were still with him, other than the ones at either side, gripping his forearms.

"Just ahead?" one muttered.

"Yes. It's supposed to be unlocked."

They stopped. A doorknob clicked. They led him inside, then a hand loosened the drawstring. The hood tickled past his nose and came free. Nat took a fresh breath of cool air and blinked into the brightness. As his eyes adjusted to the light he saw he was in an office, standing at a desk. Seated behind the desk was Clark Holland.

Nat exhaled loudly, almost laughing in relief. He had never been this happy to see anyone, although it was clear from Holland's face that the feeling wasn't mutual.

The escorts quickly disappeared, shutting the door behind them. Holland didn't even bother to say thanks.

"Maybe now I can finally get an update," Holland said. "What happened to your arm?"

Nat began to shiver. The sweat on his back felt like melted snow, and his legs were limp. He looked down at his arm and saw that the bleeding had stopped.

"There was a knife. What the hell just happened? Who were those guys?"

"BfV, most likely. German domestic intelligence. But when I ask for help from the Germans I'm not exactly picky, so who knows for sure? Could even be contract employees. Effective, though, judging from the results."

"They hooded me."

"I noticed."

"They scared the hell out of me, if you really want to know."

"They have their own way of doing things. I don't question their tactics as long as they produce the desired results. In exchange they sometimes offer the same courtesy to me, especially when I'm operating on their turf. You look like you could use a drink. I'm afraid all we have is water." He shouted toward an open door to an adjoining room. "Neil? Come take care of our visitor, please."

Neil Ford, the young agent who had tracked him down in the university library, came bounding around the corner with a first aid kit, a schoolboy grin, and an open bottle of Volvic mineral water.

"Hi, Dr. Turnbull." Like they'd just run into each other at the mall.

"Just super to see you, Neil."

"Same here!"

"I think Dr. Turnbull's being sarcastic, Neil."

"Oh."

"Glad I'm not the only one who hasn't lost his sense of irony," Nat said. He was still pleasantly amazed to be in one piece, but his relief was giving way to anger.

"I wouldn't complain if I were you, considering what almost happened."

"Me dying, you mean?"

"Oh, he wasn't going to kill you."

"Comforting that you're so sure. Then what did he want?"

"Same as me, I'd imagine. An update on your progress. Names, dates, whatever you've found out. You know, the things you're supposed to be reporting every day."

"You killed him for that?"

"Please. *They* killed him, and it was their call. I'm not here to make a nuisance of myself."

"Are you officially even here?"

"Do you really expect an answer? Drink some water, then I'll explain. Although you may want a second bottle before I'm finished. Just pretend it's Gordon Wolfe's cognac and the news shouldn't bother you at all."

"That bad?"

"Qurashi was a persuasive man. If he'd ever gotten a chance to sit you down for a confidential chat, just the two of you, you might have told him anything."

"You knew his name?"

"Saeed Qurashi. Iranian national. Contract employee of MOIS, the Ministry of Intelligence and Security. He's been following you since Zurich, more or less. One of his pals in the U.S. stole your cell phone."

"The one who called Karen? If she's in any way—"

"Relax. I told you, she's covered. Even better than you were just now."

"This Qurashi. I think I saw him in Bern, dressed like a house-keeper in the hotel. He may have copied the files off my laptop."

"You might have reported that, you know. But as it happens, we already knew. Did it occur to you that your friend Berta might have invited you up to her room expressly so he could do that?"

"You really think so?"

"We're not sure what to think about her. But that's a topic for later. Qurashi was an agent, but he's better known as an interrogator. A good one. Meaning a bad one."

"I thought 'enhanced techniques' weren't really torture anymore?"

"I'm not talking about something as tame as waterboarding. Not that you'd find it tame, but Qurashi wasn't equipped for it. Care to see what the BfV found in his hotel room?"

Holland hefted a large shopping bag onto the desk with a heavy clank. First he pulled out a pair of electrical clamps hooked up to wires.

"God knows what these are supposed to attach to."

Nat locked his knees. Holland dug into the bag again.

"Looks like he had an AC adapter for every specification. Careful traveler, our man Qurashi. Prepared for outlets of all nations. But I've saved the best for last."

Holland held aloft a blowtorch attached to a canister of propane.

"Believe me, he wasn't planning on using this to make crème brûlée. As I said, he was very persuasive."

"I get the picture."

"Yes, well, in case you need a further reminder of what's at stake—Neil, could you bring me those intercepts?"

Neil Ford emerged again from the back, this time with a manila folder. He pointedly avoided looking at Nat as he handed it to Holland, who slid the folder across the desk.

"NSA intercepts, all from the past week. Most of these calls are between Qurashi and a control in Berlin, who we still haven't identified, by the way, so don't feel too damn smug. Take a look."

"Who's 'Gateway'?" Nat asked.

"MOIS code name for Bauer. 'Ferret' is you."

" 'Ferret'?"

"I'm told it's a compliment. Read on."

All his recent movements were detailed. So was an order, issued the previous day via the Berlin control, to "retrieve Ferret for questioning. Use all means at your disposal."

"Does Bauer know this is happening?"

"He certainly wouldn't have any objection. The more intense the competition, the more likely he gets what he wants. He may have his own people out there looking as well. He claims otherwise, of course, and the German government has ordered us to keep our hands off him if we want their continued cooperation. Which is why it would be just fabulous if sometime in the next day or two you could actually wrap things up."

"Not likely. I'm not even close."

"I was guessing you'd say that. But maybe now you see the urgency, if only from a selfish point of view."

"You've driven home the point well enough. Maybe too well."

"Meaning?"

"Meaning I was the wrong choice for this job. I teach and I do research. Sometimes I even deal with administrators and tenure committees. But that's as risky as it gets in my line of work. Iranian thugs with blowtorches are more than I bargained for. For me or for my daughter. Hire Berta. She's crazy enough to finish the job, and she probably knows a lot more than she's letting on. Better still, you don't even have to hire her. Just turn her loose and put a tail on her. That way you won't have to pay her expenses."

"Sorry, Nat, but you're our man. Once you're in, you're not out until we say so."

"You make it sound like the Mafia."

"The Mafia pays better, and plays for lower stakes. With Bauer, we're talking about a man whose little black book could help someone build the world's next nuclear weapon."

"What if I quit anyway?"

"There are things called tax laws, passport rules, travel restrictions. Do you really think you could get very far in your work with us opposing you at every turn?"

"I'm glad you've decided to play fair."

"And I'm glad you mentioned Berta. She's next on the agenda. Neil, did you load the video?"

Neil called out from the next room.

"Yes, sir. Ready to roll."

Holland picked up a remote and gestured toward a TV in the corner. The screen flickered to life. Static and snow gave way to a grainy image with a time signature.

"That's the Baltimore storage facility where the boxes were. You've already seen the video of Gordon. Our analyst concluded you were right. He seemed to be carrying something beneath his pants. This footage is from the same day a few hours later, right after the power outage. The alarm system is computerized, and even though backup power kicks in immediately, the system takes a few minutes to reboot. Whoever knocked out the line must have known that. But the surveillance cameras never lapsed. Watch closely. This first shot is from the rear of the lot."

Ghostly images of traffic whizzed past on a highway just behind the fence. Then a dark form appeared, climbing over a Jersey wall from the highway. The form threw a stiff tarpaulin over the barbed wire and then scaled the fence. Someone with decent agility, reasonably young, but not very tall. Wool cap, dark clothes. Smudged face, probably greasepaint.

"Now we move to the camera in the hall, outside the locker."

The figure passed just below and headed straight for the door. Even through the loose contours of the sweatshirt Nat could tell it was a woman, the same way a baggy peasant blouse hadn't hidden all her curves the first time he saw her in the courtroom.

"Jesus H. Christ."

"So you finally recognize her?"

He could only nod. Over the next few minutes Berta proceeded to pick the door lock and haul away all four boxes, toting them to the back of the lot without having to pass the front entrance, where the deskman would have still been on duty. She dropped them into the bushes from the top of the fence. He cringed. No wonder the corners were dented. Nat felt like he had been punched in the chest.

It made sense, though, after what he had learned from Christian Hermann, not to mention Willis Turner. And it was easy to see what must have happened next. Berta had flown into a rage when she realized Gordon had removed the most important folders, so she took out her frustration by planting the boxes at his summer home and then phoning the police. Getting him arrested gave her free rein to look for his hiding place. Perhaps she was counting on the pressure of an arrest to make Gordon spill the beans. Or maybe she had killed him, to keep that from happening. Either way, her next step would have been to seek help from the one expert who knew Gordon best: Nathaniel Turnbull.

Nat doubted she had counted on any competition from the Iranians. Unless, as Holland suggested, she was working with them. If so, then who was Willis Turner working for?

Holland turned off the television.

"I guess this means I need to ditch my partner," Nat said. "You were right. It was a bad idea."

"Actually, I was going to suggest you stick with her a while longer."

"You really do think I'm nuts."

" 'Keep your friends close, your enemies closer.' "

"An FBI man quoting the Godfather—that's a new one."

"Actually it's originally from Sun Tzu, a general in ancient China. But still good advice, especially when someone is holding out on you. I suggest you threaten to quit, like you were just doing with me. You can even tell her I showed you this little video."

"What if she still doesn't tell me what she's got?"

"Just try it. And Nat?"

"Yes?"

"Don't forget to check in. Each and every day. After tonight, I'd say you owe me."

For once, Nat agreed.

BERTA WAS WAITING for him in the deserted hotel lobby. She didn't look happy.

"How'd it go at the bank?" Nat asked.

She shrugged, noncommittal.

"Well, I've been thinking. We seem to have accomplished just about all we can as a team. Maybe after tonight it would be better to go our separate ways."

She was aghast.

"But I have the money for Göllner. And I can get more if you need it."

"Keep it. The money's not important. Besides, Göllner doesn't want to see you."

Nat hadn't yet told her that the opposite was true.

"That's not fair! I took you to him, and I still have other leads!"

"Like what?"

"Well, leads from the interrogation transcript, once we have it."

"Fine, then I'll pursue them on my own. I speak German. You act like I've never done this before. So unless you've got something more to offer—"

"But I do have more!"

"Then tell me. Right now."

For a moment she said nothing. Her inner struggle was evident. She paused, lips pursed, like a spoiled little girl with a big secret, determined to hold her breath until her lungs burst.

"Come on, Berta. Now or never."

The words tumbled out in a rush.

"It's Erich Stuckart. He's alive. And only I can show you where to find him."

TWENTY-FIVE

ERICH STUCKART WALKED into the rain to retrieve his morning paper from a mailbox marked "Schmidt," a stooped old man on a soggy lawn. Nat recognized him from the photo in Berta's portfolio, the one shot he hadn't been able to identify until now.

The two of them watched from across the street through the streaked windshield of a rental car. Nat had picked it up that morning expressly for this trip.

The way Berta had explained it the night before, Stuckart had faked his fatal car accident with the help of a Munich policeman. Another cop had let her in on the secret. Supposedly West German intelligence was in on the scheme, doing a favor for a Cold War source. Now you could visit his headstone at a local cemetery, where an urn of ashes was stored in a small vault. Nat wondered if the irony of using a crematorium as a stage prop had enhanced Stuckart's satisfaction with the ruse. A whole new life, and he didn't even have to change his monogram.

In fact, he'd barely changed his neighborhood. Hohengatow was just across the Havel River from the Grunewald. Sail four miles downstream and you could dock at his father's old villa on the Wannsee. A few blocks farther and you'd be at the house where the Wannsee Conference was held. Talk about balls. It was the one detail that had finally convinced Nat that Berta's story must be true. Because who would ever make up anything so bizarre: that a fellow so desperate to escape his past would nonetheless settle just upstream from the site where his father had earned eternal infamy as an architect of Hitler's Final Solution.

"Nice house," Nat said to Berta, as they watched Stuckart shut the door behind him.

"He still has the family's old motorboat. It's considered a vintage model now."

"You say he slammed the door in your face?"

She nodded.

"Hard to believe you only tried once. By your standards that's practically sane."

"He threatened me with the police."

"Well, I'll threaten him with the CIA. Or better still, the *New York Times*. You wait here." They had already agreed he would go it alone, even though she was still pouting about it. "Don't worry. I take very good notes."

"As long as you're willing to share them."

"Here's something else I'll share. Göllner wants to see you when we go back this afternoon. He seems to think you have something to do with the people who've been poking around his place lately."

She frowned and wrinkled her nose.

"I work alone. You should know that as well as anyone."

Nat watched her reaction carefully. She seemed genuinely puzzled by the accusation. Good. Also, to his relief, no one had followed them on the drive out to Hohengatow. The lonely road had been quite empty at this early hour. Qurashi's death must have left the Iranians shorthanded.

"Well, you can take that up with Göllner. At least this time he'll let you in the door. Now if I can just get Stuckart to do the same for me."

Nat stepped into the chilly rain.

Stuckart answered his knock. Even at his advanced age, his resemblance to photos of his father was striking—the long face, the narrow, sloping nose, the undersized mouth, the wide-awake eyes, like those of a lurking owl, watching for prey. There was a calmness to his demeanor that was hard to reconcile with the monstrosities he had engineered. But, no, Nat reminded himself, that was his father's doing, not the son's. No real guilt here, except by association. As far as he knew.

"Herr Schmidt?"

"Yes?"

"I'm Dr. Nathaniel Turnbull, a historian from the United States. I was wondering if I might have a few minutes of your time?"

The door was already closing. Nat put his foot forward like a pushy salesman and held out his hands. He wasn't usually so aggressive, but he wasn't often this close to such valuable memories.

"I'm aware of your real identity, so that's not an issue. I have no wish to make it public knowledge."

Stuckart pushed harder and raised his voice.

"If you please, sir. I have nothing to say to you and I never will."

"I haven't come to ask about you. It's about Kurt Bauer."

This at least made him stop shoving the door against Nat's foot.

"Look," Nat said, "just let me tell you exactly what this is and isn't about."

Stuckart let go of the door, but didn't back away. He was breathing heavily. Nat dropped his hands to his sides, but kept his foot in place.

"Whatever you tell me will go no further than my notebook," Nat said. Stuckart began shaking his head. "*Unless*—" Nat raised a finger in warning. He felt like a bully, but what the hell. No matter how young Stuckart had been during the war, he had nonetheless been a Nazi, and from the looks of his house he was still living off the bounty of his father's high rank. "*Unless* you choose not to speak with me. In which case I know quite a few other historians who would love to know where you live and what your real name is. There are also a few journalists who would find the story of your so-called death quite amusing, although I doubt your friends in law enforcement would care for the publicity."

"I did *nothing*! I was a damned boy, and I only wish to be left in peace."

"I understand. And Kurt Bauer was only a boy, too. But he's not anymore, is he? And he has gotten to keep his name without ever having to disappear."

Stuckart shook his head. He still looked exasperated, but he backed into the hall.

"Fifteen minutes. No more."

He led Nat to a sitting room. A tiny woman with white hair and sparkling blue eyes peeped around the corner from the rear. She looked terrified.

"It's all right, Marlene. No need to phone anyone. Why don't you take Snowflake for her walk?"

A white toy poodle, immaculately groomed, showed its face at the mention of its name. The woman called after it and the two of them disappeared. Stuckart remained on his feet as they listened to the jangling of a leash, the click of tiny paws on a tile floor, the back door opening and shutting. Stuckart then settled into the middle of a grand old couch and glared at Nat.

A lot of old money was on display here—mostly in heavy oil paintings from the nineteenth century in gilded frames. Mounted high on a far wall was the head of a stag, flanked by fierce-looking boars, tusks shining in the gloom. Nat wondered if they had been killed in the Grunewald. Stuckart's father had almost certainly held conversations beneath their gaze as well, perhaps even with Hitler, and almost certainly with Himmler. Bad spirits galore. The glass eyes of those dead beasts had witnessed it all.

"You disapprove of me living this well, don't you?" Stuckart said. "I can tell by the way you look at everything. Your smug superiority. Well, let me tell you something, I am not afraid of your threats. I, too, have friends in the news media, and certainly with the police. If you fail to keep your word, you will hear from them, and for a long time."

"It sounds like we have an understanding, then. In that case we should begin."

Nat took out his notebook.

"You and Bauer. You were school chums, correct?"

"In fact, we are still friends. Not everyone is so narrow-minded as some people."

"What was he like then?"

"The same as now. Smart. Sober. A careful man who decides what he wants and then goes and gets it. He also knows the value of loyalty. We both do. In fact, if you really want to talk about Kurt Bauer, it would be much more productive to speak with the man himself. I am sure he would be quite happy to arrange an appointment."

"Maybe. Although I'm told he isn't too eager to discuss the war years."

"Of course not. No German knows how to have that discussion properly. Not anymore, because everyone has already made up their minds about how to feel about you. Before you even say a word they decide what you must have been like, and their judgment is always final."

"Let's not talk about Germany, then. What about Switzerland in the summer of '44? You and Kurt were in Bern, weren't you?"

Stuckart eyed him carefully and said nothing. He reached into his shirt pocket for a lighter and a pack of West cigarettes. The lighter chirped, and he inhaled deeply.

"Yes. We were in Bern. But we hardly saw each other. We were too busy for fun by then. Too preoccupied. I might have seen him in passing once or twice, but that was all."

A lie, of course, but Nat decided to save his ammunition and revisit the question later. No sense pissing the old man off just as he was warming up.

"Preoccupied with what?"

"Isn't it obvious? Everything was coming down upon our heads, and upon the heads of our families. We were doing all we could to secure our futures."

"Kurt's future seemed to end up a little brighter than yours."

"Because he is wealthier, you mean? That is not everything, you know. Even the Nazis didn't believe that."

"Not just wealth. Power, influence. Stature. Kurt Bauer can go out in public under his own name and everyone is fine with that. A Stuckart, on the other hand—"

"You'd be surprised how much of that so-called stature is because of the money. And he is part Jew, you know, which is an advantage nowadays. Not that it shouldn't be, of course."

"Bauer is Jewish?"

"Not Jewish. But he has Jewish blood. There was that whole thing with his sister's marriage."

Nat had never heard a word of this, and he suspected Berta hadn't either. The odd thing was the way Stuckart seemed to revel in the information, as if he had just brought the man down a few pegs. The two men's relationship seemed complex, to say the least, and Nat wondered what lay at the heart of it.

"His sister's marriage? I'm afraid I'm not familiar with that."

"She was supposed to marry an SS man. But it was called off after the background check by the Racial Office. Some ancestor turned up, ages earlier, a great-great-grandmother or something, who turned out to be a Jew. So, naturally—"

"Were there other consequences?"

"Not any real ones. There was never any question of that. His family was far too valuable to the war effort. There must have been thousands of those marriage background checks, and I never heard of a single one that led to anything beyond a few broken hearts. But of course Kurt's father didn't know that. The poor man panicked, nearly had a breakdown. And once you let certain people in the Gestapo see this sort of fear, well, I'm sure you can imagine how they might choose to take advantage."

"Bribes?"

Stuckart shrugged, but a sly grin said he knew better. Maybe Göllner also knew better.

"Was that why the family left for Switzerland?"

Stuckart shrugged again, and this time he didn't smile. He took another long drag from his cigarette before speaking.

"As I said, Kurt and I hardly saw each other in Bern. I never had a chance to ask."

"This news about the Jewish ancestor, then—you heard that from other people?"

"I may have seen Kurt in Berlin just before he left. We were both still too young for the draft, so we had time for socializing, such as it was, with the blackout and all. They even closed the beer gardens, you know. Worst decision the Cripple ever made."

"Did your father know about this problem with the Bauers' ancestry?"

"Of course."

"And he didn't order you to stop seeing him?"

"You know, people always assume that any German in those days would have simply been appalled to find out that a friend had even a drop of Jewish blood."

"Can't imagine why they'd think that."

"See? You are the same. And in my case, it is only because of my father, and some meeting he supposedly attended, and a single law that bears his signature. Say what you will, but I am not at all ashamed of my father. He was a legal technician, nothing more. They asked him to draft laws and he did so, just as he was obligated to do. Not by the German Reich, but by his professional code of conduct. The same way that any lawyer would defend some criminal, some murderer, to his very last breath if that was his duty. Does that mean the lawyer is complicit in the murder? Of course not."

"Yes, I see your point." The last thing Nat wanted to encourage was further lecturing. "So his Jewishness didn't bother anybody, then—is that what you're saying?"

"It was merely some old blood, a mistake made long ago by a distant relative. Or not a mistake, but you know what I mean. I suppose there was some reaction among a few people. But no one of importance. His girlfriend, for example. If anything, she was probably pleased by it. Not because she was a Jew, of course. More because of her politics. I always suspected that deep down she was a little Bolshevik."

Stuckart laughed, the smoke issuing in bursts.

"What makes you say that? Because of this little group they were mixed up in, the White Rose?"

Stuckart's smile disappeared.

"I don't know a thing about any of that."

"Nothing?"

"Quite right."

"But wasn't Bauer arrested? Surely you heard about that. He was interrogated by the Gestapo, even put into prison for a while."

"I don't know."

"Your best friend goes to jail for five months and you don't know about it?"

"We were friends, not *best* friends. And if these things indeed happened, then it must have been during a period when I didn't see him much. There were a lot of bombings of the city in that period. Life wasn't exactly proceeding in a normal fashion. So when people went missing from your life for a while, it didn't seem out of the ordinary."

"I see." Lying son of a bitch. But why cover for Bauer on a matter that, presumably, would make the man look good, even noble? "What else do you remember about Bauer's girlfriend?"

"Not so much. It was a poor match. My father detested her. But all the same he was fine with letting her dine in his house, because that is the kind of man he was."

"Tolerant."

"Of course. His duties and his work he kept to one side, his friendships and his hospitality he kept to another. As is only proper."

"Of course." Nat wished he had all this on tape, if only for the circuitous marvel of Stuckart's rationalizations. He had heard some splendid examples over the years from Germans of that era, but this was a virtuoso performance.

The discussion of Bauer's girlfriend, however, had jarred loose his memory of Berta's findings on the deaths at Plötzensee Prison, plus all those photos of the elderly Bauer arriving at the site on the fourth day of every month, flowers in hand.

"This girlfriend. I suppose you're referring to Liesl Folkerts?"

Stuckart tilted his head and gave Nat a long, silent look, as if reappraising his questioner. His next words emerged with great deliberation.

"How much, exactly, have you dug up on old Kurt?"

Was it Nat's imagination, or had Stuckart's tone contained a hint of gleeful malice? Yes, this was a complicated friendship.

"Bits and pieces. She died, didn't she? Some misadventure at Plötzensee Prison?"

"She was killed in a bombing raid. There was a big one that night, and the prison took a direct hit. A few people even managed to escape as a result, but Liesl was buried under a collapsed wall. Kurt was inconsolable."

"I thought you didn't see him any then?"

"This was all secondhand, of course. From mutual friends. As for myself, I, uh, didn't see him again until—"

"Switzerland?"

"Of course."

"Let's go back there for a second."

Stuckart shrugged and reached again for his cigarettes. He stubbed out the first one even though it was only half finished.

"As I told you, we hardly saw each other in Bern. I recall running into him once on the Kornhaus Bridge, but that was about it."

Nat consulted his notes from the Swiss surveillance reports.

"This meeting on the bridge, would that have been on the twentieth of July, 1944?"

"I have no idea. It was so long ago. That could have been the date, but I would hardly describe it as any sort of 'meeting.' "

"Well, I'm not sure what else you would call it. You and Kurt were witnessed together on the bridge. Then both of you walked to a house in Altenberg, where you were inside for several hours."

Stuckart was stone-faced, silent. Nat continued.

"A few days later you visited him at his room at the Bellevue, where his family had a suite. You stayed two hours, then the two of you had dinner together on the terrace, where you were also seen chatting with members of the German legation. One of them was a new addition to the staff of the Gestapo."

Stuckart exhaled twin plumes of smoke through his nostrils. A long column of ash drooped from his cigarette, on the verge of collapse.

"Where did you come by this ludicrous hearsay?"

"It's not hearsay. It's a surveillance report by Swiss intelligence. An original, not a copy. Swiss agents observed a third lengthy meeting between the two of you as well. It was also attended by the new staff member of the Gestapo. Maybe now that I've refreshed your memory you could fill in some of the details?"

"I'm afraid that isn't possible."

"Isn't possible, or isn't desirable? Why keep protecting Bauer?"

"Look, when I said earlier that Kurt Bauer and I were still friends, perhaps I was being a bit boastful. We are in touch from time to time, but we really don't see each other. Not face-to-face, or out in public. So, naturally, we never have occasion to revisit these old conversations, meaning that my memory of any time we may have once spent together has faded over time. Quite a bit, in fact. Do you see?"

"Yes, I see. And I'm beginning to understand your friendship. It's based on mutual leverage, because you both have something to hide. For you, the Stuckart identity. For him, something that happened during the war, here or in Bern. In a strange way you're still valuable to each other. In fact, I wouldn't be at all surprised to learn that he helped arrange your little vanishing act, in that fake accident. You probably didn't have the right connections at the time. But he did. And he was glad to help, because if his own secret ever got out, well, that would be almost as embarrassing as having people know you were the son of a convicted war criminal."

"I think it is time for you to leave, Dr. Turnbull."

"I think so, too. Your memory's not getting any better."

Nat stood. Stuckart struggled to his feet.

"Remember," the old man said, "you have your threats, but I also have mine. If you do not keep your word, I will not hesitate to take action."

"Don't worry, Herr Schmidt. I know how to keep a secret."

"Oh, I am not at all worried. You're the one who should be worried."

For all the excitement of the encounter, Nat realized as he was describing it to Berta that he really hadn't learned much new information. As a result, she was suitably unimpressed. The one item that seemed like a genuine revelation—verification that Liesl Folkerts had been Bauer's girlfriend—bounced right off her. Meaning she probably already knew. He considered telling her that he had found her stash of photographs, then decided against it. No sense bickering just before their important meeting with Göllner.

"You should have called me in," she said. "I could have gotten more out of him."

"You'd have only gotten us thrown out of the house quicker. Besides, Göllner's transcript should tell us what Stuckart was trying to hide."

"Maybe."

They grabbed a quick lunch at a nearby Imbiss. Feeling upbeat about their prospects, he ordered a Schulteiss lager with his Currywurst. Maybe they would soon have something to celebrate.

When the appointed hour arrived, Martin Göllner was waiting for them on the sidewalk outside his building. It was immediately clear he was in no condition to transact business.

His body was flattened against the pavement with his black overcoat fanned out around him like the garments of a melted witch. Two policemen stood over the body while a third taped off the scene. Göllner's skull had split on impact. The crack oozed pink foam like an overripe melon. Blood pooled around his open mouth. His house slippers had somehow remained on his stocking feet.

Nat looked up toward the fifth floor, where lace curtains blew out from Göllner's open window. Was it his imagination, or did he hear the oompah blat of a tuba issuing faintly from the neighbor's nonstop Oktoberfest? One of the policemen pulled back the flaps of Göllner's overcoat. No papers of any kind were visible.

"Come on," Nat hissed. "Let's try to get in while there's still a chance."

They dashed through the building's open front door, and they were out of breath by the time they reached the fifth-floor landing. Brassy music was indeed playing loudly from the apartment across the hall, and Göllner's door was ajar. They passed through to the living room with its flapping curtains. No sign of any documents. They reached the door of the bedroom just as a middle-aged cop in plastic gloves looked up from Göllner's bureau.

"What's going on? Who the hell are you?"

"We, uh . . . had an appointment with Herr Göll . . . uh, Mannheim."

"Well, this is a crime scene, and you've fucked it up enough already, so don't move a muscle." He approached them with a weary air. "Identification, please." Exactly what Nat had hoped to avoid. "C'mon. Both of you."

The cop scanned the entry stamp in Nat's passport.

"American," he muttered. "You arrived only yesterday?"

"Yes."

"From where?"

"Zurich."

"What is your business here?"

"I'm a historian. Here's my university ID. Mannheim was an old Gestapo man, named Martin Göllner. Was he pushed?"

The policeman took the ID while ignoring the question.

"Someday we'll be through with all of these people," he said. "Then there will be no more of their messes to clean up. Then all we'll have is old people dying the way they always do, with no complications from the past. My partner will want to speak with both of you."

A half hour later they were back on the sidewalk, having just finished speaking with a detective, who said he might want to talk with them later as well. Nat watched as Göllner's body was carted to an ambulance. His only sorrow was of a professional nature, and not simply because they had missed out on the transcript. Göllner's death meant that another portal to the past had closed forever. One less eyewitness to the most murderous era in history.

He now had to confront the issue of Berta Heinkel. In revealing the whereabouts of Stuckart she had presumably placed her last card on the table, and no matter what Holland said, Nat needed to get away from her. The woman trailed death like the train of a wedding gown, and he didn't want to be the next person to trip on it. It was time for a clean break.

"Maybe we could come back later," Berta said. "See if we can get in."

"I've no doubt *you* could. You're pretty skilled in that department."

"What do you mean?"

"Larceny of all kinds. You're the expert."

"I admitted I was overzealous at the archives, but—"

"I was talking about the storage locker. The way you followed Gordon there and then broke in. Climbed a fence, wore a cap. You should see the surveillance video—you're a star. For a plain old historian you really are multitalented. You can jimmy a lock, fake a license, seduce a source. Seduce. No wonder you like that word. It's your best trick, pun intended. So I'm sure you'd be able to get into this dump. But you heard the cop. There were no papers found. Nothing suspicious except the way he died, flying out the window in his overcoat. So tell me, did you break into the jail, too, on the night Gordon died? Or did you just pay someone else to mix too many pills into his dinner?"

Berta's mouth was agape, her eyes shocked. He had blindsided her, and for the first time since they'd met she seemed truly flustered. Even the confrontation over her thievery at the National Archives hadn't unstrung her like this. When she finally spoke, her voice was a whisper.

"Pills? What are you talking about?"

"Ask Willis Turner."

"I didn't kill Dr. Wolfe. I could never kill anyone. You'd know that if you really knew me."

"I don't think I'm willing to take the risk of really knowing you. Turner and Holland would be happy to take your offer, though. Why don't you call them?"

"When did you talk to them?"

"Does it matter?"

His cell phone rang.

"That's one of them now, isn't it?" she said. "I guess you've missed your time to report in on me. Like an informant."

"You should know. You're the one with the Stasi file."

She slapped him, hard, then turned away just as her face dissolved into tears. He had expected the anger, but not this. She sobbed as his phone rang again, but as he stepped toward her she broke into a run, coat flapping, just like Göllner's must have done as he sailed to his death. Let her go, he told himself. Wasn't this exactly what he wanted?

The cops were watching the dustup with interest, so he turned in the opposite direction to take the call. The screen showed that it was from a blocked number.

"Nat?"

It was Steve Wallace, his archival source at the CIA.

"Jesus, Steve, how'd you get this number? Never mind. Stupid question."

"I'm on an official line, so I'll keep it short. Still can't really help you. The properties in question remain unbearably hot. But seeing as how most of the heat is coming from our poor cousins across the Potomac"—the FBI, he meant—"I can at least advise you strongly to check your e-mail, preferably within the hour. But I'm expecting compensation. I understand you may have pictures?"

"I do indeed. And I'm a good sharer."

"Great. Send them all. And don't call back."

"That hot, huh?"

But Wallace had already hung up, which was answer enough. Nat looked around. More cops were arriving, and more gawking bystanders. No sign of Berta, thank goodness, although he didn't feel as relieved as he would have expected. Did he miss her? Or was he just wondering where she might be headed without him? Perhaps she had one last source up her sleeve.

He caught a cab back to the hotel. She had checked out only moments earlier. Paying on his card, of course. He pocketed the receipt and went straight upstairs, figuring he had better check right away for Wallace's e-mail. The CIA man had seemed to imply there was some sort of electronic shelf life.

There it was, waiting with a simple "FYI" on the message line. Also clamoring for attention was a message from Berta. He clicked on it first. Judging from how long it took to come up, he was half expecting a photo, maybe even the one of Stuckart. A final peace offering. Instead, it was a brief farewell.

"Sorry I was such a disappointment. Best of luck. Regards, Berta."

He had expected more. He clicked on the Wallace e-mail, which also got straight to the point:

"OSS paperwork shows shipping of the four boxes handled in Bern Nov. 8, 1945, by Gordon Wolfe and Murray Kaplan. Kaplan on OSS payroll, Dec. '44 to Dec. '45. Current address: 14147 Palm Bay Court, Candalusa, Fla."

A live source, then. Someone who might have a key memory. More to the point, it was information unknown to Berta Heinkel. Now that the Iranian with the blowtorch was dead, she might well be his main competitor. It was enough to convince him to find another hotel room for the evening, so he signed off and caught the U-Bahn to

Alexanderplatz, checking his flanks at every stop. He took a room on the twentieth floor of an ugly high-rise and logged back on to his laptop to Google Murray Kaplan. The local wireless server was terrible, and it took forever to boot up. Even then, the search came up practically empty, although it did produce a phone number for Kaplan. He dialed it.

In Florida it was noon. Kaplan's wife said her husband was out back. He came on the line and seemed wary when Nat said he wanted to reminisce about Gordon Wolfe. He nonetheless agreed to a noon interview the following day.

Nat looked up Candalusa, Florida. It was just below Daytona Beach. He reserved a seat on a midday flight to Miami with a connection to Daytona, then booked a car and an oceanfront motel. All set. After an early dinner from room service he stretched out on the bed fully dressed, telling himself he would check in with Holland in an hour. He'd then call Karen, just to make sure everything was okay.

Twelve hours later he awakened cold and out of sorts. It was 8 a.m.

Nat was irritated about oversleeping, but he was also refreshed, and for the first time in days his mind was lodged firmly in the twenty-first century. His thoughts were of anything but Nazis, or even Germany. Instead, he wondered if Karen's grades had come in, if the Wightman police had yet recovered his phone, and whether he would still be welcome on campus if his current work dismantled what was left of Gordon Wolfe's legacy.

A call to Holland was overdue, but Karen was who he really wanted to talk to. Alas, it was 2 a.m. in the States, and even she wasn't that much of a night owl. So he brewed a cup of instant coffee while watching television, feeling lonely and far from home.

Then his phone rang. Karen's number popped onto the display. Serendipity.

"Hi! I was just—"

"Dad! He's in the house!" She was breathless.

"Who is? Where are you?"

"Someone broke in. I heard him downstairs, so I climbed out the window, onto the roof above the porch. Now I'm in the yard, but I can see him in your study. He's looking for something."

"Jesus, Karen! Call 9-1-1."

"I did. The police are coming, but I'm scared. He's at the window now. Omigod, I think he sees me!"

"Get out! Now. Run to a neighbor's, or down the street. Go!"

"He's opening the window! He's coming!"

"Go, Karen! Just go!"

The call ended. Nat was frantic for more. He dialed back and got a recording, Karen's cheerful voice asking him to please leave a message. His imagination filled in the blanks, and in his mind's eye a man who looked like Qurashi chased the barefoot Karen across a dewy lawn while the neighbors slept, oblivious. The man grabbed a hank of her hair and wrestled her through the backyard to his car in a rear alley, while the cops pulled up cluelessly out front and shined flashlights at an empty house. Nat saw an equipment bag on the backseat, unzipped. Electrodes and a blowtorch.

He tried the number again with no success. Then a third time. Nothing but the maddening recording, Karen's voice so full of youth and optimism. And here he was, jaded old Dad, unable to raise a finger because he was off in Berlin, dabbling in someone else's history while his own needed him so urgently. For want of a nail. Posterity would deem him a no-show in this disaster, a failure to his daughter. Damn, damn, and damn. And where were the feds? Damn Holland and his promises, and damn himself.

Nat paced the tiny room. He banged his fist on the wall and cursed loudly. He needed fresh air, but he didn't dare leave for fear his cell phone would lose its signal in the hall or the elevator. Three minutes passed without a word. Then four, then five. He considered calling his ex-wife from the room's bedside phone, but he couldn't face that yet. He was too certain of her reproach, and knew he deserved it.

Eight minutes. He tried Karen's number, knowing he would never again be able to bear listening to this recording if the worst came to pass. He couldn't even stand it now.

"This is Karen," she chirped. "Please leave your name at—"

"Call, goddamn it!" he shouted.

Someone in the next room pounded on the wall for silence.

"Fuck off! Call. Please just *call*."

Nine minutes.

Then his phone rang, her number on the display.

"Karen?"

A man's voice: "Dr. Turnbull?"

"Who is this? Where's Karen?" In his panic, Nat imbued the man's words with a heavy accent and the worst of intentions.

"This is Sergeant Wilcox, Wightman Police. Your daughter's fine, and the suspect is in custody. Would you like to speak to her?"

"Yes." The clouds lifted. The storm passed. Nat exhaled with something between a laugh and a sob. "Put her on, please."

He sank with relief onto the narrow bed. For the moment, history had decided to give him a pass.

TWENTY-SIX

NAT DIDN'T CALM DOWN until two hours into his flight across the Atlantic. A call from Holland an hour after the break-in hadn't exactly helped matters.

"Where were your men?" Nat asked right away.

"We had just canceled the detail. When a week passed and no one came poking around, we figured they must not be interested. If it's any comfort, it was your papers they wanted. They weren't after Karen."

"I guess that's why he came through the window, chasing her."

"He thought she was a nosy neighbor. He didn't even know anyone was home."

"What are you, his attorney?"

"Look, I'm sorry. We screwed up, but it worked out. We even got your phone back. Any way you look at it, it's another player off the board."

"But how many are still on it?"

Silence.

Nat hung up before Holland could ask for an update. The news of his trip to Florida could wait. Holland's German surrogates were probably still following him anyway.

Karen, at least, was now safely accounted for. Nat had asked Viv Wolfe to take her in for the rest of the evening, and Viv had seemed grateful to have someone else's needs to attend to.

"Just keep her away from Gordon's cognac," he said. "On second thought, maybe she could use a shot. I've talked to her mom. She'll come by for her at noon."

"Susan, you mean? As in, your ex-wife and the woman I've known for twenty years?"

"Yes, Susan. Karen will be staying with her in Pittsburgh till I'm back for good. Hopefully with some better goddamn security."

"You never should have relied on those people, Nat. Not that they've stopped keeping an eye on me, of course. Every time I go to the bank it's like a presidential motorcade."

Karen, for her part, tried to act like the whole thing had been some wacky summer adventure. But Nat wasn't fooled. She was even too flustered to come up with an appropriate verse—although not for lack of trying. As she spoke by phone from the back of a police cruiser, Nat was amazed to hear her turning pages of a book.

"Did you actually take *The Complete Poems* with you when you left the house?"

"It's the one thing I had time to grab before I jumped out the window."

"Next time try for a butcher knife."

He finally mastered his own emotions about the time the stewardess brought his second complimentary drink—he had upgraded to business class, figuring the FBI owed him at least that much. But his day never quite got back on track. When he landed in Miami he discovered that his connection was canceled and another flight wasn't available for hours. He didn't pull into the parking lot of the Sea Breeze Motor Lodge in Daytona until almost midnight. Jet-lagged, he then slept until 10 a.m.

He awoke to realize that the room was a bit more depressing than he'd bargained for, with rust spots and torn wallpaper. At least there was a balcony with a sliding door to let in the salt breeze and the sound of the breakers, and when he flipped back the curtains there were no lurking Iranians or prying lawmen. Just him, alone with his rattled nerves and a lingering sense of foreboding.

Or so he thought until he left for breakfast.

Standing on the breezeway was Berta Heinkel, smoking a cigarette and wearing an unseasonable sweater. She spoke before Nat could recover from the shock.

"What time are you going to see him?" she asked.

"How long have you been here?"

"Since seven. Answer my question. When is your appointment with Murray Kaplan?"

"How in the hell do you know that name? When did you fly over? How'd you even know where to find me?"

"Like you said, I am a woman of many talents. I simply put one of them to use. Haven't you wondered why your laptop is so sluggish?"

It took him a few seconds to add it up.

"Jesus, what did you do, put something on that farewell e-mail?"

"A spyware program that sent me your keystrokes. But at least I have the decency to tell you. I'll even clean it out for you. Interested in breakfast?"

Amazing. She was better than either the FBI or the ham-handed Iranians. And as he watched her trying to maintain her coolness, he couldn't help but have mixed emotions. Sure, he was angry. But he also pitied her. She looked tired, beleaguered. The cloud of cigarette smoke lent her features the wispy grayness of an apparition, some Euro ghost far removed from its usual haunts. He was beginning to understand why, now that he knew more about her background as a zealous teen. She had been duped by the state into believing that snooping was not just okay but a civic duty. Then her grandmother had died before she could apologize, or maybe even before she realized that she *should* apologize. Bad enough to have done that at all, much less having it revealed to all your West German colleagues. And now she was broke, homeless. Yet here she was anyway, ready to resume the chase.

"Well? Are you hungry or not? And I really will fix your laptop for you. But only if I'm allowed to sit in on your talk with Kaplan. I'm following you out there, either way, so you might as well let me."

Nat shook his head, half in amazement, half in exasperation.

"C'mon, then. The appointment's at noon. We'll talk about it while we eat."

The best they could do was a Denny's, but at least it wasn't crowded. And was it his imagination or was the fellow at the next table the same guy he had just seen back at the Sea Breeze? At least he wasn't Middle Eastern, and there was certainly no law against eating at the same place as another motel guest. Maybe he was an FBI tail. Or maybe Nat was just getting paranoid.

Berta left to use the washroom, and Nat took the opportunity to phone Willis Turner for an update. He got a recording instead, and when he started to leave a message the tape ran out. Typical, he supposed, but it left him a little unsettled. Mickey Mouse town or not,

Turner didn't seem like the type who went very long without checking in.

"Hand me your laptop," Berta said as she slid back into their booth. He hesitated. For all he knew, she would install something even more intrusive. "You can watch, if you like. Maybe you'll even learn something."

He took her up on the offer and moved to her side of the booth, looking over her shoulder as she worked. He was mildly unsettled to find that he still found it arousing to be this close, bunched up against the softness beneath her sweater.

She tutted at the state of his security software.

"You're about three years overdue for an update. You made it way too easy for some snoop to get in."

You should know, he thought, wondering again what must be in her Stasi file. Their eggs arrived just as she finished, and he moved back to his side of the table with a sense of relief.

"Tell me the background on Kaplan," she said.

"Don't you already know?"

"All I learned from your keystrokes was that you Googled his name and made travel arrangements to come see him. In that sense, I suppose I am still at your mercy."

He considered telling her nothing and then asking the Kaplans not to let her in. But a scene like that would probably scare them off.

"He was an OSS man in Bern. All I know is that he worked with Gordon in shipping the records. If any funny business went on, maybe he'll know."

Shortly before noon they drove out to Candalusa, Berta following Nat in a rented red Chevy. Kaplan's house was long and low, white stucco and jalousie windows, with a carport at one end. They headed up the sidewalk, scattering a gecko. A short, lively woman with gray hair in a bun answered the door. Looming behind her was a tall, paunchy fellow with a slight stoop. Both were tanned to the point of leathery.

"Doris Kaplan," she said. "And this is Murray. Oh, there are two of you!"

"Nathaniel Turnbull. And this is Berta Heinkel, my, um, graduate assistant."

"So you want to talk about Gordon Wolfe," Murray said. "I had a feeling somebody might be calling about him as soon as I saw his obit.

We used to live in New York, and still get the *Times*. This is about those records, isn't it?"

"Well, yeah. Mostly."

"I've been telling Murray for years he ought to get this stuff off his chest," Doris said.

"Maybe I don't have anything to get off my chest," Kaplan said, not looking pleased.

"Oh, maybe not, Murray. But you two make yourselves comfortable. Then we'll see."

She led them to a Florida room in the back, wall-to-wall windows, all of them cranked open, with a view of a canal behind the back lawn. A rowboat that had seen better days was overturned in the grass.

"Lemonade or iced tea?" Doris asked.

"Tea, please."

Berta nodded in agreement. So far she hadn't said a word. Maybe she was worried about her accent. To some American vets it was an instant turnoff.

"And I hope you brought an appetite, 'cause I've got fresh shrimp salad."

This, at least, was a subject Kaplan could warm to.

"Caught the shrimp last night. You just hang a Coleman lantern on the dock and dip a net. Twenty years ago you could fill it in ten minutes, but the water's not what it used to be. Wouldn't matter so much if you didn't have to watch for gators. One of 'em got a jogger just last week. Young lady down by the golf course."

Berta glanced with alarm toward the canal, as if a gator might emerge any second.

"Sounds creepy," Nat said.

"*Florida*'s creepy," Kaplan replied.

"But you came from New York?"

"I was a dentist in Queens."

"That's not where I would have pegged the accent."

"Grew up in West Virginia. Hartwell Springs. My dad kept the books for the local mining company. We were the only Jews in town. It's where I met Doris."

As if summoned by her name, Doris carried in a tray laden with plates, forks, a bowl of gloppy-looking shrimp salad, and slices of white bread. She set it on a folding TV table. Kaplan waited until she was gone before commenting.

"Sorry 'bout all the mayo. Doris has a very high opinion of Miracle Whip."

But it wasn't bad, and Nat was grateful that at least one of the Kaplans was already in their corner. Murray might need some coaxing.

"So, where would you like to begin?" Nat said.

"I went over all this business of these missing records a long time ago, with an OSS board of inquiry. Gordon did, too. They swore us to secrecy, I might add."

"It's been more than fifty years. You're free to speak now."

Doris piped up from around the corner.

"See, honey? I told you that was the case."

"Yeah, well, there's things besides secrecy laws. Loyalty to your friends, for one."

"Well, for what it's worth," Nat said, "I think he really would want you to talk to me."

"You did say some nice things about him at the service. I looked up the coverage on the Internet."

If Kaplan had gone to that much trouble, he probably also knew about their falling-out, so Nat decided to level with him.

"We had our problems toward the end, but when it came to history we were always after the same thing."

Kaplan nodded but said nothing.

"How long had you known him when you two were assigned to this records detail?"

"He'd come on board in late '43, the first of our flyboys. Dulles liked him 'cause his German was good. I'd been with the OSS about a year. I was in dental school there when the war started, and I got stuck when the borders closed. I met Dulles on a train to Geneva and he offered me a job on the spot. I figured, what the hell, serve my country while I'm biding my time. Worked out pretty good, I guess."

"Did you work with Gordon much?"

"We downed a few beers now and then, but professionally I hardly ever saw him."

"Is that because he was out in the field a lot?"

"That was part of it, I guess. Plus those months in the hospital."

"Hospital?"

"He never mentioned his leg injury?"

"I, uh, always thought he got that from a flak wound."

"Hell, no. He came down without a scratch. Healthy as a mule. This was toward the end of the war. Some half-assed infiltration operation that went FUBAR on him."

"Infiltration? Into Germany?"

"That was the word around the legation. Don't know if it was true. I was never privy to that stuff."

Finally, something to flesh out some of the cryptic items from the National Archives.

"This operation, was it called 'Fleece' by any chance?"

"Coulda been. Never heard a name, though. All I know is that everyone said it was a cock-up from the get-go, and that he came back with a pretty nasty wound."

"From a firefight?"

"Can't say."

"Can't or won't?" Doris shouted the question from the next room.

"*Can't*, dear. And you're not helping. Let the young man ask his questions."

"So you don't know any more details, like what it was about, or who was involved?"

"That's right. None of that was in my bailiwick."

"Does the name Kurt Bauer ring a bell? Or Erich Stuckart?"

"Neither."

He said it without hesitation. Nat studied Kaplan's face and concluded he was telling the truth.

"So Gordon never mentioned either of them to you later?"

"Not to me."

Doris piped up again.

"How 'bout to anyone else?"

"Honey, *please!*"

Nat offered a smile of commiseration, but hoped she would keep it up. She seemed convinced her husband had something to hide.

"Okay, so Gordon was in the hospital. Do you remember the dates?"

"Must have been around February of '45. Got out around the end of April. Yes, that's right, 'cause it was the day Hitler shot himself. The news had just come in over the radio."

The dates matched perfectly with the Loofbourow memo that had mentioned Gordon's transfer to the Zurich safe house.

"I guess he must have healed up pretty good, because in July, of course, we both went into Germany as part of Dulles's staff. For the occupation forces."

"What were your duties?"

"I was deskbound. Pushing papers. He was out in the ruins, poking around. Beyond that, who knows? None of those guys ever said."

"Remember anyone named Martin Göllner?"

"No."

"Ex-Gestapo?"

Kaplan shook his head.

"So then you went back to Bern in, what, October?"

"Yep. And that's when they put Gordon and me on the records detail. I wasn't too thrilled about it, because by then I was itching to go home."

"I guess everybody was."

"Not Gordon. He applied for another hitch as soon as we got back to Bern. The new station chief had arrived, and everybody figured the OSS would just keep rolling along. Truman didn't dissolve it till later."

"Gordon wanted to stay full-time? You're sure?"

"Oh, yeah. Positive."

"Did he say why?"

Kaplan shrugged and assumed a pained expression. He took a long swallow from his iced tea and lowered his voice.

"Tell me. Is Gordon's wife still alive?"

"Yeah. Her name's Vivian."

"Right. I think he mentioned her once or twice. And, well, I dunno, I just wouldn't want any of this getting back to her."

"No reason it has to." Nat turned toward Berta. "Right?"

"I have no interest in this aspect of the account," she said.

Kaplan seemed taken aback by the accent, but didn't comment. Instead, he peered toward the door, as if determining whether his wife was still listening. He leaned closer.

"Truth be told, there's a lotta stuff from back then I wouldn't even want Doris to know. We were horny young bucks a long way from home, if you know what I mean."

"I get the picture. So it was a girl, then? That's why Gordon wanted to stay?"

"Yep. And she'd gone missing."

"Missing?"

"Once we came back, anyway. He went looking for her almost every day, showing her picture around town."

"Sabine Keller?"

Kaplan seemed surprised.

"Now how in the hell did you know that?"

"Research."

"You sound just like Gordon. He was always pretty cagey about his sources."

"Did you know her?"

"No, but he showed me her picture. She was pretty. Apparently he hadn't been able to find her since he'd gotten out of the hospital."

"So she'd been missing for almost seven months. Wasn't she from Adelboden?"

"That's right. Out in some valley in the mountains."

"Did he look there?"

"Hell, he looked everywhere. Anytime he had a day to spare. Zurich, Geneva, all over Bern. Then, a few days after we got put on the records detail, he stopped. He came in one morning and you could see it in his face. It was like somebody had shut out the lights."

"What happened?"

"He said she was dead."

"Goodness. How?"

"I didn't ask, and it was pretty clear he didn't want to talk about it. A week or so later we finished. A month after that they interviewed us about the missing stuff. Then they sent us home. I guess he must have withdrawn his application to extend."

Nat was amazed. At least now they knew why Gordon had held on to Sabine's book—a sentimental attachment, nothing more. Unfortunately, that wouldn't help them find the missing records. Time to zero in on that aspect. He wondered if Kaplan would clam up.

"So this work you two did—handling the records—tell me what the drill was."

"I'll tell you what I told the OSS board of inquiry, what, fifty years ago?"

"More like sixty. Sixty-one, to be exact."

"Hell, I'm old. Well, everything was already sorted by subject. The folders were numbered, and so were the boxes. All we were supposed to do was make sure every folder was present and accounted for and filed in the right order. We logged the box number on a ledger, and every four boxes went into a bigger container, which we then labeled for shipment via diplomatic mail. We then logged the numbers for those containers on a shipping manifest. Paperwork galore, but I guess that's the government."

"So the four boxes that went missing, they were in the same container?"

"Correct. That's how it showed up on the ledger, anyway."

"Where did you send everything?"

"Some containers went to Dulles's law office in New York, some went straight to OSS headquarters in Washington. The rest went to the National Archives."

"Who decided the destinations?".

"That was above our pay grade. I have no idea. Presumably some of the information was a little more 'active' than the rest."

"Go on."

"Not much else to say. We locked up at the end of every workday, and first thing the next morning somebody came by to collect the containers we'd packed the day before, for shipment overseas."

"Who kept the keys?"

Kaplan hesitated.

"Gordon."

"They must have asked you about the day you packed up the missing container."

"They did."

"And?"

"Same routine as always. Nothing unusual."

"Did Gordon go back after hours?"

"They asked me that, too. I told them Gordon and I went to dinner, drank a few too many beers at a café down on Kornhausplatz, and then crashed at our room. We were both pretty gassed. When I woke up the next morning Gordon was right where I'd seen him last, half dressed in the other bunk, snoring like a band saw. It's all in my statement."

"And you stand by that statement?"

Kaplan shrugged, but seemed uncomfortable.

"Well, weren't you under oath?"

"The statement came from a chat with an investigator. No oath necessary."

"What about the board of inquiry?"

"Yeah. I took an oath then."

"And?"

"I was asked to read the investigator's statement into the record. Then they asked me whether the statement reflected fully and accurately my comments to the investigator. I said yes, because it did."

"But they never asked if the statement was true?"

"Can't say that they did."

"Well, I'm asking you now. Was the statement true?"

Kaplan looked toward the door, as if expecting Doris to either rescue him or tell him to get a move on. He fidgeted in his chair.

"Mind if I see your credentials?"

Nat showed him. Kaplan nodded, then glanced briefly at Berta. He didn't seem to want to deal with her at all.

"Here's how it went. We were on our way back from the job that night, before we ever had a single beer, when Gordon said he'd left something behind. He didn't say what, and I didn't ask. But he went back to get it."

"The container?"

"Maybe."

"Had he done anything that day to draw attention to any particular box?"

Kaplan placed his hands on his thighs, as if bracing himself.

"I remember he was thumbing through some folders, counting them, when all of a sudden he stopped and got this look in his eye. A cold anger, I guess you'd call it. For a while I thought he was about to lose it. When I asked what was wrong he mumbled something and just sat there. Then he shuffled through a few more items, taped up the box, and put it on the pile."

"What did he mumble?"

" 'The bastard.' "

" 'The bastard'? That's it?"

Kaplan glanced at Berta.

"I believe the full quote was 'The cocksucking bastard,' but, yep, that was it."

"Did you know who he was referring to?"

He shook his head.

"Did you ask later?"

"You're a lot more thorough than that investigator, I'll say that. Yes, I asked later. He just gave me some code name, which didn't mean a damn thing to me then and would mean even less to me now."

"Do you remember it?"

"I'm not positive, but it was something scientific, or technical, and then there was a number. Like 'Milligram.' Or 'Magnum.' "

"Followed by a number?"

"Yeah."

"Could it have been 'Magneto II'?"

Kaplan looked up abruptly, with a light in his eyes.

"That was it. Exactly."

"You said he shuffled through a few more items?"

"He pulled out some of the papers and read through 'em. He did it with a couple of folders. It made me uneasy, but what the hell. Nobody had exactly told us *not* to, so I didn't say anything. Then, like I said, he sealed it up and logged it in the ledger. Just the way I testified. And for the rest of the afternoon he was very quiet."

"Why'd you lie for him?"

"I told you. I didn't. Everything I said under oath was true. Or technically true."

"But you lied to the investigator."

"Well, that was different. Some fellow came to ask us about everything, and before I knew it Gordon was giving his version of how we'd both gone straight to a bar and then crashed in our bunks. It wasn't like I was going to call him a liar right there in front of this guy. So when the fellow wrote out the statement, I signed it. We both did."

"The investigator interviewed the two of you at the same time?"

"Yep."

"Well, that was damn stupid."

"I thought so. But believe me, at the time this was not a big deal. We'd just won the war, and a lot of people were already more worried about the Reds than a few leftover Nazis, or a bunch of old paperwork. The so-called board of inquiry was just three guys at a table. There were a dozen items on the agenda, and we were in and out in ten minutes."

"Anything else you didn't tell the investigator? And, believe me, I'm not good enough to figure out what it might be, so you're going to have to help me."

"You hear that, Murray?" Doris again, from the next room. "Either you tell him what you told me, or I will."

This drew a smile from Kaplan, who seemed to have decided, in for a penny, in for a pound.

"Maybe one thing," he said coyly. "About that girl of his. Turns out, she wasn't dead. But I guess to Gordon she might as well have been, 'cause she'd gotten hitched."

"She was married? How do you know?"

"The week we went home I'm walking through the Bärenplatz and I see her, the one from the picture, sitting on a bench plain as day."

"You're sure?"

"Positive. So I called her by name. Sabine. She looked right up."

"What'd she say?"

"She wouldn't have anything to do with me. Put her head down like she wanted me to get lost. But I couldn't just let it drop because, hell, Gordon was all torn up. So I said, 'Hey, Gordon's been looking all over for you.' Then she started to cry. So did the baby."

"She had a *baby*?"

"Tiny thing. Couldn't have been more than a few months old. I was about to apologize when this guy runs up. Local man, forty if he was a day. Tells me I better scram, 'cause he don't care who won the war, I've got no business bothering his wife and child."

"Wow."

"Yep. That was pretty much my reaction."

"Did you tell Gordon?"

"Never had the heart. Besides, once I had time to think about it, I figured he already knew. Funny thing was, I recognized the guy."

"Sabine's husband?"

"Heinrich Jurgens. Ran a little hotel where we used to billet interned airmen before a prisoner exchange. I'd handled those arrangements, so I recognized him right away. Fortunately he didn't remember me or he might have made trouble. That was the last thing I needed a week before shipping out."

"Jurgens? Was that the name of his hotel?"

"Sure was."

Nat reached into his pocket for the matchbook he'd been carrying like a rabbit's foot. It was a little worse for wear, and the cardboard was limp from Florida humidity. But the white lettering on the red cover was still boldly legible. He handed it to Kaplan, who eyed it as if it was a crystal ball.

"Where'd you get this?"

"Yes," Berta added, an edge to her voice. "Where *did* you get that, and when?"

Oops.

"Gordon left it for me, in the same box with the key to the storage locker."

"There was a box?" Berta said.

Their eyes met. The Florida room was suddenly a very chilly place, and at that moment they both knew their next destination. They knew as well that they wouldn't be making the trip together. From here on out it would be a race. She was probably already regretting she had even told him about the spyware, and he was certainly regretting showing her the matchbook.

"So was this a help?" Kaplan said, suddenly feeling left out.

"An immense help," Nat said.

To his right, Berta hastily gathered her things. She rose and headed for the door. Nat rose, too. Kaplan, sensing the meeting was speeding toward an abrupt conclusion, stood shakily and extended his right hand.

His grip was weak. Nat figured he had reached the fellow just in time. Few of the old ones remained, and a year from now their numbers would be smaller still. Kaplan opened his mouth to speak, but was interrupted by the slamming of the front door.

"Well, now," he said. "Was it something that I said?"

"She gets that way sometimes."

They listened to her car start up and roar away. Nat was perturbed but not panicked. It wasn't like she could grab a flight to Bern in the next half hour. But he needed to secure a reservation on the next available plane. It crossed his mind to even phone ahead to the Hotel Jurgens, but he decided against it. No sense risking scaring them away. But he could have kicked himself for not having waited longer in the lobby during his previous visit. For once, his instincts had failed him.

Shortly afterward he said good-bye to the Kaplans, giving Doris an affectionate peck on the cheek and even praising her shrimp salad while Kaplan rolled his eyes. But Nat figured she had earned it.

Halfway back to the Sea Breeze, a police cruiser rolled up behind him, flipped on its flashers, and pulled him to the curb. Nat watched in the mirror as the officer threw open the door of the cruiser, crouched behind it, and poked a gun barrel around the side.

"Step out of the car, hands above your head!" the officer shouted. "Do it now!"

Nat obeyed awkwardly, moving slowly.

"Turn and place your hands on the roof of your car, and don't make a move!"

No sooner had he done so than the policeman yanked both arms behind his back and cuffed him, painfully, with the metal bands jamming hard against his wrists. Not again. Was this Berta's doing? The result of some dirty trick? For that matter, was this fellow really a cop?

All he knew for sure was that in the race to Bern he had just fallen well off the pace.

TWENTY-SEVEN

THE CANDALUSA POLICE DEPARTMENT was a southern variant on Willis Turner's base of operations in Blue Kettle Lake, except these guys had better radios and packed more heat.

From the glass-walled interview room Nat could see a giant poster for Florida Gators football and a gun rack stocked with high-powered rifles. There was little he could see beyond that, because the policeman had handcuffed him to a table bolted to the floor. This must be where they locked down the drunks and rowdies before booking them.

The room was sweltering, but his warders were ignoring his questions and his requests for water and a phone call. No one had charged him, or even written down his name. They did check his driver's license, so they had at least confirmed his identity.

An hour passed, then another. By then, Berta had probably either boarded a connecting flight from Orlando or Daytona or was well on her way south to Miami on I-95. A third hour passed, and his anxiety rose accordingly.

Then Clark Holland strolled into the office, nodding to the arresting officer as he stepped into the interview room. The officer followed him and wordlessly unlocked the handcuffs. Nat rubbed his wrists. He was spoiling for a fight, but he waited for the cop to leave before unloading on Holland.

"What the hell is this all about?"

"Maybe if you occasionally picked up the phone you wouldn't be asking that question. This seems to be the only way I can get an update. And frankly, it's for your own good."

"What's that mean?"

"You'll see. Soon as you've answered some questions."

"Water first."

Holland shouted for some drinks. The cop, none too pleased to be serving as a waiter to a fed and a misbehaving out-of-towner, tossed two plastic bottles of Coke from across the room. They fizzed over when Holland unscrewed the caps.

"Cops just love you guys, don't they?"

"Glad you brought that up. Your friend Willis Turner—any idea what he did with his copies of those pictures you shot? The ones of the stolen documents?"

"I don't believe we ever confirmed I took any."

"For the sake of argument let's assume you did. Why did he want them?"

"He said it was part of an investigation. Suspicious death, remember?"

"How 'bout a real reason?"

"Why don't you ask Turner?"

"We tried. Went to serve him this morning with a subpoena and a search warrant."

"There you go."

"The server found him dead. Shot with his own weapon. Apparent suicide, according to the state police, but it's not like they've got such a great track record on this case. The search came up empty. No photos, no copies."

Nat swallowed hard. He tried to think of some reason for Turner's death other than the obvious one.

"If he knew you were coming with a warrant, maybe it really was suicide."

"More likely is that someone else knew. Your German friend, Berta Heinkel—how long has she been back in the country?"

"You don't think *she* did it?"

"Just answer the question."

"She didn't make it across the water until last night, at the earliest. And she was camped outside my door by seven this morning."

"She staying the same place as you? The Sea Breeze?"

"I think so. But by now she's probably either on a plane or sitting in an airport."

"Where's she headed?"

If Nat answered honestly, he'd have to explain the rest, and he didn't want to. But he did want the FBI to try and pick her up. Anything to slow her down.

"Home, I guess. Berlin. She's all done here. But—"

"But what?"

"Well, last time I talked to Turner—"

"When was this?"

"A few days ago. He phoned me in Berlin."

"Go on."

"He was beginning to think Gordon was murdered. Berta was his prime suspect."

"We heard that, too. False lead. The toxicology tests came back negative. The medical examiner's report was on Turner's desk, dated yesterday. Heart attack, plain and simple."

Holland's cell phone rang. He grimaced at the incoming number.

"Wait here," he said. Then he left the room.

It was a relief to hear Berta was in the clear on Gordon. But she was still the competition, and it didn't sound like the Bureau was too interested in picking her up. Holland returned a few moments later, frowning.

"Fresh news," he said. He showed Nat a photo. "Ever seen this guy?"

Nat recognized the face right away.

"Yeah, he was at the Denny's where I was having breakfast. Might be staying at the Sea Breeze, too."

"When did you last see him?"

"Ten thirty this morning."

"His name is Tim Scoggins. He's a private eye. If you check your engine block, dollars to doughnuts you'll find a GPS tracking device. Two days ago he wrote a check for $25,000 to Willis Turner. Any idea why he'd do that?"

"He was working for Turner?"

"Last I checked, PIs weren't in the business of paying their clients."

"Oh. Right. Why pay Turner, then?"

"We figure he was buying something."

"The copies of the files?"

"Possibly."

"And Scoggins told you this?"

"Scoggins's rental car was just found on the shoulder of I-95, just north of Daytona. Blood on the seat. No body."

Nat took a deep breath. Assuming the worst about Scoggins meant four bodies in two days, and he had recently met or talked to all of them. Even if Gordon's death was by natural causes, Berta and he were certainly stirring up a world of trouble.

"There's an old guy I was just talking to across town, Murray Kaplan. Maybe you should make sure he's all right."

"Will do. Just leave me his number and address."

"Who's doing all this? I mean, I know who killed Qurashi. But Turner? And this PI?"

"If they were working for Bauer, then it was the Iranians. Or vice versa. Somebody must be getting close, I guess. Maybe it's you, maybe it's someone else."

"How come they haven't killed me or Berta? Not that I'm complaining."

"Probably because you're still useful. I'd advise you both to keep it that way."

"Then I should get moving."

Holland shook his head.

"Just because they're picking up the pace doesn't mean you should panic. We'd like you to stick around until we have a better handle on recent events. Neil Ford is going to escort you back to the motel. To be on the safe side, he and another special agent will be posted outside your room. Just sit tight. Unless, of course, you've got something to tell me?"

He was tempted to tell Holland all about Bern, and the Hotel Jurgens. Maybe then the agent would turn him loose, or, at the very least, dispatch someone to beat Berta to the punch. But if the FBI got there first, and the lead panned out, then Nat would probably never get first dibs on the material, or any dibs at all. After what he'd been through, he wasn't willing to risk losing everything now. So he said nothing.

"Don't worry," Holland said. "This shouldn't take more than a day or so. Then we'll put every means at your disposal to get moving as fast as possible, to any destination. Provided you behave in the meantime. I'm tired of having to rely on other people to bring you in. At least so far you've still been warm and breathing. Next time, I wouldn't count on it."

Neil Ford seemed pleased as always to see Nat. The agent waved through the windshield as he pulled in behind Nat's car on the way back to the Sea Breeze. A second agent was with him.

By now, Berta was almost certainly winging her way across the Atlantic, and when Nat reached the motel he glumly climbed the stairs to his room. He mixed a stiff drink from the minibar, then flicked back the curtains to see if the FBI was really watching.

There they were, two Eagle Scouts in a black sedan. He turned away from the window and surveyed the room. Clothes on the floor. Laptop open. Gordon's box of keepsakes atop the TV. Time for another look, especially now that the matchbook had turned out to be important.

He emptied the contents on the bed and inspected them with renewed interest: a vial with powder for making invisible ink, complete with printed instructions typed in 1946 by Gordon himself; a German officer's cap, which may or may not have been Gordon's size; plus the key that he had already used at the storage locker and the matchbook from the Hotel Jurgens. Then there was the old crime novel that had belonged to Sabine Keller, Gordon's Swiss miss, with a dried flower for a bookmark.

He studied them awhile, as if hoping for a message. Nothing. Nor did they offer any help in eluding FBI agents.

"So, tell me, Gordon," he asked aloud. "How would an old OSS man get out of this fix?" He didn't expect an answer, and he didn't get one. "Too bad I never got any of your training, or maybe I'd know."

Or maybe he did, seeing as how there was more than one way out of the room. Nat stood and slid open the glass door to the balcony. He looked down. A long drop, but it was sandy at the bottom, with a path heading straight to the beach. Better still, no one was watching the back. The problem was how to get down without breaking a leg.

Moments later he decided upon the solution, feeling sheepish if only because it was such a cliché, borrowed from innumerable cartoons and comedies and damsels in distress. Bedsheets. The only thing available. So he packed for departure, carefully placing Gordon's items back in the box and tucking it between his shirts, and then he went to work. The Sea Breeze linens were so flimsy that he doubled them up to support his weight, twisting together the top and bottom sheets. That meant the line would come up short. He would have to jump the final seven or eight feet to the sand. So be it. He slid open the balcony door and tied one end of the sheets to the railing.

He then dropped his suitcase over the side and slung his camera bag and laptop over his shoulders, bandolier style, one on either side. Feeling like a novice alpinist about to tackle a mountain well beyond his technical skills, he then slung a leg over the rail and awkwardly climbed to the other side while gripping the sheets for all they were worth.

His feet slipped, and for a moment he dangled like an oversized spider, bumping his face against the railing. He steadied himself by bracing his soles against the balcony. Once he felt secure, he slid his left hand down the sheets, then his right, all the while bouncing his toes against the railing as he dropped.

After he'd lowered himself further, his feet slipped below the bottom of his balcony and he again dangled free, thighs bumping the overhang. But he continued to grunt his way down to the limit of the makeshift line. When he let go he jumped outward to avoid catching his feet on the railing of the balcony below. Fortunately no one was in the ground-floor room, and the view from the beach was blocked by a row of dunes.

He landed heavily and toppled onto his suitcase. But nothing seemed broken, and he was elated to have made it. He grabbed his bags and lumbered across the dunes. From there it was only a quarter mile to the fishing pier. Fishermen and beachcombers stared curiously at this fellow hauling luggage up the strand, but he paid them no mind. When he reached the pier he dropped two quarters into a pay phone and dialed for a taxi. Then he ducked into the tackle shop to wait for its arrival.

Two and a half hours later, Nat boarded a flight to Miami. Judging from the earlier-scheduled flights, he guessed Berta would arrive in Zurich around seven the next morning, meaning she could reach Bern as soon as eight thirty by train. Nat's connection out of Miami was due to land shortly after noon. At least a four-hour advantage for Berta. And that was assuming he made it out of the country before the FBI discovered he was gone. He settled into his seat, ready for the chase.

TWENTY-EIGHT

Basel, Switzerland—May 16, 1944

FIRST IT WAS THE PRICKLY SWISS BORDER OFFICIALS who harassed him, with their careful rules and smug neutrality. They kept him waiting in a locked room for five hours.

Now the besieged Kurt Bauer faced a new indignity: a wiseass American flyboy, barely older than he was. The man swaggered into the room and, without even stating his name, began asking questions. When Kurt resisted, the fellow grinned dismissively and offered cigarettes, as if a mere pack of Luckies could set everything right.

Not that Kurt was in a position to refuse. Alone and on the run, he needed allies. He accepted the proffered pack with a muttered "Danke" and began arguing his family's case, just as he had done with the Swiss.

"My father *must* be allowed into the country. Can't you make them see that? He has a factory here and possesses valuable information. Every second he is refused entry puts him in greater danger. For all I know he is already in the hands of the Gestapo. And didn't the Swiss tell you? It's not you I asked to see, it's Dulles. Those were my father's precise instructions. Only Dulles will do!"

Maddeningly, the flyboy smiled and shook his head.

"Go easy on that name. For one thing, it won't get you very far with them." He nodded through a glass partition toward a bored Swiss official, who stared dumbly at a mounting pile of paperwork. "It also won't get you very far with Dulles. He doesn't like having his name bandied about in public."

"It's gotten me this far, hasn't it?"

"Only because you lucked into the one guy here who knows what he's doing, so he gave me a call. Besides, I wouldn't call this progress. A customs inspection room in Basel isn't exactly a luxury suite at the Bellevue."

He was certainly right about that. The border post, drab and sterile in the best of times, had become a wartime way station for the lost and the stateless. It was a wretched scene—dim, overcrowded, and smelling of desperation; a wet-wool stench of herded people on the move, trapped in the chute between sanctuary and slaughter.

During his long wait, Kurt had watched a number of distressing episodes, overhearing every shouted exchange through the glass partition. An elegant woman in furs and jewelry disappeared through a door only to emerge an hour later sobbing and practically naked. But at least they waved her through. A shabby Frenchman was forced to open a steamer trunk containing a hoard of gold fixtures and knick-knacks, including several menorahs. Since he wasn't a Jew, it marked him as a thief and scoundrel. The trunk got in. He was arrested. A ragged family of seven erupted in an indecipherable Slavic tongue after the mother and three daughters made it through and the father and two sons didn't.

Officiating each transaction was a prim man in uniform who never stood and rarely looked up before he stamped the entry papers in either damning red or beneficent black.

Only moments ago, two American airmen had been escorted in. They were wet, bedraggled, and, just like the one visiting Kurt, dressed in leather flight jackets, identifying them as members of a bomber crew. For some reason unknown to Kurt they had been caught while actually trying to get *out* of Switzerland. The unsmiling deskman picked up his phone and arranged for transport to a Swiss detention camp.

Presumably all these airmen had crashed here after dropping their bombs on Germany, a realization that stirred a deep sense of loathing in Kurt. He was especially troubled by their shoulder patches. One depicted a laughing cartoon figure riding bareback on a bomb—as if their work was some sort of elaborate prank. These were the people who had killed Liesl, and they were cracking jokes and trying to escape from a country that millions of people dearly wanted to enter. Sure, Americans were dying, too, just like the soldiers of every other army in

Europe. But they did so in foreign skies and on foreign fields, while their own loved ones slept peacefully, without fear of bombs or midnight arrests.

And how come this particular flyboy was allowed to run free? What made him qualified to speak on behalf of the lofty Dulles, who, to judge from Kurt's father's description, was a wealthy patrician god with mysterious powers of benediction. He was the man who could grant their every wish, if only Kurt could arrange an audience.

"Look, the Swiss have already let my mother and sister in," he pleaded. "They came through a week ago, no problem. In fact, they *are* staying at the Bellevue."

"Did you think I didn't know that? But you're still here, aren't you? And from what I've heard, you won't be joining them anytime soon. Unless you cooperate with me."

"Cooperate how?"

"You could start by telling me in as much detail as possible how the hell you managed to get here."

How the hell, indeed. It had been more than eight months since the awful day when he found Liesl's body in the rubble of Plötzensee. After Kurt returned home on his bicycle, his father decided then and there to do whatever it took to keep his son out of the army, deal or no deal. During the three-week grace period he called upon all his connections to wangle an additional three weeks, and three more after that. Finally, and only by enlisting the help of Speer himself, his father secured a delay of six months, until May 5, 1944, and in the process delivered what he believed to be the coup de grâce, by engineering Martin Göllner's transfer to a Gestapo backwater in Munich.

Meanwhile, conditions in Berlin grew worse. By midwinter the Bauer factories were so badly damaged by bombings that production was at a standstill. Trainloads of bedraggled Poles, Czechs, and Hungarians kept arriving to keep things running, but soon they were busier carting away bodies and rubble than running assembly lines. Reinhard Bauer began to fear that unless production resumed, the arrangements he had worked out on Kurt's behalf might be voided.

The last straw came on November 18, the night of the heaviest air raid yet. Reinhard decided the next morning that the best strategy was to move his family to Switzerland, where he would set up a new base of corporate operations and resume his campaign to curry favor with the Americans. It took months to plan the move. First he had to sell it to

Speer, by arguing he could still produce important matériel from across the border. Then he secured the necessary passes and transport.

Kurt, meanwhile, stayed mostly indoors, moping around the house in a funk of grief and guilt. Within days he learned that Liesl's family had also been killed by a bomb blast, ironically within hours of her death. On some nights he didn't even bother to go to the cellar during the air raids. Ignoring his mother's pleas, he locked himself in his room and watched the fireworks outside his window, imagining he was back at Plötzensee.

In October there was news of more White Rose arrests in Munich and Hamburg, and in April there was a White Rose trial in Saarbrücken. With each such revelation he wondered how much of the responsibility lay with him. On one of his few trips out of the house he tried to visit Bonhoeffer at Tegel Prison, but was turned away at the gates. On the way back he thought he spotted Hannelore at a U-Bahn station, but she disappeared into a crowd. He wasn't sure whether to feel heartened or terrified at the prospect that she was still prowling the city. Klara Waldhorst had been hanged nine days after his release, meaning Hannelore was the sole surviving member, and the only one who might know he was to blame. But she was also his only remaining link to Liesl. If there was one thing they could still agree on, surely it was their shared sense of loss.

On the first of May, with Kurt's enlistment date approaching, his father packed up the family and commandeered a factory truck for their journey south. The going was chaotic, a maze of ruined cities, blocked highways, and impossible checkpoints. Halfway to Munich they abandoned the truck and sold most of their belongings, then set out on trains that often sat for hours at a time, exposed to attack. When they reached the frontier of occupied France, Reinhard bribed a pair of AWOL soldiers to escort Kurt's mother and sister onward to the crossing at Basel. The women took most of the family's money and remaining belongings, and a few days later relayed word that they had reached Bern and were resting comfortably in the city's finest hotel.

Reinhard and Kurt spent the next five days dodging Wehrmacht patrols and document checks until they, too, reached the border post at Basel. The problem was that the Swiss had become increasingly finicky about letting German men into the country, even—or especially—when they were as well connected as Reinhard Bauer. So Reinhard was peremptorily turned away, and Kurt, who at least had the virtue of youth, was yanked aside for further questioning. And that was where things stood now.

The American flyboy still hadn't offered a name, nor had he produced any credentials. But apparently he was going to decide if Kurt would get into the country.

Kurt had no way of knowing it, but at that particular moment the American legation, and the OSS in particular, was preoccupied with two subjects when it came to arriving Germans. One was the coming Allied invasion of France, due to take place in about three weeks. The other was the likelihood of an imminent attempt to assassinate Adolf Hitler. Thus the only two types of Germans in great demand were those who knew about German troop movements along the French coast and those who had close connections to dissident officers in the Wehrmacht high command.

Nonetheless, the American flyboy sat attentively as Kurt related his recent adventures. He took a few notes, and even winced when Kurt mentioned that the Swiss had brushed aside his father's promise to stop sending goods across the border into Germany.

"Well, you're right about one thing," the American said. "They should have let your father in. I'll see what we can do, but I can't promise anything. If word gets back to the Gestapo about what he said here, then I'm afraid he's a goner."

"How could they possibly find out?"

"How do you think? If one of those fellows out there saw fit to phone me, don't you figure some of the others might have different friends?"

"Oh."

"Yes, 'Oh.' That's the way things work in Switzerland."

"So will they let me in?"

"If I ask nicely." Kurt still didn't like the fellow, but his German was impressive. Hardly any accent, and enough slang to impress even the most cynical Berliner.

"And will you? Ask nicely, I mean?"

"Only if you continue to make yourself available to us and, of course, to the Swiss authorities as well."

"Of course. That has always been our intent. It is why my father insists on seeing—"

"Whoa. No more mentions of that name. Understood?"

"Then maybe you could at least tell me yours."

"You won't need it."

"How am I supposed to get in touch?"

"I'll handle that. I already know you'll be at the Bellevue."

"But if there is an emergency, or urgent news, how will I find you?"

The American hesitated, then scribbled something on a customs declaration form and shoved it across the table.

"Call this number. Ask for Icarus."

"Icarus like the myth? What kind of name is that?"

"The kind you had better keep to yourself. So don't expect me to write it down, and don't repeat it. Just remember it, if you ever want me to take your call."

"Icarus."

"Don't wear it out."

Kurt felt scolded, then was angry for feeling that way. If only his father were here. Reinhard would know how to deal with this brand of insolence.

"In the meantime, stay out of trouble. Let your mother sign your tabs at the hotel and avoid the bar. Too many creeps."

"Creeps?"

"You'll see."

AND HE DID. The very next evening, in fact, when he decided to have a drink. He had arrived the night before, shortly after midnight. He threw himself into bed without even bathing, then slept past noon. When he awakened he ate a huge room-service brunch and luxuriated in a tub of hot water while watching the sediment of his travels settle to the bottom. The American's warnings made him wary of leaving the room, so for several hours he kept to the family's suite. He shyly joined his mother and sister downstairs for an early dinner, averting his eyes whenever anyone else looked their way. Afterward he ordered a bottle of claret sent up to his room.

But halfway through his second glass he erupted in anger, cursing his timidity. If the stupid flyboy really wanted his cooperation, then the Americans needed to make sure his father got safely into the country. Until then, Kurt was going to play by his own rules. He stalked angrily from the room and shouted through his mother's keyhole.

"I'm down going to the bar!"

At that hour, with plenty of light remaining in a fine spring day, the place was practically empty. But no sooner had he ordered a shot of schnapps than four men burst through the door with a loud exclamation in German. Two were dressed in the black uniform of the SS, meaning they were probably Gestapo. Kurt looked away, but noticed them nudge each other after glancing in his direction. He swallowed his drink and felt a hand come to rest on his back.

"Herr Bauer?"

One of the Gestapo men had materialized at his side.

"Yes?"

"I am Gerhard Schlang, based at the legation. Welcome to Bern. We'd be honored if you joined our table for a round. With my compliments, of course."

"Thank you, but I would prefer to remain alone for now."

"Ah. Rough journey?"

"You could say that."

"For your father as well?"

"You'll have to ask him."

"So he has arrived, then?"

Kurt said nothing.

"Well, please give him my regards."

Did they not know his father had been turned away? In that case, maybe Reinhard hadn't yet been picked up by the authorities.

"I'll be sure to do that."

Schlang then startled him by thrusting his face lower, right next to Kurt's. Beer on his breath, and he lurched a bit. He and his friends must have gotten an early start, Kurt thought. All the more reason to give them a wide berth.

"You know," Schlang whispered, "just because the war is lost doesn't mean we can't make things easier for you here. Or more difficult, if that is your choice."

Kurt must have blanched, because Schlang smiled as if he had scored a point.

"Besides, some of us who have recently been in Berlin know all too well what your history is, even though your father was able to keep it out of the papers. How do you think that kind of news would play in the so-called New Germany that the Americans want to build? None of these trivial things need be repeated, of course, as long as you're agreeable."

"Perhaps we can meet later," Kurt said weakly.

Schlang straightened. His face was flushed.

"Yes. That would be advantageous for both of us. Here is my card."

He placed it on the table. Kurt didn't pick it up.

"We keep very late hours, so call anytime. Or just drop by."

Kurt finished his schnapps as Schlang rejoined his friends at a table in the back. He signed his mother's room number to the bill and stood to leave. The others watched as he hesitated, then quickly reached down to pick up the card. Schlang nodded approvingly.

Kurt cursed himself all the way up the stairs, and by the time he reached his room he had decided to retaliate. He locked the door and picked up the phone.

"Operator? Please connect me to the following number."

He rattled off the one the American had scribbled on the customs form. A woman answered on the first ring.

"Embassy of the United States."

"I wish to speak with Icarus." It made him feel like a fool, but the woman didn't miss a beat.

"Just a moment, sir."

The line clicked and wheezed. Seconds later the flyboy spoke. He sounded wary.

"Who is this?"

"Bauer. I have information for you. About the Gestapo."

"Not now, please."

"But it's important. Where can we meet?"

"You've been drinking."

"Maybe a little."

"You've been in the hotel bar, rubbing elbows with them." He laughed. "It's even worse than I expected. Christ, you're like an unexploded bomb that needs to be disarmed, and I sure as hell don't want to touch you. You're not calling from your room at the Bellevue, are you?"

"Of course."

Another laugh, and then a judgmental sigh.

"A word of advice, young Bauer. Never, and I mean never, make a call from a hotel unless you're interested in a wider audience. You'd also better unplug the phone as soon as you hang up, unless you want the Swiss police to have a microphone straight into your room. Oh, and do me a favor. Don't call here again. From anywhere."

The American hung up.

Kurt's cheeks were warm with embarrassment. For all he had endured during the previous years, he knew that in some ways he remained soft, callow, a naive practitioner in games like these. He felt uncertain about what to do next. Schlang had craftily invited him to call, but where would that lead? And what would be the consequences of ignoring Schlang? Icarus, on the other hand, had ordered him *not* to call. Was there any way around that?

He finally decided that the best answer was to simply be a boy again, if only for a few days. He would banish himself to the children's table, figuratively speaking, and not rejoin the adults until he'd had time to think things over. The decision immediately made him feel better. He lowered the shades and dressed for bed.

But nine days later his recess ended abruptly, when his father crossed safely into Switzerland. Reinhard's appearance was shocking. He had lost at least twenty pounds, and he took to bed with a fever. The doctor feared it might be typhus. For the moment, Kurt was the head of the family. It was time to get back into action.

Over the next several days he followed his father's whispered orders and visited commercial contacts and the family factory, traveling by rail. A company car met him at the rural station, and everyone was respectful as they showed him around and answered the questions his father had dictated from the sickbed. But he saw the strain in their faces, the worried look that asked if he was the only leadership that remained.

Back at the hotel, Kurt fielded phone calls from suppliers and arranged payments for the bills. A pleading telegram from one of Speer's minions asked how long it would be before the Swiss released the next shipment for export. Kurt had no idea, but, figuring that every Allied intelligence agency would intercept his answer, he replied, "Never. Expect no further deliveries."

There. Let the Americans digest that. Maybe they would realize the Bauers were doing their part to end the war. But days passed without any word from Icarus.

He stayed out of the hotel bar in hopes of avoiding Schlang. But central Bern was so compact that it was difficult to keep from crossing paths with almost anyone who really mattered. No wonder the spies loved it here. Kurt adapted by staying out of the cafés and restaurants on the most popular squares. When he needed fresh air he headed instead for the bridges spanning the Aare and wandered into the hills overlooking the city.

Ten days after his father's return, the radio announced the momentous news of the Allied invasion of Normandy. In spite of himself, Kurt was pridefully heartened by initial reports of stiff resistance. It was the boy in him, rooting for the home team, even though he knew it was in Germany's best interests for western defenses to collapse as quickly as possible to prevent the Red Army from overrunning the country from the east.

A month and a half later the news took its oddest turn yet. He was seated with his sister and mother in their anteroom early one evening when someone in the hall shouted that Hitler had been the target of an assassination attempt, plotted by his own generals. They went downstairs to find a crowd gathered in the lobby, seeking details. It was true. A bomb had exploded at his headquarters on the eastern front. Then came the bad news. The Führer had not only survived, he was expected to recover fully. A wave of mass arrests was under way.

Kurt swallowed hard. Every German in the room knew the import of the last remark. His mother and sister stared at him, and he couldn't bear it a moment longer. Throwing caution to the winds, he headed straight for the hotel bar. No Gestapo contingent this time. Doubtless they were all in a tizzy, trying to determine what to do next. It was comforting to think of them fearing for their lives and having their own loyalties questioned.

But most of his thoughts were of Liesl. This news would have thrilled her. It confirmed that the fever of resistance had spread to the very top of the German war machine. In a sense, the White Rose had accomplished its mission.

Kurt ordered a bottle of schnapps, signing for it as always with his mother's room number. He raised his glass in a lonely toast: "To Liesl." He thought, too, of Bonhoeffer, wondering if the poor man was still alive. Maybe the pastor had even been involved in the bomb plot, because surely it had taken months for the plan to come together. Kurt thought back to those first meetings at Bonhoeffer's house, and Liesl's ringing words, always spoken so boldly. Part of her attraction had always been the excitement at being part of something larger, something noble. Yet look at what had happened in the end. Liesl was dead, the Bauers were in exile, and Kurt's ideals had gone into hiding on this strange landscape of stealth. He swallowed a second shot of schnapps and asked the waiter to send the rest of the bottle to his room. Then he headed outdoors, pursued by his thoughts.

It was late July, but not very hot, and the last of the sunlight slanted on the pavement. It seemed as if half the town was out for a stroll or a drink in one of the open-air cafés. Beer glasses sparkled amber in the dusk, and conversation sounded lighthearted. You could tell everyone sensed that the war would soon end. And here, of course, there was no war at all, and no roundups or mass arrests.

Kurt crossed the cobbles of Kornhausplatz and made a beeline for the high slab of the Kornhaus Bridge. The view from there was something special. The city's skyline spread along the horizon like a medieval painting. On a clear day you could also see the snowy peaks of the Berner Oberland. But the greater attractions for Kurt were the sights along the riverbanks, down through the treetops that swayed in the evening breeze. Red roofs and open terraces. People relaxing over dinner or drinks.

He spotted a man reading his newspaper on a balcony. Next door, a woman reclined on a lounger, a portrait of leisure as she flipped through a magazine, oblivious to Kurt's longing stare. From this distance, she might even have been Liesl.

Feeling a sudden need for the company of others, he was on the verge of heading back to the square for a beer when a voice cried out in surprise.

"Kurt? Is it really you?"

He turned to see the long face of Erich Stuckart, breaking into a grin. And despite all that had happened, Kurt was thrilled to see him. A taste of simpler times, when there was nothing more important to worry about than your marks in school or how you were going to sneak your next cigarette.

"I don't believe it!" Kurt said. "Are you here with your family?"

"Just the women, except for me. We've only been here a week. My father, of course, is still in Berlin, running the ministry. Can't imagine what it must be like tonight, after what's happened. Did you hear the news?"

"Yes. Shocking."

"To say the least. Dad will be working overtime. And now he doesn't even have anywhere to unwind. Our villa was bombed, you know."

"No, I hadn't heard."

"One of those fluke shots, the pilots clearing their bays or something like that. It was the only house hit on the entire street. The rest of the bombs all fell into the Wannsee."

"I'm sorry."

"And your family? How is everyone?"

"All here. But my father is ill. He hasn't quit on Berlin, of course. But the situation was impossible, so we've decided to set up another base of operations. We're trying to contribute from here."

"Of course. I seem to have heard you ran into a bit of trouble. But fortunately that all worked out for the best, yes?"

Kurt wondered how much Erich knew.

"Yes. Except for Liesl."

"I heard. Shattering. She was so beautiful. It must be difficult for you, since, well—"

"Since what?" The words came out with more heat than he had intended.

"Well, because of all that went on."

Did Erich know more? Was he holding back simply to minimize Kurt's embarrassment, or was he being vague out of ignorance? Kurt decided to steer the conversation elsewhere.

"Were you going into town?"

"Coming back, actually," Erich said. "I've had a few drinks in the square. Such a beautiful night. But everyone was far too cheerful about the bombing, so I was heading home. You should come with me. We've got a nice house, up in Altenberg. And we're fixed pretty well for drinks, if that's what you need. I know I could use another one."

Kurt shrugged. Why not? With any luck he might even learn something that Icarus would want to know.

"Sure."

"That's the spirit."

Night had fallen by the time they reached the house, a magnificent old timbered home near the top of the hill on Sonnenbergstrasse. Lamplight shone through an arched window, seeming to beckon them inside. Erich's mother was effusive in her welcome. Kurt had always found her a bit chilly, but she was warm and generous this evening. Perhaps she was homesick.

"It is so good to see someone from Berlin," she said. "Terrible to think about what they must be going through. Did Erich tell you about our villa?"

"Yes, Mother. All about it. I'm taking him to the parlor for a drink. So no interruptions, please."

"Whose place is this?" Kurt asked, once they were alone.

"Belongs to a friend of my uncle Max. Comfy, isn't it? And well stocked, as you can see. Would you like a gin? I'm trying to be ready for when the British take over."

Kurt laughed.

"Gin would be fine. You're supposed to have it with tonic, aren't you?"

"Yes, but we don't have any. How about straight up?"

"Sure. I've never tasted it."

It was strong and resinous, like biting into the tip of an evergreen, but not unpleasant.

"I'm glad I saw you," Kurt said, feeling his spirits lift. "We might have gone weeks without running into each other."

"Maybe. Although I'd already heard you were around."

"Oh, yes?"

"A certain Herr Schlang told me. Said he'd seen you over at the Bellevue."

"Oh. Him."

The room went quiet. Erich, smiling, seemed to be waiting for more of a reaction. Kurt, feeling put upon, set his drink down and stood to leave.

"Really, Kurt, it's all right." Erich slapped him on the back. "These are confusing times. You're not the only one wondering what to do next or where to turn."

"I wouldn't think you'd have much to worry about on that score."

"Oh, quite the opposite. My father could end up with a rope around his neck, especially if the Russians find him. Even our friend Schlang has his concerns. But he tells me your father seems to be on the right track."

"My father?"

"Schlang said he was seen here and there during previous visits to Bern. Apparently he was seeking an audience with, well, people who might soon be in a position of influence. I guess that's one way of putting it."

"I wouldn't know. You'll have to ask my father."

"Oh, c'mon, Kurt. Everyone knows how it's done here. I'm not expecting you to break a family confidence. Far from it. I just want you to know that, well, if there is anything you can do for my family along those same lines, not only would my father and I be most grateful, we would also be willing to help in any way we can in the meantime. And I'm sure that Herr Schlang feels the same. You see?"

"I suppose."

Maybe this explained why Schlang hadn't applied any further pressure on Kurt, and—so far, at least—had allowed his father to recuperate in relative peace. If Erich really wanted an introduction to the Americans, Kurt could try to arrange one. The Stuckart name certainly seemed likely to get the attention of Icarus.

Was it unseemly to think of using his friend this way? Yes, certainly, but wasn't Erich doing the same? He realized something else as well: Once you had dipped your toes into the cold water of betrayal and withstood the initial shock, it was much easier to contemplate a second plunge, as long as you could make it work to your advantage.

"I'll give it some thought," he said finally.

"I suppose that's all I can ask for. Truth be told, even my father put some feelers out in the same direction—toward this Dulles fellow everyone keeps mentioning. None of it went anywhere, I'm afraid. Apparently the Americans have put all of the Stuckarts on some list of 'black' Germans. But the Bauers, I'm told, have landed in the 'white' column. So anything that you might say on our behalf, well, you see what I'm getting at."

"Absolutely. How about another drink?"

"Capital!"

Kurt began to feel better about his family's prospects. Even with the dark memory of Liesl still clouding his judgment, he might yet work things to their advantage on other fronts. But his optimism was short-lived.

"You know," Erich said, while handing him a drink, "Schlang also mentioned someone else who is looking for help. Someone who is still in Germany, and I'm told you're familiar with him as well."

"Yes?"

"Martin Göllner."

He realized instantly that this must have been Erich's plan all along.

Coax him to help out, then show him they had the means to ruin his standing with the Americans, in case he was reluctant. Hadn't Schlang already hinted as much? It was powerful leverage.

Yet for the moment it only made him more determined to pursue a course of action that would benefit his family alone, and to hell with everyone else. Maybe that was always the nature of wartime once you moved beyond the front lines—every man for himself. He was certainly prepared to fight on those terms, but he knew he had better measure his words carefully with Erich.

"Yes," he said, "I know Göllner."

"Well, he has a few ideas on how to impress the Americans, and he seems to believe you're the one person who might be able to make them see things his way."

"Does he really?"

"Oh, yes. Would you like to hear them?"

"Even if I don't, something tells me that Herr Schlang will soon be asking more persuasively."

Erich laughed, then gave Kurt another companionable slap on the back. Anyone watching through the window would have thought they were the best of friends, laughing about old pranks.

"You know, Kurt, I always wondered how you got better marks than me in school. Now I'm beginning to see why."

Kurt smiled thinly, and Erich kept talking. He spent the next two hours laying out the details of Göllner's plan, and Kurt realized that his life was about to become a lot more complicated.

But he did more than just listen. He planned, too, plotting an alternate strategy, one better tailored to his own needs—not that he would ever share any of the details with Stuckart or Schlang. He could play at this game of unholy alliances as well as they could, and, in the process, not only win but also bring harm to those who had wronged him and his family.

Their meeting lasted until 2 a.m. By then, Kurt was already contemplating his next move. Best of all, he had stored up loads of information to pass along to the disagreeable American he knew only as Icarus.

TWENTY-NINE

Bern, Switzerland—September 8, 1944

ICARUS STILL WOULD NOT RETURN Kurt's calls. Nor would anyone else from the American legation.

Day after day Kurt delivered the same disappointing news to Erich Stuckart: not yet, but soon. He could tell Stuckart was beginning to doubt him. If only his father were better. Reinhard would know how to arrange an audience with *someone*, if only for show. But he was still bedridden, withering away at the Bellevue on a diet of room-service meals that he barely touched. His marching orders to Kurt grew more incoherent by the day.

Kurt held Stuckart and Schlang at bay by telling them that the Americans were too preoccupied with events elsewhere. There may have been some truth to it. The Allied armies had come ashore at Normandy and were smashing their way across France. Paris was liberated, the Rhine was in sight, and the Swiss border to France was now open to all Allied traffic. In the east, the Soviets were pushing the Germans across Poland and the Baltics. To the south, in Italy, Mussolini had been deposed and the Germans were in retreat. Soon the Fatherland would be squeezed in a vise, and, as with so many previous wars, there was already boastful talk of finishing the job by Christmas. Maybe the Americans simply didn't have time for any expat Germans, whether "white" or "black," especially when, according to news reports, they were pursuing a policy of unconditional surrender.

But just as Kurt was about to lose hope, he returned to his room after a late lunch to find a handwritten message stuffed under the door: "The Münster. 15:00 hrs. Icarus."

Finally, this was it. A meeting at the cathedral, mere blocks away.

Kurt checked his watch. Only fifteen minutes. A knock at the door made him jump.

"Yes?"

"It's Mother."

"I'm busy!"

She paused, unaccustomed to such brusque treatment, but right now he didn't care.

"Your father wanted me to remind you that you are due at the factory in an hour."

"I can't make it. A more pressing appointment has come up."

"More pressing than your family's livelihood?"

He threw open the door. She was quivering in anger. He brushed past her and spoke over his shoulder.

"Yes, Mother. More pressing. Because it does concern our livelihood. I'll explain it to Father later. Tell him it involves the Americans."

He didn't wait for her reply.

Ten minutes later he crossed the cobbles of Münsterplatz toward the towering steeples of the cathedral. No one was waiting outside, and he was early. Should he go inside?

He decided to linger by the door. To kill time he looked up at the colorful figures carved on the central portico, just overhead. Under the circumstances, they were a little frightening—a sword-wielding archangel in combat with a menacing demon, amidst a mob of the Chosen and the Damned. Not a fight you could afford to lose.

A figure brushed passed him on the right, startling him. It was Icarus.

"I meant inside, stupid," the American muttered. "Wait out here a minute, then join me. Take the row just in front of mine."

The man's manner was infuriating, but Kurt did as he was told, counting off the seconds under his breath and then pushing open the heavy door. The apse was gloomy, and the cool air smelled of candle wax. He walked through to the main hall, where a slanting sunbeam marked his path. Icarus sat in a pew toward the front, wearing the stupid leather jacket. His head was bowed as if in prayer. Kurt strolled down the aisle and slid into the forward pew, stopping when he was maybe five feet away.

"I have much to tell you," Kurt offered in a stage whisper.

"Never mind that," the American hissed. "You're here to listen. Keep your face to the front."

As arrogant as ever, but his German was still excellent. If Kurt hadn't known better, he would have guessed Icarus was from the Rhineland.

"You came across around the middle of May, right?"

"Yes," Kurt answered.

"So you've had nearly four months to get acclimated. How well acquainted are you with some of the more recent arrivals from Germany?"

Was this a veiled reference to Erich Stuckart? Kurt didn't think so. He had met few Germans other than Erich, but it sounded like Icarus was hoping for the opposite, so he played along.

"Pretty well. I've met quite a few."

"I need everything you can get from them on the current state of play in the border areas of Germany. Some of your own knowledge is probably still operative, too. Rail connections, travel logistics, what sort of papers and documents are necessary for what kind of people, or for different professions. The kinds of food coupons you'd be likely to carry. Are you getting this?"

"Yes. Should I be writing it down?"

"Hell, no. Unless you want to be arrested. But I want you to retain it, all of it."

"Okay. Travel logistics. Especially in the border areas."

"For both civilians and off-duty military. And also for guest workers with mobility, if anyone knows. What roads are still open, what trains are still running. Anything you can get."

Kurt was thrilled. Everything Icarus wanted fit perfectly in the scenario for an infiltration scheme, which was exactly what Göllner was proposing, and Kurt had his own version in mind. The man's urgency suggested the Americans were in a hurry.

"Okay," Kurt whispered.

He heard Icarus sliding toward the end of the pew.

"Wait!" Kurt hissed.

Icarus stopped, but didn't slide back. Then he spoke.

"The answer to your question is no, I can't pay you, and no, I can't guarantee you or anyone else a spot on the 'white' list, and no, you can't see the boss."

"That wasn't what I wanted. I was going to offer you something better—a firsthand source of everything you're seeking. A Gestapo man in Munich."

The cathedral was so quiet he could hear Icarus breathing, mulling it over. Kurt decided to add a further enticement.

"This Gestapo man stands ready to help any infiltrator get established inside Germany. He was recently reassigned from Berlin, so he has the seniority and the security connections to make it work."

Icarus inched back down the pew.

"And you know this how?"

"I won't tell you that. My source will only let me reveal it to Mr. Dul—"

"Shut up! Never say his name. Meeting him is out of the question. He's not in the country right now, anyway."

Probably in liberated France, Kurt guessed.

"Then I will wait."

He figured Icarus was staring a hole in his back, trying to gauge his stubbornness. For once Kurt had the upper hand.

"Okay," Icarus hissed. "I'll set it up when he's back. But only one meet."

"One is enough. When?"

"I'll let you know. But probably the first week in October."

"That's almost a month."

"If your news can't wait, then tell me now."

"No. But I'll need a day's notice, so I can have the freshest information possible."

"I'll be in touch the day before, then."

"Good. I'll be waiting."

And I'll be planning, too, Kurt thought. Planning and scheming in a way that he never had before. He would do this not only for his family and the future, but also for Liesl and the past. Because experience had taught him a painful lesson: You won only when you made the stakes personal. From here on out, that was how he would play it, no matter who paid the price.

NEARLY FOUR WEEKS LATER: Another note under the door. Another summons to the Münster—same time, same pew. Icarus again in his battered jacket, prayerfully relaying the news from on high.

"Tomorrow night, ten o'clock. Meet me at the gazebo in the park around the corner. It will be after blackout, so I'll flick my lighter and you'll follow. Stay twenty yards back and listen out for the flatfoots.

But watch me carefully. It's not a direct route, and you could end up lost in somebody's tomato patch. Got it?"

"Yes."

"Will you have everything you promised?"

"Of course."

"You'd better. Both our asses are on the line."

Icarus slid down the pew, stood, and strolled away.

Kurt walked to Erich's for final preparations. To his dismay, Schlang was also there.

"I have been in touch with our friend Göllner for the latest," Schlang said. "Railway timetables, necessary documents, everything the Americans have asked for. Study these notes, then burn them. If you're stopped on the bridge, drop them in the river."

He handed Kurt a brown envelope. The three of them then went over the tentative script for Kurt's meeting with Dulles. Schlang made Kurt recite his planned spiel several times before the other two were satisfied. But Kurt already had his own ad-libs in mind.

The plan as Schlang envisioned it was for Göllner to help the Americans establish an infiltrator in Munich. Göllner would then use the Americans' help to sneak into Switzerland. Once he was in Bern, Göllner's middleman would be Erich, which would allow the Stuckarts to get their foot in the door with the Americans, with Schlang riding their coattails. Kurt was supposed to buttress the case for both Erich and Schlang by revealing afterward to Dulles that the whole scheme had been their idea. Kurt's reward for helping out would be Göllner's silence. Everyone would hold their tongues about his role in the White Rose disaster, and Göllner would ensure that all Gestapo documents related to the matter were destroyed.

But Kurt had no intention of tailoring his actions to their needs. Schlang and Stuckart were merely a means to an end. Nor did he trust Göllner to hold up his end of the deal. Kurt, who still had his own contacts in Germany thanks to the family business, had only two objectives: to use the American mission to discredit and silence Göllner before the man made it out of Germany and to convince Dulles that he had done his best to help, no matter how the mission turned out. Any failure would have to be engineered to reflect poorly on someone else—preferably Göllner, although Schlang or even Erich Stuckart would suffice.

The next day arrived with a blast of crisp autumn breezes. Leaves swirled through the parks. A half-moon lit the way as Kurt arrived for his rendezvous, his overcoat buttoned to the neck. He peered toward the dark shape of the gazebo. A light flickered with a chirp, and he paused to let Icarus set the pace. No one seemed to be following.

They proceeded to a promenade along the edge of the park. Far below, the Aare sparkled faintly. You could hear the water rushing through the floodgates. Icarus turned onto a walkway that headed downward on stone steps. Kurt barely saw him cut right onto a poorly graded path along the steep hillside. Moments later he was pushing through brambles as bare branches snapped at his face. He could no longer see Icarus, and had to follow by sound.

They emerged into a terraced garden, its arbors covered with grapevines that had shed most of their leaves. Icarus appeared fifteen feet ahead as a moving shadow. Kurt heard the creak of a rusty hinge, then the *thunk* of wood against metal. He came to a heavy door built into a stone wall at the rear of a private garden. He pushed it open and emerged into a moonlit glade.

From there the going was easier, steadily uphill across two terraces to another small gate that opened onto a slate path. The path led to the rear door of a house, and the door opened just as he arrived. An older gentleman with a pipe in his mouth stood in a pool of light cast from a sconce in the hallway. He was grinning.

"Kurt Bauer?" he said.

"Yes."

"Welcome. I understand we have a lot to discuss."

So this was Dulles. His German was terrible, no better than that of a Polish guest worker, and the cotton candy smell of his pipe tobacco made Kurt think of vendors at Oktoberfest. For a moment he was very much a boy again, and a little overwhelmed by the role he was about to play.

Dulles led him into a cozy parlor at the front of the house, where Icarus was waiting on a couch. A fire was going on the hearth. The flames lit a glittering array of drinks in a row of crystal decanters on a side table. The room smelled strongly of pipe smoke, as if all the curtains and upholstery were imbued with its scent. Dulles dropped another log on the fire, then prodded it with a brass poker before turning to face Kurt.

"Please, have a seat."

He motioned toward a wing chair facing the couch.

"And please accept my apologies for my very bad German. From here on out we may be better off if our friend Gordon here acts as interpreter, if that's all right with you."

Gordon. So that was Icarus's name. Kurt was surprised Dulles had used it, and apparently so was Gordon. The two of them exchanged glances—Gordon's tight and a little resentful, Kurt's with a mild hint of triumph. Kurt answered in English.

"It's all right," he said, surprising both Americans. "We should speak your language. My grammar is maybe not always so perfect. But this I think will be better for us, yes?"

Another glare from Gordon. The interesting part was that Dulles wasn't missing a bit of their interplay. He just stood there puffing his pipe, eyeing them as carefully as a teacher mediating between two brilliant but difficult students.

"You did say he had hidden talents, Gordon. And, yes, I know you don't like me using your name. But seeing as how we've brought him along this far, don't you think we might as well establish a certain level of trust?"

"Yes, sir."

"As for you, young Mr. Bauer, please give my regards to your father, who I understand is ailing. I'm sorry I haven't had time to pay him a visit, but surely you can see how that might create difficulties for both of us."

"Yes. Of course."

"Henceforth, if you don't mind, I'd prefer that you use the name 'Magneto II' in any written or telephone correspondence, official or otherwise. Is that agreeable to you?"

"Certainly."

"Very well."

Gordon then spoke up, a bit brusquely, as if hoping a more businesslike tone would keep things from getting any chummier.

"Did anyone follow you?"

"Not that I could tell."

"And not that you'd notice."

Dulles gently intervened.

"You see, there's this Swiss fellow named Gustav who is paid to follow our friend Gordon, so chances are that someone has been assigned to you as well, or will be soon. Occupational hazard, I'm afraid. Fortunately this fellow Gustav isn't very good." He turned toward Gordon. "Didn't you say he's been getting a bit lazy?"

"He does like his beer," Gordon said. "Walk past enough cafés and eventually he'll stop off for a cold one. I'm pretty sure I lost him before the gazebo."

"Very good," Dulles said. "Shall we begin?"

The younger men nodded. Kurt again felt called before the headmaster. But, all in all, the atmosphere was to his liking. Dulles had a pleasant manner, a polished ease. It didn't hurt that the room was nice and toasty on such a sharp autumn night, and the firelight cast a conspiratorial glow, conducive to sharing secrets. To complete the effect, Dulles decanted a fine brandy from the side table and filled three snifters.

"How about some of this while we're working? Don't suppose your mother would mind, would she, Kurt? I know Gordon's old enough, even though he doesn't look it. That's one thing war does. Makes early drinkers of us. That was certainly my experience when I was posted here in 1917. I had a room then at the Bellevue Palace, just like you. Not bad waking up to a view of the Jungfrau every morning, is it?"

"My room looks onto an air shaft."

Dulles found this extremely funny, and laughed generously. Gordon sulked.

"So, then, young man. What do you have for us?"

Kurt went through his rehearsed spiel on the logistics of travel inside Germany. To his surprise, no one took notes. He found out why when Dulles began asking questions.

"Is the maximum limit for travel without special authorization papers still thirty kilometers?"

"Uh, yes. I think so."

"On the matter of food rations. I'm told that a good alternative to the monthly cards, especially for someone hoping to stay longer, is a special traveler's coupon, an urlauber Lebensmittelkarte, good for up to six months. Know where we might get one?"

"Not at the moment."

As the questions continued, their detail and precision made him realize the Americans had plenty of sources like him, and probably many that were better. He realized that his information on Göllner was the only way he had gotten in to see Dulles.

Appropriately enough, Göllner was the next subject. Dulles quizzed Kurt for several minutes before assuming a pensive expression and standing up from his chair. He poked the logs, sending a shower of sparks up the chimney while the embers whined. Then he sat, sipped his brandy, and leaned forward until his face was only a few feet from Kurt's.

"You know this fellow Göllner personally, correct?"

"We've met several times."

"Enough to make a judgment on his character?"

Yes, and his judgment was that Göllner was a slimy opportunist who would duck out at the first hint of real danger. But that wouldn't sell it the way he needed to, so Kurt nodded instead.

"Speak up, young man. A nod isn't going to suffice on a matter like this."

"Yes," Kurt said. "Well enough to judge his character."

"And?"

"You can take him at his word. If he says he'll help, he'll help. And I am certain he wishes to cross over. He was recently transferred from Berlin against his wishes, and I am told he is pretty much his own boss down there. All he really wants at this point is to gain favor with the Americans."

"Him and a thousand others, half of them con artists," Dulles said distractedly. "But if we're going to take the plunge, this is the time to do it. So here's what we want from him. We'd like him to help an infiltrator, one of our own people, get established and settled in. To provide enough support for our operative to stay in the area for maybe two weeks, or at least long enough to get a good look at the lay of the land and find out where the assets are and who's guarding what. That sort of thing. Then, and only then, will we be able to assist him in crossing over. Do you think he's capable of all that?"

"Yes, sir."

"Very well. I can't say I'm a great believer in this type of operation. Never have been. I've always believed that if you have an inside source, it is best to keep them in place, rather than endangering your own people. But apparently this is what they're eager for now in Washington."

Gordon, who hadn't said a word in minutes, spoke up.

"It's our best bet, sir. And it sounds solid to me, which should count for something, seeing as how it's my neck that will be on the block."

He let the phrase hang.

Kurt was stunned to learn that Gordon was going to be the infiltrator, but he supposed he should have figured as much. Gordon's fluency in German, his age, and his eagerness made him an obvious choice. The funny thing was, up to then Kurt had regarded him as an American version of Dieter—all talk and no action. But as he studied the young man's face he decided there was a lot of Christoph in him as well. If they had been on the same side, then who knows, they might even have become friends. Although all he could recall now was the man's arrogance in dealing with the Bauer family. If Gordon became a casualty of Kurt's machinations against Göllner, then so be it, as long as someone besides him got the blame.

Dulles stood to pour more brandy.

"The way I see it," he finally said, "the biggest problem for any male agent in Germany is that his cover has to explain his military status, or lack of it. All the controls on the train lines are now directed toward combing out every available man for the Wehrmacht and the Volkssturm. Unless you can account for why you're not serving, then you're apt to have trouble. Don't you agree, Kurt?"

"Yes, I do." He was pleased to see that this made Gordon angry.

"If I went in civilian clothes," Gordon said, "I could pose as Gestapo, or SD. Or maybe some sort of engineer."

"Possibly." Dulles relit his pipe. "Or you could always go in uniform. Of course, then you'd have to worry about running afoul of the MPs, unless you've got some good excuse for being away from your unit. And you'd be out there with no backup, no radio. Completely isolated. Still, with the right cover it could work, as long as young Bauer's information here is as good as he says."

"I certainly wouldn't do anything to damage my family's prospects, not with the way things stand now," Kurt said.

Dulles gave him a long look.

"No, I don't suppose you would. And if I wasn't prepared to trust you, then I wouldn't be sharing any of this. But since you're going to be the one to relay it to Göllner, then I suppose I have no choice."

Dulles turned to Gordon.

"I hate to say this, Gordon, because I know how gung ho you are. But in some ways we'd be better off sending a woman. Plenty of good covers available for them—confidential secretary to some Party functionary, or to a war-important businessman, like Mr. Bauer's father here. They never have to explain why they're not off at the front."

Gordon was crestfallen. Then his eyes lit up in the glow of the flames.

"Or you could send a pair of us," he said. "A man in uniform, me, with some sort of cover to explain why he's in transit. Plus a woman traveling as his wife, who would also be a built-in backup in case something happened to me."

"She would also double the possibility for something to go wrong," Dulles said. "But I see your point. We could spare Evelyn, but she might not be available for a while."

"I can think of someone even better," Gordon said, grinning slyly.

"You're not thinking of that waitress friend, the one we helped out of a jam?"

"She speaks the language, knows the area, and better still, she knows me."

"I'll bet, and in every sense of the word. Still, it's your neck. As long as you think she would be up to it. Do you trust her?"

"As much as I trust anyone."

"That's not the answer I was looking for."

"Yes, I trust her. More to the point is whether she trusts me. It would be asking a lot. But she does owe us, which for our purposes makes her useful. That is what you're always looking for, isn't it, sir? Useful people?"

Dulles smiled.

"You're a fast learner, Gordon. And with what we're planning tonight, you're going to have to be. You sure you're ready?"

"Yes, sir."

"And what about you, young Mr. Bauer? Can you keep a few more secrets along with the ones already stuffed in your head?"

"Yes, sir."

"Very well. We will call this operation Fleece. And it's not going to happen overnight. Both of you must be prepared to participate in a lot of advance planning."

Exactly what Kurt wanted to hear. The more time he had, the better the chances his own machinations would succeed.

"Then let's get down to work," Dulles said. "And do pay attention. From here on out, we can't afford to have a single thing go wrong."

THIRTY

ALL HOPES of overtaking Berta evaporated as Nat's plane idled on the runway in Frankfurt. A one-hour delay had already turned into three. Now something else had apparently gone wrong.

Cell phone use was banned on the taxiway, but calling ahead to the Hotel Jurgens would make little difference now. Berta had probably gotten there as early as eight thirty this morning, and it was now one in the afternoon. Even after arriving in Zurich he would have a train to catch, meaning he would be lucky to make it to Bern by five. If there was anything to be found, she would have found it, although he did wonder what sort of approach she must have used at the hotel, given her usual lack of tact.

Had she bullied the staff? Demanded to see the manager? Asked for Sabine by name? And what had she told them about herself and her curious mission? For that matter, what was Nat going to say? All he remembered from his previous visit was a wary chambermaid, eyeing him over a stack of towels.

There was also Holland to worry about. The FBI agents in Florida had doubtless discovered by now that he was gone, and although he technically hadn't broken any laws, he had certainly disobeyed a direct order. The delays had given them plenty of time to track him down. He wouldn't be a bit surprised to find federal agents waiting in Zurich.

To make matters worse, he hadn't slept at all during the flight. By now he must look like hell. He vowed to shave and brush his teeth at the first opportunity, or else he might scare away the staff of the Hotel Jurgens before he even made his pitch.

And what, exactly, *was* his pitch? *Hi, I'm looking for Sabine Jurgens, because I'm convinced my old dead mentor sent her some valuable documents, and I know this because he left behind a matchbook with the name of this hotel.* For all the certainty he had felt while sitting in Murray Kaplan's Florida room, he was having plenty of second thoughts. For all he knew, the Hotel Jurgens was now owned by some impersonal hospitality conglomerate, or the Russian mafia.

Nonetheless, he was anxious and excited as he cleared customs. There was no sign of anyone waiting for him, and no one seemed to be following as he moved briskly toward the airport Bahnhof to catch the next train to Bern.

The hotel was only three blocks from the station, so he walked straight there. His laptop and camera equipment hung from one shoulder, his overnight bag from the other. The luggage was heavier than it should have been, thanks to Gordon's box of keepsakes, still tucked between his shirts. Stupid to have brought it, perhaps, especially since by now he had memorized its contents. He was beginning to feel like a Shakespearean witch with a bagful of charms and amulets. *Eye of newt and toe of frog, wool of bat and tongue of dog.* The luggage straps cut painfully into his shoulders, and he paused to rest. Then he heaved everything back into place, rounded the curve, and saw the modest red sign for the Hotel Jurgens just ahead on the right. Blood rushed to his fingertips. He didn't pause again until he had shoved awkwardly through the door and stood before the front desk.

This time, a pleasant-looking man in his sixties was there to greet him. The fellow looked strangely familiar, which was worrisome.

"Do you have a reservation?" the man said, eyeing Nat's luggage.

"I'm afraid not."

"In that case, you are in luck. We have just had a cancellation."

"Actually, I'm not here for a room. In fact, I'm not quite sure where to begin. Maybe I should just ask if anyone named Sabine Jurgens is still associated with this hotel?"

The deskman cocked his head.

"May I ask your name, please?"

"Nathaniel Turnbull."

The fellow broke into a grin. He raced breathlessly around the partition and thrust out a hand in greeting while Nat clumsily dropped his bags to the floor.

"Dr. Turnbull! But of course! I am Bernhard Jurgens. We have been expecting you. Your assistant indicated you would be here by noon, so we were beginning to wonder if something had gone wrong. I hope your journey was not too stressful?"

"My assistant?" Nat had a sinking feeling about this.

"Yes. Miss Larkin? She presented your letter of introduction."

Christa Larkin. Berta's alias.

"And did, uh, Miss Larkin do any work on my behalf while she was here?"

"She spoke with my mother, and said that you would probably wish to do the same. We then entrusted to her care the parcel which Mr. Wolfe sent us some months ago, with instructions to hold it for you. She signed for it, thanked us very graciously, and took it upstairs to her room. She said she wanted to rest until you arrived."

"She's here?"

"Of course. My mother would not have been very comfortable giving her the parcel if she had simply taken it away into the streets. Although both of us are certainly curious to learn what is inside. As was Miss Larkin."

"Yes, I'm sure she was."

"She asked me to phone her room when you arrived. Shall I do that now, or would you rather check in first? You will be staying with us for the night, I hope?"

"Uh, sure. But why don't you go ahead and phone her?"

The deskman nodded and went back behind the counter.

Surely it was too good to be true. Nat kept telling himself that as the old fellow punched in the number. He watched with resignation as the deskman's expression slowly changed to one of puzzlement, then disappointment, while the phone rang and rang.

"She doesn't seem to be answering. Perhaps she is a very sound sleeper. Or maybe she is in the shower."

"Do you have a rear entrance?"

"Yes, but that is only for use after closing hours."

"Maybe we should go up there."

A look of concern crossed the deskman's face.

"Surely you don't think that— I had better phone my mother. She lives around the corner."

"What's the room number?"

"Three-ten. But, please, wait."

Sure. What was another five minutes when Berta had probably

been gone for hours? By now she might even be in Berlin, already writing up her results for some scandal sheet, or one of the less reputable historical journals. He saw it all clearly now, every reason for why she had become so driven. She had pursued Bauer a bit aggressively, and he had retaliated by digging up her Stasi file, which pushed her off the deep end. Her search then became a ruthless quest of personal vengeance, nothing more. She was determined to ruin Bauer just as he had ruined her. Nat felt soiled just by being a party to it, and now his bumbling had allowed her to succeed. It was not a result worthy of his calling, and certainly not of Gordon's legacy, which would perhaps also be ruined as a result. Sickening, really, now that he saw everything so plainly. He sagged into an easy chair in the lobby while the deskman punched in another number, and for the next several minutes he was lost in thought. The chase had finally done him in.

"Sir? Dr. Turnbull?"

It was the deskman, leaning over him like an orderly in an emergency ward.

"My mother is on the way. Shall we go upstairs now?"

Looking closely at the man's face, he again noted the odd familiarity of the features. And that's when everything clicked into place, striking him like a splash of cold water.

"Your mother's name is Sabine, isn't it?"

"Yes. I'm sorry, I thought you understood that."

"And you were born in, what, 1945?"

"Yes, the last year of the war. How did you know that?"

Because you were the crying baby on the bench, he almost said. The one held by the sad young Sabine as she turned away in misery from Murray Kaplan, all those years ago in the streets of Bern. This old fellow, Bernhard, staring at him with such concern, was the son of Gordon Wolfe. Same eyes, same forehead, same ears. Nat also recalled the pseudonym that Gordon had used to rent the storage locker in Baltimore: Gordon Bernhard. Another bread crumb dropped along the way.

"Are you all right, Dr. Turnbull? Can I get you something? You've had such a long journey."

"I could use some water. Anything without caffeine."

"I shall fetch it this instant."

As he watched Bernhard hustle back around the counter, the door opened and a sweet voice called out his name.

"Dr. Turnbull?"

It was Sabine, wrinkled and a little stooped, but clear-eyed and trim, and flushed with health. Like an aging farm girl in a meadow, or, perhaps, for the sake of historical accuracy, more like a busy waitress at an Alpine retreat. He stood to greet her, beginning to feel like himself again as he took her hand in his.

"I'm here for Gordon," he said.

"Yes, I know. It is a pleasure to at last meet you, after all that Gordon has told me."

A terrible thought occurred to him.

"Are you aware that Gordon is, well . . ."

"Yes," she said. "We heard the news last week." She lowered her eyes and gently released his hand. "A terrible blow. But seeing as how it has been years since I've actually seen him, well . . . Ours was not exactly an ordinary relationship."

"No, I don't suppose it was."

"Had he told you much about me?"

Nat shook his head.

"Nothing at all. But I've been finding out a few things the last week or so. Enough to lead me here."

She frowned, seemingly puzzled.

"He did not leave specific instructions for you to come here?"

"Not as such. If you really want to know the truth, I think he wanted to make it a challenge. A test, teacher to student."

"That sounds like Gordon. He never explained to me when or why you might come here. He just said to give you the parcel if you did, at whatever hour of the day."

"And now, I'm sorry to say, I might have arrived too late to claim it."

Sabine furrowed her brow in apparent confusion. This time her son supplied the answer—a bit sheepishly, Nat thought.

"Dr. Turnbull believes that Miss Larkin may have left through the back entrance. She is not answering her phone. We were about to go up and check her room."

Sabine shook her head disapprovingly.

"You see, Bernhard?"

"I know, Mother. You were right."

"Bernhard gave her the parcel before I arrived, or I never would have allowed it. But by then she was preparing to check in to her room, and I decided it would be impolite to ask for it back. She did seem very tired, but I'm afraid it was her pretty face that won him over."

Like father, like son. Because, for all of Sabine's wrinkles, the contours of past beauty remained. She must have been a stunner.

They climbed the stairs in brooding silence. Bernhard knocked loudly, and there was no answer. He unlocked the door.

The bed was still perfectly made. No luggage was in sight. Through the bathroom door Nat saw that every towel was folded in place on the rack. Even the paper seal on the toilet was unbroken.

"Oh, dear," Bernhard said. "I am such a fool."

"But look," Sabine said. "On the dresser!"

It was a small padded mailing envelope, five by seven inches, the kind you can buy in any U.S. post office. Tape had been peeled back from one end, and a flap was open.

"That's the parcel," she said.

Nat was stunned.

"All of it?"

"I don't know if everything is still inside. But it's certainly the envelope we've been holding for you."

It was too small. There was no way four folders, or even their contents, could be squeezed inside it. Even Berta must have realized that right away. Maybe that explained her convincing look of weariness. She would have been devastated. Unless, of course, Gordon had somehow shrunk everything to a more manageable size—microdots, for instance, approaching the job as a spy might have.

Nat stepped to the dresser and reached inside the envelope. There were two pieces of paper, that's all. On the first one he recognized Berta's handwriting. It was a note on hotel stationery, scribbled only hours ago:

We have come for nothing, as you can see. But to once again prove my good intentions I have decided to let you share in the bounty of our disappointment. I still have my own leads to pursue, and will be willing to share them if you are willing to share your own findings with me. I believe that I am not the only one who has been hoarding secrets. If this is your desire, then I suspect you will know where to find me soon, on the fourth day of the new month.

At the Plötzensee Memorial, she meant, when she would presumably be stalking Bauer yet again. She must have realized he had rummaged through her photographs.

He checked the second page. It was typed on an old sheet of onionskin, just like the stuff in the OSS archives. But it was dated only a few months ago:

> Dear Nat,
>   Given the various neuroses associated with our profession, I suppose you will be trying to read between the lines here for all sorts of hidden meanings. But my message to you is blessedly simple and straightforward: Look no further. Leave the past in the past. Because even when we do our work well, we can only fathom the faintest of outlines of purpose and intent. The rest vanishes forever, and none of our tools can rescue it from obscurity. Rest easy, then. Let Sabine take good care of you during your stay, and please accept my humblest regards, as well as my deepest apologies if you believe that I have led you astray.
>   Fondly,
>   Gordon

Nat sagged onto the bed. He handed the page to Sabine, who read it carefully while Bernhard looked over her shoulder.

"Oh, dear," she exclaimed softly. "I assume this is not what you were hoping for."

"No. Not at all."

"I will get your bags," Bernhard said quietly. He practically tiptoed out of the room.

Sabine waited until they could no longer hear his footsteps.

"If it is not too forward of me, may I ask what you did expect to find?"

"Old documents. A bunch of OSS materials. The key to the past for a lot of people. Gordon. Kurt Bauer. You and your son, too, if I had to guess. Am I right in making that connection?"

"Yes," she said faintly, looking very prim, even a little chastened.

"Does Bernhard know that Gordon was his father?"

She shook her head as a tear rolled down her cheek.

"Don't worry," Nat said. "I won't tell him."

"But I should. And I should tell you about all that happened. But I'm afraid that my version is incomplete, and now there are parts of it that I will never find out. Things that Gordon always kept from me. That's why I had high hopes for that parcel as well. You wouldn't believe how many times I nearly opened it to take a peek."

Bernhard clomped back upstairs with Nat's bags. Sabine hurriedly wiped her eyes and turned away so her son wouldn't see her face.

"I am going home for a while," she announced over her shoulder, her voice barely under control. She paused at the threshold and seemed to gather herself. "Bernhard, please take good care of our guest until I return. I think he would probably like to rest now."

NAT TOOK A LONG SHOWER, then wrapped a towel around his waist and unpacked his suitcase. He removed Gordon's box of keepsakes and placed it on the dresser next to the typewritten letter, as if letting them mingle might somehow produce a new and better outcome. He stared at the items in the gloom of early evening and tried to feel something—a presence or a clue, anything that might tell him what to do next.

There was only exhaustion. No spirit call and no flash of inspiration. Just the dead, dull feeling that Gordon was gone forever, silenced for all time.

He lay down on the bed, afloat on weariness and frustration, although Berta's decision to leave the package behind was oddly touching. He attributed it to the personal nature of Gordon's note. Even she hadn't been able to overlook that. Or maybe she simply still wanted his help, having implied as much. Now that they were again at a dead end, he might even consider her offer. Truly, this business of theirs was a shared sickness.

Shutting his eyes, he gave in to jet lag and drifted off. Sleep was dreamless, and it was dark when he awakened. The towel was dry, the room chilly. He was debating whether to dress for dinner or call it a night when the answer came to him, making him sit up so quickly that the bed shook.

It was a moment of sudden insight, much in the way that someone stumped by a crossword puzzle puts it down for an hour and then clearly sees every answer the moment he returns. Nat now realized what he had been missing before, and it was so easy that he laughed.

He stepped to the dresser, refreshed. Then he gathered up Gordon's letter and the box of keepsakes and took everything back to the bed, too excited now to even consider eating or sleeping. He flipped on the bedside light, and as he reread the letter everything seemed obvious. The key words leaped out like a playground taunt:

Read between the lines . . . hidden meanings . . . Look no further. And, then, Gordon's most obvious hint of all: *The rest vanishes forever, and none of our tools can rescue it from obscurity.*

Holding the letter at a low angle, Nat peered across it like a landscape and saw that it had a pebbly look, as if it had been moistened and then allowed to dry. He opened the wooden box and took out the bottle of "secret ink powder" along with the folded instructions that Gordon had written just after the war.

He read quickly. If Gordon really had used this stuff, or, more likely, something a lot like it but much newer, then all Nat had to do now was find a fluorescent light to read the hidden message. None here, and none in the bathroom. He was on the verge of racing downstairs when he realized he was practically naked. So he dressed and clattered down to the lobby with his shoes untied, taking the stairs two at a time while shouting for Bernhard.

"Phone your mother! And find me a fluorescent light, quick as you can!"

The devilish old goat, he thought. The damned troublemaker. Still provoking his old student with tricks and challenges, even after death. And thank God he had, or Berta would have gotten everything and run straight to Berlin with her treasure.

Nat could barely contain himself as they waited for Sabine. Bernhard took him to the back office and switched on a fluorescent desk lamp. The three of them crowded around as Nat held the letter beneath the lamp.

His elation turned quickly to despair as rows of faint characters appeared. It was all numbers and hyphens.

"Well, damn."

"What is it?" Sabine asked, sidling around for a better view.

"Another of his gags, I guess. See for yourself."

Sabine gasped and clapped her hands to her cheeks. Then she giggled, sounding a little like the young woman she must have been.

"It's our old book code," she said. "I'd swear on it. Unfortunately, I no longer have the book."

"The Invisible Hangman?" Nat asked. "By Wolf Schwertenbach?"

She put a hand to her heart and nodded, speechless.

"I have a copy upstairs. *Your* copy. Gordon left it for me. At least now I know why."

He retrieved it with care and returned slowly down the stairs. With

Sabine there to help, their efforts took on a ceremonial air, and he tried not to rush her. She sat at the desk with pencil in hand and a blank sheet of paper, ready to get started.

"It was how we always communicated from afar," she said, "so that my father couldn't read our messages."

He handed her the book.

"We always used page 186."

She thumbed to the right page, where the dried wildflower was lying in wait. She set the book down and looked away, blinking quickly.

"My old bookmark." So faintly that he barely heard her. "The one I was using the day we met."

She took a deep breath and swallowed hard. Then she showed Nat how the cipher worked, and it was blessedly simple. The message was a series of hyphenated numbers—12-09, 23-17, 05-11, etc. The first number in each couplet represented a line on page 186. The second stood for a letter on that line. Twelfth line—ninth letter, and so on. You couldn't have cracked it without the book.

Sabine worked steadily, pausing only once to wipe away tears.

"I knew there would be memories," she said, "but I never expected it would be quite like this. This was his gift to me, you know, his way of making sure I would remember him from his best days."

Five minutes later she was finished. The message made it obvious that, for Nat, there was still more work to be done:

Go to gun shop address. Box stored in your name.

"Something new to figure out," Sabine said. "I am sorry."

"It's okay. I know the address. It's in Zurich. And, actually, all of this makes perfect sense."

He wasn't just being kind. Because even though Gordon was still having his fun, it struck Nat that this was the only way he could have kept the hiding place secure. It was a location that only he—not Berta, not Holland or the Iranians, and not any of Bauer's old pals or minions—could have discovered. You had to have the book and the box, and, even more important, you needed Sabine's trust. Even the blunder by Bernhard hadn't come close to giving away Gordon's last, best secret. The old man had constructed the perfect labyrinth, tailored for one.

And if Sabine had died before Nat found her? Well, in that case Gordon must not have thought the folders would still be worth finding. Nat figured their contents would soon tell him why.

He made plans to leave for Zurich first thing in the morning on an early train. Bernhard fetched a twenty-three-year-old bottle of champagne from the cellar so they could celebrate the discovery in style. When it was nearly empty, Nat retrieved Gordon's box and showed them the odd assortment of items. The German officer's hat took Bernhard by surprise, but not Sabine. She fingered the brim reverently.

"I never thought I would see this again," she said.

"I was kind of hoping you'd know something about it."

"He actually looked quite good in it, believe it or not. It was a little unnerving to see him in full uniform like that."

"Gordon wore it?"

"For that terrible mission we went on."

"*You* were with him?"

"Start to finish. A wartime infiltration across the border. All the way to Munich and back."

Nat's mouth dropped open. Bernhard's, too.

"Mother, is this true?"

"Yes. An operation called Fleece." She turned to Nat. "You'll see. Or that's my guess, once you have the documents you're looking for. We can talk about it more then. I only hope you'll be able to answer all my questions. Some of it I don't even want to tell you, unless Gordon chooses to first."

Nat wanted to know more, of course, but he respected her wishes. Soon enough, he supposed. They shared a simple dinner and another bottle. Then Nat went upstairs while Sabine lingered for a long talk with her son. Already the contents of the box had changed their lives. He wondered how Bernhard would feel about everything in the morning.

Nat slept soundly and woke early in a state of excitement. He shared a quick breakfast with a very quiet Bernhard.

"Your father was a great man, the best in his field," Nat said.

Bernhard nodded, but said nothing in reply. Obviously this was going to take some getting used to. Nat packed his camera and tripod. He left his laptop and suitcase with Bernhard for safekeeping, but took along his empty laptop bag and set out for the Bahnhof. His spirits were high, but he was wary, and after only a block he began to sense he was being followed. Paranoia? Perhaps. The signs were small but disturbing. A face that seemed familiar, a lingering rearward presence that seemed to stop whenever he did.

On the train the sensation persisted. Averted eyes when he turned. A hastily raised newspaper. They were here—someone was, anyway—and he wasn't sure he could shake them. Worse, he didn't know whose side they were on.

He tried a few evasive measures as soon as he reached Zurich, ducking down alleys and into shops, speeding up and then slowing down. None of it seemed to do much good until, by chance, he spotted a place he remembered from one of the OSS documents he had seen in the National Archives. The name, Café William Tell, had stuck with him because Dulles had favored the location for its rear entrance—a door near the restrooms that led to a narrow alley out back. The alley, in turn, emptied onto the next block.

Nat played it cool, taking a table and ordering a cappuccino and a croissant. Then he excused himself to the men's room and ambled casually toward the back. Five minutes later he was free and clear, no one else in sight as he exited the alley one block over from the café. Had he lost them? Maybe. But it was the best he was likely to do. Two blocks later he stood at the door of Löwenstrasse 42, former location of the W. Glaser Waffen Shop, the one advertised on the lid of Gordon's wooden box.

The address was now home to a branch of Zürcher Bank AG, and Nat was among the day's first customers. He went straight to the information desk, where a young woman in prim glasses and a navy business suit smiled and asked in English what she could do for him. The nameplate on her desk said she was Monique Binet.

Trying to act like he knew what he was doing, he handed her his passport.

"Good morning, Mademoiselle Binet. I am here to check on the contents of a safety deposit box."

"Please, call me Monique. I shall check the status of your account."

He held his breath while Monique made a few clicks on a mouse and typed in his name.

"Here we are. Yes, you are the co-holder of the account. I'll summon the assistant manager, Mr. Schmidt. He will take care of you right away."

Nat glanced toward the glass door at the entrance. No one appeared to be waiting outside.

Herr Schmidt, grave in manner and portly in build, approached in a charcoal suit and motioned toward the back of the bank, like a maître d' gesturing toward a prime table. Nat didn't say a word as they marched down a rear corridor to a small carpeted room with soundproofed walls, a tidy, square table, and a pair of black leather swivel chairs. Herr Schmidt double-checked Nat's identification and then nodded.

"Please wait here, Mr. Turnbull. I will return in a few moments with your account box."

Shortly afterward, Monique entered with a silver tray bearing a crystal glass and a bottle of mineral water. Herr Schmidt followed. He carried a long, flat metal box of stainless steel, or maybe titanium. Nat stood, partly out of politeness, but also because he could barely contain himself. The box—a drawer, really—was about nine by fifteen inches, and roughly four inches deep. Herr Schmidt placed it gently on the table, laid a key on top, and turned to go. He paused just before shutting the door.

"Will there be anything else for now, Mr. Turnbull?"

"How much time do I have?"

"As much as you need, sir. We close at four thirty."

Roughly seven hours. More than enough.

"Thank you. I'll let you know when I'm done."

Nat sighed in anticipation as the door shut. He was so giddy he nearly broke into laughter. Then he checked himself. For all he knew, Gordon had one last gag up his sleeve.

He turned the key and slid open the drawer. No jokes this time. Four gray folders with faded labels stared up at him. Each was fairly thin. Beneath them were two letter-sized envelopes—one new, one old—and some sort of multipage memo, typed in German, with a swastika in the letterhead.

The new envelope was unsealed and bright white, and had Nat's name on it in Gordon's handwriting. The old one, yellowed with age, had a Swiss airmail stamp from long ago, and was addressed to Vivian Sherman, on Brady Avenue in Baltimore, MD, USA. It was sealed but not postmarked. Gordon had never mailed it.

Nat set the envelopes and the German memo aside and checked the headings on the folders: "Fleece," "Magneto II," "Stuckart, Erich," and "Icarus Expenses—January 1945."

It was all here.

He coughed nervously and opened the expenses file, just to see how much was there. There were three sheets of paper, each with columns of numbers and notations, nothing more. Hardly surprising. He shut it and quickly checked inside the other three folders. He was dying to read the contents, especially Fleece, the fattest of the bunch, but he needed to follow his plan to the letter, no matter how great the temptation for detours. If he was sidetracked now he might lose everything, because he was certain that Holland's men—or somebody else's men— were out there, probably still closing in.

So Nat pushed the folders aside, positioned his camera on the tripod, and methodically began shooting pictures of every page, one document after another. He didn't dare stop to read, not yet, although he couldn't help registering what each set of papers represented—agent reports, planning memos, surveillance logs, a concise dossier on Erich Stuckart and his circle of Nazi friends in Bern, and, in that final memo in German, the one separate from the folders, the transcript of Martin Göllner's 1943 interrogation of Kurt Bauer. The very one that Gordon had purchased from Göllner in the ruins of postwar Berlin. Pure gold.

When he had photographed everything, he briefly checked a sampling of images for legibility, then ejected the flash drive wafer and inserted a new one. He then repeated the process, making copies upon copies for nearly two hours more.

Finally, with that chore completed, he repacked his equipment and reopened the folder marked "Fleece." It was thirty-seven pages of black typescript on legal-size paper, stapled in the upper left corner. The lettering was faded but easily legible.

The cover page told him that it was the after-action report of Gordon Wolfe, aka Icarus, as dictated to OSS operative Frederick Loofbourow, or 493, at a time when Gordon still would have been in the hospital, being treated for his wounds. From the little Nat had already glimpsed, he was betting that this, along with Göllner's interrogation report, constituted the heart of the matter. Or, as Gordon had once boasted, "*Live* ammunition. Pick it up and it might go off in your hands. *Boom!*"

Nat poured a fresh glass of water and checked his watch. Still plenty of time.

He began to read.

Live ammunition indeed.

THIRTY-ONE

OPERATION FLEECE
Report of ICARUS (543), as dictated to 493
Prepared February 2, 1945

On Monday, January 8, 1945, the two of us (myself and Swiss national Sabine Keller, of Adelboden) departed after sunset from Schaffhausen accompanied by a guide. We crossed the Swiss border in a forest two miles northeast of Thayingen, opposite the German village of Binningen. Cloudy, no moon.

The guide departed. He had advised us that we would pass three roads before reaching Binningen. It was completely dark and we could proceed only by compass, East 12. After passing the second road we came to a third where we saw a family riding in a farm wagon. We hid behind a stone wall and ran on. We had to cross a brook and decided to jump. We stopped at a barn so I could change into my officer's uniform. From there we reached the station at Binningen.

I bought tickets to Singen and we were requested to show our papers. The train had neither lights nor windows. The station at Singen is in ruins. In conversation with others we learned that papers are investigated in Singen by the Gestapo, and all its men are members of the SD. They carry pink identification cards, signed by Kaltenbrunner, nothing on the back, and on the left-hand side a photograph of the bearer. We stayed at Singen for two hours, and at 22:00 went to Radolfzell, where we spent the night at the station after the sentry examined our papers.

The narrative went on in this vein for several pages, chock-full of details about how to move around in enemy territory. Nat was entranced as he imagined the young Gordon Wolfe, looking sharp and sinister in his officer's cap and uniform, inching his way toward Munich with the pretty Sabine at his side. They must have been terrified.

In the early going, their luck held. They hopped their way east along the north shore of Lake Constance, first to Friedrichshafen, then to Lindau. Then they headed north, crossing Bavaria on a train to Buchloe, where they endured further document checks and slept overnight at the station. From there they caught trains to their target destination of Munich, where they sought out their local OSS contact.

His name was Helmdorff, and he managed a factory that was part of the Bauer industrial empire. His services had been arranged by Kurt Bauer, who was referred to throughout the report by his code name of Magneto II. Helmdorff gave Gordon and Sabine lodging in the cellar of an empty building at the factory.

Gordon and Sabine then split up, apparently by prior arrangement. She ventured into the city accompanied by Helmdorff while Gordon initiated contact with Göllner.

> Helmdorff instructed me to telephone Göllner from Theresienstrasse 4, where I could get a direct connection with the Gestapo office. He drew me a map, explaining how I could find the telephone booth on the first floor.
>
> I reached Göllner by telephone at 09:30 and asked if I could meet him at his home. He sounded very agitated and cut our conversation short. He asked me to leave my present location at once, and said I could see him at 11:00 at his office.
>
> Before the bombardment of last November, the Gestapo kept their offices in the Wittelsbacher Palais in the Briennerstrasse. Now their HQ are in the Polizei-Kaserne (see attached sketches). Göllner has his room in building Block Nr 1, 3rd floor, 4th room on the eastern side.
>
> I was uneasy with the idea of entering the Gestapo-Kaserne, but as I did not know whether Göllner would see me otherwise, I went. I entered the barracks, showed my military passport and told them I was Major Lehrer and wanted to see Sturmbandführer Göllner. The girl at the reception desk let me straight through.

Göllner seemed rather afraid and shut his door. He told me he was no longer able to accompany me to the border, nor would he be able to cooperate with us due to circumstances that had arisen during the previous two weeks. He said he had informed Bern of this development, and was therefore very astonished by my arrival. He explained that his original instructions had been arranged through Gerhard Schlang and Erich Stuckart, both of Bern, but that Magneto II and his contacts had handled more recent messages. He blamed them for any miscommunication.

Feeling somewhat desperate, I told him that my cover was still sound, and that my papers showed I had been a good soldier in Russia, awarded the Iron Cross, and that since then I had served admirably with the German legation in Bern. He replied that he would try to make alternate plans so that he might still accompany me.

Miss Keller and I stayed again in the cellar of the factory, accompanied by rats and the sound of air raid sirens, due to bombing in the city center. I briefed Helmdorff on my new plans. Miss Keller was not comfortable with the arrangement, but Helmdorff insisted it was quite safe and said I should contact Göllner from the same telephone at the same time the next day.

In the morning a noticeably agitated Helmdorff drove me to Theresienstrasse 4. At 09:30 at the telephone booth, I was approached by three officers in SD uniforms and arrested. I was taken directly to the Polizei-Kaserne, where I was questioned by Kriminal-Inspektor Siekmann. He questioned me off and on for six days. Throughout this time I maintained my cover.

Good Lord. The man had endured *six days* of confinement and questioning in the heart of Munich's Gestapo headquarters. Nat had to put the report down to collect himself. All these years without the slightest idea, nor had Gordon offered a single hint. And what on earth had Sabine done in the meantime, especially since she had been left at the mercy of Bauer's man, the duplicitous Helmdorff? Nat read on.

During this time I stayed in the so-called "Gestapo-Hausgefängnis" barracks, behind the burned-out Wittelsbacher Palais, in a cell together with five other companions. The food was very bad. The first four days I was in irons, day and night, also during transport from the jail to the barracks for questioning. But everyone was very orderly and I never heard from any of the fellow-prisoners about any bad treatment. Even the prisoners of the concentration camp Dachau who worked in their striped uniforms in front of the jail seemed in reasonably good spirits.

In the course of Kriminal-Inspektor Siekmann's questioning, it became apparent that he was attempting to build a case against Sturmbandführer Göllner. But, curiously, he did not know that I was an American, nor did he seriously question my cover, except to the extent he believed I was in league with Göllner as part of some traitorous operation, supposedly in cooperation with the Allies.

On the fifth day, Kriminal-Inspektor Sickmann told me that he was sure that I would be sentenced to death based on other evidence they had compiled, but asked whether as an alternative I thought it would be possible for me to return to my position with the German legation in Switzerland without making the Allies suspicious. This way I could report back on their plans, and find out which Germans in Switzerland were cooperating with them.

Nat shook his head in wonder, not just at all the machinations but at the way Gordon presented everything in such a straightforward fashion—the leg irons, the interrogation, the threat of execution, even the bizarre sight of the prisoners from Dachau.

Göllner was apparently not helpless in these affairs, and on the sixth day, a Friday, he visited me. He brought books, cigarettes, fruit, and sandwiches. He explained in some agitation that my presence had placed him in a difficult spot and said that a previous antagonism with Magneto II was to blame for our situation. He told me that Magneto II had been his source two years ago in exposing a student resistance organization in Berlin in exchange for personal considerations for Magneto II's family. Three members of the resistance group were executed. Of course, I was surprised by these revelations, and knew that they did not bode well for Miss Keller and me.

Boom. There it was, at last. The Bauer bombshell. Nat was almost shaking with excitement. No wonder the old arms maker had dispatched two foreign governments and all his minions to track down these folders. And no wonder Berta had been willing to ruin her career. She must have had an inkling of this. All she had lacked was proof.

And what did this mean for Nat? A professional triumph, he supposed. But by now the quest had become so entwined with personal connections that his usual feelings of elation were muted. These were not the remote doings of long-dead strangers. History had put on a new face, and it was unnervingly familiar. He turned the page for more.

> Göllner said that he was now secretly promoting Siekmann's plan to return me to Switzerland as a double agent, saying that this was the only possibility that my life would be spared. But he said this plan would only work if Siekmann released me before Monday, in only three days. This was because a Gestapo courier had been sent by plane on Thursday to Kaltenbrunner in Berlin, to notify him of Siekmann's plan to send me back to Switzerland. In Berlin, the falsity of my cover would doubtless be discovered. Fortunately all lines of radio and telephone communication from Berlin to Munich had been cut, and it was impossible to send letters without great delay. However, the courier would return by plane on Monday. Göllner said he would attempt to engineer my release on Saturday. I would then have to leave immediately for the border with Miss Keller. Göllner would face difficulty once my cover was blown, but he said this was preferable to my remaining for further questioning, and possibly revealing the full extent of our plan.

Gordon was indeed released on Saturday night, after he fed Siekmann some fake information at Göllner's suggestion. Siekmann assured him he would not be impeded when he tried to cross the border back into Switzerland. Gordon then headed straight for Helmdorff's factory to retrieve Sabine.

> Helmdorff was very surprised and agitated to see me. Miss Keller said that Helmdorff had been trying to convince her to return to the border without me, and that she had been unable to move around the city because Helmdorff had locked her papers in his office. After speaking with us he said that he had to use the

telephone to arrange for another location where we could stay that night.

I secretly followed him to his office, upstairs in an adjoining building. The rooms were empty and dark, but I heard him pick up a telephone. He was not able to reach an operator for several minutes. He then asked to be connected to Kriminal-Inspektor Siekmann. As soon as he did so I entered the room and approached him from behind. I was able to pull the phone wire out of the wall before the operator connected the call. We struggled briefly. I wrapped the phone wire around his neck and held it tight until he was no longer breathing. I then found Miss Keller's papers and returned them to her. We left immediately for the train station.

Nat took a deep breath. Gordon had killed a man with his hands, a Bauer minion who had nearly done them in. He wondered if Gordon had told Sabine. Probably. Death was such common currency in those days, and they were fleeing for their lives.

He read on. More train journeys and document checks as they made their way south. Their only close call was with a nosy sentry in Singen until they met a guide near the border town of Binningen. Gordon changed back into civilian clothes, and the guide began leading them to the frontier crossing. Then all hell broke loose.

We left the road and followed a railway line and reached a small wood. We came to a crossroads with a signpost pointing toward Binningen when suddenly we were shot at by German machine guns. It was dark, but there was no cover. Our guide was armed and he fired toward the muzzle flashes in the trees, but the shooting continued. Our guide was hit and fell backward on the tracks. Miss Keller and I dropped to the ground and rolled into a ditch. I pulled our guide by his boots into the ditch with us. He was groaning but did not appear to be conscious. The gun was still in his hands and Miss Keller took it and fired back. Soon the firing from the wood stopped.

We tended our guide's wounds with a kit that he carried, finding sulfa powder and bandages. There was more gunfire. We then heard the movement of soldiers crossing the tracks in the dark to either side of us, at some distance. By then I had taken the gun from Miss Keller, and I fired in both directions. Their muzzles flashed, as did ours, revealing our position, and while taking return fire I was hit in the right leg by several shots at once. I remained conscious but dropped the gun and was in great pain from that point onward. Miss Keller shouted for the soldiers to stop firing, and we gave ourselves up. Our guide was dead. They left him in the ditch and took us with them.

So here was Gordon's war wound. In the *Daily Wildcat* exposé, the student hacks had practically made fun of his limp, implying he might even be faking it. No doubt the FBI had fed them that version. Shameful.

Gordon learned that the soldiers who ambushed them were part of an SS patrol that had been dispatched to the area that very day, with orders to disrupt further border crossings by Germans. Had Bauer or Helmdorff had anything to do with the deployment, or had Siekmann relayed the order after the courier returned from Berlin? The timing was certainly suspicious.

Two of the SS men carried me to a truck, where I was shoved onto the front seat, bleeding heavily. The guard stood on the running board, looking for enemy airplanes as they drove to a small farmhouse which seemed to have been abandoned. There was almost no furniture. An Untersturmführer was sitting at a small table with an oil lamp along with a radio operator and half a dozen soldiers. He offered me Jamaica rum while a medic attended to my wounds somewhat roughly. The men checked our papers and emptied the contents of our bags. Miss Keller was taken to another room, and we were interrogated separately for the next hour. They said we had no authorization to be in the area. Seeing my military passport and finding my uniform in the bag, they claimed I was a deserter. I became very weak from loss of blood, and they put me in another room, where I fell asleep.

Breakfast consisted of ersatz coffee, dark bread, and blood sausage, but I was too weak to eat much. I had a fever, and the medic put more sulfa powder on my wounds, which were still very painful. At some point I blacked out. When I came to, it was dark outside and I was on the floor. I had regained some strength but was at first disoriented. For a while I thought I had been abandoned until I heard noises from the adjoining room.

I stood with difficulty and made it to the doorway. A candle was burning in the other room, where two soldiers were forcing themselves on Miss Keller. The first wore a shirt and was naked below the waist. The second was bare-chested, with his trousers around his ankles. He was mounting her while the first one watched. Neither noticed me. One of their guns was propped against the doorway, so I took it and fired, hitting the first soldier. The second one stood and tried to reach his weapon, but he tripped on his trousers. I shot him twice in the head before he could get up. Miss Keller dressed and we left the house.

(Note from 493: At this point in his dictation, Icarus became extremely upset, cursing loudly and thrashing in the bed. Fearing he would do damage to the dressings on his wound, I summoned a nurse, who called for further help and then sedated him. I remained throughout the afternoon and evening while he slept. Later that night we concluded our work after he had eaten dinner. The balance of his report follows. Afterward he asked repeatedly about the current whereabouts of Miss Keller. As instructed, I replied that this information remained classified, whereupon he again became disorderly and demanded that I leave the room.)

Outside the house Miss Keller found that the others had gone on patrol and had left the truck unattended. She helped me onto the seat, and we drove until we had nearly reached the spot of our ambush. We got out of the truck and entered the wood. I could move only with difficulty and was in great pain. We must have covered several hundred yards when I again blacked out. The next moment I remember was awakening in the back of another truck in Schaffhausen, in Switzerland. According to Miss Keller we had crossed the frontier at 03:52.

The narrative ended. It was devastating material—callousness and heroism hand in glove. Gordon had killed three men and had witnessed the gang rape of his lover. Viv was right. Part of Gordon had never come home from the war, and now Nat knew why. It had been forever left behind in a cell in Munich and a farmhouse at the border.

There was an appendix of seven pages that Loofbourow had also recorded, in which Gordon documented various details that Sabine and he had observed along the way, complete with sketches. Much of it concerned conditions in and around Munich—which factories were still running, what was available in the markets, the coal supply, observations on troop positions and gun emplacements.

But the most notable item came last, when Gordon weighed in on the reliability—or lack thereof—of Kurt Bauer. It was useful to Nat because it indicated which way the wind must have been blowing at the American legation with regard to the Bauer family. Its harsh tone also showed how desperate Gordon already was for vengeance. In a sense, Gordon was rendering his first judgment as a historian, and its strong opinions foreshadowed the style that would later mark his scholarly prose.

> **I am well aware that the inclination in this case will be to regard Magneto II's misdeeds as youthful errors in judgment, if only because of his family's perceived importance in rebuilding an industrial base for a new democratic Germany, as a bulwark against Soviet influence. But this forgiving attitude should not be allowed to obscure two important truths:**
>
> **1) Magneto II's story to us was a dangerous and intentional lie which led to the death of an OSS guide, plus the injury of one OSS operative and the brutal rape of another.**
>
> **2) Magneto II's purported role as a resistance figure has been severely compromised by his evident betrayal of his colleagues to the Gestapo. Although personal considerations may have clouded his judgment, and his young age was almost certainly a factor, it should not be forgotten that his actions resulted in the executions of three courageous individuals.**

Good for you, Nat thought. Although it seemed clear that his recommendation had ultimately been ignored. No wonder Dulles had wanted these files shipped directly to Donovan in Washington. Already covering up for the new captain of industry in the fight against the Reds. It explained why Gordon had been so enraged when he came across the files, and why he decided to steal them. The only question now was whether his muttered exclamation—"the cocksucking bastard"—had been a reference to Bauer or to Dulles. It must have been infuriating to learn that the boss who had put your life on the line had sided with the man who almost killed you. It also explained why the CIA would still consider these items too hot to handle, as Steve Wallace had said. That told Nat the Agency probably had other documents, still classified, which must have at least offered an inkling of these events.

Next he read Göllner's interrogation transcript. It was every bit as juicy as promised—more sticks of dynamite to obliterate the Bauer legacy. The rest of the items were mostly supporting documents for the main event. A flurry of memos between Dulles in Bern and Loofbourow in Zurich told him that Gordon had endured two surgeries on his leg after his return from Munich. There was also a Loofbourow memo on Sabine, saying that her father had been sent a lump-sum payment in Swiss francs to cover the expenses of hiding her after the Fleece fiasco, not only to keep her out of the hands of Swiss authorities and local German operatives but also to make her unavailable to Gordon.

Nat then turned to the two sealed envelopes. Being a historian, he opened the oldest first—Gordon's unmailed letter to Viv. It was dated May 15, 1945, a week after the Germans surrendered. He must have still been recuperating at the Zurich safe house and hadn't yet discovered that Sabine was "missing."

Dear Viv,

I am writing to tell you that I was wounded in my right leg during an operation, but that I am healing nicely and soon expect to be up and about. The doctors promise that I will be almost as good as new. I have been invited to accompany a postwar reconstruction team into Germany, and will be doing so this summer.

It has been a strange experience to lay in bed all these months here in Zurich. Hours pass when all that I do is listen to the whine of the tram cars on the tracks, or the passing conversations of people in the streets. They sound much happier than they did a year ago. Laughter seems to be returning to the city now that the war has ended. You can sense a collective lifting of spirits.

This gladdens me, because in some small way my work may have played a role in helping to end the war, or, at least, more of a role than I would have played as a gunner on a Flying Fortress. Unfortunately, much of what I did will by necessity have to remain a secret.

Yet, in other ways my spirits are sinking. I suppose that my wounds are partly to blame, and also the knowledge that I might never be able to walk again without some degree of pain. But I must confess that my greater pains are emotional, due to a matter that is all too close and personal to us both. I regret to tell you that this matter is almost certain to cause you pain as well.

I have met a woman, Viv. And I do not say that lightly, or in the sense of some mere passing affair. It has developed into something quite serious and complex, and the experiences she and I have shared during these past months have at last convinced me that it will be impossible for me to leave her behind.

None of this has anything to do with any lacking in my feelings for you. I know that will not be any solace to you, but events here have stirred up feelings more powerful than any I have ever experienced before. My greatest regret is the pain you will feel as a result.

Because of this, I expect to be staying in Europe permanently in one capacity or another, even after my duties with the occupation forces have ended. I therefore bid you a regretful but heartfelt farewell, in the fervent hope that someday you will find a way to forgive me.

If it is any consolation, I am no longer the high-spirited young man you knew before the war, cocksure and happy-go-lucky. I don't believe that my experiences have made me a worse person, but I am indelibly changed, and perhaps you would not have recognized me or wanted me in any event.

With love and affection,
Gordon

Oh, my. What was Nat supposed to do with this? He was certainly never going to show it to Viv. He opened the next envelope.

Dear Nat,

So what do you think? Is this proper recompense for all that I've done to you in the past? I like to think so, but I need one last favor. Please share the findings with Sabine, especially the letter to Viv, which, as you can see, was never mailed. The rest is at your discretion. I'm trusting you'll handle everything in the best interests of all concerned.

Fondly,
Gordon

A weighty statement, that last one. It made Nat responsible for the legacies of several people—Viv, Sabine and Bernhard, Bauer, perhaps even Holland and all the feds. Granting him that sort of power was the old man's greatest possible gift, yet also his most burdensome. Nat had better get it right, beginning now.

The first order of business was some careful logistics. Fortunately, he had already given the matter a great deal of thought. He placed the two envelopes back in the steel drawer and locked it shut. The four folders went inside the bag for his laptop. Then he removed his right shoe and sock. He stuffed one of the flash drives, with all its important images, into the sock and put it back on along with the shoe. He stood, opened the door, and called for Herr Schmidt, who arrived promptly.

"I'm taking some of the items with me. The rest of them I'm leaving behind."

"Very good, sir." As if Nat had just chosen the perfect wine.

Nat handed over the key and walked out of the bank into the warm sunlight of late afternoon. It felt good to breathe fresh air again after being entombed with all those memories. Glancing in both directions, and detecting no sign of danger, he set out for the Bahnhof.

Two blocks later, Clark Holland stepped from a storefront and blocked his way.

"Greetings from sunny Florida, Nat. Sorry you couldn't stick around."

Before Nat could move a muscle, Neil Ford arrived at his right shoulder and a third agent sidled up on the left. Nat lunged at the gap between Holland and Neil, but six hands immediately clamped down.

They had him.

And what that really meant, of course, was that they had everything else, too.

THIRTY-TWO

H OLLAND WAS UNABLE to resist the temptation of a victorious sneer.

"Your laptop bag looks a little heavy," he said. "Neil, why don't you take it off his hands."

Neil rummaged through it, showed the four folders to Holland, and then took it to a black Mercedes that had just rolled to the curb. A rear door opened. Neil put the bag on the backseat and shut the door. The automatic locks slammed home.

"And now your camera, please," Holland said.

Nat glumly handed it over.

Holland clicked through enough frames to satisfy himself that this time the flash drive actually had something on it.

"Very good," he said, ejecting the wafer into his hand. "Next for the hard part. Neil, please take Mr. Turnbull into the men's room of this fine establishment here and search him head to toe for anything he might still have on his person. Thoroughly, please, like they taught you at Quantico."

"Aw, c'mon," Nat said. "You've got your chip."

"I've got *a* chip. Neil?"

The young agent nodded. Nat followed him inside the restaurant, and they trooped toward the restrooms in the rear.

"Your boss isn't very trusting."

"Sorry, sir. But it's—"

"Stop. Don't say it."

"Yes, sir."

The bathroom smelled like those soap cakes that go in urinals. Neil locked the door behind them and frisked Nat efficiently—head to toe, just like Holland wanted. If the Swiss police had burst in, both men would have been arrested on morals charges, assuming that the Swiss still bothered with such things.

"You're going to have to remove your trousers and shirt," Neil said. "Also your socks and shoes."

Nat undressed, but left his socks on. Neil rummaged through everything else.

"Socks, too."

Nat sighed and did as he was told. As he peeled off the right sock he took care to keep the wafer from falling out.

"Hand them here, please."

Neil held each sock by the toe and shook hard. When he shook the right one, the flash drive wafer clattered to the tile floor.

"Dr. Turnbull!"

"If you knew what was on it, you'd hardly blame me."

Neil shook his head. Nat dressed without saying a word. By the time they stepped back onto the sidewalk they were both wearing such hangdog expressions that Holland burst into laughter. Neil handed over the second chip.

"Guess I can't blame you for trying," Holland said cheerily. "But look at it this way, Nat. You've done a great service to your country. And I mean that. We'll be acting on this material immediately. Believe it or not, I do intend to uphold my end of the bargain on first dibs. Not that you haven't already read some of the juicier stuff, I'm sure."

"A lot of good that'll do me without the copies to back it up."

"As I said, first dibs."

"When?"

"You know better than me the way those things work. However long it takes, I suppose."

Years, in other words. If not decades.

"Can I at least have my camera back?"

"All in good time," Holland said. "And don't forget to submit your expenses. In fact, have a nice meal on us. Take that old Swiss woman and her son, too. You've earned it."

The federal entourage climbed into the Mercedes, and the car pulled away from the curb. Nat made sure to offer his most forlorn expression to give Holland something to remember him by. He guessed they'd be heading straight to the airport to catch a flight to Berlin. Then on to Bauer's house.

Good for them. Nat didn't begrudge them their victory. In fact, as the car eased out of sight, he felt downright triumphant on their behalf, and he broke into a huge, relaxed grin.

He took his time before making his next move, in case they or anyone else had posted a tail. First he returned to the Café William Tell, where he apologized profusely for having walked out on his breakfast. He then enjoyed a fine lunch, tipping extra generously.

Heading south, he passed a leisurely hour by strolling to the Fraumünster for a look at the Chagall stained-glass windows. Impressive, even inspiring. Or maybe that was just the mood he was in. Finally convinced that the coast was clear, he returned to the Löwenstrasse branch of Zürcher Bank AG shortly after 4 p.m., where he sought out the unflappable Herr Schmidt and announced that he would like to retrieve a few more items and then close the account. It would take only a few minutes, he said.

Once the door had shut on the small room in the back, Nat unlocked the steel drawer and removed both envelopes. He pocketed the old one for delivery to Sabine. Then he pulled out Gordon's note from the new one. When he unfolded it, out dropped the third and last of the flash drive wafers, the copy that even Holland hadn't counted on.

Nat signed the proper forms for Herr Schmidt. Monique then escorted him to the glass door up front. It was 4:29 p.m. She had a set of keys, ready to lock up for the day.

"Au revoir," Nat said cheerily to Monique. "Auf wiedersehen," he called out to Herr Schmidt. Switzerland was such a wonderful place.

He set out for the Bahnhof, and this time no one stopped him. He detoured briefly to an Internet café, where he logged on just long enough to plug in the flash drive and copy the images onto an e-mail attachment. He sent one copy to his own address, and another to Karen for good measure. He told her that all was well and that he expected to be home within a week.

He bought a beer at the station just before boarding, and when the train was safely out of the Bahnhof he toasted his smiling reflection in the window of the railcar. For the moment, he could even live with the idea of letting Kurt Bauer think that he, too, had just won. Nat felt certain that very soon, perhaps as early as this evening, Bauer would be exulting in his triumph, believing that never again would he have to answer to anyone like Nat or Berta.

And that was fine with Nat. Because his newest hunch, the one he had developed while reading the "Fleece" report, plus other recent items, might yet provide enough leverage to make even a shamed Bauer break his silence. But only if his hunch was true—and there was only one way to find out. Nat took out his cell phone and punched in the number for Steve Wallace, his friend at the CIA. Wallace had told him not to call, but what were friends for?

Being a reliable employee, Wallace answered on the first ring.

"Hi. Don't hang up."

"Make it fast. Very fast."

"I don't need information, just a favor. An easy one."

"Sure it is."

But when Wallace heard Nat's request, he actually agreed. Furthermore, he promised to do it. He knew just the person. One phone call to Berlin ought to do the trick, he said.

Nat then phoned Sabine.

"I have something important for you to read. Several things, actually, but some of it I need to download and print out on your office computer. Think you could get Bernhard out of the way for an hour or so? I doubt you'd want him to see any of this before you've both had a chance to talk things over."

"Come straight to the hotel. I'll take care of it and meet you there."

She was waiting at the front desk. Within half an hour Nat had printed out the images from the pages of the "Fleece" report. He handed Sabine the copies along with Gordon's aging letter. She nodded grimly when she saw the heading. Then she took everything back to the breakfast room along with her reading glasses and a cup of tea.

"Bernhard will be back soon. Please ask him to mind the store and not to disturb me."

Nat waited quietly on a couch in the lobby. He heard her sob once, but the only other sound was the occasional shuffling of papers and the rattle of her teacup in its saucer. Bernhard arrived and accepted his marching orders without a word of protest. You could tell he sensed that something important was in the air. A few minutes later his mother emerged. Her eyes were clear, her expression resolute. Just the sort of woman you could depend on to get you back across the border when all the odds were against you.

"Come on back, Dr. Turnbull."

Bernhard glanced over from the desk but didn't say anything. Sabine shut the door behind them and Nat took a seat.

"Tea?" she said.

"Please."

Sabine had just brewed a fresh pot, and she poured them both a cup. Then she sat down and looked into his eyes.

"Painful reading," she said. "It made it all so fresh."

"I can only imagine. So what happened between the two of you? Afterward, I mean."

"Bernhard happened."

"That I figured. But how come you didn't, well . . ."

"Marry Gordon?"

He nodded.

"I would have. Happily. But by the time I learned I was pregnant, they were keeping me out of sight. And of course by then I was all in a panic. Because, you see, I was certain the baby was the spawn of one of those terrible SS men. A little Nazi incubus. They had raped me several times by the time Gordon shot them. There was a third soldier, too. He also raped me, but he had gone on patrol. It was a miracle we made it back at all, with the shape Gordon was in. Some farmer in the woods helped us those last few miles or I don't know what I would have done."

"What happened when you finally got to Schaffhausen?"

"A contact met us, and the wheels began to turn. They took Gordon away to a hospital. Dulles and his people debriefed me, then packed me off straightaway to my family in Adelboden and told them to keep me out of sight. When the morning sickness began, I knew I wanted to end the pregnancy, but my father wouldn't allow it. So he moved me away again, to an aunt's house in a further valley. Someplace where my father knew Gordon would never find me. That was okay with Dulles, too, because they wanted to bury all of this as fast and as deep as possible.

"I still tried sending him messages, but nothing ever got through. I wanted to use our code, but by then I had lost the book. Yesterday was the first time I've seen it since."

She had it with her now, tucked into her purse, and she pulled it out while Nat watched. She thumbed it open to the front, where her name was written in the hand of a young woman.

"Then Mr. Jurgens came along. Wilhelm had always had his eye on me. Once he had been after my father to arrange a marriage, but even my father wasn't that old-fashioned. Not then, anyway. A kind man, really, but so old. Or that's how it seemed when you were twenty, as I was. He was forty-four, a businessman. He owned this hotel and several more properties in the city. And he was very kind. I suppose he must have been, to marry some stupid pregnant girl who had shamed her family. My father and he worked it all out between them, like a real estate transaction. He bought off my father's shame, and in return he got a pretty young wife to help run his hotel.

"By the time I gave birth to Bernhard, Gordon had left for Berlin with Mr. Dulles. And then when he returned, well, I suppose you can figure out the rest. He was heartbroken when he found out, and I was, too. Because even by then I could tell it was his baby. One look at little Bernhard's face and you could see it in every feature."

No wonder she had burst into tears when Murray Kaplan came along.

"So when did Gordon get back in touch?"

"It was years later, the month after Wilhelm died. That's when the first bank notice arrived. It told me I had a new, numbered account at Zürcher Bank and said that deposits would be made quarterly. I thought at first it must be something Wilhelm had arranged to be done in the event of his death. But the next day a letter arrived from Gordon explaining everything. I tried to stop the deposits, but the bank refused. Gordon had set it up in a way where he had that kind of control. He said to think of it as my OSS pension. From then on, the payments came every quarter. I got the latest one just a month ago. Over the years I have given a lot of it away. Charities and churches. But frankly it has helped us through a few rough times. It helped pay for Bernhard's first house."

"Did he ever visit?"

"Not once. I think we both knew what a disaster that would be. But he always sent a letter, every quarter. It's how I learned about you. About everything except, well, all of this." She gestured to the report.

"Did you write back?"

"Of course. To his office address. He was very clear on that point. Have those letters turned up as well?"

"No. Not one."

"Just as well. He loved his wife, you know. But I don't think that he was ever the same person again."

"Viv didn't think so, either."

The comment hung in the air while they sipped tea.

"This money he wired you," Nat said. "Do you mind if I ask the amount? It's important for me to know, believe it or not."

She told him. It was a perfect match for the number Holland had mentioned weeks earlier, while smearing Gordon's name. So, yes, Gordon Wolfe had indeed blackmailed Bauer, but only for payments that went straight to one of Bauer's victims. Gordon must have taken great pleasure in being able to make the man squirm even as he showered generosity on Sabine. And he must have found some way to convince Bauer that killing him would only release the secrets to the world at large. That way, Bauer had no choice but to keep playing along. Until, of course, he found a way to fight back, by offering the secrets of his nuclear black book to whoever could locate Gordon's buried treasure first, an action that had unleashed the resources of two powerful governments.

It meant that the storage locker in Baltimore had no longer been safe or adequate. That was why Gordon had gone to such lengths to secure the materials here in Switzerland, locked beneath layers of his own cryptic clues, with Nat holding all the keys.

He wondered briefly how the old man had managed to transport the files here. With a quick visit? By mail? Via some trusted courier? Who knew? Either way, he had fooled them all. Maybe the feds now had his secrets, but so did Nat. And he knew just what remained to be done with them.

They drank more tea, and talked a while longer about the past, and about Bernhard, and what this would all mean to the boy. Or to the man, rather. Bernhard was sixty-two, for goodness' sake.

"What will you do next?" she asked.

"I'm leaving tonight for Berlin."

"To see Bauer?"

"As soon as I've wrapped up a few loose ends."

"What if he refuses to meet with you?"

"If the loose ends are what I think, then he'll see me. Maybe not for long, but long enough."

Sabine paused, and then glanced with distaste at the "Fleece" report.

"Something tells me that my story won't be remaining a secret for much longer."

"It will if you want it to."

"Do you mean that?"

"Absolutely."

She sat quietly for a moment. Watching her face, Nat figured she was reviewing all of the possible consequences, for better and for worse.

"But if you keep this silent, Bauer wins."

"Not really," Nat replied. "He still won't have the one thing he always wanted most."

"Perhaps. But he'll still have respectability. His reputation. His family's place in history."

"Yes. He'll still have all that."

"Then use it. However you need to. Just give me a day or two. Enough time for Bernhard to get used to what it all means."

"Is five days enough?"

"Yes. But why five?"

"That's how long it is until the fourth of June. It's the one and only time I'll know exactly where to find Bauer. Alone, and out in the open."

"Then here's to the fourth of June." Sabine clicked her teacup to his. "Do what you must. And good luck."

THIRTY-THREE

Berlin—Monday, June 4, 2007

KURT BAUER BOUGHT FLOWERS from the kiosk at the Beusselstrasse S-Bahn station, just as he always did. The vendor was nearly as old as he was, and her fingers were just as gnarled. Kurt handed her three euros and grasped the bundle of wet newspaper, wrapped at the stems. It was a spring bouquet, mostly daffodils. Liesl would have liked the scent. He waited for the light to change and slowly crossed the highway.

The walkway took him over a bridge, high above a stinking canal, and then across a busy Autobahn. A desolate route, perhaps, but that was how Kurt preferred it. All too soon he would be too feeble to walk, and he would have to journey here by limousine. Too bad. Half the appeal of his monthly pilgrimage was his use of public transport and the way it let him blend into the surroundings, just like any other Berliner.

He turned the corner onto a narrow lane, which had been buckled and bowed by the large trucks of a nearby shipping firm. The lane ran alongside a high brick wall that had once surrounded the prison, the very wall Kurt had viewed from his cell for five months running. He paused to catch his breath, and shifted the bouquet to his left hand. Then he entered the stone courtyard of the Plötzensee Memorial.

It looked as if he had the place to himself. Good. Other visitors made him uncomfortable, especially young ones. If you were of a certain age and dressed in a certain way—prosperously but conservatively—they tended to regard you with suspicion, or outright hostility. As if you were Hitler himself, come to gloat over the dead.

Kurt never bothered anymore to go inside the site's centerpiece, a brick shed that had been built to resemble the old death house. Once had been enough. The hangman's meat hooks lined a far wall. They gave him the shakes.

He was also unsettled by other elements. There was an interpretive exhibit with grainy photos and thumbnail bios of the most prominent victims, plus a supposedly comprehensive roster of all 2,500 people who had been put to death here by the Nazis. Well-meaning, he supposed, but there was not a single mention of Liesl in all the fine print, for the unfair reason that she had been killed after her release. Kurt had long ago complained to the fools who presided over the place, but they merely shrugged and directed him to their equally indifferent superiors.

So he always paid his respects out in the elements, rain or shine, journeying deep into his memory while groping for contact with Liesl's soul. At times he was taunted by the drifting fumes of his own factories, which were only a mile from here. The smoke traveled the same route that the bombers once had, swooping in from the west.

He raised the daffodils to his nostrils and sniffed, to mask the fumes. It was then that he realized he wasn't alone after all. Someone had just stepped out of the shed. *Mein Gott!* It was the American, the researcher who had been working with that damned nuisance of a girl. Bauer recognized him from the surveillance photo, the one the Iranians had passed along. Helpful people, the Iranians. Kurt had been rooting for them. But they were of no further use now that the Americans had come up with the desired product. A pity, he supposed, although Kurt had learned long ago not to form emotional attachments in this sort of business. In the end, whoever could deliver the goods was always the preferable option.

The American stood in front of the shed, staring brazenly. Hadn't he gotten the news that the whole thing was over? Stupid pest. And— oh, no—what was this now? Bauer spied a camera lens poking from behind the far corner of the building, aimed like the barrel of a sniper rifle. It could only be that damned girl, meaning she was in direct defiance of a court order.

He would have thought she would have had enough of him by now. The people he hired had apparently dug up sufficient damning material to ruin her, although Kurt had never bothered to read it. Well, if that didn't stop her, there were other methods. Like the one he had used against Martin Göllner, once the old snoop had finally outed himself.

The American turned away and headed for the front gate, where a taxi had just pulled up. Good riddance. But, no, he wasn't leaving. Instead, he was helping someone climb out of the back—a woman, even older than the flower vendor, her hair as gray as the skies. She was dressed like an East German, frumpy and proletarian. It had been seventeen years since reunification, but Kurt could still always tell.

The woman stood slowly. She turned toward the sun, and Kurt's breath caught in his throat. For the briefest moment, the contours of her face struck a deep chord of memory, sharply enough to make him recall the nauseating smell of wet wool on hot tile, from a rainy morning long ago. Then the moment passed, and in relief he realized he had been mistaken. Kurt now saw that she was just someone's grandmother, or elderly aunt. Or maybe just an old friend of the American's. He raised the honey-scented daffodils to his face to get the stench of wet wool out of his head. His moment of panic had been a trick of sunlight and shadow, and of the strong emotions that were always at play whenever he visited this sacred ground.

Kurt cleared his throat, as if preparing to deliver a speech. He then stepped forward with his bouquet. Too many defilers here this morning. It was time to lay the flowers on the ground and move on.

HAD BAUER SEEN HER YET? Nat believed he had. The old man had even seemed to flinch, but now he was turning away and crossing the courtyard with a bunch of flowers in his hand—a memorial bouquet, just like the ones in all of Berta's photos. And was Berta still lurking around the corner like a gremlin? Yes. There was her lens. Maybe the sight of the old woman at Nat's side would lure her out of hiding. Everything was according to plan. Now all he had to do was keep from blowing his lines.

Nat had enjoyed a fruitful five days since his big discovery in Switzerland. On the previous Thursday morning he had arrived at a hulking gray building on Normannenstrasse in eastern Berlin, just as it was opening for business. The top floors were now a museum. You could tour wood-paneled offices and conference rooms where a grim fellow named Erich Mielke had once presided over East Germany's

Stasi, the notorious secret police. But downstairs, where linoleum and plastic prevailed, it was still business as usual in a way, because people continued to come here regularly to pry into the secrets of others. Except now the members of the public were the ones doing the snooping, by poring over the dossiers that the Stasi had once compiled on them.

It wasn't easy getting permission to look at the Stasi files, especially on short notice, but Steve Wallace had apparently worked his magic. The only concession was that Nat wouldn't be allowed to use his camera, although he could take as many notes as he liked.

He had been there before, of course. You couldn't very well be a professor of twentieth-century German history and *not* go there. Because for all the renowned record keeping of the Nazis, it was their successors in East Germany who had created the nation's true archival wonderland—six million dossiers in all. Load them into a single drawer and they would stretch more than a hundred miles, from Berlin to the Baltic Sea.

The files included the gleanings of as many as two million informants, from a nation of only seventeen million people. In other words, if you had attended an East German dinner party with sixteen other guests, chances are that at least two of them—possibly including you—would have been informants. The voluminous pages offered heartbreaking tales of wives ratting on husbands, and husbands on wives. Parishioners on pastors, and pastors on parishioners. Parents on children, and, as Nat already knew in Berta's case, children on parents.

Berta was far from alone in this behavior. So far the agency had identified roughly ten thousand informants younger than eighteen. Nat knew now that Berta had come here last year to view her own file. By doing so, she had joined a procession of several million other citizens of the former East Germany who had peered through this disturbing window onto their past.

On his arrival at the front desk, Nat's name got quick results. A supervisor was called from the back to assist him. She was dressed in black, with her hair chopped close to the scalp—a no-nonsense type who doubtless knew a string-puller when she saw one. She had set aside the requested file in advance, and now she brought it out from behind the counter and ushered him to a private viewing room.

"I hope you realize this is a very special exception," she said sternly as they reached the door. "Normally you would not even be allowed."

"I'm aware of that. And I thank you." She said nothing in reply.

Nat settled in at a small table and picked up the file for Berta Heinkel, informant #314FZ. It was quite thick.

At first the contents were fairly routine. Her profile as a loyal citizen was well documented, including her membership in the Young Pioneers up to age fourteen, followed by the usual transition to the Free German Youth.

It turned out that Berta, too, had been informed on. Hardly surprising, although the list of informants was disheartening—three classmates, a schoolteacher, a principal. What an appalling way to grow up. He thought of Karen, a child of divorce, yet far more sheltered as a college freshman than Berta had been at fifteen, or younger. One girl mooned over poets and boyfriends. The other had consorted with security goons and professional snoops, thoroughly schooled in suspicion.

The informants' reports almost invariably concerned episodes when Berta had complained about the way the state was treating her grandmother—a poor housing allowance, occasional harassment, frequent requests for police interviews, and so on. Maybe this explained why Berta had tried to keep her grandmother in line by reporting politically risky comments. A girl's misguided attempt to keep small transgressions from growing into bigger ones. A stitch in time saves nine.

The last report filed against Berta was the most notable. A friend named Hans Koldow stated in September 1989 that she had made a wild accusation of government complicity in the recent death of her grandmother. Berta had apparently stated the belief that a fatal auto crash had been anything but an accident.

"Perhaps these statements were not actually so malicious, seeing as how she was suffering terribly from grief at the time," Hans wrote charitably, or as charitably as a stool pigeon could. "I nonetheless felt it was my duty to report them."

Had anything come of his complaint? The file didn't say so, and Nat doubted it, because by then the East German government had been crumbling from within. Massive demonstrations in Leipzig and Berlin were on the boil. Only two months later the Wall had come down. Berta, it seemed, had been saved by history, only to succumb to it later.

Nat found one of the key items he was searching for just beneath

Koldow's report. It was a roster of everyone she had ever informed on. Only four people were listed. Three were Heinkels, and one was Hartz, just as on the summary Nat had gotten from his professor friend at the Free University.

But the summary had contained initials instead of forenames. Nat had reached his own conclusions as to what two of those initials must have stood for, and he was thrilled to see now that he had been correct:

3—Hannelore Heinkel, grandmother
4—Liesl Hartz, family friend

Their maiden names, he felt certain, had been Hannelore Nierendorf and Liesl Folkerts. That meant both of them had escaped from Plötzensee Prison, but for some reason Bauer—and, apparently, everyone else who mattered—had been convinced that Liesl was killed in a bombing raid on the morning of her release.

Nat suspected Göllner knew the truth—another little secret the Gestapo man had hoarded against Bauer, banking it for an uncertain future. That certainly would have explained why Göllner told Gordon in 1945 that only three people, not four, had died as the result of Bauer's actions.

How much had Berta known? Well, she had almost certainly heard of her grandmother's escape, from all the stories Hannelore must have told her down through the years about the White Rose. But judging from the contents of the file, Berta had barely been acquainted with the woman known as Liesl Hartz.

In fact, Berta's only submission on Liesl referred to her simply as "Mrs. Hartz," and from what she wrote it seemed clear that she had met the woman only once. The report said Berta accompanied Mrs. Hartz and her grandmother on a trip to an art gallery, and during this time Mrs. Hartz had criticized the government several times. Berta made it a point to say that her grandmother had not agreed with all of the criticisms. Nat suspected that was half the reason she had made the report. To show what a good citizen her Oma was becoming.

Berta's reports on her grandmother were similarly mild, and always added some bit of mitigating evidence. It was enough to make Nat believe that Berta had little reason to feel so guilty. After all, she had been a girl, and a very passionate and impressionable one at that.

Then he came across an item that abruptly changed his mind.

The first part of it was dated August 21, 1989, although a key addendum had come later:

> **#314FZ reports conversation with family in which subject (H. Heinkel) expressed outrage over positive news coverage in Western media of prominent West German industrialist. Subject expressed intention to denounce said industrialist, claiming he was a Nazi collaborator, and then said, in critical tone, "Why doesn't the Stasi ever do anything about people like him, instead of always bothering people like us?" (Case officer's note: Verified that subject did contact State Security offices the following day to arrange appointment to discuss this matter. Appointment never kept, as subject was fatally struck by motor lorry on scheduled day. Item referred to official inquiry. See attached summary from Investigative Report #16LB-0989-Heinkel.)**

The investigative summary, while brief, was larded with acronyms, code names, and arcane bureaucratic references that Nat could have spent weeks deciphering. But the gist of it was clear enough. Due to a security breach within the Stasi, the granddaughter's report of the pending denunciation of the "prominent businessman" had been leaked to West German intelligence. As a result, the fatal accident that occurred one week later had been deemed "suspicious."

As of November 9, 1989, the investigation was still active. But that was the day the Wall came down, throwing the Stasi into chaos. Meaning no one had ever followed up. Except Berta, of course. She apparently had her suspicions from the beginning, to judge from the Hans Koldow report filed against her that September. Then, a year ago, she had come in to see her own file. It was right about the time she "went off the deep end," according to her university colleagues, and began her downward spiral of destructively obsessive behavior.

Now he knew why. Not because she had been outed by Bauer, or figured her future was doomed. Nothing that selfish. It was instead because she had learned that her own loose lips had led directly to her grandmother's death and that Bauer himself may have helped arrange it.

It explained why she had spoken with such passion about the power of love. Nat had scoffed, foolishly so, when she later claimed she was speaking of her Oma. He had also made some crack about how her grandmother must have been her "guardian against the Stasi." No wonder Berta had cooled so quickly.

So, yes, it was love that drove her, but also shame, grief, and a burning desire for vengeance and atonement—even after her reputation was in ruins and her bank account was empty.

In the back of the folder, agency officials had listed the names of everyone who had viewed this file to date.

Berta was the second visitor. She had come in May 2006. Nat was the fourth.

The first, only a few weeks before Berta, was a lawyer with an address on the Ku-Damm—probably the Bauer henchman who had dug up the dirt and passed it along to the Free University. He, too, hadn't been entitled to see the material, meaning that Bauer had pulled strings just as Nat had done.

It was the third visitor's identity that provided Nat with his most pleasant surprise.

Liesl Hartz had come here only about a month after Berta. Like most Germans who visited the Stasi files, she had been curious to find out which neighbors and friends had been spying on her all those years. It was her address that was remarkable, so much so that it raised the hair on Nat's arms. After the Wall came down she must have moved back to the west side of the city. Perhaps she did it to be near the place where she grew up, because her apartment was in Dahlem, on a street Nat was familiar with. It was only blocks from the Krumme Lanke U Bahn stop. No wonder he had sensed such a strange presence that day with Berta. Except Liesl was no mere spirit. She lived and breathed, and her home was his next destination.

As he knocked at the door, Nat wondered how many times Liesl must have heard that sound and feared the worst. Not only had she endured two of history's most oppressive and intrusive regimes, but she had dared to defy them and, somehow, had survived.

Yet when Liesl Hartz opened her door, she did not bother with a security chain or even a precautionary glance through a peephole. She simply threw it open and looked straight into his face. Her voice was neither harsh nor challenging. Nor was it timid or cowed.

"Good afternoon. Whom do you wish to see?"

"Liesl Hartz. Or, as I expect you were once known, Liesl Folkerts."

Her eyes betrayed a flash of surprise, and she stepped back from the threshold.

"Oh, my," she said, raising a hand to her neck. "No one has spoken my maiden name for quite some time, and I'm not sure I like the idea of anyone knowing it. Who are you, and how did you find me?"

"I'm an American historian, Dr. Nathaniel Turnbull. But I hope you'll call me Nat. And, well, I found you, at least indirectly, through the granddaughter of the woman who was once your best friend."

"You must mean Berta Heinkel, Hannelore's favorite. The one who did her in, poor child, quite unwittingly."

"Oh, she knows, I'm afraid. In fact, she seems to have spent the better part of the past year trying to make up for it. It has practically ruined her."

Liesl shook her head. Then her expression took on an air of suspicion.

"I was just about to invite you in. But I would feel more comfortable about it if you could first indulge me by answering one more question."

"Certainly."

"Are you here on behalf of Kurt Bauer?" She placed a hand on the doorknob, as if preparing to shut the door.

"Definitely not. If he knew I was here, he'd probably be doing everything in his power to stop me. Because I've come to ask you about the war years, and the White Rose, and everything else that happened then."

She exhaled in apparent relief.

"Then I had better make some coffee. You're going to be here for quite a while."

She showed Nat to a couch in the parlor. The furniture was clean but threadbare, and the walls were unadorned except for a few simple prints. Her television set was a small black-and-white model, ancient, but her bookcases were full. A tea table was piled high with newspapers and magazines. The place bore all the earmarks of someone who had little money for luxuries yet had never stopped feeding an active mind.

She carried in a wooden tray with a coffee thermos and two plain white mugs.

"Milk and sugar?"

"Just milk, thank you."

"I'm afraid this coffee may be the only item of any real value that I can offer," she said. "I have my impressions, of course, and my memories. But I have none of the sort of items that historians usually think of as proof, at least where Kurt Bauer is concerned, even though I have never had any doubt since the end of the war as to what really happened. Hannelore also knew, but she, too, had nothing you would ever call proof. It's why neither of us was ever bold enough to come forward. Until, well . . . I suppose you must already know of how Hannelore died? Or was killed, rather."

"Yes, I read the report. But I wouldn't worry any longer about not having any proof against Bauer." He handed her a copy of Göllner's interrogation transcript. "Take a few minutes to read this."

Liesl slipped on a pair of glasses, and for most of the next half hour the only sound in the room was of the traffic, whisking by out front. Her eyes glistened a few times, and she paused often to shake her head, slowly and dolefully. Twice she sighed loudly and put down the papers, as if struggling to maintain her composure. But she never once shed a tear. Too much hard-earned endurance for that, Nat supposed.

As Nat watched her, it occurred to him why this case had fascinated him so much, even apart from the personal connections, and why it would probably continue to absorb him for months to come, or longer. It wasn't just the opportunity for a world-class "gotcha" in exposing Bauer, or even the higher motive of helping Holland and playing a small role in a twist of global history. It was more that this cast of players—Bauer and Berta, Gordon and Sabine, Liesl and Hannelore—perfectly encapsulated his life's work. The six of them *were* his curriculum, Modern Germany made flesh, in all its macabre and tragic grandeur.

Liesl put down the transcript with a final sigh. Dry-eyed, she handed it back.

"Keep it," he said. "I've made copies."

"Thank you. But tell me, if you have this, what could you possibly need from me?"

"Well, one thing I'd like to know is how the hell you got away from Plötzensee Prison without anyone finding out you'd survived?"

She smiled.

"That was Hannelore's trick. The bombs blew open her cell, of course, and I happened to be standing in a hallway at the time. I had just been released. Göllner himself had come to sign the discharge papers, which were still in my hand. One of the walls collapsed, and everything was pretty crazy, pretty frightening. Somehow I ended up outside, half in shock, and that's when she saw me. She took me by the arm and we ran. And that might have been it, except Hannelore had the presence of mind to place my release papers in that poor girl's hand, the one who was already half-buried in the fallen bricks. Another prisoner, I suppose. No one has ever known her name, because when the authorities found her they logged her death under my name."

"Göllner must have realized the mistake."

"I'm certain he did. He knew my face, and he would have seen hers. But he would have been glad to keep it a secret."

"What makes you say that?"

"Because of what he had just told me, inside the prison, while I waited for him to sign my papers. He told me all about what Kurt had done. His idea of a joke on Kurt, I suppose. I gather he was feeling ill-treated by his superiors as the result of all the pressure being applied by Kurt's father. Telling me about Kurt's betrayal was his only way of getting back at the Bauers. And when he heard later that Kurt thought the dead girl was me, it must have made him even happier."

"Where did you go from there?"

"We tried my house first. But by then my family had been killed, that very morning. So we went across town, to some friends of Hannelore's in Prenzlauer Berg. We barely survived all the bombings during the next few months, and then we barely survived the Russians. I was raped by a soldier in the Red Army. Hardly unusual, as you must know. Hannelore was a far better survivor. She killed one of them with a pair of scissors. She was also better than me at surviving the Worker's Paradise, at least for a while. She was quite the firebrand at first. Then they put her in prison for two years, and she was never quite as vocal afterward. Nor was I. After a while I no longer had much spirit for dissent."

"Weren't you ever tempted to contact Bauer, or confront him in some way?"

"Hannelore and I always talked about that. In private, of course. We drafted several letters to the press, laying out our case. And I found out his phone number, the one to his home. But we never mailed the letters, and I never called."

"Why not?"

"Only two things could have happened, and neither was satisfactory. Without proof, the West would have seen it as another trumped-up Communist attempt to smear a good capitalist. There were quite a few of those, you know, complete with forgeries. In some ways that would only have made him stronger, an object of pity."

"Maybe."

"Yes, maybe. Meaning maybe we could have succeeded. But then we realized what that would have meant. Hannelore and I would have been celebrated as heroes of the Worker's Paradise. Sturdy tools in the hands of our new enemy. The very people who were making others spy on us would have been richly rewarded. Besides, part of me simply never wanted to relive those days. Those horrible executions. Discovering that my true love had betrayed us. Then learning that my entire family had been blown to pieces. All in one terrible day. Those sorts of memories don't bear much stirring up. Even after Hannelore and I were both married, with new names to hide behind, we never said much about our days in the White Rose. Although I gather that toward the end Hannelore told some of her stories to Berta. Maybe that's what finally inspired the girl to try and take down Bauer."

"How often did you see Berta?"

"Only once or twice. And on both occasions Hannelore introduced me simply as Mrs. Hartz, because Berta had already heard so many wartime tales of the heroic Liesl Folkerts. Even then Hannelore suspected the girl was reporting on her. Out of love, she said, which I could never understand. All I saw in Berta was a frightening little Communist, and Hannelore knew I felt that way. So there is no way she would have ever told Berta who I really was."

"I guess you weren't very surprised to read in your Stasi file that Berta had informed on you as well."

"Not at all. Although it made me want to look up Berta's file as an informer, which I was entitled to do as one of her 'victims.' That's when I found out how Hannelore had been killed. It made me furious at the girl, of course. Her stupidity had cost me my best friend. But it also made me realize that she, too, was a victim of the state. Besides, she was only a girl."

"Kurt Bauer was only a boy."

"But his motives were wealth and self-preservation, and he was nearly eighteen. Berta was three years younger, a far more vulnerable age, and she had been indoctrinated from birth. And as perverse as it sounds, I really do believe she was acting out of love, just as Hannelore said. Surely in your profession you can see the difference between them."

"What are your feelings about her now?"

"There is still anger, of course. But there is also pity. I have heard through others that she has lost everything. She has paid a far greater price than Kurt ever did. And I would guess that what torments her most is the loss of her Oma."

" 'Torment' is exactly the word, and I'm hoping I can help her. I'd like to share these materials with her, if it's all right with you. I may even let her help me prepare an article for publication. She did show me the way to your door, in a sense. I can't say her motives were always admirable, and definitely not her methods, but I wouldn't have succeeded without her."

"You must do as you see fit. But I am told she no longer has a home. Do you even know where to reach her?"

"I'm pretty sure I will quite soon. Bauer, too. Which brings me to my last question. Are you busy this coming Monday?"

ON SUNDAY NIGHT, just as Nat was putting the finishing touches on his arrangements for the following morning, he telephoned Holland. The agent was at home, and sounded a little tipsy.

"Still celebrating?" Nat asked.

"Why not? You gave us plenty to celebrate."

"You'll also be happy to know I've completed my expense report. I'll fax it tonight if you'll give me a number."

"I hope you took me up on that offer of a nice dinner in Bern."

"Didn't have time, as it turned out. Had to head straight to Berlin."

"Berlin? What on earth for?" He sounded a little edgy.

"I had a few loose ends to wrap up. Still do, in fact, if I ever want to publish."

"Publish?"

"Don't worry, I'm not looking to spoil your party. In fact, the whole point of this call is to make sure I don't. Which is why I have only one question, and if you're smart you'll answer it."

"Try me."

"This stuff you wanted from Bauer. Has he given it to you?"

"Yes, all of it. Took up the better part of the weekend. The last debriefing session ended this afternoon."

"And it's complete? It's everything he promised?"

"That's more than one question. But, yes, everything. Our experts were even a little taken aback by the bounty. Names, contact info, flowcharts, transport networks, important middlemen, the works. Even better than expected, from what I've been told. And after seeing what was in those folders you found, I can understand why he was willing to make the deal. Completely off the record, some people in our own government weren't exactly sorry to see this stuff buried for good, either, given the way certain matters were handled, way back when."

"Good. That means I can proceed with a clear conscience."

"Oh, dear." He sounded concerned, but he quickly relaxed into a chuckle. "Am I to take it you found some way to outsmart us?"

"No comment."

Another chuckle.

"You don't exactly sound worried by the prospect," Nat said.

"Off the record again?"

"Sure."

"A few days ago I would have been. But we kept our end of the bargain—delivered everything Bauer wanted, took every precaution to assure its secrecy. If he's still not used to dealing with the likes of you—well, that's his problem. Besides, it's the Agency that stands to be embarrassed on our side, not us. Although frankly we've also made some accommodations I'm not very comfortable with. Agreeing to look the other way on some of these recent deaths, for example."

"Gordon's?"

"No. His was natural. I wasn't lying about that."

"Willis Turner, then, and the PI in Florida. Plus Göllner in Germany."

"It was the Germans who caved on Göllner. And those other two are only part of the story."

"You mean there were more?"

"This thing got pretty complicated, and Bauer pulled out all the stops. As of now we're not even certain who was responsible for half of it. Bauer, the Iranians, who knows? But today I was told in no uncertain terms that we no longer need to find out."

"So we're covering for him. Again. Meaning he'll never answer for it."

"Not in a court of law. Which should explain why I'm not really upset by what you're apparently up to. Of course, I never said that. In fact, we never had this conversation."

"Fine by me. As long as you pay my tab."

So NOW IT HAD COME to this on a cloudy Monday morning in Berlin: Nat, standing beside Liesl on the grounds of the Plötzensee Memorial. Berta, with her camera, lurking behind a wall. Bauer, stooped and wary, bouquet in hand. All the *dramatis personae*, in place for the final act.

Bauer shuffled toward the spot in the stone courtyard where he always placed the flowers. Just as he was bending over, the motor drive of Berta's camera whirred into action. Nat heard it clearly. Bauer must have, too, because he stiffened and clenched the flowers tightly. Even from twenty feet away you could see his knuckles whiten. He then turned toward Nat and strolled briskly forward, as if he had decided that this was where he would focus his anger first.

Liesl, holding Nat's arm, tensed in anticipation, and Nat decided to intervene before things turned ugly. He patted her hand and headed toward Bauer. The two men came face-to-face in the middle of the courtyard just as Berta emerged fully from behind the shed.

Bauer raised a bony finger, which quivered as he spoke.

"All of this is over, you know!" Spittle punctuated every word, flak bursts of fury. "Over! For you and for that horrid girl!" He nodded toward Berta, who had lowered her camera and was watching in rapt silence. "One call to the police and she will be arrested! They will no doubt wish to hear about you as well. I will ruin you, just as I ruined her."

No sense arguing, Nat decided. Only a full frontal assault would do now.

"As you please, Herr Bauer. But I've brought someone with me who has wanted to speak to you for a very long time. Liesl, will you please come here?"

Bauer froze at the sound of her name and clutched the flowers to his chest. For a moment Nat feared he would drop dead from a heart attack. He even felt a twinge of sympathy. Look at how far astray the man's adoration had led him—so many misguided betrayals, each of them a burnt offering at the altar of her memory. But now you could sense the dawning realization that he had built a flawed temple to a false god.

"It *is* you," the old man said, breathless. "Liesl. My dearest!"

Bauer reached out a hand, but Liesl backed away, repelled. There was no way she was going to let him touch her, and you could see that it wounded him deeply. Berta, too, had been halted in her tracks. It was clear to Nat that she had recognized her Oma's best friend and, having heard Liesl's name, she was now adding up the rest of the story, stunned by its implications.

"Yes, Kurt. It is me," Liesl said. "I have told our story to this young man. Hannelore's story, too. She was the grandmother of that young woman over there, the one with the camera. Anything else you'll just have to learn by reading about it. And by then, of course, everyone will know."

Bauer was too dumbfounded to answer, as if he was still trying to reconcile this vengeful old woman with the girl he had once loved. Liesl turned toward Berta.

"Put your camera down and come here, unless you never want to escape your past, like this bitter old man here. If you come with me, I think we will have a great deal to talk about."

Liesl held out her hand. Berta nodded, and obeyed as if in a trance. They linked arms and turned to go. Liesl called out to Nat over her shoulder.

"I will see you back at the car, Dr. Turnbull."

Berta nodded toward him, the barest hint of a smile. Gratitude or relief, he couldn't tell which. She was still stunned to silence, yet also aglow, as if she had not only finally found her answers but also had been pleasantly surprised to discover that there was more than just death at the heart of things.

As for Bauer, he remained speechless and staring, his open mouth as rigid as that of a corpse. He was an old man rooted to his memories, unable to reconcile any of what he had just seen. Turning slowly, he watched the two women climb into the taxi, the younger one helping the older. Yes, it was Liesl, so stooped and bent—his age, his era, and, also like him, fading now beneath the burdens of their shared past, a history that had at last come to claim him.

At the very moment when the door of the taxi slammed shut, the bouquet fell from his hands. The flowers were still bundled in wet newspaper, his final tainted offering upon a girl's empty grave.

EPILOGUE

January 2008

N EW SEMESTER, first day of class. Professor E. Nathaniel
Turnbull scanned the creaking rows of the lecture hall for
early arrivals.

One eager lass had already snatched a syllabus and taken a seat up
front, but the telltale lines of a stowaway iPod betrayed her true intentions. Last-minute texters hovered by the door, bent to the task like
scriveners to their ledgers. A cell phone's forbidden galaxy tune twin-
kled in a backpack.

It was 7:56 a.m., not the best of time slots for a debut course. Half
the arrivals still had damp hair from their morning showers. Some
were already stifling yawns.

Nat could hardly blame them. The name of the course certainly
wasn't sexy: History 225: Modern Germany, a Case History. The
department had given him only half an hour to come up with a twenty-
five-words-or-less description for the spring catalog, and even then it
had only slipped in as a typewritten insert: *An assessment of the Third
Reich's lingering aftereffects on postwar Germany, told through the life story
of resister-turned-collaborator Kurt Bauer, the noted industrialist.*

Only twenty-seven takers for fifty slots, but Nat wasn't worried.
Reviews would be glowing. Word would spread. By next fall they
would have to move him to a bigger room, especially after the book
came out over the summer.

His greater concern this morning was whether any of his invited
special guests would show up, including a particular student who was a
procrastinator by nature. Ah, there she was now.

Karen flashed him a daughterly smile and settled into a seat toward the back. Finally, he would be teaching in a style that wouldn't shame her. Not that he expected to win her over completely to his favorite subject. He couldn't help but notice the dog-eared *Complete Poems* poking from her backpack.

She had phoned at six thirty that morning with a verse to get him off on the right foot:

> *Mine enemy is growing old,*
> *I have at last revenge.*
> *The palate of the hate departs;*
> *If any would avenge,*
>
> *Let him be quick, the viand flits,*
> *It is a faded meat.*
> *Anger as soon as fed is dead;*
> *'Tis starving makes it fat.*

Good stuff, he told her. And as he sipped his breakfast coffee afterward he contemplated the import of those words for Gordon and Bauer, for Berta and Liesl, and, well, for every player in this saga that had consumed him for the better part of the previous eight months.

Nat had his own role, of course, although as a professional evaluator of such things he was certain his own would never turn up in any official accounting. Because, for all of the supposedly great material the FBI had gathered from Bauer's storehouse of nuclear secrets, Holland confessed later that much of it had already exceeded its shelf life. During Bauer's last few years of laying low, the various shadowy vendors, suppliers, and middlemen of the atomic marketplace had apparently moved on without him, re-forming and re-channeling their networks. Meaning Bauer had been peddling a stale loaf indeed.

That meant, in turn, that Nat hadn't exactly saved the world for democracy.

But he *had* triumphed handsomely in his own small theater of operations, the realm of academia where Gordon and he had toiled for so long. A prolific bout of further research and furious scribbling had attracted a decent advance from a publisher, followed by an even more lucrative sale of translation rights to a German publisher. Kurt Bauer's name was about to be immortalized, although not in the way the old fellow wanted. Once again, it was the broken parts that had proven to be the most interesting.

For a while Nat had worried that the man would seek vengeance. But the scorn of a resurrected Liesl seemed to take all the fight out of him. Bauer didn't even pursue his court case against Berta, much less any vendetta against Nat. As for the Iranians, if anything they were probably glad to see the old man get his comeuppance, since he had goaded them into a disastrous competition over damaged goods.

That freed Nat to handle and dispense the information as he saw fit. The hardest part was breaking the news to Viv.

He invited her over for dinner the night after his return from Berlin. Karen, who had quickly warmed to Viv after her close encounter with the would-be burglar, was there to cook the meal and soften the blow. After coffee Nat gently sat Viv on the couch and uncorked a bottle of Pierre Ferrand, Gordon's favorite cognac. He withheld the "Dear Jane" letter from Bern, but told her the rest.

There were tears, of course, but by the time he drove her home she seemed grateful for the knowledge, if only because it meant she hadn't been the one failing time after time for all those years, whenever Gordon had receded into his drinks or his anger.

"Maybe I should meet her someday," she said of Sabine.

"Maybe," Nat answered. "The way Sabine sees it, you won. You ended up with Gordon, changed man or not."

"But she got a son."

BERTA AT FIRST RESISTED his offer to collaborate on further research for the book. Even after she accepted, Nat had to move heaven and earth to secure a visa for her, and the National Archives would still have nothing to do with her—not that he blamed them.

She helped tie up loose ends in other areas, and her work was spirited, energetic. She even exhibited a newfound tact in dealing with several of their trickiest sources. All along, she stayed in close touch with Liesl. Nat never asked about the nature of their conversations, and Berta never volunteered any answers.

Nat did virtually all of the writing. He was happy to share his advance, but he debated briefly with his own ego over whether to also share authorship. Berta then surprised him by flatly refusing the offer.

The only credit she wanted was for research. The work, she said, was its own reward.

It was clear to him that she hadn't yet come to terms with everything that had happened. Nor did she seem to have any idea of how she would proceed—either professionally or socially—once the project was done. The problem went beyond restlessness or lingering guilt. It was, Nat believed, something quite German—an unfulfilled need to put everything in its proper place and to talk it out within herself, a dialogue among all her weary demons.

So when she disappeared without warning just after the first galleys arrived from the publisher, he did not try to track her down or pry into her plans. When the check for the balance of their advance then arrived by mail, he forwarded her share in care of Liesl.

The course he was about to teach was a fortunate by-product of their work. Its outline was roughly the same as that of the book. He wrote Liesl to invite her and Berta to attend the opening lecture. Liesl sent her regrets, but also her blessing. Berta didn't respond.

But Karen was here, and now so was Viv, taking a seat just behind his daughter. It was exactly eight o'clock.

Nat unfolded his notes at the lectern and uttered a few bland words of welcome. No more my-way-or-the-highway shock therapy. If anyone lagged, well, he would just have to try coaxing them along, the way any good teacher would.

Dispensing with the preliminaries, he asked the girl on the front row to please hand out the syllabus to everyone else. As she complied, he noticed movement from the doorway and glanced toward the back just long enough to see Berta taking a seat in a far corner, an island among empty seats.

He nodded. She seemed to offer a flicker of acknowledgment, or maybe he imagined it. There was no way to find out for sure, because now it was time to deliver the heart of his opening remarks, with what he hoped would be a stirring preview of what lay ahead. Students always grumbled if you used the full fifty minutes on the first day, so he wrapped things up at 8:35. He closed with these words:

"By presenting you the life of one rather venal and tormented man, I hope to show you the ways in which history is a living entity. Not just because of its survivors, and the stories they have to tell, but because of its enduring power to hurt and to heal, to create even as it destroys, to transform familiar old heroes and monuments into dust even as it raises fresh new icons from the ashes of the lost and the forgotten."

Rather pleased with himself, Nat scanned the room as the students began packing to leave. Karen nodded approvingly. Viv wiped something from her eyes.

But Berta was gone.

She must have slipped out during his summation, another disappearance without warning. Still haunted, he supposed. And still very much a German, waltzing with her past even as it enticed her down a dark stairwell.

He wondered if she could use some company.

ACKNOWLEDGMENTS

HALF THE FUN of writing this book was the month I spent poring over declassified OSS records in the beautiful reading room of the National Archives in College Park, Maryland. The staff were helpful and knowledgeable, the material was endlessly fascinating, and the setting was a treat for the eyes. Heck, even the cafeteria food was good, especially the ribs.

As I followed the paper trail of Allen Dulles through, figuratively speaking, the streets and alleys of wartime Switzerland, I most often sought guidance from the incomparable Lawrence McDonald, a veteran archivist who knows every nook and cranny. Without him, I'd probably still be floundering through the first of those sixty boxes of documents.

Among those documents, I am particularly indebted to two richly detailed field reports from OSS operatives: the April 1, 1945, report of Philip Keller, describing his arrest and interrogation during his infiltration of Bavaria, and the dramatic report of Gertrude LeGendre describing her capture by the Germans in occupied France in September 1944.

I also owe a deep debt of gratitude to Neal H. Petersen's seminal work, *From Hitler's Doorstep*, an admirably indexed and annotated collection of Dulles's wartime intelligence reports. It functioned as my road atlas in navigating the era's baffling array of operatives and code names. Another helpful tool was *American Intelligence and the German Resistance to Hitler*, edited by Jürgen Heideking and Christof Mauch.

In researching Dulles himself, I relied greatly on the fine biography *Gentleman Spy*, by Peter Grose, and also *Autobiography of a Spy*, the colorful memoirs of Mary Bancroft, who was a confidante and mistress of Dulles.

On the subject of Nazi Germany and what it means to spend your life researching that era, I owe much to Professor Gerhard Weinberg, of the University of North Carolina–Chapel Hill. Not only did he allow me into his living room to pick his brain for hours on end, but he also steered me toward other helpful historians and archivists.

On the topic of the student resistance group known as the White Rose, three books were particularly helpful: *Sophie Scholl and the White Rose*, by Annette Dumbach and Jud Newborn; *A Noble Treason*, by Richard Hanser; and *The White Rose: Munich, 1942–1943*, by Inge Scholl. *The Fall of Berlin*, by Anthony Read and David Fisher, was invaluable for its details of daily life in wartime Berlin, and *The Villa, the Lake, the Meeting* was a vital reference for all matters pertaining to the infamous Wannsee Conference of January 1942. Thanks also to the caretakers of the Dietrich Bonhoeffer House in Berlin for allowing me to roam its rooms for a short but significant period one spring afternoon.

On the subject of downed American airmen who spent much of the war in Switzerland, thanks to Captain Martin Andrews, who not only shared his own vivid memories but also his papers. For additional help on this topic I am indebted to *Refuge from the Reich*, by Stephen Tanner, and *Masters of the Air*, by Donald L. Miller.

In Switzerland, thanks to Dr. Pierre Th. Braunschweig for his observations, and also for his informative book, *Secret Channel to Berlin: The Masson-Schellenberg Connection and Swiss Intelligence in World War II*.

A NOTE ABOUT THE AUTHOR

DAN FESPERMAN's travels as a writer have taken him to
thirty countries and three war zones. *Lie in the Dark* won the
Crime Writers' Association of Britain's John Creasey Memo-
rial Dagger Award for best first crime novel; *The Small Boat of
Great Sorrows* won the association's Ian Fleming Steel Dagger
Award for best thriller; and *The Prisoner of Guantánamo* won
North America's Dashiell Hammett Award.

A NOTE ON THE TYPE

This book was set in Janson, a typeface long thought to have been made by the Dutchman Anton Janson, who was a practicing typefounder in Leipzig during the years 1668–1687. However, it has been conclusively demonstrated that these types are actually the work of Nicholas Kis (1650–1702), a Hungarian, who most probably learned his trade from the master Dutch typefounder Dirk Voskens. The type is an excellent example of the influential and sturdy Dutch types that prevailed in England up to the time William Caslon (1692–1766) developed his own incomparable designs from them.

Composed by Creative Graphics,
Allentown, Pennsylvania
Printed and bound by Berryville Graphics,
Berryville, Virginia
Designed by Virginia Tan